I0818206

Unburied Memories

David Powers

UNBURIED MEMORIES

First Edition - February 2014

This book is a work of fiction. Names, characters, places, and incidents either are a product of the author's imagination, are used fictitiously, and any resemblance to actual persons, living or dead, business establishments, events, or locales is entirely coincidental.

Library of Congress Cataloging-in-Publication Data
Powers, David.
Unburied memories/David Powers.
310 p. 22 cm.

ISBN 978-0-9914248-1-8 (hardcover)
ISBN 978-0-9914248-0-1 (paperback)
ISBN 978-0-9914248-2-5 (ebook)

1. Murder--Investigation--Fiction 2. Mystery--Fiction
3. New Jersey--Fiction. I. Title.

Library of Congress Control Number: 2014901629
Printed in the United States of America

Eerie Forest
www.eerieforest.com

For Jennifer

Introduction

I AM JOHNNY and go by John now. As a kid, everyone called me Johnny. Dad named me after his father. Grandfather John was a very tall, silver-haired gentleman who came during the holidays to visit. Grandpa sat in a large stuffed chair by the fireplace, smoking cherry pipe tobacco and sipping potent amber liquids. The glass-eyed man had few words.

My surname is Townsend, and I am descended from the famous line of Townsends who landed on Plymouth Rock in 1620. To be more truthful, my relatives originated among the row houses in nearby Hoboken. Dad once said "Townsend" is an ancient English moniker meaning "Edge of the Village."

I grew up in the northeast corner of New Jersey, in the tiny borough of Haworth. When the railroad arrived in 1872, a financier christened the additional rail stop "Haworth" for a favorite city in England. Raters frequently score the municipality as one of the best suburbs in America. The community is a rectangular-shaped town of roughly two square miles, with a population surpassing three thousand. Dutch settlers built many of the colonial stone farmhouses still in existence. When I was young, the downtown consisted of a few shops: Jim's Market, where the grammar school students could hang around following their final class, an Ace Hardware store with the supplies a do-it-yourselfer needed to carry out most 1960s home repairs, Smith's Pharmacy, a barbershop, and a welcoming United States Post Office. The main drag, Terrace Street, hasn't changed greatly over the decades.

Haworth can be a delightful habitat in the summer. The roads are labeled for trees or presidents and continue to be a haven for youth to play. Soaring oaks and maples, planted long ago by the city founders, thrive everywhere. There are plenty of recreation areas where residents engage in baseball and soccer. When autumn comes, the wind lifts the brilliant leaves to blanket the neighborhood's yards. Those without landscapers spend each weekend raking and hauling the debris to the curb. These huge piles are vacuumed up through a hose by a mammoth truck lovingly nicknamed the "Elephant." Winter is also a fine time of year. Back in the '60s, northern New Jersey seemed to get much heavier snow. Now and then, I wonder if the white powder appeared deeper because my boots were smaller. Driveway shoveled, I grabbed my Flexible Flier and joined the other juveniles sledding down the steep hill behind the high school.

Springtime is a different story. To this day, I am anxious during this season. Spring is when the murder took place.

A science magazine stated that adults don't retain memories created before the age of five. I certainly can't elicit the experience of conception, but I do recall what I consider my earliest childhood recollection. On "Date Night," Mom and Dad went out square dancing, leaving my mother's parents to babysit. Thirsty, I started downstairs, my grandparents materializing at the foot. They goggled as I uttered syllables approximating, "May I have milk?" Although perfectly clear to me, the words were obviously baby gibberish, and I didn't obtain my drink.

Sometimes, in conversation, the topic of early remembrances is discussed. The anecdote of the bemused grandparents is the tale I always recite. There is another flashback that is exceptionally vivid and, at the same instant, unreal. These tenacious visions float in my subconscious.

Born at the beginning of 1957, I had barely turned five when an event transformed my life. You must understand, what I observed was shocking for a youngster. For countless years, I tried to believe the incident never happened.

A warm afternoon: I ran around the playground climbing on everything. Children screamed and shouted. Dogs barked, and mothers cautioned kids to be careful.

The episode evolved very fast. One second I had fun playing; the next, I retreated, terrified and blubbering into my mom's neck. The world shifted in an instant.

The images that I visualize resemble jerky stop-motion movies. A young woman in a blue dress and a man are standing in the shade of the woods, beyond two boys riding a teeter-totter. The man's angry expression caught my attention. Shaking his hands, the frightening man seized the teenager's shoulders as she attempted to escape. Too far away to hear with clarity, I stopped frolicking to watch. A playmate yelled my name. Then a spirited dog jumped on my back, dropping me to my knees. When I returned my gaze, I saw the man wearing a hat hunched over, pulling the girl beneath a bush. Hair fell to her brow, as black-and-white shoes kicked desperately. Just like that, they vanished, leaving nothing, not even the quivering of a leaf. The cheerful sounds of the park remained.

I remember running to my mother, who chatted with a few ladies on a bench. Through tears, I whispered what had transpired. Always shy, I didn't want the others to overhear. Mom kept asking why I cried. The occurrence passed so swiftly, there wasn't much to tell. While explaining how a man snatched a girl and dragged her into the undergrowth, I began to rationalize the entire affair. Maybe the couple had a normal argument. I was too immature to comprehend the means grownups used to interact.

Mom and her friend Barbara crossed to the wooded section. The older woman said something, and both laughed. As they approached, my mother's face wrinkled with doubt. The pair hadn't noticed anyone or anything suspicious. She inquired if I could come see for myself, but I refused. After walking to our house, I went up to my bedroom.

That was the last time we ever spoke of what I'd seen, and the details faded from memory. . . .

Part One

The Note

Friday Afternoon—May 19, 1967

IT WOULD BE NICE if I could claim to be one of the smartest scholars in fifth grade, although to be honest, on a productive day, I'd be proud to have absorbed any worthwhile facts. The year was 1967, and I daydreamed constantly, gazing out of the Haworth Public School windows at the street traffic. Right now, it was impossible to keep my eyes off the unmoving clock hands hovering above the teacher's head. Two forty-five on a Friday; fifteen minutes remained before class ended for the week. My best friend sat to my right.

"Vince," I whispered, using the side of my mouth. As Mrs. Parker commemorated the good old days of German history, I rested assured she wasn't concentrating on me.

Bored and hungry for a diversion, he stared. "What?"

Holding forth a small folded piece of notebook paper, I commanded, "Take this and pass it up to that new guy. Say it's from Sally." The pie-faced girl always sat in the very first row. As the official Teacher's Pet, Sally May had every answer and relished rehashing your deficiencies with her comrades.

"Why?" he asked, one finger digging into a nostril. No one had the ability to flick snot farther or with more accuracy than Vince Ranzetta.

The schoolteacher droned on, "Overall, the Nazi regime enabled national economic recovery and heavy spending on the military. . ." Man, she could spin a tall tale.

"Grab the note, and give it to Billy. Tell him Sally sent it." Billy Outlaw sat two seats in front of Vince. I placed the scrap on his desk. "Come on!" I hissed.

My friend picked up and unfolded the message, glancing at me. "What the. . .?" His eyes narrowed, and my gut squeezed with a slight pang of *Hmm, maybe this isn't such a great idea.*

"Do it, pussy." No longer bold, I considered retrieving the piece of paper.

Ranzetta balled up the words and flung the chunk at the bulbous noggin. Not exactly what I intended. In a stupor, Billy raised a palm to rub the quills of his buzz cut. Looking around and at the floor, he saw the miniscule sphere and ignored it.

"Mr. Outlaw, is there anything special you want to share with the class?" Mrs. Parker questioned. Perturbed, she twisted from the blackboard, chalk in one fist and eraser in the other.

"Nah, Mrs. Parker," he answered. "I just—"

"You just what, Billy?" The instructor put the writing implements on the desk and crossed her arms. "What is so important that you had the sudden urge to disrupt the class?"

At this point, startled that she made such a fuss, I became increasingly nervous that this poor experiment at humor might backfire. Outlaw seemed like a decent kid, and I sadly wondered why I had pulled this prank.

The boy's red face matched his hair. "Ma'am, I *was* paying attention. Someone threw something at me."

The woman made a beeline across the green-and-white tiles to the wad of paper and bent over. Even with impending catastrophe on the horizon, I felt obligated to check out her backside. Not truly a mini skirt, but short enough.

The teacher peeled apart the note. "This is foolish, a complete waste of time. My students should know better." Exasperated, she inquired, "Who wrote this?"

Though I wasn't willing to put up a hand, my cheeks blushed with guilt. Vince was ready to explode.

"Don't you realize I can recognize your hieroglyphics? I grade everyone's essays and review penmanship."

Mrs. Parker had me. Under ideal conditions, my handwriting resembled the crabbed scribble of a three-year-old. Most of the time, I couldn't read what I wrote. Admitting to the document was not an option, being afraid to wind up in hot water or worse, my mom got involved.

"Mr. Ranzetta, was it you?" The instructor approached Vince's steel-and-chrome desk. Despite the scowling, I trusted Vince not to tattle. Confidently, she held the paper open, words aimed at his face. "Did you write this gem?"

"No, I didn't."

"Did you throw this at Billy? It's acceptable to express personal feelings, although not at school. This Monday, I am giving a quiz on what you've mastered about the German empire, and some of you," she stared directly at me, "need a passing grade."

"The note says," Mrs. Parker paused for dramatic appeal, "I LOVE YOU!" She enunciated the damning words and distinctly spelled each letter. *Holy crap!*

Ranzetta, comprehending that he had sent a romantic communication to a schoolmate, pivoted and glared icily. Raising a forefinger, he blamed, "That guy did it. Johnny wrote the note!" My best friend ratted on me.

"And you threw it?" the teacher sternly asked, again crossing her arms.

"Well, yeah, Townsend told me to," Vince expounded. "I don't even like Billy."

My stomach lurched. Now it appeared I had sent the love letter to the new kid. This hoax had been conceived as a quick gag.

The students were laughing—at me. Many doubled over, howling. Others smirked with mugs of amusement. "Johnny loves Billy!" a boy screeched. Outlaw looked mortified.

"It was plainly a joke!" I blurted. Nobody listened.

Three winks later, Vince and I fidgeted outside the principal's office. Through emptying halls, Mrs. Parker scolded, "What am I going to do with you? Johnny, I'm convinced you can improve. Vince, you watch that mouth, and don't do everything anyone tells you. Go explain your shenanigans to Mr. Glenn. Good luck." She sounded dejected.

A portly man in a tweed jacket scented with cheap aftershave beckoned us into the chamber. "Come on in, fellas," the principal said. We sat stiffly before the bare desk. Peering past horn-rimmed glasses, he stated, "Mr. Townsend, this is the second time in May you've visited this office. To drag Vince into this mess isn't worthy of a responsible friend. This is ridiculous, and there is no time to hear your side of it. In ten minutes, I have to be on the teeing ground at White Beaches. Mrs. Clive will enroll you for detention every day next week beginning Monday. The next time I see you, it better be because one of you is receiving the Best Student of the Year Award." Mr. Glenn conferred the standard "I am serious this time" glower and discharged us at the clerk's table.

Released and standing on the schoolhouse's steps, Vince whirled and punched my right arm with considerable strength. Reeling in pain, I hollered, "Jesus, what's the matter with you?"

"You got me detention, you imbecile. My dad will kill me!"

I saw the dilemma. Mr. Ranzetta held the illustrious title of "A-Number-One Asshole" and used a belt as the primary tool to refine his son.

"Sorry, Vince," I said, retreating. "Oh man, I can't go back next week. They'll tear me to shreds."

As Ranzetta started laughing, his lanky body jerked in a peculiar dance, joining kissy faces and clenching shoulder blades in a fake hug.

Hilarious comedy, so I giggled too. "Man, that message never reached Sally May. That would be priceless!"

"Uh, next time, you should actually sign the note from Sally, you moron!" Vince stopped boogying and chased me along the stairs.

At that moment, Outlaw came out, not grasping the full intent of the dispatch. I was not about to enlighten him. The kid had me by at least thirty pounds. "Did you guys get yelled at?"

"Yeah," Vince answered sullenly. "I get to stay after school, thanks to dumbass here." The three of us walked toward the bike rack. A big kid named Frank shouted something unintelligible from down the road. Presuming the comment had to do with the event in class, I flashed the middle finger. My frustration heated again as he snickered and sauntered past.

"Hey, let's go to Jim's and get candy," Billy suggested. In possession of a few extra bucks, I decided to spring for chocolate bars to make up for the bother. Even though the market was out of the way, there was no hurry to return home in case my mom discovered what had happened. Eventually, I needed to explain the reason for getting detention.

Ranzetta led, pedaling like a madman. Billy owned the nicest bicycle, a shiny silver Schwinn Sting Ray, yet he fell behind. The Outlaws lived in a swank residential neighborhood, so I inferred the family had lots of money in the bank. I had a fairly good bike, a green Western Auto Flyer, still too tall for me. Vince rode a beat-up red Murray undeniably purchased from a yard sale. The Ranzettas definitely had no dough. Jokers laundry-clipped to his rear wheel made an amazing sound buzzing against the spokes.

Whooping, Vince veered off the sidewalk onto a trail slicing through the forest. The kids in town always referred to these six acres of trees and overgrowth as the "Woods." Legends proliferated. Fabricated stories retold fear-provoking accounts of murdered pioneer ghost sightings or cannibalistic tribes of homeless people hiding in caves. The Woods was the largest unpopulated land in the village and the spot we went to play. I never explored the whole thing and don't suppose anyone has. There were too many wild places overrun with vines and poison sumac. Even knowing the myths were untrue, I was always edgy in the Woods.

We leapt over berms and ducked under drooping branches. I listened to Outlaw puffing and gave the stocky youth credit for trying. Ranzetta skillfully skidded out the tire on the last turn, emerging into sunlight on the path leading to downtown. Backpedaling, we braked to a screeching halt before Jim's Market. Sometimes, my mother stopped here to pick up a gallon of milk or sack of flour when there wasn't enough time to go shopping at the A&P in nearby Closter. Tempting ads for cigarettes and beer plastered the insides of the windows.

With care, Billy and I leaned our bicycles against the concrete wall as Vince unceremoniously ditched his in the gully. A bell jingled as we entered the darkened market. The air always smelled rank in Jim's, like something sour required mopping. Ranzetta wandered the aisles, trailing fingers across merchandise. Occasionally, he peeked back, a dangerous gleam in his eyes. I prayed the boy wouldn't try to swipe anything. With Vince, everything became a test. The suspicious pout of Jim's wife tracked us throughout the dingy establishment.

"Let's buy the candy and get the hell out of here," I pleaded, as he shoved boxes containing batteries into the side pockets of his baggy sweatshirt. "Jesus," I muttered.

Despite the situation, Outlaw tried to appear calm. As a sweaty sheen beaded his forehead, I wondered what the kid thought and if he might bolt.

Vince ordered, "Go up and pay. I'll meet you outside." Complying, I guided Billy to the cashier. Jim's always stocked an assortment of world-class sweets.

Anxious to withdraw, I grabbed a pack of candy cigarettes for Ranzetta and Atomic Balls and Sugar Daddy Pops for myself. Outlaw loaded up on Boston Baked Beans and Gold Mine gum. After telling him I would treat, I deposited the goods at the register. The woman tried to keep an eye on the store, while counting out the mountain of pennies covering the glass counter.

"What's your friend doing back there?" she inquired, putting the confections in a bag. Quiet, I gave her an "innocent and stupid" expression.

Billy responded smoothly, "His mom needs a few personal items." I peered at him with surprise. Under pressure, he was a cooler character than I'd previously suspected.

As the owner handed me the change, Vince walked to the exit. Lifting an arm to push the handle, a large carton of Mallory nine-volt batteries fell from a pocket, clattering to the linoleum. Hastily, he scooped up the cells and shouldered his way to the sidewalk.

Outlaw followed my lead running out the screen door and to our bikes. Ranzetta wrenched the Murray off the ground and effortlessly leaped onto the frame. Glancing backwards, he pumped hard, the roaring playing cards simulating a motorcycle. I hustled to start my bicycle rolling, balls slamming against the middle bar. Equipped with a lower seat, Billy's Sting Ray flew ahead.

"You boys better stay away!" Jim's wife screamed by the doorway. "I remember your parents and can find out where you live!"

"Jesus Christ," I moaned, struggling to catch up with the others. Already, I had gotten into mischief twice today, and it wasn't even four o'clock.

Vince aimed toward the Woods, to our hideout. Originally named the "Fort," we used the location to play Cowboys and Indians or Commando with friends. Now used to hang out, I renamed our place the "Shack."

The Shack had been slapped together with miscellaneous junk scavenged on garbage days. Before school, we used bikes to cart off rubbish neighbors cast by the curb. Ranzetta and I initially wanted to build a tree house. Most of the timber was not sturdy enough, so we settled on a dwelling cobbled from old lumber. Fervently working on the building during the course of one weekend, we promised to complete the project later. That never happened. We were still proud of the clubhouse, especially the hubcaps decorating the walls. To a certain degree, the wooden floor kept out a few of the bugs.

The space beneath a fir was dubbed the "Parking Garage." When at the hangout, Vince always leaned his bicycle on the tree. Billy and I did the same.

Since our guest hadn't visited our hut, we provided the grand tour. Not loads to see: a frayed rope swaying below a bough, soda cans and litter strewing the ground, and a square structure eight feet wide and six feet tall. I hoped Billy liked the Shack, yet felt embarrassed imagining this dump from his perspective.

"This is awesome!" he said eagerly, searching for a spot to sit. The interior of the cramped shanty reeked of the instances some twit unwisely peed in the corner.

"Pull up a chair," I offered, chucking a threadbare carpet sample. A cloud of dust filled the hovel as he flopped to the earth. I nodded at Vince, who was unloading his loot. "What did you think of that?"

"I, uh. . .," Outlaw stammered, appearing nervous to be alone with us. "Man, we won't be able to go back there again," he finished, undoubtedly worrying about losing his daily sugar fix.

"You didn't take anything," I soothed. "We paid for our stuff. Sure, you and I ran out of the market, but we can always tell our folks we had no idea what was going down." Internally, I considered the same complication. Patronizing Jim's with my mom on a regular basis, it was purely a matter of time before she found out. "Forget it, man." I parceled out the allotments of delicacies.

Ranzetta used a stick to poke into a crack in the planking. "I use those batteries in my radios," he murmured, not looking our way. Hefting a package, he started reading the label.

"How much do you need?" I asked sarcastically. Vince always strapped a Japanese transistor radio to the seat of his bike and played the latest pop hits at full volume distortion. The Ranzetta residence scarcely resembled the Townsends' home. The house was literally on the other side of the railroad tracks. Haworth didn't have a bad part of town; however, it had a rundown prewar section by the Oradell Reservoir. My parents spoke of that neighborhood in an unkind way and weren't the biggest fans of my friend.

Vince glanced up and mumbled, "I give them to my dad, and it's a mystery what he does with them. It helps keep him off my back."

Subject dropped, I said, "Fine. In the future, please refrain from drawing us into your grand larceny schemes. I got enough problems."

With that concluded, we dove into the sweet stash. The sun shimmered through the slats in the Shack as we ripped apart wrappers. A spring day under the trees was nice, far from authority and schoolwork. One could be isolated here, with only the songs of the blue jays, chattering squirrels, and distant muted traffic.

"What are you guys doing tomorrow?" Billy questioned, between popping golden gum nuggets into his maw.

Vince spun, as if just noticing our company. "Why?"

"Did you ever see the big rock?" I surmised the kid was trying to fit in.

"What rock?" Ranzetta inquired, suddenly attentive. Tongue tinted blue, a sugar cigarette hung in the crease of his mouth, James Dean style.

"A couple of years ago, a group of friends took me deep into the Woods, to a site in the middle of nowhere. There's an enormous boulder in a clearing. They say the stone is a prehistoric altar or something, witches, sacrifices—I saw it myself. It's really fucked up."

Wondering if Outlaw attempted to impress us by cursing, I asked, "Where is it located?" Curious and excited, I bit hard on an Atomic Ball, possibly chipping a molar.

Now that the boy gained our consideration, he continued, "Not positive. I went with my cousin Ray and his buddies. Up that way, I figure." Squinting, Billy pointed into the shadows. "If you want, we can find it. The rock is boss."

Abruptly rising, Ranzetta paced around the clubhouse. Bouncing a box of batteries, a display of contemplation lined his lean face. "I heard of that, too. Paul talked of a place in the Woods with a gigantic stone called 'Ceremonies.' That's where he parties with his classmates." Vince's older brother was laid back, notwithstanding the sucker punches the teenager loved to administer when least expected. "I've got nothing else happening. Let's meet here in the morning."

"Count me in—if I'm not grounded, of course," I chuckled, standing.

As an early riser, I like getting out of the house. I suggested meeting at seven-thirty and urged the guys to pack a variety of snacks as provisions for the exploration.

Leaving fulfilled, I sensed we had added an important member to the gang. Summer approached, and school would soon recess. Life looked pretty darn good.

Friday Evening—May 19, 1967

Saying farewell to my pals, I reluctantly swung toward home with the uneasy sensation that punishment waited patiently at the door.

Our family lives in a perfect example of suburbia: tree-bordered boulevards, three- to four-bedroom houses with garages for one or two automobiles, and large yards. As I mentioned before, the name "Townsend" means "Edge of the Village," and frequently that translation appears accurate. We lived on the fringe of town, a mile from Haworth's bustling little downtown. A steep hill separated the borough, and I griped of friends being far away. Near neighboring towns, we typically went beyond Haworth to shop or visit. In northeast New Jersey, traveling through five or six different communities in a short span is the norm.

The Garden State is a massive suburbia with many people commuting to Manhattan. Jersey inhabitants usually call New York City the "City," as that is where our identity is generally associated. A majority of television and radio broadcasting comes out of the metropolis. Even the sports teams hail out of NYC. Bergen County does have its own newspaper, the *Bergen Record,* the sole source for local information.

I live on Franklin Street. Most of our neighbors are nice, and as I glided downhill, I waved at Mrs. Campbell, sitting on her veranda. Dad parked his old black Dodge Matador station wagon in the driveway, so I assumed he left work early. I had hoped to head off any incriminating news with Mom first.

Constructed in the mid-1950s, our house was painted sunny yellow with white trim. Mighty oaks bounded the road, and clipped bushes graced the facade of the two-story residence. Brown spots receded as the lawn regenerated after a harsh winter. The one-car garage sheltered my mother's Chrysler. I put the Western Auto Flyer indoors and rolled the door closed. Remorsefully, I stepped into the dark laundry room to the aroma of cooking. The washing machine initiated the spin cycle. Above the knocking noise, my parents talked animatedly in the kitchen. Doorframe cracked ajar, I cocked an ear at the top of the stairs.

"Helen, Johnny has got to start applying himself," my father complained. Pans clanged, followed by running water.

Mom groused, "I can't understand why the boy does these things. Wish he would act more like Jane."

Jane was my sister. Already considered the wunderkind of the family, the five-year-old excelled in kindergarten.

"Yes, well, you baby him too much. The kid is ten. Where is he, anyway?"

"Should be here any minute. Probably with that Vince," she groaned bitterly. Keeping Dad serene was challenging, as my mother had the quick temper.

Returning to the metal garage door, I slammed it shut. No use avoiding the inevitable. I stomped up the stairway and burst into the bright kitchen. Roused, Django sidled against my legs, meowing. My parents swiveled in astonishment as I planted the impressive pair of textbooks on the table. *Such a hardworking student!*

"Ah, the prodigal son has arrived!" my father exclaimed, bowing from the waist. My mom, irritated, scrubbed at a stain.

"Hi," I said enthusiastically, thinking of a distracting topic. "We learned German history," I bubbled, striving to act and sound fascinating. "Those dirty Nazis were a bunch of—"

With an upraised soapy yellow dish glove, she terminated my speech. Dad served in Korea. War was not a topic any of us discussed in public, and my mother refused to ridicule different cultures. "Where were you?" she questioned harshly. "Johnny, you ought to have been here an hour ago to do homework. Supper will be ready soon. Go upstairs, and wash up." Frowning, she eyed the muddy pants. "Tonight, I'm doing a load of laundry, so put on clean jeans and throw those filthy things in the hamper."

Bedecked in fresh clothes, I pondered again when the inquisition might commence. *What if my parents talk about me all the time and don't even know what occurred this afternoon? Am I that big a loser?*

Jane helped set out the plates. "Hi Johnny," she gushed, showcasing a cheerful smile and a mouthful of missing teeth.

"Hey, Sis." Even though I loved her, a sizable age gap divided us. Often, I was not in the mood for never-ending little-kid babble.

"I made yummy chocolate cake by myself!" Pink ponies jumped along the ruffled fabric of her dress. Blond hair stuck out at angles.

"That's swell," I said. "Santa" delivered an Easy Bake Oven to my sister last year. The petite green stove utilized a 100-watt light bulb to concoct "lip-smacking" meals. To me, every recipe bore a resemblance to dog turds. During the winter, the toy dried my socks when I came in from the snow.

My father entered and precisely angled a mirror on a chair so the family could view the new living room television at the dinner table. As he switched on the newscast, Mom brought in a platter of pot roast and a few bowls of vegetables. Dad said grace, and everybody dug in.

For the first part of the CBS broadcast from New York City, a reversed image of Jim Jensen read a list of the day's top murders. A tally of the death toll in Vietnam followed the commercials. The news was both depressing and fascinating. A few weeks earlier, the station went too far with gruesome coverage. The producers sent a scuba diver underwater to film a crashed plane at the bottom of the Hudson River. Through the polluted murk, a woman's cheek pressed against the aircraft's window, hair floating eerily above the shriveled skull. Still strapped in, her eyes opened wide, mouth gaping in absolute terror. Restful sleep remained intermittent for days.

Wolfishly, I devoured whole chunks of braised beef while my father inquired about my day. I nearly choked on the sinewy meat. *This is it. They want me to spill the truth, or they'll trap me in a half-assed lie.*

Concerned, my mother asked, "Johnny, on Wednesday, a parent and teacher conference is scheduled with Mrs. Parker. Can we assist you with homework? How are your grades?"

"Okay, I guess."

"Helen, may I please have some of those delicious carrots?" Filling his plate, Dad shifted the spotlight on me. "Son, are there any other incidents you need to discuss?"

"Uh, no," I replied, using a *less is more* approach.

Conspiring, my parents made eye contact across the table, Mom arching her eyebrows.

"Seriously, Johnny? Nothing comes to mind?" she demanded.

"I got detention," I mumbled, gawking at the mound of overcooked green beans.

After I clarified what happened and left out unnecessary key details, my mother ranted and raved endlessly—quite dreadful. Jane stared in dismay.

Finally, my father turned away, attracted to Marine helicopters lighting up the fleeing Viet Cong in the Que Son Valley. The orange napalm explosions were gosh-darn spectacular on the Trinitron. "Whoa," he breathed, holding knife and fork ready.

Dismissed, I went to my bedroom hearing a reporter examine crumbling relations with Russia. Briefly surveying the street from the front window, I lay on the bed and cracked open the math book. Minutes later, the numbers blurred, and the formulas dissolved. I had the entire weekend to solve the problems and study for the history test. Rereading a few *Mad* magazines, I returned downstairs to watch *Bewitched.*

The sitcom was comical. In this episode, Darren, the witch's husband, received a futuristic car from his mother-in-law, Endora. Ultimately, Darren finds out the vehicle is stolen. Jane tittered at everything, and I questioned if she even appreciated the humor. Mom laughed too, although she was unusually subdued. Brow furrowed, she peered at me in distress.

Allowed to stay up late on Friday evenings, I enjoyed *Bonanza* before going to bed. Inspired to roam the Woods with Vince and Billy, I fell asleep.

Ceremonies

Saturday Morning—May 20, 1967

I WOKE WITH A SHOUT, not exactly shrieking.

The dream has a recurring theme. The vision usually starts off the same: I'm at a playground, running with many children. Mom keeps watch. The day ends, the playing field is vacated, and my mother has gone home. The place is in perpetual flux. Components of the jungle gym dissolve or change dimensions. Nothing makes sense, suspended by chains or sliding the ramps. The park is no longer enjoyable—I am anxious. There are urges to go to the bathroom. Time for dinner, but I'm not certain where that is. How can I not remember? I come to these grounds routinely. Shifting trees hem in two sides of the green. Instinctively, I stay away from the foreboding woods.

Night arrives, unseen. In some dreams, the bold moon rises high. Often, the atmosphere is so black, I pray for an astral body. I should be confident with my ability to locate my house, yet the street names are unknown or nonexistent. Confused, I continue walking.

The sidewalks are safe, and I gaze up at illuminated residences, overhearing garbled conversations. This must be the correct way. A few avenues are dark, as if the buildings are abandoned. Running, I avoid those roads. Terrible things maintain pace in the bushes; however, when I cease, silence. An interloper stands in the shadows, wearing a familiar hat. Wanting to ask for help, I can't speak. Fighting the clamping sickness of escalating panic—I am forever lost.

These exhausting dreams usually end with a monster chasing me through the streets, something unholy breathing on my neck. Prudently, I don't dare turn to look.

Infrequently, I force myself to wake. Other times, merely being frightened jolts me conscious. The grey light seeping in the windows highlights the roping cowboys on the wallpaper. No use falling back into a nightmare, so I shuffled along the hall to stream lemonade. Everyone was still asleep.

Django followed, rubbing my leg and yowling frantically. The Persian craves breakfast. In the kitchen, I ladled a few scoops of Puss 'n Boots, joining him with a nutritious bowl of Quisp.

Jane appeared, wiping sleep from her eyes.

"Would you like your favorite this morning?"

"Please," she replied, clambering into the chair, half asleep.

To encourage my sister with reading and writing, I poured Alpha-Bits. Habitually, she lines up the soggy ABCs on the tablecloth. Once, she spelled the word "biology," which I considered very advanced.

Chomping on text, Jane eyed me seriously. "Why are you constantly getting in trouble, Johnny?"

"Why?" I mumbled, not liking this direction.

She peered deep into the cereal, as if the solution floated. "Just wondering," she answered with a sly smile. Absorbed, my sister returned to sorting red vowels with a spoon.

Walking to my room, Mom came from their bedroom. I heard my father snoring.

"Where are you off to this early, Johnny?" she inquired, already peeved.

"Uh, going to ride around on my bicycle," I responded with gusto, "with Vince and another guy named Billy."

"Who is this Billy? What's his last name?"

Knowing she didn't think much of Vince, I needed to make my latest friend more palatable. "Outlaw. The family lives on Owatonna Street." A nice neighborhood, so my mother is reassured. "Billy's a new student at school. He moved here from Pennsylvania or Ohio. Billy's smart and says he can help with math," I ad-libbed.

"Well, be back for lunch, and be careful." Above my dad's sleeping form, the blue eyes of Jesus judged me before the bedroom door closed.

Pop Tarts in my bag, I mounted my trusty iron steed and started toward Vince's house. Although we settled on meeting at the Shack, I decided to catch him at home. Up early, Mr. Reynolds dug holes in the side yard, not seeing me pass.

The Ranzettas lived in a dilapidated dwelling on the far side of town. From the lane, the residence did not look too bad, while the inside was a rundown mess. Painted a dated shade of teal, the structure had a wide porch and black shutters on most windows. Gliding into the gravel driveway, I leaned the two-wheeler against the fence.

In the backyard, Bosco panted as she tested the chain. Luckily, the dog didn't bark. I had tried approaching the pit bull once, giving up for good meeting her ill-tempered glower.

Vince inhabited the third floor, a converted attic. Even though the vaulted chamber was freezing in the winter and hot as hell in the summer, his room is a neat hangout. Ranzetta tacked rock and roll band posters on the sloped walls and played albums on the hand-me-down RCA record player he received from his brother Paul.

At this hour, I was reluctant to knock on the front door. I tried to avoid Vince's parents as often as possible, especially Mr. Ranzetta, who always stared menacingly past the neck of a beer bottle. Grabbing a handful of lima bean-sized gravel, I cast the pebbles high against the bedroom sash. After a few unsuccessful shots, Vince's shadow grew, then vanished, annoyed to be disturbed. Eventually, he exited the rear, pulling a T-shirt emblazoned with the words *"Smooth Move Ex-Lax!"* over his head.

My friend wasn't an early bird, so I wisely kept silent. Filling a pot with clear water for Bosco, Ranzetta uncovered his bike from a sheet of canvas. "Let's skedaddle," he said, spitting a loogie of accumulated night snot.

Vince led the way, whipping through the deserted town, leaping up and off sidewalks in daring fashion. Tired or not, the boy had one speed—fast. He cleverly avoided going past Jim's by taking a narrow, garbage-lined alley.

There were a few entrances into the Woods. Vince chose a path that snaked beyond the duck pond, across the boulevard from the Borough Hall. Behind a white gazebo, the constricted opening could only be located by standing directly before the encroaching shrubs. The humid air glistened on my skin like morning dew. Disgusting cobwebs caught my hair as we dived below hanging vegetation. I wondered if Billy would be at the Shack and if the legends were true.

Outlaw stood waiting, excited that we made an appearance. "Hey, Vince, Johnny," he greeted, hands jammed in pockets.

"What's shakin', bacon?" Ranzetta called, braking. Appreciative of his friendliness, Billy grinned and nodded. Vince didn't respond to many people.

"Hi, Billy," I said, hopping off the bicycle. "Man, it smells like ass out here."

"That's the skunk cabbage. Polecat Weed is quite a remarkable flower," he declared. "That foul odor attracts pollinators."

"Yeah, right," I said. Crinkling my nose, I started to think the kid was a bookworm.

"Are you armed with pig stickers?" Vince asked, brandishing a worn blue Boy Scout knife. Wielding the bayonet, he put on an exhibition, stabbing make-believe foes. With an exaggerated flourish, Ranzetta polished the edge on his jeans and put the blade in a pocket.

"Nah, but I did bring snacks," I replied, patting the knapsack.

Outlaw produced a worn, canvas-sheathed canteen and a vial of insect repellant. He asked if we wanted any.

Vince answered, "Later. I'll cover defense, while you ladies can be in charge of food and first aid. So, Billy Bob, how do we get to this humongous boulder of yours?"

Proud to own a nickname, Billy hitched up baggy dungarees. "It's this way. As I said before, I only went to the rock once." Billy pointed to an overrun trail angling into the wilderness.

Numerous times, we had nosed around the periphery of the Shack. Venturing to roam this footpath, we gave up when the tract became impassable.

"Lead the way," I requested, swinging a leg onto the bike.

"It will be easier if we walk," Ranzetta advised, strutting purposely toward the path.

The sun burned away the mist, and the trees created slanting shadows as we followed him down the track. The heat intensified. Glad that Outlaw brought refreshments to share, I craved my own supply. The route seemed shorter than I recalled, and our group soon became inundated by a curtain of ropey, dangling vines.

Searching for an opening in the climbing plants, Vince pulled out the knife and extended the microscopic machete. "Over that way!" Billy yelled, specifying a stretch behind a giant oak.

After weaving our way past the creepers and scrub, we stood in a small expanse. A circle of stones confined the remnants of a fire containing blackened soup cans. Ranzetta kicked a tin, sending puffs of ash soaring.

Two pathways headed from the camp. "Do you have any idea which one to take?" I asked. The trail to the right ended in a swampy bog, so I hoped Outlaw picked the left.

Naturally, we wound up hiking the squishy course. In the beginning, we jumped from dry clump to dry clump, without being drawn into the mire. Before long, my Converse high-tops submerged into the muck. The sneakers would need to be clandestinely washed before my mom found them. Ready to suggest turning back, firmer ground returned. Billy gained the lead and moved swiftly. The morning grew very hot, no breeze. He began to perspire profusely through the white T-shirt, as swarms of pesky gnats veiled our heads. Futilely, I swatted the pests or ran faster than they could fly.

"Billy, you got any brothers or sisters?" Vince inquired, drinking from the canteen. His face was shining, and stringy dark hair stuck to his forehead.

The boy seemed worried, explaining how his brother enlisted in the Marines and was shipped to Vietnam. "Ed's been overseas a couple of months, and we sometimes get postcards." Morose, he sounded as if he wanted to cry.

"Don't sweat it man," Ranzetta said, gripping Outlaw's arm. "As a Marine, he'll be fine. Your brother's getting high and getting laid."

Billy smiled thankfully. "Yeah, I guess you're right, but it's kind of scary. Mom and Dad don't discuss the war much, at least, not in front of me." Taking a prolonged slug, he spun the cap and resumed trudging on the footpath.

Vince gave a wry smirk and shrugged. Often, I had no clue what my friend talked about and wished for an older sibling who might school me in more adult topics. I understood "getting high," but remained fuzzy on why Billy's brother needed to lie down.

The terrain inclined between pine trees. I had no impression any hills existed at the Woods, as the topography looked flat from the exterior. I couldn't see ahead and the overgrown path drove us to hop over rotting logs.

Outlaw warned, "Heard a few copperheads live out here. Have you guys seen any?"

"Last year, I saw a garter snake at the pond," I replied. Picking up the reptile by the tail, I had chickened out when the serpent struck back. Now, I used extra care stepping on anything.

Ranzetta was responsive to my abhorrence to serpents and spiders. At every opportunity, he brought up the topic or tried fear tactics. "Later, we can go snake hunting," Vince proposed, giving me a mischievous glance. Grimacing, I flipped him the bird.

"The rock is up here someplace," Billy huffed. Now drenched in sweat, he repeatedly turned to verify we still followed.

The three of us emerged through a tangled archway of bushes into a round clearing almost fifteen yards wide. A boulder eight feet long dominated the center. It was easy to perceive the four-foot-tall, table-shaped stone as an altar. Flecks of quartz and mica flickered in the sun as we circled. Never noticing any other large mineral formations in the vicinity, I speculated uneasily of its origin.

The cluttered space held beer cans and bottles. Logs and boxes rimmed the perimeter. Paul definitely partied here.

"Check this out," Vince whispered sinisterly, pointing to one section of the stone. "Blood. Now, I understand why they named this place Ceremonies."

We examined the surface where he ran a digit. Indeed a stain, yet weather worn, the substance was tough to identify.

"Shit, yeah," Ranzetta breathed, nose close, sniffing the spatter.

Nauseated, not wanting physical contact with the rust-colored pigment, I touched the sticky mottle to hide my building stress. Brain pounding, I stumbled to the corner of the glade to slump on a milk crate. *Get me out of here!*

Billy walked to me, handing the canteen. "Johnny, are you feeling well? Your skin is rather pale."

"I'm fine, just hot," I answered, gulping the liquid and hoping for the swampy sensation in my sinuses to ebb.

Vince scratched at the blemish with the blade's edge, the sound grating. A white object was barely visible in the weeds below the rock. Poking in the unhealthy grass, I unearthed a miniature skull, using a twig to lift the dome by the eye socket. "Look at this."

They rushed to survey my find. "Most likely a cat, too small for a dog," Vince mused.

"Yes, I agree it is *felis catus*," Billy murmured, taking the head. Inspecting the cranium at every angle, he prodded at the sizable canines.

In the ground, a silver disk glinted from the curved depression formed by the skullcap. I took the stick and dug, hooking the tip under a loop of leather. The soil released a collar, the ring the size of a feline's neck. With thumb and forefinger, I cleaned off the round tag and tiny bell.

"Banshee, 268 Frank St."

Outlaw peered over my shoulder. "That's where you live, Franklin Street?"

"Yeah, if that is what 'Frank' means."

"The owners shortened the address to fit on the identification badge." Pleased, he positioned the skull on top of the boulder, a ghastly hood ornament.

Ranzetta accepted the neckband, scoured off more dirt, and handed me the article. "Let's see where that is. Maybe the owner will give us a reward for telling what happened to their pet."

Doubtful, I remained silent. We lived at 322 Franklin Street, so I knew the residence lay up our road and on our side. I didn't want to put the grubby thing in my pocket. Wrapping the leather in paper, I shoved the wad in the pack.

"Let's split," I urged, leaving the hilltop.

Before long, we hunkered down at the clubhouse, and I passed around the Pop Tarts. Lethargic, I was done for the day. My head still hurt, and I just desired going home to watch television or nap. I informed my friends that I had to do chores.

"Let's find 268 on Sunday," Vince suggested. Billy nodded in accord.

"Sure," I consented.

We barged from the Woods and into the open by the duck pond. Families edged the water, throwing bits of bread to the mass of quacking birds.

On the way home, I checked out the number on the animal collar. Mr. Reynolds lived at 268 Franklin Street. Somehow, I was not thunderstruck. My neighbor oozed oddness.

Headache cured by a hearty lunch of peanut butter and jelly sandwiches, I spent the afternoon pulling weeds in the flower beds. Dad worked on a project in the basement and regularly came outside to evaluate my progress.

"What about that section, Johnny?" My father gazed at an aggressive mass of dandelions overtaking the yard. Strolling to the garage, he returned with a sharp implement. My dad taught me methods to sever the plants at the roots with the forked piece of metal. "That's the only way to kill them for good."

The hot and sticky day dragged on, and the golden yellow flowers were endless. Looking up the hill, I wondered how Mr. Reynolds' cat wound up at Ceremonies. Was the feline beheaded? Where was the rest of the body? I reminisced on Pastor Richards' sermons of animal and human sacrifice. The Bible contained many macabre stories.

Summoning me inside, my father patted my back. "Nice job, Son. The deal with weeds is that there will always be more tomorrow."

I concurred and went to view TV with my sister. Spanning the couch, we tuned into a rerun episode of *Gunsmoke*. As Matt Dillon and Doc argued, I found myself unable to concentrate. I envisioned what had caused those evil bronze stains on the altar-shaped rock, at a hidden place named Ceremonies.

Sunday Morning—May 21, 1967

I stirred from another fitful sleep. As the substance of the dream evaporated, I vaguely recollected something regarding a darkened school building and the inability to pinpoint my class. There had been a haunting tone to the nightmare, and although I needed further slumber, swung out of bed.

The edgy mood might be related to the fact that I hadn't yet studied for Monday's history test. Sliding the thick schoolbook onto my lap, I paged to the required chapters. The book included a few alluring gory illustrations on German warfare, but the words were pure drudgery. I finished two-thirds of the reading and reviewed the notes. My illegible doodle had no value. I was totally screwed.

Following a quick breakfast, I went outside for a breath of air and to sample the weather. The sky was hazy, and I expected today to be a scorcher. After a while, Jane came out to play. We pitched a rubber ball back and forth until Ranzetta and Outlaw rolled up.

"Hi, Vince!" my sister exclaimed fondly. "Who's your friend?" On tiptoes, she pointed shyly.

"I'm Billy," he responded, raising a hand. Jane smiled and said hello.

With introductions complete, I wheeled the bike to the curb. "Jane, go indoors," I directed. With a grin and a wave, she skipped into the house through the garage.

"We're gonna speak to the owner of the collar?" Vince asked. Again, he wore the same *Smooth Move Ex-Lax!* T-shirt.

"Yup, I know the place," I replied, gesturing up the lane. "Mr. Reynolds." Extracting the neckband from a pocket, I jingled the bell.

Ranzetta put on his best Dracula impersonation and lisped, "Mr. Reynolds, ve are here to offer information pertaining to vour cat. Ve haf discovered that a blood fiend kidnapped poor Banshee and sucked vim dry." A good Bela Lugosi imitation: we laughed.

"Let's check it out," Outlaw said. "Later, I have to attend church, so I can't stay that long."

Steering up the road, I pulled to a stop. "Hold up!" Once again, Mr. Reynolds was in the yard, burrowing. A dreadful premonition emerged, and I fought the urge to change course.

"Come on, let's talk to him," Vince said, riding to the driveway.

Aware of our presence, my neighbor dropped the trowel. At a kneeling position, he squinted warily.

"Mr. Reynolds?" Ranzetta called, sweeping hair off his brow.

The man got up and walked toward us, square face indecipherable. "Yes, what can I do for you fellas?" Of average height, he appeared to be in his late forties.

With a twirling motion of his finger, Vince signaled me to display the collar.

Nervously, I said, "We found this badge with your address and wondered if your cat or dog was missing." Holding out the neckband, the bell jingled as Mr. Reynolds took it from my palm.

"Hmm." He questioned softly, "Where did you come upon this?"

Billy answered, "Yesterday, in the woodland by the municipal building."

Mr. Reynolds' forearm muscles flexed as he turned the object over, weighed the identification tag, and then passed it back. "I've never seen this and have at no time kept an animal." The man stared each of us in the eyes.

We peered at each other and at my neighbor. "Then why does this pet ID tag show your house number on it?" Vince accused.

Mr. Reynolds' voice raised, and his white cheeks splotched red. "I told you, boy, it's not mine!" His gloved hands clenched into fists.

"Thank you, sir, sorry to bother you," I said gently, wanting to defuse the situation. *The dude looks like he's going to burst a blood vessel.*

Undeterred by Ranzetta itching to extend the interrogation, Billy and I headed downhill. With a disappointed grunt, he accompanied.

"What was that about?" I inquired near my driveway.

"That fucker is lying," Vince responded with disdain. "You could tell, right?"

"I don't know, maybe, who knows? Does it really matter?"

Billy snorted. "That guy lied through his teeth. Wow, I thought he was ready to freak out on Vince." Scowling, he complained, "Gotta go. Need to be at Sunday school at eleven."

"Okay, man, see you later." Outlaw rode off, the undersized bicycle straining.

"Pwaise Gwod!" Ranzetta cried, mimicking a hillbilly preacher.

"What do you want to do now?"

Agitated, he replied, "Sorry, I'm taking off. My parents said we're visiting my grandma."

I knew that meant a trip to the old folks' home. Vince hated that place, finding the nursing facility depressing and stinking of bodily fluids. Never entering one, I imagined a houseful of shambling zombies.

The afternoon was expended weeding, followed by a few more hours studying. By day's end, I felt better about the quiz, but worse in the matter of Mr. Reynolds.

Monday Morning—May 22, 1967

The air in the bike's tire was low, so I walked to school. The overcast sky and weather report predicted rain. Mom provided the plastic green poncho that I rammed into the book bag. As I ambled by Mr. Reynolds' yard, I caught a flash of movement in an upstairs window.

In class, a few kids continued to taunt me about last Friday's love letter. I ignored them. Fortunately, I passed the history test. Vince surreptitiously peeked at my multiple choice examination, trying to steal the answers. As a friend, I should help, but I also reckoned he could do the work himself.

Monday Afternoon—May 22, 1967

Our class assembled in the gym to view *Duck and Cover,* a dated black-and-white instructional film teaching the techniques to survive a nuclear holocaust. The principal presented the movie several times a year which featured Bert the Turtle using his shell to miraculously withstand an atomic explosion. When I was younger, the flick rattled me. Now, we found Bert laughable.

Detention crawled, and I had difficulty staying awake. Marching home, I elected to utilize a shortcut through the Woods. A squat masonry bridge spanned a stream trickling into the thicket. It was hard to distinguish where the brook started, and I pretended the stinky effluent came from a secret well. Scrambling below the arch, one can hike skunk cabbage-lined banks or use steppingstones to cross. The clouds drizzled, and the leaves afforded shelter.

Lonesome, I sang, *"There was a turtle by the name of Bert, and Bert the Turtle was very alert."*

I thought of my classes and again of Ceremonies. Even though I was afraid, I wanted to search Ceremonies for more evidence. The interior of the Woods was crisscrossed with different footpaths. I concluded the general locale of Ceremonies could be found by listening to the cars on Whitman Street. On our trip Saturday, I clearly heard motorists on the east side. The creek flowed to the opposite end, so I preceded downstream, keeping the traffic noise to my right.

A scuffling noise surprised me. A bearded man entered the path. "Hey, little fella," he said, drawing on a non-filtered cigarette. Waiting on the margin, I let him pass, inhaling the stinking combination of nicotine and sweat. Vigilantly, I stared as the hippie blended into the foliage, long hair flopping over the stitched peace sign on his green army jacket. Startled, I had no interest in going back the way he traveled.

Adhering to the main byway, fully in tune with my environment, the drone of traffic diminished. For a while, the burbling water and the breeze high in the leaves were the exclusive sounds. Dank air held the faint tang of combustion. As the odor strengthened, I paused to get my bearings: five o'clock and no idea where I was. Still by the brook, I had no indication of the distance to Ceremonies or where to exit the Woods. *I should have left a trail of breadcrumbs.*

Around a curve, I walked into an acrid, bluish haze. Last week, I watched a forest fire episode on one of the nature programs. The bug-eyed host cowered by a stampede of spooked antelope. Petrified, the khaki-clad entertainer screamed into a microphone.

The sky stormy, I had to head home. A faint glimmer in the foreground made me curious. The spark originated at a tall chestnut. Checking for company, I observed the smoke drift and embers smolder inside the hollowed-out trunk. From what source did a tree start burning deep in the Woods? Worried that it was arson, I assumed the entire area might incinerate if I didn't return and tell my parents. They could phone the fire department. A funny idea came to mind. Yellow spray sizzled at the silly attempt to drown out the blaze with my own human hose.

Below the chestnut, the route meandered upward past a stand of pines. The region looked familiar. The pinecone-peppered pathway merged into the broader trail that I had trekked with Ranzetta and Outlaw. With a relieved grin, I ran up the footpath.

I entered the glade, soaking in the surroundings: the ring with tree limbs and boxes thrusting up against the edges, scatterings of liquor containers and cigarette butts, and most importantly, the huge rectangular boulder that lay in wait beneath threatening thunderheads. Now that I was on my own to scrutinize the stone, it appeared larger and more imposing. *How the hell did it get here?* Knots once again tightened my stomach. *The skull isn't there!* I stopped, convinced that Billy had left the feline cranium perched upon the darkening stain. Had it had fallen, or had some kids taken it? I was braced to hightail it home, but I had to know. Circling the rock, I pushed aside the weeds and grass with a sneaker—*nothing.*

Near Vince's scrapings, a metallic object glittered in a slight cavity on the boulder's exterior. I peered at a bronze disk. *"Diablo, 268 Frank St."* The tag hadn't been here two days ago. The badge clattered to the stone as I scanned the circumference. *Crap!* Shaking the feeling of being spied upon, a shiver ran along my spine. Except for the single passage, the bushes and reeds formed an impenetrable barrier—*trapped!* As if turning on a shower head, the clouds released a torrential downpour. The sky ignited and rumbled as I cleared the hole in the shrubs. Drenched, I ran through the rain, pulling the poncho from my knapsack.

Part Two

Mr. Reynolds

Saturday Evening—October 23, 1971

VINCE, BILL, AND I CROUCHED in the rhododendrons behind Mr. Reynolds' split level. The sun had recently set at six o'clock. Although the temperature was mild for October, a damp chill rose from the ground. My neighbor had a very nice home and kept the property tidy. The spacious backyard had a redwood patio that contained deck chairs and a spick-and-span barbecue. Light leaked around the blinds of an upper window.

"John, give me the telescope," Ranzetta whispered, stretching out a palm. I passed the Christmas gift of a few holidays past and described how to work the focus.

"Yeah, yeah, I got it." Aiming the instrument at the residence, he scanned the windows and twisted the lens. "Can't see a goddamn thing. The image is fuzzy."

"Turn this, bonehead," I instructed, grabbing at the knob on the eyepiece. Vince scowled, nudging away my hand. After a few adjustments, he continued the vigil.

Bill brought a pair of walkie-talkies and gave me one. "I'm going to the far end for a reconnaissance. Use channel 8," he said, melting into the darkness. Fine-tuning the squelch cut the electronic hiss of white noise.

"Testing, testing," blared from the tiny speaker. Vince glared as I quickly reduced the volume.

Talk button pressed, I fancied myself Bill Cosby in *I Spy*. "Copy, do you detect anything?"

"A lamp is on in the basement," Outlaw responded. The radio clicked again. "Why don't you rendezvous over here?"

"Ten-four."

"Follow me," Ranzetta breathed, leaping to his feet and running across the yard.

We huddled by Bill in the mulch beside a garden shed. Reaching for the telescope, he trained the lens on the windowpane. "There's movement, shadows, can't make out much. Someone is definitely in the cellar."

Vince army-crawled toward the dwelling. "Ranzetta!" I rasped as he crossed further, elbows pumping. Straightened, he signaled to stop. Two digits forked to his eyes, he proceeded to wriggle to the side of the small casement. Looking in, the yellow glow illuminated the long face. My friend stayed still for a while, and I tried to imagine what was so compelling.

"Vince," I mouthed, gesturing wildly. "Vince!" Engrossed, the boy waggled a finger with impatience. A moment later, he glanced backward and beckoned us forth.

Outlaw eagerly inquired in a hushed voice, "Should we go there?"

"I guess," I sighed. "That is one crazy dude." He returned the telescope.

Instead of creeping, we ran stealthily to the casement. Ranzetta pointed and made an exaggerated leering pout. "This guy, what a big-time perv," he chuckled.

Against the spotted glass, I noticed tables and woodworking tools. "Is Reynolds down there?" Bill asked.

Vince replied, raising eyebrows, "I didn't see him, but I can hear sanding. Do you realize what that stuff is?"

The apparatus appeared to be odd benches constructed of wood and leather, none of which I recognized. *Exercise equipment?*

"Is it a torture chamber?" Outlaw wondered.

"That's right, a torture chamber for getting fucked," Vince choked, unable to smother giggles.

Peering through the haze, I discerned straps and chains fastened to a few of the mystifying devices. I pondered if this had something to do with the missing neighborhood cats.

"That's sex furniture. The kind where people get tied up and spanked or whipped. Once they start crying, you have your way." Ranzetta seemed quite proud of this knowledge.

After consuming this disturbing information, I questioned dryly, "When did you become the expert?" Entranced, my friend didn't reply. The harsh sound of a power drill broke the silence.

"Let's vamoose," I urged. "This is insane!" Standing up, I rushed to the shrubs.

Vince laughed as we scurried from Mr. Reynolds' house of horrors.

Cabbage Night

Thursday Afternoon—October 28, 1971

BEING TEAMED UP WITH KAREN SCHMIDT in chemistry lab was working out. In September, I enrolled as a freshman at Northern Valley Regional High School, located in the neighboring town, Demarest. "Here," Karen said, handing me a vessel filled with vinegar. "Titrate," she ordered.

Stumped, I mumbled, "The instructions say to place the beaker under the burette." I was glad to be paired with Karen; the pretty classmate proved exceedingly intelligent. To top it off, my laboratory partner's body had developed nicely.

Typically laughing with her friends, now the girl stared with disdain, snatching the beaker from my glove.

Stationed at a lab bench across the room, Bill spoke animatedly with his lab partner. The teenager had thinned out in the last few months and now stood taller than me. The spiky red hair had grown much longer, too.

"Do you need any help?" I asked. Eyes narrowing, Karen shook her head in dismay. Letting my lab partner complete the balance of the project, I thought: *Man, this girl is great!*

Friday at Noon—October 29, 1971

"What are we doing tomorrow night?" Ranzetta questioned. A cheeseburger worked its way into his yap.

Lounging around the cafeteria lunch table, we tried to look hip. This was my favorite evening of the year, the nightfall before Halloween—Cabbage Night!

Cabbage Night or Mischief Night was the witching hour for mayhem. The local teenagers gathered in mobs and wreaked havoc upon the neighborhood and one another with shaving cream, eggs, toilet paper, or whatever else might be bought or stolen. The night before Halloween mirrored the closest thing to anarchy I had ever witnessed.

"Smash pumpkins?" I answered smiling, suggesting the usual. "Ring doorbells and run? Set garbage on fire?"

Solemnly, Outlaw contemplated activities. Suddenly, his freckled face beamed purposefully. "Let's bomb Mr. Reynolds."

"Sounds like a terrific idea to me," Vince professed, standing to return the lunch tray.

He returned to settle in with his feet propped up. I concurred, "Yeah, that is one sick bastard." Thinking of the sexual contraptions in Reynolds' basement, I admitted to being slightly turned on, but also sensed something very wrong was happening there. Besides the unaccounted-for cats, additional considerations lurked in my mind that I could not quite capture. Ever since finding the cat skull, my haunting nightmares of being lost in the park frequently involved an individual resembling my neighbor.

Bill broke the trance, asking, "Got the goods ready, John?" He grinned, stoked and ready to go.

"Yes, sir," I replied, snapping a crooked salute. A year ago, I had arisen at daybreak on Halloween and foraged the streets and bushes for cast-off Barbasol containers and valuable items jettisoned by fleeing juveniles. Painting the cylinders flat black, I equipped the guns with lengthened nozzles that spurted foam eight to ten feet. Now feeling akin to the older kids, I couldn't wait for the fun to begin.

Ranzetta whipped his shaggy mop and declared, "I have a bunch of firecrackers, plus two M-80s to blow up."

Outlaw slapped the table with enthusiasm and hurried off for the next lesson.

Cabbage Night—Saturday Evening—October 30, 1971

At dinner, my mother questioned warily, "Johnny, are you going out tonight?" Jane gave me a stern glare and then crossed her eyes.

"Yes, Mom," I answered, grinding pepper on the catsup-covered meatloaf. "Just gonna hang around with the guys."

"With Vince and Bill?"

"Yup. I mean, yes." Ingesting a large forkful of chunky mashed potatoes, I prayed for the cross-examination to end.

"John, let's not have a repeat of what occurred last Halloween," my father requested, serious and amused in the same smirk.

The previous year, we were caught red-handed soaping up the cars of the Petersons, a nice couple living directly behind our house. What set my mother off was seeing "Suck My Dick!" scrawled across the windshields.

Face burning, I murmured, "Yes, Dad."

"And you need to be in by ten o'clock," Mom added firmly.

"May I go too, Johnny?" my sister inquired, rabid to wear her new princess costume.

"Jane, you are not coming with us this evening." Rising to carry the plates into the kitchen, I granted more kindly, "I'll take you trick or treating tomorrow after school." As I loaded the dishwasher, the anchorman discussed attempts at detente to ease tensions between the US and USSR.

Using a black garbage bag to stow the stash hidden in the basement, I met Outlaw and Ranzetta on the adjacent block. Troops of kids assembled, and Haworth police cars patrolled the neighborhood. When headlights approached, we ducked beneath the nearest shrubs. I passed around cans of shaving cream.

"Killer. This one is chock full," Vince said, shaking a canister and spritzing foam on Bill.

"Not cool, man!" he shouted, jetting white froth on Ranzetta's jacket.

"Hey!" I admonished. "That's to squirt on others, not us." My pals both holstered their weapons.

Showing the lads toilet paper rolls stuffed with flour, I enlightened, "We can chuck these powder bombs, and they'll explode."

Vince produced a pack of firecrackers and inserted several into the ends. "Now they definitely will." After a few guffaws, we prowled the boulevards.

I indicated a monstrous carved pumpkin sitting on the stoop of a house, set back from the road. "Fuck yeah, mash that motherfucker!" Ranzetta urged.

Bill ran up the sidewalk and onto the portico, hefted the decoration overhead, and slammed the squash on the front steps. The gourd ruptured in an orange cloud of seeds. *Kersplat!*

"Holy smokes!" I exclaimed, sprinting helter-skelter along the avenue. Falling to my knees, I convulsed with laughter.

Astounded at his hasty, deviant actions, he chuckled, "Oh man, that was far out!"

Vince slapped Bill on the back before chasing a group of squealing little kids, coating the wee ones with layers of shaving lotion.

An hour elapsed, roaming the streets egging houses, throwing toilet tissue, and spraying more revelers with foam. In one garden, we found rotting tomato plants and enjoyed splattering the mushy fruit against the residence's walls. Keeping to the secondary roads, the three of us wisely avoided the huge parading groups of older teenagers chanting and picking fights.

"Quiet," Bill cautioned, pointing to an oncoming patrol car. Concealed by a hedgerow, we braced to strike.

"Get ready to run; these fuses are short," Vince warned, passing out the firecracker-infused flour bombs. The vehicle was now thirty feet away. Smoothly flicking a Salem lighter, he lit all three. "On my signal," he commanded. "Now!" Ranzetta hooted as the cords neared the end. Hurling the tubes at the oncoming police cruiser, we watched eagerly. Flying high, mine exploded in a white shower above the roof, while the remainder erupted as direct hits against the passenger window. The automobile jerked to a standstill.

Vince screamed, "Run" and vanished.

Grabbing Bill by the sleeve, I yelled, "Come on!" and pursued Ranzetta.

The cop exited the car and shouted. In the darkness, Outlaw created a racket, slamming into lawn furniture and pinwheeling into a rose bush. Vince could not be found. Evading via another yard, we slid behind a fence. Provoked, neighborhood dogs barked as we caught our breath.

"Hey," Vince whispered, hiding by a rack of firewood. "Funny meeting you fellas here."

I giggled until Bill demanded for me to shut up. "Ow, my leg!" he cried, wincing in pain.

"Sorry, bro," I consoled. "Let's get going."

"Mr. Reynolds?" Ranzetta asked, sneer creasing his face.

"Let's do it," Outlaw replied gamely.

In the shelter of shadows, with Bill groaning, we hustled in and out of backyards, arriving again by Mr. Reynolds' shed. The house had the same light on upstairs, although no one appeared to be home.

Having saved a few eggs, I shared the embryos, one each. "So what's the skinny?" I questioned.

"Check these out," Vince answered with hushed anticipation. In his palm rested a duo of red cardboard cylinders, each an inch and a half long with green fuses. *M-80s!* The explosives looked menacing. "These are the equivalent to a quarter stick of dynamite."

"Where did you obtain these?" Bill inquired, picking up one of the charges to examine.

"Paul gets the basic parts and gunpowder through the US mail from China. Once, I helped put the M-80s together. Any extras are sold to his chums. One idiot blew a friggin' pinkie off," Ranzetta specified with wide-eyed awe.

Unbidden, I conceived a diabolical plan. "Let's throw these bombs on Reynolds' porch and then egg the freak as he opens the door." Immediately, I wanted to take the idea back. *What if he sees us?*

"Oh boy!" Vince exclaimed, slipping out his trusty lighter.

"Let me do one," Bill pleaded, eyes shining with promise.

"Sure, buddy." Ranzetta relinquished one M-80 and transferred his egg. "Give John your yoker so he can hold onto them while we torch these suckers."

The squad circled with care to the front of the building, below the veranda. The facade hid in gloom.

"After I ignite the fuses, we throw these fuckers over the railing and run across the street behind those hedges. When old Mr. Reynolds comes outside to see what the big ruckus is, we egg him in the schnoz," Vince suggested, pantomiming bewilderment.

Cautiously, he lit the tip of the fuses. The freight train was now in motion, too late to leap the hell off. When Outlaw threw his M-80, the stick rolled up against the welcome mat. Laughing, he took off running. Ranzetta tarried before lobbing overhand. The firework landed with a knock, as I traversed the road cradling the three eggs.

In an instant, I recorded Bill's smile of expectation, freeze-framed into a grin of astonishment as the initial bomb detonated. *Whump!* I turned to watch Vince's rushing shape silhouetted in the flash of the second explosion. *Ka-boom!*

"Jumping Jesus on a pogo stick!" Vince bellowed, crouching. *"Oh, my God."* His voice sounded muffled, and my ears buzzed in the now-deafening silence.

Anxiously standing by to see the result, a few lights appeared along the street, and a few doors opened. Where were the cops? Mr. Reynolds' home remained dark. Disappointed, we stared at each other.

"Should we go?" Outlaw asked, pupils the size of half dollars.

"Hold on," Ranzetta replied, clutching an egg. "I think he is—"

"What?" Bill yelped. Out of the corner of my eye, I glimpsed a pair of strong, seizing fists. A large, nondescript character wearing an old-fashioned hat towed him into murkiness.

Eggshells dropped, as Vince and I flinched in shock. In terror, we dashed down the lane.

"Wait a second!" Ranzetta huffed, gripping my arm. His skin gleamed with sweat. "We can't leave Bill there. Who was that? Is it Reynolds?"

Bent over, side in stitches, I gasped, "Don't know. I ain't going back there." Wearily slumping to the curb, I held my head. *Fuck!*

"John, we've got to go." Determined, he reached out a palm.

Drawing me to my feet, we retraced our steps. A block away, we snuck through yards within sight of the residence. Lamps now lit the entrance and windows on the lower floor.

"Oh no," Vince moaned. "That asshole's taken Bill." My friend rocked, rubbing his temples with both hands. He was losing it.

"We can't do anything," I said, trying to stay calm. "Let's go to my house. My mom and dad will figure out what to do."

Dubious, Ranzetta sharpened. "You're telling your parents what we did?" Nervous, his fingers scratched a cluster of blemishes.

"Let's first look in Reynolds' windows," I suggested. Deliberating again, I changed my mind. "No, we're walking home."

As we entered the kitchen, my knees trembled, stomach oozing sour. When Mom saw my pale face, her mouth registered worry. "Is Billy with you?" she questioned.

"Uh, ah, no . . . he's, ah—" I yammered. Chest throbbing, I wondered if a heart attack hurt this much.

"Mrs. Outlaw called. Something has happened, and she needs Billy home now."

"Well, he's um—"

"Where is Billy, John?" Angry, my mother yelled, "Vincent?"

"Mrs. Townsend," he began. "Bill was—"

The kitchen telephone rang. Now by the sink, Dad answered, "Hello?" Impassive, he listened closely. "Alice, I am very sorry for your loss." The receiver hung up with a click.

Gravely, my father addressed us. "Billy's brother lost his life in Vietnam. Mr. and Mrs. Outlaw just found out. Bill is home." Abruptly aged, he said to Mom, "There will be a military service for Ed next week, when the Marines ship his remains to America." Turning to me, my dad said, "Mrs. Outlaw requested that, for now, don't contact Billy. As you might expect, the family is extremely upset." Before leaving the kitchen, he glanced compassionately once more at my mother.

Primed to cry, she hugged me and then awkwardly squeezed my friend. Jane watched the scene from the doorway.

Saying goodbye to Vince, we questioned if Outlaw was okay and how he escaped.

That night, I dreamed of being trapped in Mr. Reynolds' basement. None of the windows opened. The stairs rose endlessly as the arch fiend ensnared my legs, pulling me under.

Friday Afternoon—November 5, 1971

Mom informed us we'd be attending Ed Outlaw's funeral. I had been to Grandpa John's last rites, which was closed casket. Although I never met Bill's brother, I hoped to not encounter a stiff.

Bill stayed out the entire week. Karen now seemed resigned to my ineptitude. Happy that my chemistry partner clarified a few of the procedures, I cleaned up and put away the lab equipment when she absconded with friends.

The ceremony commenced at three o'clock in the afternoon. My mother asked the school's permission for us to leave early. Uncomfortable, I yanked on a tie and grey jacket. Jane wore a black dress, thrilled to be formally attired. We perched in the backseat of my father's station wagon. On the ride to the funeral parlor, he explained that New Jersey didn't have a military cemetery. Ed Outlaw would be buried in George Washington Memorial Park with full honors. Dad said Ed's luck ran out when he trod on a landmine. Wondering what parts survived, I tucked in my trousers.

Drakes' Funeral Home was a sprawling Queen-Anne style mansion. The roof supported flanking round towers capped with green cones. The Drake twins welcomed our clan past huge oak doors and ushered us along a series of muted hallways to the Sunset Forever viewing room. Between displays of medicinal-smelling white lilies, I spotted the deceased in a Marine uniform, lying motionless in a bronze coffin. *Jesus, he looks like Bill!* A few unoccupied foldout chairs filled the rear. Thankful to be so far from the action, I scanned the alcove. Bill sat in the first row, dressed in a dark jacket, head lowered. Mrs. Outlaw grieved against her husband, eyeing their dearly departed son.

The energetic minister recited a few prayers, followed by an uplifting eulogy exalting the fallen fighter. "Edward Albert Outlaw died a hero for the United States. Forthwith, we'll emulate this young man's courage as he walked through the valley of the shadow of death." The pastor swiveled benevolently to the parents. "Life on earth is temporary. We will see our loved ones for eternity in Heaven. Let us commend Edward to the mercy of God." Bill's mother sobbed uncontrollably, almost tumbling off the seat.

Family members and friends gripped the podium, summarizing the lieutenant's lifetime or reliving sentimental memories. An earnest soldier told a heartfelt yarn of Ed's ability to offer humor in any situation. Choking up, the man stepped off the platform, unable to continue. During the depressing speeches, I heard people sniffling and was relieved when the service ended.

In the funeral procession, Dad tailed the lead automobile's flashing beacon to the cemetery. The long line of vehicles had right of way under the traffic signals. Mom tried to start light conversation, but eventually stopped. A string of chanting longhairs stood near the gate. In large block letters, one yellow poster read "Drop Acid NOT BOMBS!" Swaying handmade signs proclaimed "Send Them Tractors Not Tanks!"

Outraged, my father cranked the window and roared, "Go back to Russia, you pinko communists!" Rolling up the glass, his face flushed crimson. Simmering down, he apologized to my mother, "Sorry, Helen." She laid a palm on his arm.

Jane and I glanced at each other and kept silent for the procession among the tomb markers.

An honor guard secured the US flag-draped casket. The circle listened to a few more consoling words and shed another round of tears. A Marine folded the cloth and gave the triangle to Mrs. Outlaw, while a Navy seaman played "Taps."

A crew lowered the coffin into the grave as the earnest minister preached, "We therefore commit Edward's body to the ground: earth to earth, ashes to ashes, dust to dust, in the sure and certain hope of the Resurrection to eternal life." The cleric scooped up a fistful of dirt, murmured a blessing, and flung the clay into the hole.

Before throwing a paltry clump on top of the box, I locked eyes with Bill. Blinking, he turned elsewhere.

Monday Morning—November 8, 1971

Bill returned to school. In the morning, I saw him in the hallway and inquired how he was doing. "Fine," he responded, going off to class. Hoping for my friend to show up at lunch, I held off probing into what had materialized at Mr. Reynolds'. Bill didn't appear at the midday meal.

Tuesday Morning—November 9, 1971

Talking before study hall, Ranzetta advised behaving normally toward Outlaw.

"Hey!" Vince shouted in the corridor. Forlornly, Bill pulled books from a locker. We went over and leaned against the cabinets.

I asked gingerly, "Are you coming to lunch?" Bill stared.

"Why not, fucknuts?" Vince questioned, expression alternating between resentful and concerned.

"You guys just bailed on me. *You ran away!*" Outlaw answered furiously. A glint of ember sparked his eyes.

"John and I bugged out, but we did come back for you," Ranzetta explained, spreading arms in frustration. "Bill, you weren't there. Then we went to John's house, and your mother phoned to say you came home. And she told us to let you alone."

Ashamed that Vince had been the one wanting to help, I remained silent.

"Following the explosions, we hid behind those shrubs, and then you disappeared. What happened? Who grabbed you?" Impatiently, he inquired, "Was it Reynolds?"

Bill regarded us with a hint of a smile. "I'll tell you at noon. Right now, I have geometry."

In English class, I conjectured what had transpired with Bill. Cabbage Night was wild. Meditating on the funeral service, I had to turn my thoughts aside; they were too melancholy. I hoped an extraordinarily long time passed before the next burial.

Composition had become one of my favorite classes. My sentence structure improved, and Mr. Price appreciated my stories. On most essays, I scored As or Bs. The teacher's arms flailed passionately as he looped the classroom, elucidating transitive and intransitive verbs.

Finding myself gaping at the back of Karen Schmidt's head, I speculated on what she could be thinking. Karen's golden brown hair reached down, braided in a lengthy ponytail. I had chemistry that afternoon and looked forward to seeing my laboratory partner. The prior evening, I even read over today's experiment. For the first time, I was prepared.

Tuesday at Noon—November 9, 1971

"Christ, my mom is a wreck," Bill said to Vince, as I set the lunch tray on the cafeteria table. Sliding up a chair, he glanced at me. "My mother was hysterical when she told your dad to not call me. On Cabbage Night, while we fucked around, a CNO walked up to the house and—"

"What's a CNO?" Ranzetta interrupted.

"Casualty notification officer," Outlaw continued. "The CNO communicates to the family that a member has died in action. They explain the procedures: delivery of remains, funerals, and any assistance. The officer brings a chaplain to illuminate why God picked your kid to blow to smithereens. Cocksuckers," he muttered bitterly.

We ate for a moment before I asked, "My father said Ed got killed by a landmine?" I felt horrible for Bill, yet thirsted for these morbid details.

"Yeah, in a fucking Vietnamese rice paddy. After two years stationed stateside, he volunteered to deploy for a second tour. I told him he was crazy."

Having seen a zillion war movies, I imagined a line of infantry marching single file through a field, one man vaporizing in a puff of bloody mist, the rest wailing and dropping for cover. *Jesus.*

"Now life's a drag at home. My parents barely speak to each other, and I pretty much fend for myself, still eating lousy leftover funeral food. What's weird, they sealed the door to Ed's bedroom, like it's some sort of holy shrine."

"That's awful," I agreed, wanting to change the subject. "Can you tell us about Cabbage Night? What happened?"

Outlaw thrust the tray aside, the chicken Parmesan uneaten. Ranzetta nabbed the cookies asserting, "Now we're absolutely gonna fuck up that douche bag."

"Mr. Reynolds let me go. Your neighbor should have told my mom and dad or notified the police. When the M-80s exploded, he probably came out the back of the house circling behind us. God knows how we didn't see or hear him. Reynolds grabbed me, and you both split. He shoved me to the mud and sat on my legs. That guy is very powerful. I kept apologizing and begged to be let go, scared shitless. Reynolds didn't say a word and vanished. I thought he followed you. Afterwards, I booked."

"Then you get home and find out your brother is pushing up daisies," Vince stated. "That is messed up, for sure. I wonder why he didn't call your parents."

Bill had a faraway stare. "I don't care. Maybe he still will. Honestly, I could give a fuck."

Thursday Afternoon—November 11, 1971

When I entered the chemistry lab, Karen stood chatting with a schoolmate. Pausing, they turned as I dumped the books on the granite counter.

"Hey, John. Do you mind swapping lab partners?" Steve questioned bluntly. Caught off guard, I fumbled for a response.

The girl appeared sympathetic to my reply. I surprised myself, answering, "Of course, I mind. Why?"

"I really hoped. . ." As he gaped at Karen for encouragement, she crossed her arms, watching with amusement.

"Look, Steve, you heard me the first time. Unless my partner feels like switching, I suggest returning to your desk." Exhaling, I peered at Karen, who grinned. The doofus sighed, leaving dejected.

"What was that all about?" she inquired, entrusting me with a laboratory scale.

"Nothing," I responded, smiling. "Karen, I'm practically failing this class, and it is way too late in the semester to change horses."

"You're implying I'm a horse?"

"No, no. . ." I stuttered. "I purely meant—"

"John, you're going to pass. If you want, I'll help you. Science isn't that hard if you apply yourself. Measure four grams of this potassium," Karen said, passing a brown glass bottle. As our hands fleetingly touched, I tingled. Pressing up against the lab table, I hid my growing excitement.

Damn, life sciences are starting to get interesting!

Party Time

Friday Afternoon—November 12, 1971

THE GANG ASSEMBLED IN VINCE'S ATTIC BEDROOM after school. The Ranzettas' finances appeared to be improving, and I observed a few shiny appliances in the kitchen. He blasted a song titled "Black Magic Woman" by a group named Santana. I plopped into a red inflatable seat alongside the homemade audio speakers. Frustrated, slipping off the uncomfortable plastic, I got up and sat on the edge of the bed.

"What's wrong, John, you don't love my groovy chair?" Vince yelled, bobbing his head violently to the guitar riff.

"That crap is for pussies!"

From the carpet, Ranzetta picked up a pair of wadded underwear and hurled the nasty rag. "Fuck you!" he laughed.

Bill courageously tried the stupid chair. Pulling its plug, he announced, "I get what you mean. This thing sucks!" The balloon deflated in a screeching hiss as the boy fell off to the side snorting. It was good to see my friend clown around.

"You losers suck!" Vince shouted, lowering the volume on the mint Lafayette solid-state stereo. He slid to the floor, back against one of the vertical walls. "So, do you fellas want to party this weekend?"

"What are you talking about?" Outlaw inquired, standing by the window.

"Nothing too complicated. We get a shitload of booze and hang out at Ceremonies."

"Ceremonies?" I asked. "That place with the big rock in the Woods?"

"Uh, yeah. What other Ceremonies are you aware of? Everyone goes there to party," he replied, exasperated.

Bill spun to question, onboard and captivated, "Where should we get the hooch?"

"Paul will purchase the beer, if we provide the dough."

Vince mentioned that, even though his brother was a minor, the clerks didn't question his age at many liquor stores. The scruffy beard and surly manner helped.

Not anxious to return to that loathsome site, I said, "Sounds great."

Outlaw gave the thumbs up, planning to get together Saturday.

Saturday Evening—November 13, 1971

The chilly wind howled as the three of us loitered outside Ron's Smokes and Spirits. We agreed to discretely meet Paul at five o'clock p.m. in Demarest. Bill and I balanced atop ten-speed bicycles while Vince popped wheelies along the street on a brand-spanking-new orange Raleigh Chopper.

"Where'd you get that?" Outlaw questioned. The bike was one sweet ride.

"Paul." In figure-eights, Ranzetta winked, keeping a hand on the T-bar-style shifter.

There were rumors of his brother selling reefer at school, and it was exciting to associate with a drug dealer.

"Tight!" I congratulated. Even wearing a down jacket and beanie, my face turned numb.

Bill rubbed palms and said cheerily, "At least the beer stays ice-cold. What kind of suds are we getting?"

"Inexpensive," I answered, passing a fiver. Most of my summer money from cutting lawns spent, I was strapped for cash.

"Indeed," Vince allowed. "If the alcohol is cheap, we can get more."

Paul noisily pulled to the curb in a green 1968 Plymouth Road Runner, throttling the engine once for effect. At nighttime, he wore sunglasses and a worn leather jacket.

"Nice wheels," I said appreciatively.

Proud, Paul nodded at the car. "You kiddies want me to buy beer?"

Vince transferred the pool of bills. "Quarts, please."

The senior smirked and disappeared into the store as we paced the sidewalk. An eternity later, he exited and delivered two paper bags to his brother. "There you go, fellas. Now, you boys owe me."

"Any change?" Vince inquired.

"Yeah, right. You're welcome," Paul chuckled, slapping the outstretched hand. Flashing a peace sign, he ducked into the automobile and peeled out.

With diligence, Bill and I strapped the paper bags to the bicycle racks and tagged after Vince into the darkness.

I hadn't been to Ceremonies in years, but heard the local teenagers had worn a direct route through the Woods to the hangout. Ranzetta had the foresight to tape a flashlight to the handlebars and piloted the way. The glare bounced wildly, creating spooky moving shadows everyplace. "Be mindful of those bottles," he cautioned, as steam billowed from his silhouette. The rough trail carved amid the trees, and the glass clashed with every bump.

Not looking behind, I called from the corner of my mouth, "Outlaw, you okay back there?" Vince traveled at his usual breakneck pace, and I feared losing sight of the beacon.

"Yeah, buddy." His speech vibrated as he hit a rock. The ten-speeds were not designed for off-road use, and I fretted about puncturing the thin tires.

Warmed by exertion and anticipating our destination, I peered sideways into the forest. No moonlight, pitch-black. Scary. *Of all places to go to drink a few beers!* The sharp odor of smoke reminded me of the time I beheld the burning tree. "Are we almost there, Vince?"

"Up here." He pumped the bike up a slight incline into clusters of pine. I switched to a lower gear and followed.

Distinct voices and bawdy laughter drifted between the timbers. The pungent smell of charred lumber deepened, and a faint radiance became visible amongst the growth. Vince skidded and dismounted, leaning the bicycle against a trunk. We untied the bags.

Ranzetta grabbed a sack, unveiling a thirty-two-ounce bottle. The lamp aimed at the trademark, he bawled, "Iron City! This stuff tastes like goat piss." Twisting off the cap, my friend poured half the container down his gullet. Surprised, he smiled, "Not bad. Go easy, John, we have to make the liquor last." Vince grinned, conveying liquid courage. "Just kidding."

I quaffed a snootful of the amber brew and handed the quart to Bill, who finished it off before launching the dead soldier into the shrubs. "Give me more," he belched.

Skeptical, Vince supplied a fresh bottle. "Here you go, brother." He handed me a lager and continued up the path by foot.

As we entered the clearing, a moment expired before anyone noticed our arrival. Pallets blazed in a corrugated metal ring, and a dozen candles wavered high on Ceremonies' altar.

"Hey, Ranzetta! How's it hanging?" a drunken male welcomed.

"What's up, Larry?" he hollered to a couple of guys on milk crates, clutching cans of ale. Ten kids circled the bonfire, smoking and drinking.

Vince tilted his bottle as we moved closer to the flames and sat on a fallen tree. As I gulped the Iron City, ice bits tickled my throat. People say beer is an acquired taste, but the folks in Pittsburgh certainly perfected recipes to ferment a damn fine alcoholic beverage. Ranzetta flared a Marlboro and passed me the pack. I leaned toward the lighter and stifled a cough as the harsh smoke seared my chest.

Bill hungrily guzzled a brewski. We clinked glass. "This is the life!" he celebrated, butt drooping from his lip. It was hard to believe my friend was smashed.

We bullshitted about school, girls, and sports; everybody, more and more tipsy. The tinder scorched my face while my spine remained glacial. Halfway down the second quart, I left the gathering to void my bladder. Cocked backward watching the steaming arc of piss, I wobbled on wooden legs. Away from the fire, it was lonely and frigid. Unnerved, I shivered, zipped up, and hastily returned through the opening to the safety of the group.

I scrutinized the huge centerpiece dominating the flickering space. The rock seemed even larger than I recollected. As the uncanny glittering surface danced in the guttering light, I considered Mr. Reynolds. Snapping off a few lengths of board, I rekindled the inferno.

Vince stared. "Where were you, Johnny, milking it?" Stroking, he illustrated the classic gesture.

"Yeah, I was milking my humongous python." With both hands, I imitated jerking off a monstrous schlong. The crowd roared as I resumed drinking.

Bill's muttering caught my attention. His nails scratched off the Iron City sticker. Glancing at me with soot-irritated eyes, he mumbled, "They say it's supposed to be good luck if you peel off the label."

"Who said that?" I picked at my own red-and-white logo.

After a big mouthful, Outlaw replied, peering deep into the coals, "You know—*them!*" Those fucking schmucks that makes up shit. Those pricks that decides fucking everything. *Fuck!*" Finishing the barley pop, he chucked the container into the embers. The glass sizzled, popped, and turned obsidian.

For a spell, the group sat in silence, mesmerized by the flames. I reflected on why this place might be named Ceremonies and wondered if the title went back to the Lenape Indians. Imagining ancient, bloody rites, I soon felt claustrophobic.

Three females quietly entered, abiding by the sparks to thaw their palms. I had never seen these teenagers in class. The young women, bundled in heavy coats, appeared older. Vince's friend, Larry, nonchalantly said, "Laura, I didn't think you'd show." Lowering to a seat, the scrawny boy folded an arm around her neck.

The other two were introduced as Cindy and Mary, sophomores from a different high school. Sliding over a few inches, the dark-haired beauty sat beside me on the log. Mary found a spot by Vince.

As I uncapped another cold one, Cindy questioned, "May I have a sip of that?"

"Sure." I appraised her profile, sharing the bottle. The girl wasn't at all bad-looking.

Accepting a deep swig, she regarded me. "Delicious," Cindy muttered sarcastically. After recognizing the brand, she squinched her brow. "This oil is swill. What's your name?" she inquired, licking her lips.

"John." I wondered if she sat close to me because of the free alcohol.

"It's swell meeting you," Cindy said, extending a gloved hand. The firm grip lingered.

By the heat, we relaxed, drinking and eavesdropping on lively discussions. Cindy fired up a joint. "Do you want a toke?" she asked, offering the weed.

"Okay, thanks." I took a hit, trying not to choke. Holding in the vapor got easier as we swapped the reefer back and forth. Blandly, my brain melted.

Bill drank, detached, not saying a word. I worried about his present state of mind. Very drunk by now, Cindy's warm shoulder pressed against mine. My eyes shut, the world spiraled upside down.

My eyelids fluttered wide to see her fiddle with an earring. "Can you help me with this, John?" Seductively, Cindy held out the tiny ornament. In the dimming firelight, I studied the pierced hole in the lobe of her delicate ear. Wrapping the ring in my palm, she whispered, "Take it."

I gazed around the campfire. Ranzetta was locked in a lustful kiss with Mary, while Larry unzipped Laura's jacket, a paw roaming under her shirt. Bill glared at the ground.

As I fumbled with the earring, Cindy said softly, "Careful, John. Don't hurt me." Disclosing the pin, she took my hand, bringing the circle to her cheek. Shadows played along the curves of the girl's face, and I became enthralled in the depth of her eyes. For an instant, I thought of Karen.

"What the fuck, Outlaw!" Vince complained. Lager glistened in a darkening stain across his jacket.

Bill stood before the fire pit, holding a foaming bottle aloft. The glass shattered on the stone altar as he staggered through the gap.

Vince and I stared at one another in astonishment. "Let's go, Casanova," I urged, rising.

Annoyed, he nodded and gave Mary a final, sloppy kiss. "See you on the flip side, baby." Ranzetta ran into the dusk yelling.

"Where did he go?" I blurted. At the bicycles, Vince shined the light into the trees. Bill's two-wheeler rested in the same place. Tracking the beam, I had difficulty focusing.

"I don't know. Let's split up to search for that lunatic."

The Woods blurred and enveloped me. "But we only have a single flashlight," I argued, hoping to stay united.

Vince produced an extra penlight from the bike bag and clicked the switch. "John, I'm not a Boy Scout, but I'm always prepared. Go there," he ordered, pointing to a footpath coiling behind Ceremonies. "I'll head back the way we came."

Ranzetta hurried away as I aimed the modest ray at the unfamiliar path. Never imbibing so much and not ever being high, I felt befuddled and queasy. Tunnel vision and standing upright were problems. Gasping in a lungful of frosty air, I trudged down the trail, boots catching against rocks and roots. Vines and low-hanging limbs snagged on my jacket, smacking the side of my face. Drunk or not, I was freezing.

Ahead, a faint splintering crash. "Outlaw!" I called weakly. No response, although the crackling stopped before continuing. "Bill?" I mumbled, peering into nothingness.

Inebriated, I persisted. "Men will be men," I cackled. Here, the foliage converged, and the anemic glimmer narrowly reached three yards. Chasing a stumbling outcry, I moved faster, grabbing tree trunks to remain erect. *Holy Jesus, what am I doing out here?*

"Outlaw!" I shouted. "Come here!" The words sounded hollow. Pushing deeper and deeper into the wilderness, I realized the pathway had vanished. In circles, I swept the weak beam, watching my own footprints freeze in the mud. I was short-winded from exertion, and puffs of vapor drifted into the flashlight's incandescence. Winter's denuded vegetation leaned inward. *I'm going back!*

Hastily reversing, I followed the tracks until they dwindled, the ground too hard. I endured, finding a fork in the route.

Which way? "Bill!" I screamed. "Vince!" *Shit!* Kneeling to examine the earth, the bulb dulled as the batteries drained. Terror-sweats beaded my collar. A few crystallized scuff marks turned to the left. "That away," I murmured, scrambling to unsteady feet. Now weaving through the brush, I yanked at branches, panicking.

As I blindly raced, the course darkened; the horizon smoothed and mirrored the background. Too late to react, I skidded, falling heavily onto a glassy sheet. Sliding uncontrollably, the penlight flew, my gloved hands grappling for purchase. I pinwheeled ninety degrees until a foot caught a frozen root, revolving me in the opposite direction. My body slammed against a thick log. Panting, I saw the lamp seven yards distant, the twinkle aiming away. On my knees and struggling to stand, my legs splayed. Collapsing and cracking the crisp ice, my elbow dipped into the biting water. "Ouch!" I cried to whoever cared. Wincing, I cautiously scuttled to the dying glow.

The penlight lay on a glossy patch, the ray facing a heap of wood. Mind sharpened by the sudden jolt of impact, I strained for the flashlight. Something white emerged near the pile of twigs. *What is that?* On my stomach, I wondered why the curved object looked familiar. As I painfully writhed, my breath fogged the sheen. The dotted line tracing the contour resembled thread—stitching! *That's a shoe!* While gaping at the footwear, I hooked fingers into the insole. Pulling, I questioned why I bothered messing with an old shoe. The ice fractured as the item stubbornly came free. Dirt and leaves sloshed from the inside, soaking my glove. Disgusted, I released the article. An image of a woman in a dream—a hatted man fighting with a girl wearing saddle shoes. *Did that happen?*

The light's intensity faded rapidly. Disoriented, I had to find my bicycle and get home. The temperature lowered as I rested a temple on a forearm, drowsy, drifting to sleep . . . *Get up!* I crawled and placed the black-and-white shoe above the sticks.

Fully elevated, I scanned, attempting to memorize the area. In the nighttime, the trees appeared identical.

With concentration, I skated across the ice, reaching the main trail. Marking the path with three rocks in a triangle, I heard voices echoing in the distance.

"John!" *Bill?*

"Numbnuts!" *That must be Vince!*

I barked, "Over here!" Moving toward the cries, relief warmed my heart. Beckoning lights fueled my legs.

"Where the hell were you?" Vince demanded, a huge, goofy grin plastering his face. "Did you get lost? *Jeez.* We walked everywhere calling your name. Bill thought you shit yourself and went to your house." Farting, he piddled on a stunted sapling.

Outlaw spread his palms and shrugged. "Sorry, man. This whole thing with my brother has me fucking bonkers." Cheeks burning, he smiled sheepishly.

"You sure were drunk as a skunk," I acknowledged, overjoyed to find friends. "Vince, this piece of crap flashlight has kicked the bucket," I joked, swinging the cylinder flaccidly beneath my belt buckle.

"If dingdong here hadn't run off like a maniac, you wouldn't need it, and maybe, just maybe, I might have gotten laid." Vince shoved the penlight in a pocket. "Let's flush this toilet."

Bill laughed. "Fine with me, Mr. Hefner. I am going home to a toasty bed."

I arrived at eleven p.m., nervous to confront my parents. With my jacket filthy, reeking of alcohol, cigarettes, and pot, it didn't take a doctor to diagnose my intoxication.

Adopting a bold approach, I strolled straight through the front door. My mother and sister reclined on the couch viewing the late news. Commentators deliberated the escalating hostilities between India and Pakistan.

"Hi, everyone, I'm bushed and gonna go to bed," I slurred, heading toward the stairs.

"Did you enjoy yourself tonight, Johnny?" Mom questioned, evaluating my red eyeballs and mud-splattered coat.

"Uh, yeah, we rode on our bikes until I fell." I aped normal behavior, keeping my tone steady and eyelids wide open.

"Another awesome Saturday evening riding around in the dark, huh, Johnny?" Jane teased, smiling sweetly.

"Goodnight," I said, slinking to the solitude of my room.

Before sleep found me, I contemplated the implications of a saddle shoe lost in the Woods.

Sunday Morning—November 14, 1971

I dreamt of an ebony horse mired in a peat bog. Poised on the slick edge, I witnessed the heroic battle. The stallion's coat gleamed with sweat, terrified eyes pleading for aid. Helpless and companionless, what could I do? The steed and pit dematerialized, replaced with an abandoned playground. Goats roamed amid the blackened equipment. The swing set's corroded chains screeched, resembling fingernails dragging across a chalkboard.

Hesitantly, I sat upon the unoccupied cracked leather seat. Below, legs pumped, propelling me higher and higher. Momentum building to loop round the top, I tried to stop. Sneakers aligned, the scenery moved, while I remained stationary. *How was I still going faster?* Dipping rearward, rough hands pushed against my shoulder blades—*claws!* I craned my neck to see.

Wake up, wake up!

No longer at the park, I cowered behind a smoldering barbecue as shuffling feet ceaselessly searched.

Wake up! Wake up!

The Shoe

Tuesday Afternoon—November 16, 1971

KAREN POURED ACETIC ACID into a large Styrofoam cup. With the help of a thermometer, I registered a thermal reading. Deftly adding sodium hydrogen carbonate, she peered through safety glasses. "What is the temperature now?"

The mixture foamed to the top of the container. "Up two degrees," I replied, documenting the results in the lab journal. Proudly, I put on a display smelling the froth. "The bubbles are carbon dioxide!"

Karen beamed. "Maybe you'll wind up becoming a scientist yet. So what's this about getting drunk out in the Woods last weekend? Somebody said you were lost?" My lab partner no longer smiled.

"Oh, that," I answered guiltily. "Saturday evening, I hung out with a few friends drinking beers. Who told you that?"

"I have my sources," Karen whispered confidentially, collecting the goggles. Up close, her warm brown eyes were amazing. "John, I wondered if you felt like studying tonight for the chemistry test on Thursday." Class finished, she started gathering papers.

"Uh, sure," I responded coolly, inside jumping up and down. *Wow!*

"Come by at seven-thirty," Karen commanded. "You know where I live, right?" I nodded. Leaving the lab, she called over her shoulder, "Don't be late."

Tuesday Evening—November 16, 1971

Mom hustled by the oven fixing the evening meal, elated that a schoolmate volunteered to assist with my grades.

Jane sat by the dinner table working on a class project. Constructing a realistic replica of the United States Capitol from cardboard, she glanced up, riveted. "Who is this girl?"

"Karen is her name, and she's in my chemistry class," I replied. "What are you building?" Even though the architecture was unmistakable, I sought to change the trajectory of the conversation.

"The Capitol in Washington, DC, where Congress meets. Johnny, weren't you taught that in your American History class?" Jane needled.

Curious, my mother questioned, "Who is the family? Did I meet her parents?"

"No idea, Mom. 'Schmidt' is the last name," I answered, blushing.

"Johnny's got a girlfriend! Johnny's got a girlfriend!" my sister sang with glee.

"Knock it off, Jane!" I said, louder than expected.

"Quit it, you two," my mother ordered. "Be quiet; your father is napping."

After supper, as I was dressing to go to Karen's, I stared at the disappointing reflection in the bathroom mirror. My tangled, dirty-blond mop looked greasy, and the fattening zit pulsed angry red. "Jesus," I moaned, giving the pimple a hard squeeze. Allowing one more pout, I snapped off the bulb.

The Schmidts lived by the golf course on the other side of Haworth. Sweating beneath the jacket, I biked up to the large green residence on Westview Terrace. This upper-class development had been built around the time Karen moved to town.

The windows burned with light as I nervously climbed onto the broad porch. Running fingers through my hair, I inhaled and rang the bell. A shadow crossed the curtains, and the door was yanked wide by a tall gentleman in a pinstriped suit. Steel-blue eyes judged my attire. This flinty fellow had to be Karen's father.

"Yes?" he inquired suspiciously. "Son, are you selling magazines? If you are, we don't want any."

"No, sir. My name is John Townsend, and I'm here to study with Karen," I blurted.

A woman appeared, twisting to shout, "Honey, a young man is here to see you!"

The solemn couple continued to rubberneck until Karen's exasperated voice rose from behind, "Dad, let him inside."

Mr. Schmidt reluctantly unlocked the screen and stood aside.

Scraping my feet on the mat, I extended a hand to Karen's father. "It's very nice to meet you, sir. This is a beautiful house," I said, surveying the comfortable foyer. The man hesitated before shaking my hand. Then, I introduced myself to Mrs. Schmidt, who acted friendlier.

"Over here, John, we'll work in the dining room," Karen invited. Clad in jeans and a flannel shirt, she looked fantastic.

"John, what can I get you to drink?" Karen's mother asked, as we sat at the elongated table.

"Water, please, Mrs. Schmidt." Tonight, I had to be on my best behavior.

Karen opened a notebook, and I produced mine from my book bag.

Demeanor hard to read, she gazed at me. "Are you prepared for this?"

"Ready as I'll never be," I smirked.

Following an hour and a half going over notes, we discussed what might be on the exam. Karen's parents watched television in the front room, occasionally studying me. Karen patiently explained the chemical formulas. "John, you'll do okay. Don't overthink the multiple-choice answers." Finished, my tutor lowered her pen.

I was having an outstanding time and genuinely liked Karen, but finding that shoe in those damn Woods hadn't left my mind. Fixated on the shoe, I hadn't been sleeping lately. *What should I do?* A lonely desert panorama adorned one wall of the dining room, and a few family photographs decorated the opposite side. I considered one image of Karen as a cute, toothless toddler posing beside an older girl. *A sister?*

Eyes direct, Karen questioned, "What is it?"

"Huh?" *What is she talking about?*

"What's that weird expression?"

Guardedly, I took a sip of water from the glass. "What do you mean?"

Annoyed, Karen started to rise. "Fine, don't tell me."

"Hold on," I implored, raising a palm.

Gauging my plea, she sat again. "Why?"

"You're pretty smart. Are you familiar with decomposition?"

Stunned, Karen leaned backward. "Did you say 'composition' or 'decomposition'?"

"Decomposition. You wanted to understand what was bothering me. Outdoors, how long does a dead body take to disappear?"

Incensed, she glanced into the living room. "That's not funny. Christ, what an asshole."

Dazed, I gaped, perplexed. *What did I say?* The chamber's temperature had dropped twenty degrees.

"That's plain mean. I believe it is time for you to go home!" Abruptly standing, her seat banged against the chair rail. Karen's face turned bleak as a winter storm, holding back tears.

"Sure," I said rising. The parents now gawped with concern. "I'm sorry, I—" *What am I sorry for?*

Shoving books in the knapsack, I passed the television, heading for the exit. Karen remained cross-armed at the dining room table.

"Goodbye, Mr. and Mrs. Schmidt," I mumbled, sliding outside. Bewildered, their eyes met. Gently closing the door, I stood on the stoop, questioning what had occurred. The lamps flicked off, and the deadbolt slammed home. Alone again—in the darkness of night.

Wednesday at Noon—November 17, 1971

The gang met at the usual bench for lunch. Vince ate the customary well-done hamburger and fries. The sandwich was sliced in half, my friend saying "partitioned bites" are "a civilized way to eat."

"Bill, if you ever want to talk, let me know," I offered, between mouthfuls of overcooked spaghetti.

Nibbling on a ham sandwich, his cheeks reddened with embarrassment. "Thanks, but I'm doing better."

"That's hardcore shit to deal with, man," Vince commiserated, shaking his head. "Can't imagine what I'd do if Paul got hurt. I worry a lot about the assclowns my brother hangs out with."

"Well, anyways, I'm here if you need me," I finished lamely.

Scanning the space for Karen, I brightened, seeing a tall brunette in the cafeteria line, despairing when the stranger pirouetted.

"Have you guys met Karen Schmidt?" I inquired.

"The attractive girl that's your lab partner? Yeah, she's in a couple of my classes," Outlaw responded. "Karen's definitely a brainiac. Why?"

"Was wondering if you knew anything about her. She transferred here two or three years ago."

Ranzetta spilled globs of catsup over his French fries. "John, do you like her? Isn't she the chick whose sister got killed, or is that story an urban legend?"

Bill scratched his scalp. "It's true. When their daughter vanished, the family departed and returned recently to Haworth. I can't recall the facts."

My friends saw the trauma I tried to suppress. "Oh, crap," I muttered.

Fascinated, Vince asked, "What's the damage? What happened?"

"Nothing," I replied. "I think I said something dumb to piss her off."

"Don't sweat it," he chuckled, wiggling a bloody potato wedge. "They always come back."

Wednesday Afternoon—November 17, 1971

Lunchtime complete, I had study hall in the library for an hour. Sitting in a cramped cubicle trying to unsnarl impossible math formulas, I caught Karen enter with a band of schoolgirls. Desperate to talk to her but afraid to make an ass of myself, I miserably observed the group discreetly banter. After ten minutes of scolding my id for being such a wimp, I made my move.

As I strode forward, she looked up in recognition. The withering glare lowered my confidence to the cellar.

A petite blond sat next to Karen. "What are *you* doing here?" she questioned crabbily.

The friend's flashes of dismissal turned comical as I stammered, "Karen, can I please speak to you a second?"

The girl shot a leveling stare, muttering, "Fine." Irritated, she followed me to the far side of the room. I pulled out her chair and sat across the desk. "What do you want?" she snapped. "Make it quick. I have to get back to my friends."

"I didn't know what happened to your sister. To tell the truth, I found out today. That was a real question I had, and the answer hadn't anything to do with your family."

"You made fun of me, referring to dead bodies. That's sick."

"No, as I told you, I had no prior knowledge." Not the ideal time to grill Karen about her sister. "There is this, um, thing that I needed to ask you. You're good in science, and I don't have any other friends who can help." I also liked her, keeping that fact a secret.

Karen scowled and leaned over the tabletop. "Ask me again, John."

"Are you busy this Saturday?"

"Why?"

Deciding to come clean, I said, "There's something I can show you in the Woods. I think it's a body."

Time lapsed as she grimly dissected my countenance. "Okay, I'll bite. Why do you presume you located a corpse?"

"Last Saturday, I slid on ice while searching for my friend. Then, I found a shoe sticking from the ground. It looked suspicious."

"Really. So you unearthed a shoe. I can't mention to my folks I'm going unaccompanied into a forest with a boy. You're not screwing with me?"

"No, Karen, no way. Seriously, I'm not making this up," I responded. "And I get that I'm strange, but—"

"You got that right," she agreed, rising to leave. "I'll get back to you."

Thursday Afternoon—November 18, 1971

I kept glancing at Karen during chemistry. Focused on the examination, she was oblivious to my attention. Handing in the paper, I caught up at the door.

"How did you do?" she asked. Long, dark locks bounced as we walked down the hallway.

"Ah, guess I did pretty well. On a few stumpers I picked, 'All of the above.' That may have been a huge mistake. We'll see. Thanks for helping me on Tuesday."

"No problem. On Saturday morning, be at the end of my street at ten o'clock. Wait there; I'll meet you." Karen vanished into a classroom.

Thursday was definitely improving!

Friday Evening—November 19, 1971

"Jane, please pass me the plate." With a fork, my mother gored a thick slab of rib-eye. "Be sure to eat those peas and carrots, too."

"Johnny's the one who doesn't eat his vegetables!" my sister alleged with a knife.

"Dear, don't point. It's impolite. I'm mindful your brother hates healthy food, but I treat all my loved ones equally." Punished for loving sweets, she dumped an extra-large portion of greens onto my dish. God, I hated lima beans. "Did you have fun studying at the Schmidts the other evening? The young lady's name is Karen?"

Dad stared at me, startled.

"Yes, she prepared me for the test."

My father faltered, face aghast, "John, you went to the Schmidts?"

"Yeah, there's a classmate in chemistry class who helped me cram for the chem exam. Karen's awfully smart."

Gloomily, my mother scooted in her chair. "Thinking some more, I knew that name sounded familiar. Yesterday, I talked to Barbara on the phone. Mike, remember that teenager who disappeared nine or ten years back? Everyone searched for that child, then the family left town. I wasn't informed the Schmidts returned."

Picking at the green seeds, I remarked, "They moved back to Haworth. Vince said Karen's sister had been kidnapped."

"Barbara recalled her name as Angela, and unfortunately, the poor girl was never found."

Excited, Jane chimed in, "That's the same as those lost kids on the posters at the post office."

"That's correct, honey," Mom concurred wistfully. "And we've already taught you not to speak to strangers. Be very cautious. Not everybody is nice."

Later, falling asleep, my mind concocted visions of puppy dogs, sunny days, and ice cream. I wish!

Saturday Morning—November 20, 1971

I squatted on an icy curb a block from the Schmidts' house. Bundled up, I resembled an Eskimo. My feet hurt, and my cheeks were numb. Wind blew out of the dreary sky, and the temperature had to be in the teens. Runny snot glistened and froze on the sleeve I used to wipe my nose. A fluffy white blanket fell overnight, and the golf course bordering the road became a winter wonderland. A figure approached, outfitted for a polar exhibition, making it challenging to verify any identity. Standing, I squinted through watering eyes.

"Yes, it's me, John," Karen said dryly.

"Hey," I greeted, flapping a glove.

The girl tucked her mittens into the pockets of a red coat, the faux-fur hood shielding much of her features. Shifting awkwardly, she questioned, "How did you get here?"

I pointed stiffly to the front tire of the bicycle, poking out behind a tree.

"What did you tell your parents?" I inquired.

"Told them I was visiting my friend Melissa. Keep your fingers crossed they won't telephone her house." Karen peeped anxiously past her shoulder.

"Do you know the shortest way to the Woods? Can we cut over the golf course?"

"Sure," she responded, peering at the links. "Follow me. This is the ninth hole, and traversing the seventh fairway, we should get fairly close."

"Karen, as I said the other day, I'm real sorry about your sister. I didn't intend to be insensitive."

"Angela vanished when she was fifteen. I was young and hardly remember her. There are pictures of my sister, but my parents don't discuss what happened. Angela is a painful subject." Karen led downhill into a sand trap and ascended to the teeing ground for the number-six hole. Looking back, our footprints trailed into the distance.

"The police never found her?" I asked hesitantly.

"No, they didn't. Many times, when another person is nowhere to be found, the reporters ring our number to add content to a story. The investigations upset my mom and dad. We relocated to Arizona when I was seven and returned to Haworth several years ago. Eventually, my folks comprehended they wanted to be near where Angela's memories still lived. Not accepting what happened is tough. Over this way."

Emerging onto a road headed to our destination, I questioned, "Did you ever explore the Woods?"

"A few times with friends, although my parents get nervous if they can't monitor where I am. They always want me to stay around home, which drives me nuts. One time, my dad notified the cops when I just went downtown with Melissa. My mother and father demand I leave a note or call. I was having fun that day and forgot. I appreciate their fears, but seriously, the mollycoddling is awful." Karen exposed frustration and then smiled. "How's life at your house? So, you've got a sister?"

"Jane's perfect, smaller and smarter," I grinned. "That's a huge shock? As an older brother, I try to defend her, yet most of the time, she's actually protecting me."

"That must be nice, to have a sibling. Being an only child with a missing sister . . . I mean, everyone recognizes that Angela's gone."

For a while, I walked in silence, not versed in the manners to respond. As we landed on an avenue adjacent to the Woods, the sun emerged through the haze. Steaming black patches spread as the slush melted on the salted street. The day turned pleasant, and my mood lifted.

I guided her to a slight opening between the trees. "Come on, we can go in here." I hoped not to get lost. Glancing up at the blue sky, I set my bearings. If I kept the sun on my right side, we would be headed in the proper direction. Footprints in the snowflakes should facilitate retreat, if necessary. "Ready?" I asked.

Karen's lips pinched. "Yes, show me what you found."

The woodland was surprisingly luminous with most of the limbs stripped bare. Hiking along the trail, our feet slid on sleet-encrusted leaves and I was glad that we wore boots. At a break in the path, I stopped and removed a Pop Tart from an inner pocket. Tearing the wrapper apart, I handed over half.

"Gracias," she said, pleased. "Blueberry. These are my favorite. Mom keeps these stockpiled for when the Russians strike."

I laughed. "Maybe that's why my mother hoards so many. She buys Ring Dings and Yodels by the case. Scientists say Twinkies and cockroaches will survive the apocalypse."

Shyly watching one another, I finished the snack and threw the silver casing on the snow.

"Honestly? Pick that up, John. A starving animal could choke on that."

Abashed, I fetched the wrapper, fluttered the crumbs, and stowed the trash in a pocket. "Sorry," I mumbled.

Karen nodded in mock exasperation. "Thank you." Staring down the route, she questioned, "Is it that much further?"

"Not too far," I answered, with exaggerated aplomb. "I marked the way with rocks. With any luck, we can find them below this snow."

Warm now, I pulled the beanie off. Karen pushed away the jacket's hood, shaking out her hair. The familiar copse of pines arose. We were on the trail to Ceremonies.

"Stop," she sighed. "Look!" Up ahead, a flock of turkeys leisurely crossed the footpath. A Kodak Instamatic appeared from a zipper as Karen crouched and composed. One of the wild birds gyrated at the mechanical click.

I inquired, "You own a camera?"

"You said we are going to find remains. I carried one to record evidence. That's why we're here, correct?"

"Yes," I responded. Sober and in bright daylight, my fuzzy party remembrance seemed absurd. "To be frank, I saw something the other night and now feel ridiculous. The object wasn't a real body."

"Let's see what you discovered," Karen said, pocketing the camera. Eagerly, she hiked onward.

Rounding the bottom of Ceremonies, I easily located the three stones indicating the trail. The sun had defrosted the markers. "Turn that way," I directed. The ground became perilous where the fresh powder carpeted the soil. "Watch your step," I advised. "There's ice under here. Very slippery. I almost broke my neck."

The trees thinned at the spot where I had fallen. The low-heeled shoe, now dusted with crystals, rested on the same stack of twigs. "There!" I exclaimed.

Karen knelt by the mound, baffled. "This is just a shoe."

Punctured, my heart sunk into the muck. "Yes, a shoe that is. . ."

"John, why do you assume someone is buried here?" Walking to me, her air softened.

I hesitated, oscillating betwixt candor and secrecy. Explaining the childhood memory of the fight between the man and woman might be problematic. The repeating nightmares were simply dreams. Besides speaking to my mother that horrible day, I hadn't told another soul, forcing the visions into my cavernous subconscious. So many years had passed, and I wasn't clear anything illegal had truly transpired.

"Tell me!" she coerced. "Tell me why you brought me out here."

I sat cross-legged by the shoe while Karen settled on a log, expression perplexed.

Breathing deeply, I began, "When I was five years old, around the time your sister went missing, I may have witnessed a terrible event. One day, I went with my mom to the playground. . ."

Karen listened intently as I revealed my recollection. "That was it? And your mother at no time followed through? Why didn't she call the police? Angela's tragedy was all over the news. Christ, your parents should've made the connection!" she yelled furiously.

"That's easy for you to say now. Just out of diapers, there's a strong possibility I didn't make any sense."

Karen formed a snowball and dropped it. "You said you found this thing sticking up in the ice?"

"Yup, I skidded and fell down there. Getting up, I happened to notice an object with the flashlight. I took the shoe and stuck it on that pile."

Retrieving the camera, she took a few photos at different angles. Meticulously whisking the powder, Karen snapped a few more.

"That's a saddle shoe," I said. "Do you remember the old-fashioned black-and-white kind?"

"Yes, I do," she admitted faintly, releasing the Oxford from the snow and brushing off the remaining flakes. Sizing the footwear alongside a boot, Karen commented, "The shoe is larger than mine, although it doesn't appear adult. I wonder if any information is stamped inside." She closely inspected the insole. "Nope, there's no number in here, or the ink is worn away."

With care, Karen laid the shoe on the solid terrain. Wearily, she asked, "So now what?"

"Karen, I'm not sure. I mean, like you said, it's merely a shoe."

For a while, we sat in peace. A boisterous grey squirrel hopped around in the snowdrift, effortlessly crawling up a tree. The scenery dazzled, white topping everything. A jet's contrail traced high above, hopefully flying to Bermuda, not Newark.

"Will you talk to your mother and father?" I had no inkling what I wanted her to do.

The girl pondered, hand buffing aside a layer of snow. "Um, I doubt it." Karen pushed on the glaze, as if testing strength. On her knees, with a mitten she polished the glassy surface, eyes boring into the frozen water. "Can't see a thing. The ice is thin. There are only rocks and leaves."

"When I fell, I crashed through a patch, and you're right, it's scarcely a few inches deep. I got a bit wet." Rubbing my sore elbow, I needed to say more constructive words, yet had nothing.

"From what you recollect, a man and girl fought, and he drew her into the bushes? This took place at that playground on the east end of the Woods?"

"Yeah, that happened a very long time ago, so I'm not positive how old the woman was. But, I recall she wore shoes similar to that one."

"What? Why didn't you say that before?" Karen shouted.

"I'm sorry," I said softly, attempting to placate her. "Now, you must get what a nitwit I am for dragging you out here."

She laughed. "John, I don't think you're stupid, and I enjoy having you for my lab partner. You're funny, and even though you don't realize it, smart."

I flushed as Karen stood sweeping snow from her pants. "Come on, time to go."

"What should we do with the shoe?" I questioned.

Karen produced a plastic bag. "Here, you're in charge of the evidence. Stay still." Aiming the Instamatic, she captured a photograph of me exhibiting the shoe, the moment ominous and exhilarating.

On the return trip, we talked of school, the latest movies and music. The bicycle pulled free of the snowbank. As I tied the sack to the handlebars, my eyes followed Karen striding to her house. Wondering if the girl might twirl to look backwards, my heart leaped with joy when she waved.

Saturday at Noon—November 20, 1971

Inconspicuously hiding the saddle shoe behind the summer tires in the garage, I went up for lunch. Ravenous, I asked my mother, "Where are Jane and Dad?"

"Your father took your sister to the hardware store. The faucet upstairs is leaking, and he's picking up a set of washers," she replied, liberally scooping a mountain of orange macaroni and cheese onto the plate. Mom added a glass of milk, and I mixed in a generous helping of Nestle Quick. "What were you doing out this early?" Joining me at the kitchen table, she ate fruit and crackers.

"Karen and I went for a walk," I answered, concentrating on the pasta.

"Hmm," my mother murmured, intrigued. "What is Vince and Bill's opinion on this?"

"They haven't found out. Yesterday, you were telling us about Karen's sister. She got kidnapped?"

"Johnny, it's very likely Angela was abducted; however, no one knows for certain. Barbara said she didn't return home when classes recessed for the day. A teacher noticed the girl leave, and that was the final time anyone ever saw her alive. Everybody looked for Angela. The cops even used tracking dogs. The neighboring towns organized search parties, but in a few weeks, they had to quit."

I gorged myself on more cheesy noodles without chewing. After the abundance of nature, I could eat a gazelle. Putting the dish in the sink, I asked my mom to ferry me to the Teaneck Public Library.

She gawked at me. "This is rather unusual on a Saturday. Are you writing a paper for school?"

"It's for a project," I hurriedly responded. "I'm doing research on the history of Haworth. That's what the report will be covering."

The rock salt on the library steps crunched underfoot as we crossed into the welcoming warmth of the old brick building. While Mom wandered to the periodical section, I descended to the basement to pursue old issues of the *Bergen Record*.

The reference librarian handed me rolls of microfilm from the spring of 1962. "Sign this form. See me if there are any questions on using the reader."

Threading the earliest film into the machine, I browsed for newspaper pieces explaining Angela's disappearance. Not finding a thing, I skimmed faster and faster, my eyeballs drying as the text whizzed by. *This is a complete lost cause. Why am I doing this? On the weekend, I should be home watching American Bandstand.* Envisioning Karen, I slowed. The word "Hunt" caught my curiosity. Pausing, I viewed the article "Haworth Police Press Hunt for Woman's Body" on the second page of the Sunday *Record* dated May 6, 1962.

> HAWORTH—Authorities are seeking a 15-year-old Haworth girl who has been gone for nearly three weeks. Angela Schmidt was seen walking away from school on April 19. Police scoured the adjoining towns of Closter, Dumont and Demarest. No evidence of foul play is detected; however, Haworth Police Chief Thomas Edwards is soliciting assistance in this inquiry.
>
> "That could be your youngster," he said. "Please call the Haworth Police Department with any knowledge you have, no matter how insignificant. Help us find Angela."
>
> Over the last several days, rescue workers and cadaver dogs have combed local wooded areas without result.

Scrolling in reverse, I found another artifact on April 20. The headline was "Haworth Girl Lost."

> HAWORTH—Police appeal for support in the investigation of a missing female residing on Westview Terrace in Haworth. Angela Schmidt, a student enrolled at Northern Valley Regional High School, never reached her house after class Thursday night.

> Yesterday afternoon, a faculty member described seeing the girl leaving school property alone. The father, Scott Schmidt, said Angela usually takes the bus home as the distance is too far to walk. He pleads for everyone's aid finding his daughter.
>
> Angela wore a light-blue dress and a dark coat. The girl is 15 years old, has brown hair and weighs approximately 95 pounds. Contact the Haworth Police Department at once with any tips.

Feeling odd reading the dated material, I had difficulty associating Angela and Karen Schmidt with what I perceived ages ago. There was one supplementary item, dated May 18, 1962, headlined "Search for Haworth Woman Called Off."

> HAWORTH—The hunt for 15-year-old Angela Schmidt, a Haworth resident, has ended. Haworth Police Chief Tom Edwards issued a statement this morning. "The department will continue to search Haworth and the surrounding regions for Angela, although at this point in time, we don't expect to develop any new leads. Rescue teams have concluded multiple area-wide and in-depth investigations. Oradell Reservoir is an enormous body of water and is still being probed."
>
> Chief Edwards asks citizens to telephone the Haworth Police Department with any information.

Not finding more, I unthreaded the microfilm reader and coiled the spool into the can. I hadn't learned much new, but seeing the stories in print were troubling. Depressed, I ascended the stairs to spot my mother reading a *Good Housekeeping* magazine. Glancing up from a feature illustrating what to wear to an ice cream social, she smiled and then frowned at my expression. "Did you find what you needed?"

I dredged up a grin. "Sure, Mom. Let's go home."

Master Plan

Monday Morning—November 22, 1971

I HELD THE END as Vince shimmied up the taut rope. Resembling a monkey wearing gym shorts, he rang the bell and slid, decelerating with his feet. My friend hit the deck and tossed me the manila line. "John-Boy," he said, "this gymnasium is the perfect venue to prove your masculinity!"

Grabbing the cord, I looked up. The rope attached to the ceiling rafters was insanely long. "Clamp with your legs," Ranzetta instructed. "And try not to fall," he advised, thumping hard on my back.

"Jesus," I moaned, heaving myself up inch by painful inch. At the halfway point, I peered downward to see him wrenching the rope tight, grinning. A line of boys stared, anxiously anticipating a turn. *Don't look down!* Scads of kids didn't achieve the top, and I considered quitting. *A little more!* Edging higher, my arms quivered with fatigue. *This is no time for low blood sugar.*

Incessantly optimistic, Outlaw called, "You can do this, John!"

At the top, I grunted, overreaching for the bell. *One more foot!* Legs losing friction, slipping, I endeavored to slow myself with burning fists. Toppling, my ass hit the glossy oaken floor with a painful thwack. Embarrassed, I got up, hiding the rising blisters.

"Nice head!" Vince brayed.

Resignedly starting sit-ups on a mat in the corner, I asked, "Hey, do you guys want to ride to Rudy's after school?"

Bill's palms were behind his neck, torso pumping. "Sure," he huffed. "Forty-seven, forty-eight. . ."

"Starving now," Vince grunted. Flipping, he showed off, doing one-handed pushups.

"That's it. I'm done," I complained, examining my raw sores. The President's Physical Fitness Challenge occurred in one week, and I wasn't prepared. Outlaw and Ranzetta smacked of Marines in training. Cross, I left the gym rubbing my bruised ego.

Monday Afternoon—November 22, 1971

Bill and I relaxed on one side of the worn red vinyl booth, while Vince sprawled on the opposite seat. Rudy's had the tastiest pizza in Closter and had become a personal favorite. The pepperoni slice sold for thirty cents and came served on wax paper. I watched the golden oil pool and drip onto the red-and-white checkered tablecloth. The heat of the brick ovens warmed my toes, and the aroma of the baking food was mouthwatering.

"John, you must be famished," Bill mentioned, indicating the extra piece of pie.

"Uh, yeah," I mumbled, glancing at the clock. I hadn't mentioned that Karen was joining us.

The bell jingled as Karen entered, clothed in a stylish blue ski jacket. Removing her sunglasses, she slid onto the bench beside Vince.

"Would you be kind enough to move that big ass over a bit?" Karen requested, glaring sideways. I wasn't sure if the attitude was an act; I could never tell if girls were serious.

Amazed, he exclaimed, "Oh, you're the lab partner with the dead sister!"

Karen's expression soured. Pausing for a moment, she neatly rebounded. "And you're Vincent Ranzetta, the one whose brother sells dope to the seventh and eighth graders."

"Touché, Mademoiselle," he chuckled, satisfied with the quick retort. I was always astonished at what flowed out of his trap. Vince was a smart kid, and I hoped he wouldn't follow in Paul's footsteps.

"Hey, what about me? Don't forget, I got a dead brother!" Outlaw proclaimed, raising an arm.

No one answered. I said sarcastically, "Apparently, the Townsends are the only ones in town with a normal family."

"Um, looks like you are the one with an abnormal family," Vince refuted, around a mouthful of sausage. Karen and Bill laughed.

Casually, I pushed the additional wedge of pizza and a napkin over the table. "Here, Karen."

Startled and charmed, she murmured, "Thanks."

"So, is this your new girlfriend, John?" Ranzetta questioned, dumbfounded. "Better than the old one, that's for damn sure!"

Karen seemed entertained as I replied, "Karen's no more than a friend, Vince. There was no other—"

"John and I were just engaged, at fourteen," she interrupted. Everyone roared, especially Bill, who spewed half his drink on the table. As he wiped up the mess, I left to buy her a soda.

When I returned, the three earnestly evaluated our idiotic health teacher. "Remember yesterday, when Flaherty stated it was impossible to catch germs from a toilet seat?" Outlaw asked, poking fingers down his esophagus.

"Ha! I dare Mr. Flaherty to sit in those revolting stalls in the women's lavatory," Karen said, giggling. "Girls are way nastier than boys!"

"How do you know? Ever been in the men's room?" Ranzetta inquired.

"No, and I never will," she responded, disgusted.

Impulsively, I professed, "I want us to break into Mr. Reynolds' house." The idea surfaced sometime during the day, perhaps while clinging to that damn rope.

Bill appeared stunned; Karen, confused. Animated, Vince squawked, "What?"

"Are you out of your friggin' mind?" Outlaw sputtered.

"Quiet," I shushed, glancing throughout the restaurant. A worker gracefully spun a large pie high in the air. I whispered, "Something is wrong with Reynolds, and we should find out what he's up to."

"Who is Mr. Reynolds, and why in the world do you need to get into his home?" Karen asked.

Ranzetta took an extended gulp from a glass. "Mr. Reynolds kills cats and builds sex contraptions in his dungeon."

"Whoa! Vince, we're not positive of that," Bill avowed defensively.

"Damn right, he does!" Ranzetta glowered.

I summarized what we had learned. "Vince could be accurate, Karen. When we were kids, Bill took us into the Woods to a huge boulder nicknamed Ceremonies. That day, we found an animal collar and a skull from a cat. The address on the identification tag was up my road and belonged to Mr. Reynolds. At his house, he got worked up, swearing he never had any cats. Later, I hiked to Ceremonies and saw a different animal collar with the same address. Then, before Halloween, we snuck up and looked in his basement window. There were a lot of unusual things down there, but I'm not sure what they were for."

"Sex furniture!" Vince leered.

Karen gaped as the lad slid a digit in and out of a cupped hole in his other hand. "Do you believe this has something to do with—?"

With a raised palm, I silenced her. "I don't know."

"Have to do with what?" Outlaw questioned ardently.

I was unwilling to discuss with Vince and Bill the night I found the footwear or the day Karen and I located it again. They might conclude I was a fool or keeping secrets.

Irritated at being cut off, Karen said, "John, you're asking your friends to illegally enter a neighbor's residence without explaining the complete story. Either you spill it, or I will."

Annoyed, I sighed. "Tell them, if you want."

The guys pivoted keenly to Karen, who shot a flat stare my way. "When John was small, he played at the park in his neighborhood and—"

"Are you referring to that playground by the Woods? Double slide and rocking animals on springs? That hippo is the best," Ranzetta declared.

"Yes, the one with the purple hippopotamus," I answered. "My mother and a friend were there. Something happened."

Intensely, she continued, "John recollects seeing a man and young woman fighting, disappearing in the Woods. The incident sounded violent from his description."

"That was so many years ago, and I forgot most of what occurred—seems unreal now. When Bill ran off at the party, we started searching. I fell on a sheet of ice and discovered a half-buried shoe. The footwear is comparable to what I recall the girl wearing. That got me thinking—"

"That you found her sister's sneaker?" Vince inquired.

Karen shrugged. "Angela was her name. On Saturday, we checked it out. John tripped out, convinced there was a body. In a frozen swamp, he showed me a saddle shoe, one of those black-and-white Oxfords."

Spellbound, Outlaw asked, "Karen, when did your sister go missing?"

She told him: April 19, 1962, when Angela was walking home from school.

"Goddammit it to hell!" Vince exclaimed. "That has to be her shoe. Did you educate your girlfriend about Cabbage Night?"

"No, not yet. Karen, we threw a couple of fireworks on Reynolds' porch."

"M-80s!" Ranzetta reiterated, "equal to a quarter-stick of dyna—"

"Somehow, Reynolds crept up and grabbed Bill, then let him go. We don't know why he didn't notify the police or his parents." I omitted my idea to egg Reynolds and how I ran off like a coward, abandoning Outlaw. That was too much minutiae.

"Let me understand this," Bill articulated. "John, you've deduced your neighbor—Mr. Reynolds, the cat killer—hauled her sister into the Woods and—" Outlaw glanced at Karen for consent before proceeding, "killed and buried Angela where you found this footwear. Is that correct? Although the guy is a kook, he did release me without telling my mother and father."

"Close enough," I answered. "Her sister has to be somewhere, right? Angela didn't simply vanish off the face of the Earth." Karen rounded up crumbs on the plastic tablecloth with a tissue.

Ranzetta pulled his ear. "Yeah, she has to be someplace. What's the next step, phone the fuzz?"

"Not now," I responded. He relaxed.

"What does breaking into Reynolds' house get us, other than arrested?" Bill asked uneasily. "I must say, I have serious reservations."

Karen raised her eyebrows. "And I'm still lost. How does this Reynolds tie into my sister? Is it solely on account of a few missing cats?"

"Reynolds is the neighborhood freak," Vince decreed. "That fella is a complete nutcase!" Fingers rapidly circling both ears, he crossed his eyes. "When we talked to him, that mental case reminded me of Norman Bates."

I snorted. "An oddball for sure, but the dude from *Psycho*? That fruitcake was totally off his rocker." That old movie always creeped the shit out of me.

"Townsend, you're the one that wants to bust into his crib," Ranzetta hissed.

My friend had gotten me on that one: I did suspect Mr. Reynolds. I expressed compellingly, "So who's in? Entirely okay if you're not, I won't blame anyone. Hold on, don't answer." Using a napkin, I ripped the outline of Italy into four ragged pieces. "Write 'Yes' or 'No.'"

The pen rounded the table, and I tallied the votes. "Yes," I read. "'Yes,' 'Yes,' and obviously a final 'Yes' for me."

Outlaw questioned, "Any ideas on the tactics to accomplish this undertaking?"

Eagerly, Vince answered, "My brother has an associate—"

"No, we don't need anyone else involved, particularly Paul's henchmen," I said.

"Let's not do this half-assed," Karen insisted. "First, we must formulate a strategy, select equipment, survey the site, and finalize the operation before execution. Gentlemen, I am not getting caught." Dark eyes narrowing, she was dead serious.

Ranzetta's whoops rang from the storefronts outside the pizzeria. Parting, we agree to hash over details later in the week.

As I walked Karen home, flurries drifted beneath the streetlights. The girl handled herself nicely when she met my two best friends. Karen might change the dynamics of the group, but I didn't care. I just needed her nearby.

Tuesday at Noon—November 23, 1971

As Karen joined us at our lunch table, her schoolmates stared incredulously. "What's going on?" she inquired, biting a peach.

"Hey, Karen," Bill greeted, feet propped on a chair. Vince waved hello, claws slick with grease. Tuesday's special had been labeled "Country Fried Chicken."

I scanned the room, content nobody was within earshot. "As you suggested, Karen, we should find out Reynolds' schedule. Is that what you meant by surveillance?"

Nodding, she quizzed, "The man's unmarried, right? No children?"

"Not that I've ever seen. He lives alone."

"John lives the closest. Can you keep an eye on your neighbor?" Ranzetta recommended.

"Every day, I go by his house on the way to school. At seven-thirty, the car is gone. In the afternoon, it's not in the driveway. I assume Reynolds goes to work, but I have no clue when or where."

"What about Saturday or Sunday?" Outlaw asked, rapping a pen against a textbook.

"Generally, he's home on the weekends. The automobile is parked outdoors, so it's easy to tell."

This project may take more effort than I imagined, I thought.

"That's one part of it," Karen granted. She opened a scratch pad to the last page. "If we know when he departs, how much time do we require inside?"

Looking at one another, Bill replied thoughtfully, "An hour at most."

Quickly making a notation, she returned her gaze. "Where can we get in?"

Enthusiastically, Vince offered, "Easy, we could pick the lock."

Amused, Karen questioned, "Any experience doing that?"

"How hard can it be? Bend a paperclip or a wire and—"

Smirking, she considered, "Let's save that for Plan B. Anyone else have any other brilliant ideas?"

"Forcing a door or smashing a window produces substantial noise and furnishes evidence," I answered.

"A backup key may be concealed above the doorframe or under a stone," Outlaw advocated. "My parents stick one below the doormat."

"That is the easiest," I allowed. "As far as Vince's idea, I've seen people get a lock jimmied with a piece of plastic. You slide a thin card in a slot in the frame to trip the lock."

Ranzetta chucked. "Where did you see that, on *McMillan and Wife*?"

"On *Columbo*," I responded. "Just one more thing—" I muttered, doing a shaky Peter Falk impression. That earned a feeble laugh.

"Very interesting," Karen said, back on track. "John keeps tabs on Reynolds. Can somebody check for a hidden key?"

"Sure, I'll do it," Vince volunteered, raising a hand. "Sneaking around at midnight is right up my alley." A second later, he added, "I'll also practice picking a lock."

Fastidiously jotting that down, she asked, "What does that leave us?"

"Karen, you should take the camera and flash cubes," I suggested. "Everybody has flashlights. Bill, you can pack the walkie-talkies."

"And wear dark clothing," he warned. "While Vince searches for the key, I'll develop a map of the building and yard."

"Sounds like a plan to me," she ended, closing the pad.

Tuesday Afternoon—November 23, 1971

Karen swept back her hair and adjusted the goggles. Smiling, she held a beaker of distilled H_2O in her rubber gloves. A stirring bar lolled at the bottom. "Time for the potassium iodate."

I poured the oxidizing agent, followed by sulfuric acid, cautiously blending the fluid with a glass wand. In went the premixed Solution B, which we continued to agitate.

"Nice job!" Karen praised, placing the beaker on the electric stirring plate. Switching on the power shaped an amber spinning vortex. "Now for the final step. Solution C, please."

Adding the hydrogen peroxide, I stood aside to watch. The chemical reaction cyclically alternated between clear, amber, and blue. "Wow, that's unreal!" I exclaimed. "This is the best lab experiment we've done yet."

"Yes, the Briggs-Rauscher Reaction is undeniably the winner!" my lab partner affirmed passionately.

Results logged, I regarded Karen. "Are you okay with what we're plotting to do?" Personally, I had a jillion second thoughts.

Pensively, she said in a low tone, "Breaking into someone's home isn't a normal activity. As I mentioned before, I've lived a sheltered life and haven't gotten into any real trouble. I can rationalize our actions by telling myself we're not doing it to steal; we're attempting to establish if this Reynolds character is bad news. . ." Karen struggled to express the appropriate words. "I owe it to Angela to make sure nothing dreadful happens to anymore girls."

"Karen, we haven't proved Reynolds had any contact with your sister—or anybody else, for that matter."

"I'm clutching at straws." Tugging off her black gloves and setting them on the bench, she questioned, "You've known Vince and Bill a long while?"

"Ranzetta, since kindergarten, and Outlaw, from fifth grade, when he moved to town. Vince acts nuts, but he's a great guy and is like a brother. I admit his relatives are shady."

"What about Bill's family?"

"Similar to yours, I guess. Large house and nice parents. Mr. Outlaw is an orthodontist. There's a pool and trampoline in the backyard. After Ed got killed, Bill hasn't been the same."

Karen nodded sympathetically. "I know how that is."

I blurted, "Will you go see *The Andromeda Strain* with me?" For the last few days, I'd been preparing to ask her to the movie. I was terrified of rejection.

"Sorry, I already went with Melissa," Karen answered, shaking her head.

"Oh, right," I mumbled. Sensing my cheeks turn barn red, I hastily wadded papers into my rucksack. *Oh, man, I am such a tool.*

"John, I'm just kidding," she teased. "I sorta wanted to observe your reaction. That will be fun. I love sci-fi stuff." Karen unfurled her fingers in the Vulcan salute.

Still recovering, I said ruefully. "Uh, okay. That was—"

"Stupid, I won't do it again," she interrupted.

"Actually, I was about to say 'mean.'" I was smiling, but hurt. "Believe it or not, I was scared to death to even ask you."

"I'm sorry, John. If you were afraid of me, consider how you'll feel asking my mother and father." Karen registered my dismayed pout. "Don't fret. They'll let us go. My parents naturally need to be confident I'm safe."

Mentally, I played the entire scene over and over, using different lines: *Mr. and Mrs. Schmidt, can I have your permission to take Karen to the movies? Mr. and Mrs. Schmidt, Karen would like me to accompany her to a film. Is that cool with you?* The pitiful speeches included stuttering, forgetting essential parts, and finally, her mother and father shouting "No!"

"Earth to John!" she called, snapping me from the stupor. "It'll be fine. Can you come by tomorrow night for another chemistry study session? We can cover math, if you prefer. Together, we'll bring up the movie. I'm sure everything will work out."

Thrilled that Karen agreed to our date, I couldn't wait to see her again, praying the Schmidts were in a congenial mood Wednesday evening.

Wednesday Evening—November 24, 1971

Encapsulated in a thermal cocoon, I headed up Franklin Street. "Say hello and Happy Thanksgiving to Mrs. Schmidt for me," Mom had reminded. Euphoric that I was reviewing schoolwork, she delightedly gave me a brown bag of freshly baked chocolate chip cookies.

Standing to pedal up the lane, the nighttime air refreshed my flushed skin. This time, I'd potentially overdressed with too many layers. Approaching Mr. Reynolds' residence, I saw the seeping oil stains designating where the station wagon usually parked before the double doors. 6:45. *Where is he?* I braked to a stop near the same bushes we hid behind on Cabbage Night. *Why doesn't he park in the garage?* The same glow originated from the upstairs window on the right corner of the house. *Is that Reynolds' bedroom? Does he continuously leave on the light?* A bundle the size of a shoebox lay on the stoop. Reynolds hadn't come home yet, or the box wouldn't have been left outside.

Karen's mother answered this time, surprised as I surrendered the gift. "My mom wishes you 'Happy Thanksgiving.'"

"That's real nice. Please thank her." Closing the door, she directed, "My daughter is in the dining room."

Karen asked, "You brought me homemade baked goods?"

"The chocolate chips aren't for you. They're for your parents," I scolded.

"Oh, I see how it is," she said, bemused.

"Just kidding," I taunted, unveiling wrapped cookies. "There, got you this time!"

"Touché, Monsieur Townsend," she chortled.

Silently, we read the assigned chemistry chapter, surreptitiously peeking at each other. As Karen assisted me with complicated algebra formulas, Mr. Schmidt materialized out of nowhere. "How is it progressing?" he asked, holding a worn Bible.

"Great, Dad," Karen replied, lip twitching in a mischievous grin. "John is ready to ask you something."

Goaded, I breathed deeply. "Um, Mr. Schmidt, a movie is playing in Closter titled the. . ." I floundered and stalled.

Karen's father crossed his arms, the religious book resting under his chin. "Are you asking to take my daughter on a date?"

"Uh, no, Mr. Schmidt, certainly not."

"John!" Karen chided. "Dad, on Saturday we're going to that new feature, *The Andromeda Strain*. He merely wanted your approval. I think the Bible thing is alarming him."

Fervently, the man focused on me. "Who exactly are you?"

What the hell? "John Townsend," I mumbled.

"Son, I know your name. The question is, who are *you*? What are your inspirations? Where is John Townsend headed? What will be your profession after school?"

Swallowing, I searched for help. Karen smiled encouragingly.

"Well, sir," I began, "after graduating from college, I hope to get a decent job. All my life, I've prepared to be an engineer or scientist." Never contemplating the future, I spontaneously improvised a bogus career.

Nodding, he peered over spectacles. "That is a worthy life plan and requires perseverance on your part. Tell me of this motion picture you desire escorting my daughter to. Are there any beatnik or hippie characters?"

"The previews look intriguing, and I've heard the film is excellent. A deep-space satellite crashes into our planet, and scientists research techniques to prevent a fatal virus from exterminating mankind. I didn't notice any longhairs, as my dad calls them."

Mr. Schmidt bowed approvingly and frowned. "Honey, you'll need to bring a girlfriend."

"Melissa can go, Dad." Karen glanced at me and shrugged.

"Thank you, sir. I won't let anything—"

"Bad happen? I am secure knowing you will not. Have a nice time, and bless Mrs. Townsend for the heavenly cookies." Softly drumming the Bible, the intimidating man left the room.

Staring at each other, Karen laughed. "That wasn't so horrible."

"I wasn't ready to have your friend act as our chaperone." Disappointed, I sulked.

Miffed, she questioned, "You'd rather we didn't go at all?"

"Of course I want to go. That's cool, if Melissa comes along," I answered sharply.

"John, give it time. My father has to get acquainted and trust you. Melissa has acted as my best friend since I moved back here. Like your pal Vince, she'd never let me down. Rest assured; it'll still be fun."

"I'm sure," I grinned. "Saturday will be awesome, and I can't wait!"

The Paris Sport sailed noiselessly through the night. Frigid wind brought stinging tears as I swung by Jim's Market. Jim and his wife were restocking cases of toilet paper. Dropping the bicycle into low, I cranked the pedals to ascend Tank Hill, the steep ridge dividing the town. I had been disillusioned reading the knoll was named after a long-gone spring-fed water tank, not for war machines. Mr. Schmidt had asked who I was and what I proposed to do with my life. At fourteen, I had lots of summers to lock that down. But maybe not.

The derailleur clicked into top gear as I descended Tank Hill, avoiding ruts and potholes. At the head of Franklin Street, I slowed to check on Mr. Reynolds. The driveway remained vacant, and the delivery lingered against the door. Rolling to a halt, I wondered who had shipped the parcel. Leaning the bike against a mailbox, I stole into the yard and onto my neighbor's shadowy porch.

I tilted the carton toward the streetlamp. To: *Martin Reynolds.* As I squinted to decipher the From: *address*, high beams illuminated the trees bordering the road. An automobile approached. *Jesus!* The package fell as I leapt up and ran to the corner, ducking underneath a shrub.

A dark station wagon with dual headlights and pseudo-wood side paneling pulled into the entrance. This had to be Reynolds. The engine shuddered as the lights snapped off. Slowly, the driver side creaked open, and I saw a black boot lowered to the pavement. A figure exited and walked to the rear of the car, popping the tailgate. Yanking out a bulky duffel bag, he easily draped the pack over his shoulder. With a free hand, the male closed the vehicle and strode toward the portico. Again, I speculated why he didn't utilize the large garage.

The man stopped and peered to the right, then the hat swiveled my way. *That's undeniably Reynolds, and he sees me!* Dizzily, I held my breath. Moving past my vision, footsteps crossed the threshold. The door unlocked, lanterns brightening the front yard. Between leaves, I watched him bend to lift the box. Rising to scrutinize the stamp, I noted a business suit and an apron or bib tied around my neighbor's waist. Inscrutably, he vanished from view, the latch clicking shut. *Should I try to look in the windows?* Not pushing my luck, I hurried to retrieve the bicycle.

Thanksgiving—Thursday Morning—November 25, 1971

I pleasantly tumbled out of bed to the aromatic scent of Mom cooking dinner. When I entered the kitchen, she glanced up, forearm halfway inside a huge turkey. "Happy Thanksgiving," my mother scowled, towing an oddly shaped object from deep within the carcass. The purple organ bounced as she lobbed the mass into the sink.

"Morning, Mom," I responded, slumping at the breakfast nook with a bowl of cereal. Django vaulted up, purring and grinding his jaw in my hair. *When did the cat get so roly poly?* Scratching behind his ears, I nudged away the milk. Django blinked his green eyes and jumped to the counter. "Who's coming today?"

My mother rattled off a list of relatives. "Johnny, can you please vacuum and help Jane clean and dust?" As I nodded tiredly, she inquired over the fowl, "Did you give Karen's mom the cookies?"

"Mrs. Schmidt said 'thanks,' and Mr. Schmidt called them 'heavenly.'" Gratified, my mother rammed a metal thermometer into the bird's ribs and shoved supper into the oven. I added, "Karen and her friend Melissa are watching *The Andromeda Strain* this Saturday. I'm going too and hoped you could please drive us to Closter."

Giddily, she asked, "Is this your first date?"

"Mom, it's not a date. We're just seeing a movie."

"Oh, I loved group dating," she reminisced sadly.

Jane ran by, holding a bottle of Pledge and a cloth. "What's happening, big brother. Got a fancy date?" Energetically, she flapped the yellow rag in the air.

"This isn't a date," I repeated, flustered. "And whatever it is, it's definitely none of your concern."

"Johnny, I'll be glad to bring you. Let me know when. Can Jane go too?"

"What? No way am I taking her!" I yelled.

"Take your sister," Dad ordered, pouring coffee. "And you should sweep the walkway and steps before the hungry hordes arrive. Dear, whatever is cooking smells wonderful." Grabbing the newspaper, he retired to the living room.

"Jesus wept," I carped, rinsing the dish. *This date is turning into a circus!*

Luckily, the balance of the day was loads of fun. A belly-busting spread, followed by a variety of pies, stuffed my stomach to the bursting point. Afterward, while the men loosened their belts to nap or cheer for televised football; I played Monopoly with Jane and my cousins. Braving the elements, we even chased each other outside the house in a game of tag.

When Uncle Terrance came into the living room searching for his pipe, I questioned if he ever saw anyone wearing a square apron.

"Masons, or Freemasons, put on garments similar to what you described. Masons are an ancient, clandestine society that meets in local lodges and frequently helps needy charities. There is a mysterious initiation if they vote you in."

Picking up his smoking supplies, Uncle Terrance hurried to drum up a fresh beer.

That night, I lay in bed, pondering Mr. Reynolds and the Freemasons. *Who were they?* The flip clock glared 3:13 a.m. as I awoke from a disturbing dream full of snakes. Wide awake, I stared out the front window. The winter trees resembled the picked bones of skeletons. *What if he goes to regular meetings each Wednesday evening? If so, we could get into his house then.*

Chilled, I crawled beneath the warm comforter to sweat, wondering how to know when Masons gathered. Then I slithered into the same damn nightmare.

Saturday Afternoon—November 27, 1971

Loaded into the Chrysler Imperial, I occupied the passenger seat, while the girls filled the rear. Mom had picked up Karen and Melissa at the Schmidts', and we were now en route to the theater in Closter. Melissa Logan turned out to be the blond defending Karen in the library.

Both nervous and excited, my mother jabbered like a madwoman. Humiliated, I watched her tune the radio to big band music from the forties. Glancing in the mirror, she questioned, "Melissa, do you live near Karen?"

"Yes, Mrs. Townsend, two blocks away on Eastview Terrace."

"Quite a nice neighborhood. And you're a freshman, too?"

"That's right, ma'am. This year, I'm in plenty of the same classes as Karen and John."

I remained silent as the conversation bounced to and fro. Jane became absorbed in the gossip. Mrs. Schmidt and my mother chatted before we departed. I was relieved they got along. Before leaving, Mom contributed money for admittance and a surplus for snacks. Patting my head, she urged me to be a gentleman. My initial time out with young women, I was not very sophisticated.

At the mall, my mother gave one final caveat, "Enjoy yourself, and don't forget what I said. I'll pick you up at three o'clock." The tickets each cost $1.65, so I used the change to purchase large buckets of buttered popcorn and soda.

Self-consciously walking into the jammed hall, I was the odd man out. The three girls talked and joked amongst each other, not paying me any mind. Sliding down a row of empty seats, I felt appeased when Karen waited for me to follow. "Thanks for taking us to this movie, John. I'm having a swell time." Smiling, she passed the popcorn.

"Thanks, me too," I concurred. The chamber darkened, and the previews commenced. Karen appeared radiant in the dancing light.

As the film began, my sister gasped when the infected residents of a small New Mexico town transformed to grit. I loved the underground Wildfire laboratory facility and killer laser beams. *The Andromeda Strain* was a terrific flick, and I looked forward to telling Bill and Vince. I considered reaching to hold Karen's hand, but didn't have the courage.

Leaving the cinema, the girls included me in the recap. "John, what would you do if your neighbors suddenly began keeling over?" Karen inquired.

"Simple, I'd survive drinking Sterno," I asserted.

"Yuck," Jane giggled. "Pickled liver!"

Everyone laughed and kidded until the maroon Chrysler arrived. I held open the door.

"How was the show?" Mom asked, leaving the parking lot.

"Fantastic!" I replied exuberantly. "Dad should bring you to see it."

"Lots of nudity!" my sister exclaimed, leaning past the seat.

Shocked, my mother reprimanded, "You told me the film is rated G."

"Mrs. Townsend, entering the sterile laboratory environment, each scientist is sprayed with antiseptic. The camera didn't reveal any parts below the chin," Melissa amended.

"Oh, thank goodness," she said. "Johnny, why don't you switch the radio to whatever you want?"

I searched the dial, catching Cousin Brucie's modulation on WABC: "Now, heavy soul from my man Isaac Hayes." When I boosted the volume, the smooth funk of "Shaft" filled the cabin. Although Mom started to object, she refrained. Jane sang along to the "Shut your mouth" lyric, soon joined by the others. The tune *was* racy, come to think of it.

Tuesday Afternoon—November 30, 1971

Ranzetta held my feet and counted, a steely expression commanding continuance. "Fifty-seven, fifty-eight. Go, buddy. Fifty-nine, you can do it. Fifty-nine, almost sixty. . ." *Forty more, I can do this!* "Let's go, John, keep going. You must complete a hundred." A vital organ tore in my side. Appendix? *Just get me to eighty!*

Outlaw consummated the compulsory workout and moseyed by to watch the sport. "Christ, John. Why did you eat so much baloney at lunch? Don't break foul on me, man, you mustn't give up."

Mr. Block, the athletics teacher, shouted across the gym, "Mr. Townsend, we haven't got all day! Eventually, I need to get home and see the wife and children."

Hearing the acid remarks, classmates stared in my direction. As my abdomen strained, people circled.

"Eighty-two!" Vince yelled to the crowd, pressing hard on my sneakers.

Bill roused a fevered chanting, *"John, John, John!"* Drawn to the hubbub, kids wandered into the gym. "The poor guy's face will explode," a girl twittered. "Townsend won't finish. What a loser!"

Eight more to go! Head pulsing, my ass desperately clenched a balloon of gas. Considering how the flatulence might bounce off the polished floor, I nearly giggled. Not acceptable. My bronchi were on fire and I was having difficulty breathing.

"Three more sit-ups! Townsend, you can't be the only student, other than Chumpy here, to fail the President's Challenge. Dig in!" Even Mr. Block's crew cut looked angry.

Ninety-eight, ninety-nine, one hundred, ughh—Falling backward, panting, my entire body radiated pain. Cognizant of the audience applauding, Ranzetta pulled me straight. "Nice job, girlfriend," he congratulated, smiling.

Outlaw stretched and chuckled. "Oh, brother, you were about to blow a gasket. Seriously, you must take better care of yourself."

"Sure, I'll lay off the fried foods," I groaned, leaning over and gripping my knees.

Wednesday Afternoon—December 1, 1971

Vince took a sophisticated drag off a Kool, mentholated pollution engulfing his hair. "Nat King Cole used to chain-smoke these motherfuckers," he exhaled, tapping brittle ashes into the breeze.

"Why is that?" Bill questioned, checking out a group of junior schoolgirls traipsing up the steps.

Another hit: exhaust jetted out of Ranzetta's nose. "Cole thought the nicotine improved his vocal range. Dead as a doornail at thirty. Lung cancer."

Our laughter echoed off the football field's bleachers. Wincing with abdominal pain, I hoped a few muscles were sore from the sit-ups and nothing very serious.

"What's so funny?" Karen inquired, sitting beside me. She wore sorrel gaucho slacks and a colorful formfitting Mexican blouse.

"Lung cancer," Vince responded, extending a cig.

"Oh yeah, the Big C, always a gut-buster," she grinned, shaking a hand to decline the smoke.

He lowered his volume. "Outlaw and I cased the joint last night and located the key."

"For real? Where was it?" I asked.

"The moron hides the spare under the front mat," Bill replied proudly. "I was right, piece of cake."

"And I've picked locks at home and managed to open several using a standard paperclip," Vince announced. "Paul provided a multitude of helpful tips."

"Nice," I grumbled.

Outlaw unfolded a wrinkled piece of paper and flattened a drawing onto the aluminum bench. "For your consideration, I created this beautiful diagram of Reynolds' property." My friend specified Xs with a forefinger. "This mark is the main entryway. Here's the garage, and another doorway is at the rear. Presuming the key is for the front, we'll also try that. The backyard is unlit, and no one will see us."

"Better than the street side," Karen acknowledged, reversing the sheet. "Can the neighbors sight the door?"

Bill extracted a pen and hurriedly sketched. "This is the house behind Reynolds'. These are the neighbor's viewpoints," he directed, dabbing small rectangles. "A hedge of trees and bushes separate the yards." The boy drew an arrow to the back door. "This is the one place they could see us. It's an upper bay, maybe the master bedroom. The other windows, specifically the lower, are blocked by shrubbery. This is definitely the preferred way to get inside."

"While Bill and I were there, we peeked in the shed and found a mess of picks and shovels," Ranzetta shared.

"Meaning?" I questioned.

"Just that the guy loves digging," he answered.

"I found out when he is not there," I said, nervously kneading my neck. "Mr. Reynolds is a Freemason and apparently attends meetings on Wednesday evenings."

"By what method did you learn that?" Karen inquired.

To avoid heckling from Vince or Bill, I left out our study sessions. "Wednesday, his car wasn't there, and I scoped out the house. Reynolds came home, so I hid and watched. My neighbor wore a funny cloth with blue markings. On Thanksgiving, I talked to my uncle, and he says the Masons wear that type of apron. The Freemasons are a secret men's club that—"

"Yes, I've heard of Freemasons!" Karen exclaimed. "My dad has one or two friends who are members. My mom wouldn't let him join once she decided the organization was an evil cult—'Satan's Little Helpers.' Sorry to interrupt."

Amenable with her interjecting anytime, I nodded.

"Oh, you mean Manson, that maniac in California?" Ranzetta jabbed at Karen, tittering crazily.

"No, Vince, not Charlie Manson. Masons!" she giggled. "Seriously, I think they're an association of old farts who adore secret handshakes and silly costumes. The affairs are nothing but an excuse to get hammered."

"How do we differentiate if the Masons meet every Wednesday or once or twice a month?" I asked, swishing away a thunderhead of choking smog.

"There are many lodges all over Bergen County. The newspaper lists locations and meeting times," Outlaw suggested.

"Thanks, I'll check the paper tonight," I promised.

Bill brushed his corduroys while Vince stomped out a cigarette. "Keep on truckin'!" Ranzetta urged as they sauntered off.

Karen and I viewed the Norsemen training on the football field. I cleared my throat. "Yesterday, I was considering college. Do you ever worry about the future?"

Tucking a strand of hair behind an ear, she gazed at me. "Every waking minute. My parents are continuously discussing the school I'll attend or what major. The whole exercise is exhausting."

"It's easy for you, since you're so intelligent."

"Ha, I'm not that smart. To be honest, I study constantly. That's the only thing I do. John, it's as if I'm destined to replace the life Angela missed. Make my mother and father proud."

"Karen, how do you determine what to be when you grow up? I mean, when you start working? What are you intending to do?"

"That's a thought-provoking question. Sometimes, I picture a profession in the medical field. Other times, because of Angela, practicing law or even becoming a police detective crosses my mind. Currently, my folks say I should be a doctor. What are your intentions?"

"Beats me. My father works for General Foods, but I don't know what he really does. I get a kick doing the projects in those chemistry labs."

She beamed, impressed, "Ah, you strive to be a scientist!"

"Fat chance, my grades suck. I hate homework. Maybe I'll join the military."

"Funny. Well, you'll have to improve your scores. Concentrate on math, chemistry, physics, and biology. Writing skills are important, too. Basically, you need to excel in those subjects. The positive news: It's not too late."

I thought of the ways my low GPA could affect my life. Wanting to be with Karen burdened me with contemplating a career. House, cars, whippersnappers . . . *Jeez, it sounds so fucking expensive!*

Seeing my turmoil, she patted my arm. "John, don't stress out. Breathe. Just take one day at a time. Remember, we're freshmen."

Giddy from her touch, I laughed. *That's right, I'm still fourteen!* "Yeah, there's lots of time. We've got all the time in the world."

Wednesday Evening—December 1, 1971

In the cellar, I flipped through a stack of old newspapers, searching for advertisements or notices listing Freemason engagements.

Dad descended the staircase, stopping halfway, hand on the banister. "What are you looking for?"

"Trying to find an old movie review."

"How was your outing with the Schmidt girl?" he questioned, watching as I sorted the bin.

"We saw *The Andromeda Strain*. That is a sensational film, and I wanted to read the critics' comments."

Thoughtfully, my father nodded. "The reviews are in the Thursday entertainment section. Good luck locating it." Humming, he continued to the workshop and began tinkering.

Ready to give up, I found a page listing the regional societies. Shriners, Elks, Knights of Columbus, and at the very bottom, under a square and compass symbol: Freemasons.

Interested in Masonry? Please Feel Free to Stop By

> Come by and speak to our members. Ask any questions you might have regarding our special fraternity. Please make an appointment with the brethren to talk at greater length about the Masonic Order. It can take many months to join, so if you're fine with that, we look forward to meeting you.

The announcement included an index of lodge addresses, the closest in Tenafly.

Bi-Weekly Meetings – Every Second and Forth
Wednesday – 7:30-9:30 PM.

Last week had been the fourth Wednesday of November, which had significance. In my bedroom, I checked the calendar. Wednesday, December 8, was the next Freemason meeting in Tenafly. *Bingo!* With a red crayon, I circled the date.

Haunted House

Friday Afternoon—December 3, 1971

YESTERDAY, I INFORMED EVERYONE we should meet to discuss the final plan to break in and search Mr. Reynolds' residence. The crew acted doubtful or anxious, realizing the date was just a few days away. Flipping out myself, I guessed the sudden reality of what we were undertaking finally hit home. Up to now, my idea had served as a childish game. Vince suggested gathering after school at the old, abandoned building near his neighborhood. The local kids tagged the spooky estate the "Haunted House." Karen said she had to help her mother first and could catch us there in an hour.

Unless someone divulged the Haunted House's location on Lake Shore Drive, you might never know it existed. The paved street deteriorated into a rutted dirt roadway tracing the banks of the Oradell Reservoir. Peering closely, an urban explorer might spot a decrepit mailbox bending in the bushes. Visitors to Number 26 seek a narrow, overgrown path, once the long gravel driveway.

Ranzetta, Outlaw, and I parked the bicycles inside the detached garage, sheltered from the icy wind and flurries. Swirling newspapers and beer cans cluttered the greasy earth and in the rafters rested the remnants of a green canvas canoe. The frigid temperature reduced the lingering smell of used motor oil and urine.

Covered with distorted cedar shingles, the two-story homestead was tinted white. Fancy carved ornamentation adorned the doors, window frames, and under the eaves. Tall brick chimneys flanked the steep roofline. In the abode's heyday, the residence must have been considered a mansion. Nowadays, with peeling paint, busted panes, and a sagging roof, the building marked time until demolition. The Haunted House was always an adventure.

I followed the fissured concrete sidewalk leading up to the structure. Snowdrifts cloaked vegetation choking the yards. Young saplings thrust limbs into many of the gaping windows. "Who do you think was here?" I inquired, signifying the fading footprints in the powder.

"Apparently, your mother," Vince wisecracked.

The dwelling received the three of us past the wide-open front door and into the spacious hall. In dripping red enamel, the word "PIGS" greeted guests. The graffiti looked recent. A coating of snowflakes sprayed the entryway and fanned out below the windows. The same footmarks dissolved into dust.

Archaic floral wallpaper unrolled to different degrees. A flight of stairs ascended to the shadowy second floor. Although the handrail survived intact, spindles lay strewn across the moldy carpet, resembling pulled teeth.

"Hello!" Ranzetta bellowed, echo reverberating throughout the house. "Where's your girlfriend?"

"Karen's not my girlfriend, and she'll be here later."

"Fellas, check this out," Bill whispered reverently. Beaming, he stood over a huge pyramid of excrement evacuated in the nook of what used to be the formal dining area. The table remained, with one chair. A forbidding mural dangled crookedly from a wire. Outlaw lifted a chair leg and poked the turd. "Frozen stiff," the boy apprised, dropping the wood to the planking with a thud.

The dung heap reminded me of last summer, when we played "shit on a stick." For those that never participated in this challenging game, the rules are very simple. A contestant takes a dump someplace outside, and the other competitors try to find the load. Whoever returns first with a verified lump of poo at the tip of a branch scores 20 points. More credits are awarded for size, consistency, minutes to locate, etc. Shit on a stick is mighty fun on a hot day. Bill had an uncanny knack for this sport.

Individually, we toured the lower level. A dilapidated bathroom with claw bathtub and demolished toilet hung off the hallway, copper pipes torn out of the walls. When I opened the medicine chest, a solitary, gleaming straight razor rested on the cracked shelf next to a package of styptic powder. Curiously, I picked up the blade and restored the shaving tool with distaste. Mirror shut, I regarded the splintered reflection of my pale face.

In the sizeable kitchen, the maple-stained cupboard doors drooped or, torn off hinges, lay scattered on the buckled linoleum. Shattered crockery crunched underfoot, and the sink contained burnt rags and a large tureen of snail shells. Rat and mouse turds peppered the counters. Pensively, I gazed past the ripped curtains into the desolate backyard. Tattered boxers wilted from a single string on the raked laundry pole.

The living room won the award for Most Depressing. Light filtered through an amazingly intact picture window onto a worn oriental rug protecting warped hardwood. A duo of couches and an outrageously ugly high-backed chair angled in mute conversation. Rectangular marks on the wrinkled wallpaper hinted of missing family memories.

The furniture overlooked an antiquated television set in the corner. At five inches wide, the greenish screen stared out of a fancy mahogany console. The antiquity should be featured in a museum. It appeared the owners stood up and walked out during an episode of *The Honeymooners. Who would do that?*

Strolling onto the stoop, I inhaled crisp air and watched for Karen. I recalled the day I saw a spirit. Years ago, Vince, Bill, and I, plus a couple of neighborhood kids, used this home and land to play Army. Split into platoons, we used Daisy pop guns to shoot clumps of clay at each other. Someone yelled, "Ghost!" Everybody ran screaming into the yard. Breathing hard, I glanced at an upper sash, glimpsing a gruesome visage of an elderly lady. In disbelief, my friends sneered at my tale. Late at night, I still wonder about that apparition.

A loud crash ended the daydream. In shock, I peered into the streaked living room window. Vince yanked a round object from the TV's guts.

Marching into the foyer, I shouted, "What are you doing, Ranzetta?"

"Vacuum tubes implode," he expounded with glee. "Quite harmless, actually. Glass goes in, not out." Vince swung and threw the black sphere. Flabbergasted, I vaulted to the side as the ball mashed into the stairway. More rods clattered down the steps.

Muttering, I grabbed the orb slowing to a stop. "Jesus, you could have killed me!" Ranzetta laughed hysterically as Outlaw leaned in the kitchen doorway, shaking his head.

Karen and Melissa warily entered, wearing bright winter jackets. Surveying the ruins, Melissa asked, "What the hell is happening in here? We heard you monkeys halfway to China."

Karen frowned at the bowling ball. "It wasn't me," I stated, setting the projectile on the floor. "Can I talk to you a minute?" I requested, pointing to the dining room.

"That's so disgusting." She goggled at the turd pile, covering her mouth with a mitten. The brown-capped chair leg caught Karen's attention.

"What's Melissa doing here? I thought we were attempting to keep this quiet?" Exasperated, I felt betrayed.

"This afternoon, she saw the plans written in my notepad and wanted answers. Melissa's my friend and can help us."

"Help how?" I questioned testily.

"Melissa will stand watch outdoors and alert us if Reynolds returns early. On the night we pull off this caper, it will also be easier for me to leave if my parents think I'm going to her house."

Calming under Karen's cool stare, I inquired, "Is she the only person that knows?"

"Of course. Can we please get out of here? That makes me barf."

"It's frozen," I responded dryly.

In the main hallway, we found the others sharing candy bars. "Is everything okay?" Melissa asked, distributing chocolate.

I turned to Vince and Bill. "Here's the deal. Melissa is now on the team. While we're inside, she'll be the lookout."

"What the fuck! Excuse me, I meant, what the fudge, ladies!" Ranzetta exclaimed. "Bring the whole damn school, if it pleases you."

Scowling, Melissa perched on the bottom step of the staircase and rubbed her arms. "Couldn't you boys find anyplace warmer than this shithole for a meeting, like the library?"

Vince's eyes rolled. Outlaw approached, extending a palm. "Hi, my name is Bill. Welcome to the lineup. Hope we don't get caught or killed."

Melissa accepted the handshake. "Outlaw, I'm aware of who you are. You're in all my classes. *Remember?*"

"Yeah, well I, uh—" he stammered, bashfully focusing on the ground. "I, um—" Picking up four spindles, Bill deftly juggled the batons aloft. Karen's friend reached outward, snatched a club, and chucked the wood out the front door.

"Perfect," I said. "Everyone is introduced, so we'll get started. First off, I agree with Melissa that it's freezing in here and literally a shithole, but this place is more secluded than the library. Let's make this brief and get home before dark. Secondly, I suggest we go upstairs; there's additional room."

As the group draggled single-file up the groaning staircase, I cautioned against a tread placidly waiting to snap a careless anklebone. At the stairhead, the letters "FILTH" were scrawled in the same red, runny pigment. A trio of bedrooms and a tiny bathroom comprised the floor plan of the upper level. The collapsed roof in the smallest chamber massed over a crib. Through the gap, the sky dimmed to orange. I chose the largest room. The master bedroom held a matching pair of rusty bed frames and an armoire whose hatches bulged, exposing hangers of rotting material. A soiled mattress littered with condom wrappers completed the furnishings.

"What happened to these people?" Karen questioned, bewildered. "They just ran off and left their belongings?" The last of the sunlight bathed her face.

"My dad claims a family lived here following the war," Vince answered, excitedly pacing. "The husband returned home after serving in Europe. While the lieutenant buggered his wife, the cuckoo daughter snuck in and ruthlessly murdered both parents with a hatchet. Forty whacks!" Ranzetta parodied hacking motions above the beds accompanied by high-pitched grunting. "Then our pint-sized Mary took care of baby sister!" he yelled, pointing at the small bedroom. "The girl chopped off their goddamned heads and buried the skulls in the rose garden on top of Fido."

"That's Lizzie Borden, doofus," Melissa giggled, cracking up.

"Oh, yeah," Vince conceded, grinning. Tale concluded, his countenance darkened. "Seriously, folks, something fucking atrocious must have occurred here. Don't know about you, but I feel the bad karma scraping behind my eyeballs."

"Let's review the layout of Reynolds' property," I requested. The hour was late, and the sun had set beyond the trees.

Outlaw angled the draft toward the muddy illumination. Karen indicated a rectangle at the rear of the house. "Here is where we enter. You guys found a key under the doormat. With some luck, it will open the back door. If not, Ranzetta gets a chance to utilize his lock-picking skills. If that doesn't work, I'm lost." Crossing arms, she was all business. "The idea is, get in and out without anyone suspecting."

Bill inquired, "What exactly are we looking for?"

"Your mama," Vince quipped. Outlaw faked a lunge as Ranzetta withdrew, smashing into the wardrobe.

I re-examined what we saw at the basement window before Halloween. "Check for items that are unusual. Try not to touch his stuff, and leave everything as you found it. Just search the place. Melissa will monitor one of the walkie-talkies across the road." Glancing at her, I reminded, "If you see or hear anything funky, don't hesitate to warn us. We'll exit to the neighbor's backyard."

"What time?" Bill asked.

Karen squatted, outlining a map in the soot. "On Wednesday, we'll meet at Madison Avenue and Franklin Street at seven p.m. Go to the Italian restaurant on Franklin; the parking lot is a secure area to hide the bikes. John thinks the Masons' meeting starts at seven-thirty and ends at nine-thirty. That's not ample time, and the lodge in Tenafly is a short drive. To be safe, I don't want to be in Reynolds' home longer than a half hour or forty-five minutes." Chilled, she pulled the wool further over her ears. "Boys and girls, let's not fuck this up." Karen ground out the drawing with the heel of a boot.

Sunday Afternoon—December 5, 1971

The weatherman forecast heavy precipitation that Saturday evening, for once, on target. The blizzard commenced at ten-thirty p.m., and by dawn, almost three feet of powder had accumulated. As the flakes continued to descend during the day, Dad and I shoveled every few hours to keep pace. Maintaining a snow-free driveway was backbreaking drudgery, especially when the plow flung fresh mountains of slush. Later, as the weather let up, Bill stopped by with a toboggan. We towed Jane to the slope by the high school and had a super afternoon sledding.

Monday Morning—December 6, 1971

At six a.m., Jane and I sweated by the kitchen radio, hoping to hear class had been canceled. Six more inches fell in the night, and we prayed that was enough to tip the scales. Tuned to WOR, John Gambling read a long list of school closures. Jane gesticulated with a hand, tilting an ear toward the speaker. "Shush. He's coming to us." In euphoria, we jumped as Mr. Gambling announced a day of freedom.

"What are you kids doing today?" Mom asked, passing out cups of steaming hot chocolate. "I mean, after Johnny finishes clearing the pathways," she stipulated, glancing my way. Dad had already left for work.

"Can John and I ice skate at the duck pond?" my sister proposed.

"Maybe we'll drive over when the Department of Public Works has plowed and salted," my mother said, gazing out the window. The snow was halfway up the pole to the birdfeeder. "The yard sure is beautiful," she murmured.

Subsequent to shoveling the driveway and sidewalk, I toiled on a plastic car model. The telephone rang, and I overheard

Mom speaking for a few moments. "Johnny, the call is for you!" she hollered.

"Hello?" I said into the receiver.

"John, it's me, Karen."

"Oh, hi, Karen," I answered, surprised. The line clicked as my mother disconnected.

"Are you skating at the pond?" In a monotone, she gave the impression another topic hid beneath the query.

"Funny, we were discussing that earlier. After lunch, my mom is driving us, if the streets are passable." Fingers cupping the microphone, I inquired in a lower voice, "Everything all right?"

"That sounds great. John, I'll be at the park at two o'clock. See you then."

Hanging up the handset, I meditated on what Karen had been getting at.

The sun came out, and by lunchtime, the roads were passable. My mother dropped us off by the duck pond. The snow had been pushed to the edges and the park was very crowded. On the ice, Karen and Melissa whirled.

As Jane and I sat on a bench lacing up our boots, the girls gracefully skidded to a standstill, showering us with flakes. I thought Karen looked dashing in a red headscarf and white blades.

"Wow, you guys are good!" my sister exclaimed admiringly. Several days a week, she took intermediate lessons at an indoor rink and was no slouch herself.

Standing, I slid along, ankles immediately begging to quit. Gamely, I labored and did my best to remain vertical. The threesome of skaters performed advanced moves, Karen and Melissa impressed by Jane's abilities. Before long, my feet could take no more punishment, and I sank into a snowbank. Karen glided above the frozen water and sat beside me, her cheeks rosy.

"What did you need to talk to me about?" Opening a Pop Tart, I offered her the unbroken piece.

"Thanks. Hard as a rock, yet still tasty," she said, examining the filling. "John, you are always so prepared." Proudly, I smartly snapped the two-fingered Cub Scout salute.

Snack finished, Karen disclosed, "The snowstorm might have altered our agenda."

"To what degree?" I asked. Jane and Melissa pivoted each other in dizzying circles.

"Our strategy was to use the back door, but with the new snowfall, your neighbor may see the tracks."

Stunned, I smacked my forehead, confounded I hadn't considered that. "Yikes, what do we do now, go in the front?"

Dusky eyes studied me as Karen shrugged. "Do you want to postpone?" Plucking the empty wrapper, she shook it and put the foil in a pocket.

Deliberating, I watched Melissa chase Jane on the thin ice. My sister laughed, the blue scarf trailing behind her, flapping. I weighed pros and cons.

"John, it's up to you. We'll do whatever you decide," Karen promised. "Come on," she urged, pulling me upright. "Don't worry; I'll teach you how to skate. Falling is the easy part." Carefree, we cut grooves until my mother returned.

Arriving at a decision, I waved goodbye as the girls got into Mr. Schmidt's car. Before the door closed, I raised a finger, signaling a go-ahead. Karen smiled with satisfaction and stuck up her own thumb. Green light!

The Break-In

Wednesday Evening—December 8, 1971

I REACHED DOMINIC'S RESTAURANT several minutes before seven o'clock. Even though the Italian food smelled appetizing wafting out the open kitchen door, I had a nervous knot in the pit of my stomach. In the parking lot between banks of snow and garbage cans, I overheard the cooks banging pans and shouting. Not busy for a Wednesday evening, a cluster of waiters came outdoors to chat and get stoned.

From the mist, Vince, Bill, Karen, and Melissa arrived simultaneously on bicycles. "Dude, that was a scary ride. Black ice everyplace!" Ranzetta complained, tapping out a Winston. "Smoke 'em if you got 'em," he advised, offering the pack. Karen accepted a coffin nail and lit up. Hesitantly, she took a puff and coughed. Embarrassed, the girl hid the cigarette by her side. Remembering Nat King Cole, I flicked mine to the pavement.

"Everybody's here," I affirmed, relieved. "Do you have the walkie-talkies?"

Outlaw presented the pair and gave one to Melissa. Standing close, he demonstrated the talk and volume buttons. "Breaker, breaker, good buddy," my friend transmitted, smirking.

"Ten-four, Big Daddy," Melissa responded, smiling. Bill chuckled and presumably blushed; it was impossible to tell in the dark.

"Did we bring lights?" I asked, displaying a dented red-and-silver magnetic Eveready. Everyone held up a flashlight. Vince eased the tension by placing the beam below his chin, generating a ghoulish grin. The bulb blinked and went out. Irritated, he vigorously rattled the batteries and worked the switch.

I handed Ranzetta the Eveready. "I have a spare," I said, retrieving a backup searchlight from the backpack.

Karen produced a camera. "If you need a photo of evidence, let me know, but we should be extra careful no one notices the flash outside."

"Well, then, I suppose we're ready," I declared. "Since we're using the front entryway, Vince will snag the key under the welcome mat. If it works, we follow him inside while Melissa keeps watch from across the street. Anything else?" The group shook their heads. "All right. Let's go."

Leading the crew through a clump of trees and snow-covered backyards, we hid behind a hedge near Reynolds' residence.

The Ford station wagon left a faint pair of tire imprints in the slush. I was glad the curved sidewalk and front porch had been shoveled and were now footprint free. Illumination seeped from the same upstairs window. The neighboring buildings were silent.

"Hold tight. I'm going in," Vince said. Crouching, he scuttled onto the stoop. Soon holding high a shiny object, the boy eased the front door and signaled. Nodding farewell to Melissa, the rest of us hustled across the icy roadway.

Huddled in the vestibule, Ranzetta shut and locked the entrance. Hot, I took off my hat. Hyper, holding a forefinger to my lips, I listened for a few seconds before establishing the house was vacant. Reassured, I exhaled.

"Big Momma," Outlaw said softly into the walkie-talkie. "Do you copy?"

"Copy, Big Daddy. Coming in loud and proud," Melissa's tinny voice answered.

The team expected direction. "Bill and Vince, search the garage and basement," I ordered. "Karen and I can explore the remainder of the premises. If you find something, keep us informed. And stay aware of the time."

As they disappeared along the hall, I followed her to the front. The chamber resembled any other living room with drab carpet and cream-colored walls. A plastic slip-covered couch, a set of chairs, and a television completed the decor. *Popular Science* magazines crowded the coffee table. In a recess, a tall case accommodated dusty books and knickknacks. I shielded the ray as Karen skimmed text. The volumes had titles referencing medicine and engineering, nothing unusual.

A long table and a hutch enclosing china furnished the dining area. The alcove appeared unused.

"There is no artwork," she noticed. Scanning the unadorned walls, I concurred.

In the kitchen, the slightly fatty odor of recently cooked food floated in the air. Cabinets enclosed shelves of canned goods and cookware. Dirty dishes and pots filled the porcelain basin. Karen scrutinized a low pile of mail on the Formica-topped counter. Perusing one envelope in particular, I peered past her shoulder. Addressed to Martin Reynolds, the dispatch came from an Elizabeth Reynolds in Ohio.

"Sister?" I assumed.

"Could be, or wife," she mused. "The man is old enough to have a daughter, or Elizabeth may be a distant relative."

Inspecting the refrigerator, I found eggs, bacon, and six-packs of Schlitz beer. The icebox chilled a bag of frozen peas and four large items shrouded in white wax paper. The pieces were unusual, so I drew one out. Secured with freezer tape, the parcel weighed seven or eight pounds. The word "Chapman" was printed on the bottom. The name sounded familiar.

Rummaging under the sink, the girl shook a super-sized box of rat poison. "Come here," I beckoned.

At the refrigerator, Karen examined the bundles. Her eyebrows rose questioningly, and she touched the writing. "The Chapmans live a few streets away. Let's check these ones," she suggested eagerly. The text on the leftover articles said "Dolin," "Price," and "Smith."

"This is my next-door neighbor!" I exclaimed, feverishly shaking the package labeled "Smith." "The family owns the Haworth pharmacy. And 'Price.' Mr. Price is our English teacher."

"Open it," Karen directed, suspending the beam high. Jittery, I stripped off the adhesive and unrolled the parchment. "What is that?" she swallowed in disbelief.

"Get a closeup." I gagged, resisting the impulse to retch. "That's an animal. A skinned rabbit or, or a cat. Do you see a head?" As I held the rock-hard carcass aloft, Karen positioned the camera. The flash flared, leaving a pinkish-white afterimage of muscle, fat, and bones. "Will we photograph the other ones?"

"That's nauseating," she responded, pulling a pad and pen from a pocket. "If you don't mind, I'll just write the names."

Sealing Reynolds' dinner, I returned the corpses to the freezer. "Let's case the upper rooms," I implored, hankering to vacate the kitchen.

A stairway led up to a three-door hallway and a short corridor, reflecting a tiled lavatory. Karen said hurriedly, "John, we've already been here twenty minutes. Let's split up. Get the bathroom and this bedroom. I'll search those two rooms."

In agreement, I entered the small bedchamber, encompassing a single bed topped with a worn quilt. I slid the closet door, shining the flashlight inside. Woman's clothes swayed on padded hangers, and cardboard cartons loaded a shelf. The air stunk of mothballs. A shoebox stored a pair of out-of-style women's shoes.

On the corner of the mattress, I flipped open a cigar box full of old black-and-white snapshots. Most of the photographs depicted the same men, women, and children encircling Christmas trees or birthday cakes. More images recorded bygone vacations. Quite a few of the same folks posed by vintage automobiles, historical buildings, or landscapes. A fair-haired woman appeared in numerous prints beside a boy of varying ages. Reynolds and his mom?

The bath consisted of the standard fixtures, all fuchsia. In the vanity, I found a metallic item protected by cloth. Unraveling the packet, Karen startled me. "John, you need to see this!"

Excited, I tailed her past the hummingbird wallpaper into a bedroom aglow from a desk lamp. "It's decorated for a little girl," Karen revealed breathlessly.

This was where the light stayed on, everything pink and feminine. A ledge near the ceiling paraded dolls of every size. Stuffed animals roamed the comforter, and a large illustration of an angel floated above the headboard.

"This *is* interesting," I muttered. A framed photo of Martin Reynolds and a youth of six or seven was centered on the nightstand. "Do you think that's his daughter?" Karen shrugged. "Okay, I'm going to check on something. Once you finish up the other bedroom, let's find Vince and Bill." As I walked away, a flashbulb lit the corridor.

The eight objects sheathed in fabric wound up being razor-sharp knives and a rectangular honing stone. Rolls of paraffin paper and freezer tape filled the bathroom cabinet.

"Holy Toledo!" Karen exclaimed in the doorway. As she leaned to snap a photograph, my eyes shut, just in time. "Replace the scalpels; we'll consider them later. In ten minutes, I want to be far away from here."

Returning downstairs, Karen commented that the master bedroom contained nothing of significance.

Two doors occupied the space between the foyer and kitchen. Voices penetrated the door adjacent to the front of the residence. Twirling the knob, the fellas stood in the midst of the double garage, turning as we entered.

"Look at this junk!" Ranzetta burst out, aiming my flashlight at various wooden contraptions.

"What are these?" Karen asked, appalled. "Torture machines? Are these devices designed to crucify people?"

"Close enough," he replied. "This is Reynolds' playroom. The lousy fuck builds the equipment in the basement before lugging them up here to test."

"You mean for—" she murmured.

"On the nose again, Miss Schmidt," Vince answered, beaming. "That deviant drags some poor unlucky soul home and submits them to God-knows-what horrors." Assorted whips and shackles covered iron frames bolted to the paneling.

"And what might this be?" Bill inquired, holding a frightening zippered leather mask.

"Whatever it is, I don't want to find out," I responded, noticing the painted-over windowpanes and insulated walls. "I guess we know why my neighbor doesn't park the station wagon in here. Let's wrap up the photos and get out of this place."

Karen snapped images of leather-clad crosses and a toolbox brimming with surgical implements.

Laughter exploded across the room. Ranzetta lashed a lengthy flog, pretending to thrash Outlaw bending over an elaborately constructed rack. "Take a picture, Karen. It's worth a thousand words," he leered.

The camera flashed. "Seriously, you are out of—" she began and paused when the walkie-talkie sputtered static.

Bill hastily telescoped the antenna as Melissa's distant voice whispered, "A car came down the road and is slowing. Oh shit, it's turning into the driveway!"

"Let's get going!" I yelled, running into the house.

The radio screeched again. "A Ford is parking," she said frantically. "Someone is exiting the vehicle. Clear out now!"

"The basement!" Karen hissed. "There's no time. We've got to hide there."

Ranzetta yanked the cellar door and navigated the steep steps.

"This way!" Outlaw barked. Grabbing my arm, he flipped on the beacon and led the way to a narrow wood-slatted door set in the cinderblock. "Quiet," Bill breathed, closing the gate and clicking off the light.

Overhead, a door opened and slammed closed, followed by heavy footsteps crossing the floor. For a while, I felt vibrations of movement: a flushing toilet, running water, a chair scraping the linoleum. Then silence.

"John, I may have left your flashlight in the playroom," Vince mumbled desperately.

"Shut up!" I muzzled. The burrow was pitch dark, oppressive, and foul-smelling. *What is that stench?*

"Reynolds must be eating," Karen conjectured. "When he falls asleep, we can sneak away."

The thought of my neighbor's meal coiled my stomach. *And that putrid odor!* Putting a hand over the lens, I turned on the bulb. Three faces of fear hovered in the gloom.

"What in the fuck are you doing?" Outlaw scowled angrily.

"Ugh, it smells like a rotting animal in here," I moaned, wigwagging the flashlight around the cobwebbed den. A collection of white sticks were stacked in the far corner. *Are those bones?*

"Holy shit!" Ranzetta choked out. "Is that. . .?"

Karen snatched the light, kneeling before the mound. "Cat," she mouthed.

Holed up in the airless tomb, something clattered upstairs. Neck creaking, I blindly charted shoes traversing the ceiling and, finally, the click of a latch.

"Did he leave? Did Reynolds go?" I asked.

"Fuck me. I think he's in the garage!" Outlaw blurted. "That wasn't the front door."

"Take off your shoes," Karen commanded. "Kids, we're getting the hell out of here." Hauling off her boots, she clutched them while swinging open the crawlspace gate. "Hurry!" Karen summoned, fleeing into the basement.

In our stocking feet, we skulked up the flight of steps, every squeak stopping my heart. The group edged toward the exit, past the garage. Vince eased wide the screen as we beat it across the lane, falling into a snowbank. Entry locked and key returned under the mat, my friend arrived, winded.

"Jesus Christ!" Melissa cried. "I thought you guys were toast."

Thankful for freedom, I started giggling. Karen's chum stared in surprise as we hooted deliriously. Observing Vince wrestle Bill in the powder, she joined the hilarity. "Okay, okay," I said, composing my emotions. "Put your shoes on and go home." Hastily, I brushed crusted ice off my socks and jammed my soggy feet into boots. I didn't care if my toes were cold and wet—I'd never been happier.

Jane and Mom stared at the television. *All in the Family* had premiered earlier in the year, and its popularity was rising in the reruns. "Johnny, come watch this!" my sister begged. "This comedy is pretty funny. The dad's a complete moron."

The sitcom was indeed comical. In this episode, a black household had moved next door to the Bunkers. Archie Bunker, the racist father, delivered one stupid line after another.

Assessing what my friends and I had done, I felt anxious to talk with them at school and get their impressions. Reynolds was bonkers, and we were fortunate to leave the place in one piece. I worried that the maniac had seen us leaving.

Ranzetta left my flashlight!

What would my neighbor do when he found the Eveready? I didn't hear the laugh track on TV. The euphoria following our escape faded, substituted with strong apprehension.

Thursday Morning—December 9, 1971

Flashbacks pursued me throughout the day, always on the brink of reviving a meaningful memory. In the nightmare, Karen took snapshots of a basement and garage. Dazed by the camera's spark, I could not focus and asked her to stop. Costumed in a black wizard's cloak, Martin Reynolds began a tour of an extensive mansion. Stitched on the white apron's shield, a skull insignia was cleverly enhanced with the ears and whiskers of a cat. There were way too many rooms. What happened to the windows? *Where was Karen?* Candelabra brightened the abundant feast. Faceless entities gathered around the buffet, watching the guest of honor bite into the furry main course.

Thursday Afternoon—December 9, 1971

Appreciating the normality of chem lab, I listlessly stirred copper sulfate into hot water.

"How did you sleep?" Karen questioned. "John, you look drained."

"I've slept better," I answered, pouring a half-liter of the saturated solution into a shallow container. "What about you?"

Gingerly, my partner set the vessel on an undisturbed sideboard to grow a seed crystal overnight. "Not good. I keep being reminded of the meat in that icebox. What if we'd been caught? That guy is certifiably nuts."

"Totally," I admitted, removing the laboratory coat.

"I'm dropping the film off at the pharmacy. Can you go with me?"

"Smith's Pharmacy?" I responded, jolted awake.

"Yes, why? Downtown is on the way home." Karen's air changed with comprehension. "The Smiths may view their name in the freezer pictures."

"Precisely. In fact, I'm not even sure if Smith's develops film in-house or sends it elsewhere for processing. If they do, I wouldn't enjoy explaining those photographs. That is, if that eviscerated thing really was their family cat." Frowning, I tried to recall the last time Frisky had come into our yard. I was glad Django was an indoor cat.

"Did you get a chance to speak to Vince and Bill today?" she asked. I shook my head. "Melissa and I talked over what we found, and her opinion is to contact the police."

"She might be right. Let's take the Instamatic cartridge to K-Mart after school. Then we can review our next steps. Are you able to ride that far?"

"Why, do I appear feeble?" Karen pouted, flexing her calf.

"Uh, no," I answered, embarrassed. "It's just that you live on the other end of town."

"John, I own a ten-speed, too. My Schwinn will kick the ass of whatever you got."

"Paris Sport," I growled defensively. "My bike is a Paris Sport."

Karen charged down Tank Hill, head tucked low, hair streaming. Glancing backward as I neared, she pedaled furiously. At the bottom, the girl allowed me to glide close, then grinned and pulled past. This continued the entire way into Closter. When we came to a halt at the discount store, my chest ached.

With a cable, I locked the bicycles together. The blue Varsity Schwinn *was* nice. "Give me a minute," I huffed. "My chain needs lubrication. That's for certain. And I believe the tires require air, too."

"Oh, you're funny," Karen laughed, drawing the film from her jacket. "Let's drop off this bad boy."

We weaved between clothes racks to the photographic lab at the rear of the shop. While she filled in the processing slip, I idly gazed at the hunting counter. Weapons leaned against the wall. The salesperson extended a scoped rifle. Sliding the bolt back and forth repeatedly, the gentleman returned the firearm. I elbowed Karen, who was inserting the envelope into the deposit slot. Alarmed, she gasped in recognition.

As we spied on Martin Reynolds through an array of golf clubs, the salesman intently pointed out features on different pump-action shotguns. Hefting one of the guns, my neighbor thoughtfully laid the hardware on the sideboard and ran a hand along the barrel. Price discussed, Reynolds opened a wallet, holding out his identification and permit. The clerk vetted the cards before setting red boxes of shells on the glass. *You gotta be kidding!* That was it, I'd seen enough.

"Let's leave, Karen!"

Rushing from the store, I considered what we had gotten ourselves into. Obviously, my neighbor killed the community's cats and lived an unorthodox sex life. Definitely a sicko. The questions were: Had he done something illegal? Did the man have anything to do with Angela's disappearance or anyone else's?

Unlocking the bikes, we rode to the garden center to wait. A few minutes later, Reynolds departed K-Mart carrying the brown paper-wrapped scattergun in the crook of an arm.

Karen looked troubled. "Sorry for getting you into this mess," I apologized. Feeling crappy, I had made a huge mistake and didn't know what to do.

A slight smile crept to the corners of her lips. "John, you can't win if you don't play."

Karen let me ride beside her the whole way home.

Friday Morning—December 10, 1971

"Johnny," my sister whispered urgently, shaking me conscious. "A car is outside!"

"What?" I mumbled, dreaming of a lost lake irradiated by pitiless moonlight. Alone, I teetered upon the rocky bank, stark naked. Fanged rabbits hopped over my hoofed feet. "Jane, what's wrong?"

Conspiratorially, she pressed a single finger to her mouth. Orange Clackers hung from her other hand, the plastic spheres clicking gently. "There's an automobile in the middle of the lane with no one in it."

I crawled from bed and stumbled to the frosty window, stubbing a toe on the desk. "Ow, shit!" Peeping through the blinds, I saw what appeared to be a grey Volkswagen Beetle. Highlighted by a streetlamp, the driver's side door hung ajar. "So what?" I grumbled, releasing the slats and sliding under the fleece.

"That's not normal," my sister responded. "You should go investigate. The Bug is stopped on a curve, and somebody may smash into it. As a good citizen, you'll have to notify the police."

"Yeah, right!" I took another glance; it all *was* peculiar. "What time is it?"

"Two-thirty. I happened to look out front."

"At two in the morning?" I asked, rubbing my eyes.

Jane cupped hands, imitating binoculars. "Go ahead, big brother. I'll keep watch up here."

"You do that," I said, tugging on jeans and a jacket on top of my pajamas. Noiselessly, I descended the stairs. My house had a rear door in the laundry room, and I twisted the lock and tiptoed into the backyard. The air was icy and still. The silvery half-moon created mysterious shadows below the trees. Thankful for the meager illumination, I wished for a lamp.

As I rounded the corner, brittle snow crunched underfoot. My sister was correct about the unnatural way the vehicle angled. Squatting behind a bush and surveying the area, I could not detect the driver, but noticed the muffled sound of a radio. The music came from the automobile. On full alert, I inched onward. The environment seemed different and dangerous.

Resolutely, I proceeded toward the VW. Louder, the song cross-faded to the Doors' "Riders on the Storm." Beneath the direct glare of the streetlight, it became difficult to determine if the interior was truly unoccupied. "Hello?" I called. "Anyone there?"

With more bravado, I vigilantly circled, trying to peek in the glass. The open door was foreboding, maps and cigarette packs crammed into the side pocket. Beside the radiance of the dashboard, the inside of the automobile remained dim. A silver tube lay upon the driver's seat. *A flashlight!* When I slid the button, the intense beam set the red upholstery ablaze. It was bare, except for an Afghan blanket spread on the bench. I squinted up the hill. Apparently, the Bug had rolled to the bottom. *From where?* This car didn't belong in our neighborhood.

I had to at least propel the vehicle off the roadway. Grasping the basic theory of manual transmissions, I reached into the cabin and jiggled the eight-ball shift lever. The Lizard King's lurid lyrics surrounded me. The keys were in the ignition; a white rabbit's foot dangled on the keychain. I shouldered the out-of-gear VW against the curb and pulled the parking brake. As I extracted the key and placed it on the seat, the Bug died.

Jane waited impatiently by the washing machine. "What happened?"

"Nothing. The car rolled downhill." Exhausted, I wanted to sleep.

"Johnny, I saw you pushing it to the edge."

Handing her the flashlight, I pleaded, "Yeah, yeah. Go back to bed. We've both got school in a few hours."

My sister studied the dented Eveready, mystified. "Oh, neato, you found our light. Mom searched everywhere for it."

Periodically, the rest of the night, I checked if the Volkswagen moved. Awake when the alarm eventually rang, I still contemplated the flashlight. Switching off the alarm's racket, I went again to the window. The Beetle had vanished.

Tiny

Saturday Evening—December 11, 1971

I STARED FIXEDLY AT A MOUNTAIN OF COLOMBIAN GOLD. Heaped upon a green cafeteria tray, the gilded marijuana rested alongside an unfinished balsawood model airplane. In the background, Vince's brother raved about the quality of the herb, repeating the phrases, "Can you dig it?" and "Don't worry; it's copacetic."

Reality surfaced as I noticed my name mentioned. We were hanging out in Ranzetta's bedroom listening to Rod Stewart's "Maggie May" when Paul ambled in carrying the platter of weed. "Yeah, man, I need some backup. Can you dig it? Bill and John can ride shotgun. Vince, I swear it won't take long. As a bonus, I'll give you guys a couple of joints for helping out. Are you down with that?"

The high-school senior took a deep hit, passing the purple bong. "No, thanks. I'm fine, Paul," I declined, holding up a palm.

Red eyes bore into me with disbelief. "Come on, don't be a pansy. A little toke won't hurt you, Townsend." Teaching me how to regulate the choke, he held a flame to the packed bowl. As the murky water burbled, I mellowed out. *This dope is dy-no-mite!*

Vince observed our reaction to his brother's request. When nobody refused, he finally replied, "We simply have to drop off the pot in Lodi? The dude pays you, and we're gone?"

"Yeah, bro, it'll be copacetic," Paul reassured, scooping the dope into a plastic bag. "Time to boogie, fellas!"

Outlaw and I slid across the stiff, cold vinyl into the Road Runner. In the cramped backseat, I detected the delicate bouquet of beer and smoke. Paul shoved the cannabis under the bucket seat, and the powerful automobile rumbled to a start. Igniting a spiff, he handed the dregs of a bottle of Jack Daniels to Bill. My friend knocked back the liquor, grimaced, took one more belt, and relinquished the whiskey. The alcohol seared my esophagus, followed swiftly by an agreeable, warm buzz. Colorful Christmas decorations blurred past the small side window. The hypnotic psychedelic music put me in a trance.

"Watch this!" Paul bellowed, flooring the 330-horsepower V8. Hurtling onward, my skull banged against the glass as the vehicle swerved and lurched ahead with each violent shift of the Hurst. Keyed up, he flipped the finger to a Camaro receding from view. Outlaw faced the rear, laughing.

Paul swung the steering wheel into a darkened parking lot behind two-story apartments. This must be the lovely town of Lodi. "Let's take off. Get out," he ordered. Vince tipped the front seat as we eased to the sidewalk.

Perception altered by sour mash and maryjane, I trailed the Ranzettas through a maze of garages and buildings. Climbing the crumbling brick steps, we stood before a peeling doorway framing spider-cracked glass. The tarnished brass number read 117B. At another rental, angry cries accompanied the crash of splintering wood.

Knuckles raised, Paul paused to whisper, "This block is in a rough part of town." A switchblade magically appeared from his shirtsleeve. Smiling, he winked. "Just stay cool." After four quick raps, we moved away and waited.

"What?" a harsh female voice called. Not seeing anyone, I bent to catch Bill gazing at a twitching rat lying on its belly, sans tail. Bloody footprints crawled from the rattrap on the end of the stoop. *Ah, the missing appendage.*

Vince's brother tilted backward and yelled, "Yo, we're here for Tiny!"

"Who is?" A shadowy figure leaned out an upper window.

"Paul. Let us in, Shirley."

An interior glow backlit someone sluggishly descending a staircase. A leathery claw slid aside the tattered, lacy curtain. Squinting, a middle-aged female pulled the door to the chain's limit. "Who are these kids?" she questioned, frowning.

"They're my brother and his friends. Hurry up, Shirley, he's expecting me."

Scowling, she pushed the door to release the latch and allow us entry. We followed the woman up the dingy stairwell. On the landing, a stockpile of pizza boxes flickered in a bluish glimmer. The unholy funk strengthened as we left the last pocket of fresh air. As we turned the corner into the cluttered living room, cowboys on horses raced inside an aged Magnavox. Shirley announced, "Paul and his little gangster friends have arrived." Grunting, she activated a dim lava lamp.

The man sat, feet elevated, in a La-Z-Boy lounger. The definition of obese, Tiny held the record for the most disgusting human of all time. Topping a quarter ton, in this poor illumination, his features were difficult to distinguish. His black hair and bushy beard blended with dark clothes. Paul's business associate melted into the deeply stained chair.

"Come closer," Shirley coaxed. Smoke spiraled as she kindled a miniscule cigar.

Tiny's grimy face cracked, exposing gleaming dentures. He inquired in a whiney falsetto, "Hon, can you unplug the goddamn TV?" The crone terminated the blazing Indian genocide, and he asked, "Paul, did you bring the marijuana?"

"Yeah, it's outside, man. The deal is for five hundred. I'll need that up front."

"Well, of course, Paul. I'll hand you the five hundred dollars when you give me the pound of marijuana," Tiny wheezed. "I don't receive many guests. It would be pleasant if you boys relaxed a minute and visited." The bloated head swiveled to the left, indicating a sheet-covered couch.

"Sounds really fun, but we gotta go. I have other commitments; dig?" Paul's eyes flitted around the space, lingering on a partially open doorway.

"Sit, sit, sit," the slob urged, languidly clenching a forty-ounce bottle of King Cobra.

"Okay. Only for a second. I should get these guys back."

The four of us sunk into spongy cushions as Shirley faded into the kitchenette. I took in the living quarters. Unruly bundles of newspapers and pornographic magazines spilled onto cases of adult diapers. Within a forsaken aquarium, dusty plastic plants drooped on a ceramic diving bell.

"Why don't you turn that on, kid?" the beluga requested. His tumescent tongue rolled in his mouth, resembling a dying eel.

"What?"

"Switch on the fucking light. Christ almighty, I'm asking you to flip on the motherfucking bulb for the fishies!"

"Let him alone," Paul warned.

Tiny's tone bothered me, but stoned, I didn't perceive the swollen slug as any real threat. There was no way in hell he could ever leave that chair. To be on the safe side, I extracted my ass from the sofa and triggered the fluorescent tube. Examining brown objects at the bottom, I recognized the sharp-toothed jawbones of desiccated fish.

Back on the couch, Shirley entered, holding a silver tray loaded with bacon-wrapped pigs in a blanket. Carefully, she set the plate on a coffee table and passed us folded birthday napkins. "Enjoy them, boys. These appetizers are homemade, my mama's recipe," the woman purred, lying a palm on Tiny's shoulder. Always polite, I picked up a slippery hors d'oeuvre. Pretending to bite the funny-smelling sausage, I craftily hid the mini-hotdog in the tissue.

"What is it young blood, you hate my wife's cookin'?" Tiny asked, annoyed. Washing away twin itty-bitty pups, a blobby paw reached for an extra fistful.

He was observant for a guy who hardly moved his neck. I answered, "These are tasty. I'm saving mine for later. I had a big dinner."

Tiny concentrated on Vince's brother. "I gotta appraise the product before any bread changes hands." A shiny coating of bacon grease glistened on his blistered lips.

Agitated, Paul responded, "Friend, this transaction isn't the first time we've done business." Staring again at the cracked door, he asked, "Are we by ourselves here?"

Although Tiny didn't blink to confirm our isolation, Shirley's eyes darted toward the bedroom. *Had they seen?* I tried to capture Paul's attention as he glared at the fleshy mound. Outlaw, also concerned, casually elbowed Vince.

"Fine. Since, you've always been a decent customer, we'll go get the stuff. Then you can check it out. Believe me, you won't be disappointed. This shit is primo high grade," Paul promised. "Let's scram, guys."

"How about you youngsters visit while we wait for him to return?" Tiny requested, smiling. A massive thigh hid his mitt.

"Nah, I don't think so." Paul stood and motioned.

We tailed him downstairs and out the entryway. "What was that bullshit?" Vince demanded, rushing to the car.

"The deal didn't feel right. I've sold reefer to that douche a million times, but never this much. That felt like a setup."

"Somebody was in the other room," I whispered.

Paul gestured to stop within eyeshot of the Road Runner. Giving the all-clear sign, we hastily entered the hardtop. Across the lot, two pairs of headlights blinded us, blue orbs rotating on the automobiles' roofs.

"Shit!" Paul shouted. "Tiny's a fucking narc!" As one of the undercover police cruisers lunged to block our car, Paul keyed the ignition, dropping the four-speed into first gear. "Hold on!" he roared. The muscle car jerked forward, slamming into the bumper of the lead cop.

"Go, go!" Vince screamed. Cussing, his brother gunned the engine, forcing the fender aside. Metal rasped and crumpled beneath my shoulder. The Plymouth accelerated, bouncing out of the apartment complex. Bill and I twisted to view the undamaged vehicle in hot pursuit.

"The police are coming!" I hollered loudly.

When Paul pitched the Colombian Gold into my lap, I jumped as if the ganja burned. "John, be ready to throw that crap out of the car." In terror, I cranked the triangular windowpane, peering at the rear glass. The spinning flashes were close; the smashed cruiser was joining the hunt. Speeding 80 miles per hour through a residential neighborhood, Bill frantically searched for a seatbelt.

Paul cried excitedly, "Catch you on the rebound!" Amused, he flipped a toggle below the dashboard before braking hard and yanking the wheel to the right. The automobile fishtailed as the motor revved, our car shooting down a deserted side street.

"Smokey lost us!" Outlaw hooted in relief. "What did you do?"

"Used an old bootlegger trick. Disconnect the brake lights, and the fuzz can't tell you're slowing down. The chase vehicle can't decelerate fast enough to make the turn," he laughed, shaking a fist.

Paul zigzagged among numerous avenues before pulling into an abandoned gas station. "Give it here, John," he commanded, reaching for the bag of grass. Disappearing behind the structure, the boy reappeared after a few drawn-out minutes. "That's good enough for now. I'll pick up the stash in the morning."

"Paul, the cops saw the Road Runner." Never had I seen Vince this frightened. "The authorities can run down the license plate and find out where we live. We're fucked!"

"This isn't my car," his brother replied calmly.

My friend questioned in disbelief, "What do you mean, it's not yours?"

"The Plymouth is stolen," I deduced.

"During the summer, I ripped off this beauty in PA and swapped the plates. There's no possible way the fuzz will find us. That fat turd doesn't have my last name or address. Naturally, I should lay low for a while."

Relieved, Bill inquired, "Why did he double-cross you?"

"Who knows?" Paul responded. "The narco squad must have something on that tub of shit." Brooding, he muttered, "Maybe it is time to start a different career."

Paul drove onto a secluded plot of land, killing the engine. "Don't leave anything inside," the senior advised, running fingers along the sensuous length of the automobile. He released the trunk, and out came a gasoline can. "Such a shame," he murmured, sloshing fuel into the interior of the Plymouth. "Brother, you do it. I can't," Paul said despondently, tossing the container in the backseat.

The group retreated as Vince lit a strip of cardboard, throwing the torch in the window. The Road Runner blazed as we absconded through the weeds. As I ducked under a barbed-wire fence, the energy of the explosion baked the smile on my face.

The Frame

Wednesday Afternoon—January 12, 1972

"WHAT'S THAT GONNA DO?" Bill looked uptight as we departed the high school.

"Get the police involved. After planting the evidence, we notify the cops," I answered.

"You're going to get us suspended, if not arrested. That's outrageous! John, we don't even know where that shoe came from or who owned it," he said harshly.

"Incognito, we use a pay telephone and tell law enforcement to search Martin Reynolds' yard and the Woods. Say we think he's a murderer."

Grabbing my arm, Outlaw stopped. "The dispatcher will hear a dimwitted kid and decide the caller is instigating a hoax. This is absurd!"

"Yes, you're absolutely right. Using the phone is foolish. A letter can be sent to the Haworth Police Department. It should include a diagram marking where to scout in the Woods for dead bodies. That's more sensible."

"What if the officers are unable to establish grounds to take him into custody? Wasted days digging and finding nothing. The fuzz will be pissed. Isn't it illegal to falsely accuse someone of a felony?"

"Of course, but don't you think Reynolds is responsible for Angela's disappearance?" I continued walking.

"Could be," Bill said, catching up. "What do we do with the goddamn shoe? Stick it in the back of his shed? Won't that appear to be a setup? Why would your neighbor stow proof of a murder in his own yard?"

"Psychos always preserve a memento to remind themselves of the kill. That sick shit gets those screwballs all hot and bothered. We don't have to explain why he kept the trophy. Let the lawmen work that out for themselves."

Outlaw, deep in thought, kicked some stones. "Do you intend to inform the others? Did you let Ranzetta in on your scheme?"

"Keep him out of it. That guy's got enough drama with that crap linked to Paul. This has to stay between us for now."

"John, his brother is crazy. He tried to kill Tiny."

"They say Paul lit the apartment building on fire. I'm not sure he was actually trying to kill him."

"Yeah right! Luckily everyone escaped," Bill muttered.

"I can write up a note, and we'll hide the saddle shoe. Then, I'll put it in the mail. Okay?"`

Worried, my friend didn't say another word the rest of the way home.

Thursday Afternoon—January 13, 1972

I soaked up methods to compose anonymous communiqués viewing TV crime dramas. Deftly using a combination of clipped words and hand-printed block characters, I created a message and map. Snipping the listing for the Haworth Police Department from a telephone book, I glued the address to the front of an envelope. Affixing the stamp, I clasped the packet before my nose, contemplating its weight. I pinched my fingers to tear the accusation in half and hesitated. A pivotal moment, I hid the letter in a school notebook.

Friday Evening—January 14, 1972

Bill and I huddled in the familiar shadows of Mr. Reynolds' backyard. The cedar shed stood a few feet to my left. Riveted on the dwelling, he whispered nervously, "I don't see any movement."

I checked out the bordering windows and inhaled. *It's time!* Removing the saddle shoe from the plastic bag, I held my neighbor's fate up to the moonlight. As the Oxford dried, hair-line cracks split the two-toned leather. The texture was un-nerving, and I craved to be rid of the damned thing.

"Keep watch," I said, inching to the outbuilding. Unlocked, I eased the door, smelling the faint fragrance of manure and gasoline. In the semidarkness, I identified a lawnmower stored with shovels and rakes. *Where to put it?* Concerned that Reyn-olds might notice the stash, I discerned fertilizer bags stacked in the corner. Lifting the top sack, I located a gap I could fit the shoe in. Distressed, I wedged in my conscience and ran for the hills.

Saturday Morning—January 15, 1972

Decisively letting go, the blue metal flap of the mailbox slammed shut. Eyes squinched, I visualized my envelope rest-ing on top of dozens of other posts imprisoned in darkness, lying in wait for the mailman.

Tuesday Evening—January 18, 1972

Standing by for my study partner's return, I appraised an eight by ten photograph of Angela. Close to my age, she smiled, posing below the Statue of Liberty with two girls. The triad wore the same outfits: white shirts with plaid skirts.

"What are you looking at?" Karen inquired over my shoulder.

"The shoes," I responded, turning. Disconcerted, she set the textbooks on the dining room table. "You never told me Angela had Oxfords similar to the one we found."

Karen sat, staring at the homework. "I can't justify why I didn't tell you. Girls wore that type of footwear as part of their school uniform, so I'm not certain it signifies much."

Torn, I wanted to confess to planting the shoe and mailing the incriminating letter. It was burdensome, withholding secrets from Karen. I began to speak and then changed the words. "Yeah, you're right. It doesn't mean anything."

My insides churned. Four days had passed since I posted the accusation. During the weekend, I rode countless times past Reynolds' residence, expecting a patrol car. Endlessly, I circled the Woods, monitoring any action. Nothing. The police probably took a while to process incoming mail. Or they had detected who had sent the message and currently had me under surveillance.

"What's the matter, John? You're acting stranger than normal," Karen asked attentively.

"Sorry," I replied. "Lots going on, that's all." I hadn't confessed the disastrous drug deal or Paul torching Tiny's apartment building. Now, the most important thing was to keep her away from the trouble I started. Guilty as hell, I rode to my house, miserable.

Thursday Afternoon—January 20, 1972

Contemplating my lies to Karen, I coasted, not spotting the two Haworth police cruisers parked in front of 268 Franklin Street. Impelled to swerve around bumpers, my lungs froze at the sight of officers on the porch. Cheeks an enraged shade of red, Reynolds gestured wildly. Turning aside in trepidation, I glided home.

In the garage, I leaned against the automobile's hood. A jugular throbbed energetically, and I needed the bathroom. *What did I do?* I paced the cramped space, trying to relax. Nothing I could do, the wheels were in motion. Wait and see. . . . The initial step of an investigation might be to interrogate the suspect. Curious if the cops had explored the Woods, I sucked in a deep breath and entered the house.

In the kitchen, Mom cooked dinner. "Did you catch those police cars on your way home, Johnny?"

"Hmm?" I answered, hairline itching with sweat.

"When I came home from the supermarket, a couple of policemen were questioning a neighbor. The blue house on the top of Franklin, with the . . . I think the last name is Arnold."

"Oh yeah, noticed that," I mumbled.

"Now I'm curious about what took place. The poor man may have been robbed," she suggested, lowering the gas as the saucepan boiled over.

Upstairs, I dialed Bill's number. A few rings later, Mrs. Outlaw picked up and transferred the phone to him. Whispering, I asked to meet at the playground by the Woods. Grabbing a coat, I informed my mother I would return soon.

Settled on a bench, my friend rose. "What's the word? What's so urgent?"

Quickly, I chronicled the police presence at Reynolds. "Did you note any activity on the way here?"

"No," Bill responded. "Should we check if they're searching by Ceremonies?"

"Yes, that's why I called, but we can't look suspicious. Let's first circle on the bikes and see if something's going down."

Alert, we pedaled, not discovering anything out of the ordinary. Nearly completing the circuit, he yelled, "Stop!" The bicycle's brakes locked, skidding to a screeching halt.

A black van with a white "Police" logo across the side parked adjacent to a path leading into the vegetation. The rear doors swung wide, baring racks of equipment. Uniformed officers stood in a ring, engaged in a bull session.

"The fuzz didn't start yet," Outlaw observed. "Maybe it's too late for this afternoon."

"Sure," I mumbled. "Could be."

An unmarked vehicle arrived, and two jacketed detectives exited. Ensuing a terse meeting, the men seized flashlights and followed the patrolmen into the trees.

"There they go," he said, rubbing his chin. "Ugh, I wonder what the coppers are going to find."

I rejected the thought of tailing the investigators. "Yeah," I said shakily. "Let's go home and see what happens tomorrow."

Supper cooled on the table. "Thanks for joining us!" Jane exclaimed sardonically.

Mom animatedly reviewed the neighborhood commotion. Dad listened raptly. "Helen, what were the police doing? Did you hear what they said?"

"Mike, I drove by after picking up this lamb, and I can't fathom what they discussed. You heard of the recent break-ins in the neighborhood." Stubborn, she hacked through the mutton. "Usually, the butcher has a leaner grade of meat. This is shoe leather."

Pained, Dad dropped his utensils on his plate. "Jesus, Helen, this meal is inedible," my father groaned, spitting a wad into his hand. Crossly, he placed the lump of fat on the dish.

"What's your problem, Mike? The meat isn't that tough." To force a point, my mother stabbed a large chunk of sheep and bit down hard.

Friday Evening—January 21, 1972

The story broke on the ten o'clock newscast. Jim Jensen said, "Today, a shocking revelation resulting in a shootout with local authorities occurred in the small town of Haworth, New Jersey." The anchor's earnest visage cut to an image of paramedics loading a stretcher into an ambulance, the subject's identity hidden by bloody bandages. The camera panned to a group of looky-loos clustered in the road.

"Martin Reynolds is accused of two murders, and this number may rise following the search of a nearby forest. The suspect resisted capture, firing a weapon at approaching officers. One man obtained a slight laceration to a leg while apprehending the perpetrator. During the scuffle, Reynolds acquired a serious but non-life-threatening injury to the head. Police describe the shotgun wound as self-inflicted."

"Who's dumb enough to shoot at cops?" Jane inquired indignantly.

The television screen displayed a group detectives gazing into an excavation surrounded by snow. Shovels and picks stuck out at angles from mounds of dirt. One fellow slipped on mud or ice and avoided falling into the crater by grabbing a tree. The other agents roared in laughter.

The familiar mustachioed chief of the Haworth Police, Randy Evans, filled the box. Mom called for Dad to hurry upstairs. "Martin Reynolds is undergoing treatment at the Bergen County Jail Medical Unit," Evans said. "Enough corroborating evidence was collected on the property to make an arrest. The district's coroner is examining the remains of two exhumed females. Realistically, it takes several days or weeks before positive identifications can be made since the corpses are in advanced stages of decomposition."

The voice of a male reporter shouted, "Chief Evans, are either of the victims Angela Schmidt, the girl who disappeared leaving high school ten years ago?"

Evans said grimly, "Bob, it's too early to form that conclusion. It's feasible. Let's wait for Rich to submit the autopsy results."

The journalist raised one final point. "Sir, please tell us what exactly reopened this case."

As the chief peered directly into the camera, I quit breathing. "Last week, we received a tip from an unidentified source. A letter sent to our station detailed the whereabouts of the dead and supporting evidence. I am asking this person or persons to help by coming forward for questioning. Sorry, folks, I'll have to stop here. The department will do its best to keep the press informed as more facts become available."

The report changed to the status of building a modern football stadium for the New York Giants in the brackish swamps of the Meadowlands.

"That's utterly dreadful!" my mother cried. "Johnny, did you speak to Karen?" My father had materialized in the living room.

"No, Mom," I replied sharply. "I'm just seeing this now, same as you are."

Stern, her features tensed with misgiving. "Honey, give your friend a ring."

I wondered if the Schmidts caught the broadcast. Law enforcement presumably notified the family of the apprehension. Karen was smart enough to conclude our group could be associated. "Yes, I'll talk to her," I promised. Standing to go upstairs, I waved goodnight to my dad.

"Sleep tight, John," he said, moving aside to let me pass.

Saturday Afternoon—January 22, 1972

"I apologize. I should have told you," I said.

"What were you thinking?" Karen screamed, livid.

After lunch, I phoned and requested a meeting on the ninth-hole green. Resembling a dog, I chased the girl through the snowdrifts.

"I didn't want to involve you," I answered.

Karen continued with the same tone. "Jesus, you don't accept that I am involved. The police keep coming to the house asking questions, lots of questions. This news has ripped open an old wound, and my parents are a mess. If you care to remember, I was right there searching Reynolds' home. Just because only you and Bill hid the shoe in his tool shed doesn't suggest that accomplices can't be held accountable."

"Well, they *did* book him. The chief confirmed that the district attorney had enough evidence. The detectives most likely revealed additional incriminating items."

"Oh, no. I never picked up the prints," Karen moaned.

"What's that got to do with this? That was over a month ago."

"John, we need to get them. The film has pictures from inside Reynolds' house. And I took a photo of the exterior. Shit, there are shots of us on that roll. What if an employee views the five by sevens and makes the correlation? My address is on that envelope. What are Vince's thoughts on this fiasco?"

I hesitated before answering. "Ranzetta doesn't know about any of this. Outlaw helped hide the shoe, and I alone mailed the letter. We haven't talked since this happened. Vince has other stuff going on," I responded, hoping she wouldn't demand particulars.

Karen rode the Schwinn silently to Closter; it was definitely not the same enjoyable outing we had dropping off the film. In the pharmacy, an alphabetized rack organized the developed negatives. Paranoid, I kept vigilant as she sorted the "S" bin.

Snatching an envelope, Karen handed the snapshots to me. "Shove it in your pants," she dictated. "We can't have anybody see us pay for this."

Threading between exercise clothes, I hastily shoplifted the package down the front of my jeans and hid the bulge with my shirt. Outside, we hurried toward the bikes.

Still irked, Karen said, "The coroner is performing the autopsy on *my* sister. It'll look as if I set up Reynolds to be implicated."

"Everything will be fine," I reassured, grabbing her arm. "*We* didn't do anything wrong. As long as everyone sticks together, we'll get through this." Unconvinced, she glared. Holding up the stolen pictures, I urged, "We've got to chuck these out."

Behind the building, Karen slowed by a row of dumpsters. "Rip up the pics, and scatter the pieces in those garbage cans." The pocket knife worked nicely shredding the negatives.

"Karen," I implored, "you must realize that I'll never hurt you. Really, I simply wanted to help."

"I appreciate that, and I'm aware you hold a stake in this, too. John, you've carried that upsetting memory your whole life." In the warmth of the sun, her hostility thawed. "Reynolds is answerable for what he did, and I need that bastard to pay for killing Angela. I can't imagine who that other victim is, but that demon should be put away where he can't hurt anyone else."

"Did you talk to Melissa?"

"Yes, I discussed the police coming to our house and the news segments. Suspecting you of approaching the cops didn't come up. I now grasp why you're trying to protect your friends. You'll be obligated to handle Vincent at some point."

"Yes, you're right, and he won't be thrilled."

Monday Morning—January 24, 1972

Running into Vince in the hallway heading to class, I attempted to uphold why he hadn't been included in my plans with Bill. "You've got your hands full with Paul. So, I couldn't—"

Scornfully, he interrupted, "I thought you and me were friends. *Buddies!* Jesus, I can't believe you didn't even consult me before doing something this stupid." Irate, my friend dented a locker and stormed off to class.

Monday Evening—January 24, 1972

News of the tragedy spread quickly. Before dinner, I saw my father intently perusing a piece on the front page of the *Bergen Record*. Later, I read the story. The headline declared, "More Bodies Found in Haworth."

> HAWORTH—Police resume searching a wooded section in Haworth for victims of what is now considered the largest multiple murders in Northern New Jersey's history. Investigators located the original two women's remains on January 20, utilizing clues provided by an informant. Using cadaver dogs, four new corpses were recovered. Three are female, and one is male. Identification has yet to be released to the public. There is speculation that one of the six fatalities is Angela Schmidt, missing since April of 1962.
>
> Citizens are rattled by the grisly murders in their quiet hamlet. Lillian Campbell, who resides on the same lane as suspected serial murderer Martin Reynolds, maintains, "Mr. Reynolds was always a very nice neighbor. A perfect gentleman. When my husband Ralph died, Marty often assisted with repairs. On Christmas, he looked for my lost cat. If

> anyone has seen a chubby grey and white tabby, please contact me. Sprinkles is my only companion."
>
> Choosing not to be identified, another nearby resident said, "This horror show is giving Haworth a bad name. The kids are afraid to play outside, and it's lowering the real estate value of my house."

Tuesday at Noon—January 25, 1972

Ranzetta sauntered into lunch period with an improved disposition. "Hey, assholes!" he greeted, dumping a tray of cheese-encased pasta onto the table.

"Good afternoon, Mr. Douche Bag," Melissa quipped. Bill giggled, dropping a cookie on the floor.

"What, no hamburger?" I asked, inventorying his plate.

"For Lent, I've sworn off meat," Vince replied.

Bill reminded, "Ash Wednesday is next month."

"Talkin' about your meat, Outlaw." That earned a big laugh, and I felt happier.

"John, I was so pissed the other day when I learned you left me out of that thing." Ranzetta warily swept the cafeteria and said in a guttural voice, "I'm glad you got that fucker. Wish I'd been in on it, but—"

"Vince, you *were* in on it, just not that one part." Suddenly feeling vulnerable, I scanned their faces. "You guys are my—"

"Yeah, yeah, yeah, we're your only friends. We'll be known as the coconspirators who helped you break into a house and frame your neighbor for murder. Nice," he chuckled, glancing at Bill.

"Right on!" Outlaw agreed enthusiastically.

Leaning forward, Melissa questioned, "Did you get the newspaper? Have you read what the press has nicknamed him?"

"No," Karen answered. "What precisely has the media branded that pig?"

Excitedly, Melissa withdrew the *Bergen Record* from a bag, sliding the daily across the table. "Check it out."

The bold headline trumpeted "Inside the Lair of a Psychopath." A black-and-white halftone of Reynolds' residence was centered over the article.

> HAWORTH—Police continue the investigation into unidentified bodies unearthed in an undeveloped wooded area. An unnamed source at the Haworth Police Department recounted the interior of the suspected killer's modest two-story home.
>
> "This [man] is the worst breed of lunatic. Martin Reynolds uses machinery in the basement to fabricate contraptions that are used for torture or punishment. The garage contained many devices employed by sexual deviants to restrain movement or to inflict pain: whips, chains. The [man] had over one hundred hats in that bedroom closet. The old kind that you see in the movies. I served on the New York City vice squad for eight years and never witnessed anything close."
>
> National media has dubbed the serial killer: "The Haworth Mad Hatter."

"I remember those hats," Karen conceded. "Didn't give them much consideration at the time. Shelves of bowlers or homburgs. . ."

"Wow, now he's the Haworth Mad Hatter," Melissa mused. Reaching forth, she lightly touched her friend's arm. "I hope the detectives soon work out what befell Angela. Are you hanging in there?"

Karen frowned thoughtfully. "Sure, I guess. Am I supposed to pray one of those skeletons is my sister? That's like giving up faith Angela may still be alive."

"If it was me, I'd need to know what transpired," Bill professed. "But I understand what you mean. There'll undoubtedly be a funeral. Reliving the past—Jesus. Then the trial! Perhaps in the end, you'll feel release, closure."

"I hope so," she sighed.

Sunday Afternoon—February 6, 1972

At home, the telephone rang as I played Lie Detector with Jane and her two friends. Pushing the wand into the gizmo, a bell chimed, and the polygraph needle pointed to "False," indicating bogus testimony. Child's play. I easily deduced which suspect was the criminal.

"Johnny, it's for you!" Mom hollered from the kitchen. "Karen," she mouthed, responding to my raised eyebrows.

Pleased, I lifted the receiver. "Karen?"

"John, you were right. The coroner corroborated that Angela was one of the deceased," she said breathlessly. "We just found out."

"Oh, sorry to hear that. I mean to say, I'm relieved you'll finally make sense of what happened." At the doorway, my mother watched with alarm. "Did the investigators check who the others are?"

"The coroner authenticated the identities of five victims. The females. Four are New Jersey residents, and one is from southern New York State. Besides Angela, nobody else resides in Haworth or neighboring towns. The police are contacting the families and refused to give names. And the dots are not connected on how Reynolds became mixed up with the women. Thus far, the detectives haven't verified who the male body was, saying he could be a drifter."

"Huh. Can law enforcement test how long the bodies were interred or why the agents didn't find any clues when Angela appeared to be missing?" I recalled the old newspaper clippings. "The cops did a thorough inspection?"

"From what my parents said, scores of people combed the region for weeks and utilized dogs. Hard to say what went wrong, much of the paperwork has vanished. The police suggested your neighbor concealed Angela in the Woods *after* the search ended."

An uncomfortable conversation. "Okay, Karen. Thanks for calling, and again, I'm very sorry. You can tell me the rest at school."

"John," her hushed tone stopped me.

"Yes?"

"Not every victim is from 1962. Angela and another girl were. The other remains are recent. In fact, Reynolds buried a woman last October. John, you ended the killing spree. Bye, I'll see you later." As the line went dead, I conjured spectral voices whispering on the wires.

Saturday Afternoon—February 12, 1972

Muted, I spent the morning doing nothing. Sleep had been intermittent, and I woke with a dull headache. Slices of an eerie dream floated through my consciousness. The town's landscape transformed overnight as an ever-widening sinkhole formed in our neighborhood. Houses and churches folded, ingurgitated by the swirling maw. The world trembled and tilted.

Anxious to get outside, I telephoned Karen. So was she.

Answering the door, her mother seemed distracted. "Hello, there," she slurred.

"Hi, Mrs. Schmidt. How have you been?" I asked, not clear what else to say.

The woman stared raptly. "John, I can't stop imagining what that mongrel did to my daughter. *Christ!* My poor baby alone and pleading for help. Angela was just up the road from where you live. Why didn't anybody hear her cries?"

"Mrs. Schmidt, I can't explain that," I replied, not liking the direction of this awkward chat. "Is Karen home?"

"My daughter—"

"Hello, John," Karen welcomed, descending the stairs. "Mom, we're riding to Closter for pizza and will return by dark."

Despondently, her mother watched us cycle away. Karen spun fiercely to alleviate accumulated stress and surprised me by veering onto a side avenue.

"Where are you going?" I bellowed, struggling to keep pace.

Glancing rearwards, she shouted, "I have to see!"

The destination became evident as Karen headed toward the Woods, following the same route we used in November.

"Karen," I wheezed, heart racing. "This may not be a good idea."

Resignedly, she stated, "You were fine when you brought me here last time. What's different?"

"Back then, Reynolds was merely a stimulating diversion. Nowadays, he's a frightening reality. Shouldn't you treasure Angela as she was?" Gazing uneasily past the foliage, I questioned, "What do you hope to find?"

"John, I have vague memories of my sister. Sometimes, I do recall a few things: how she used to play dolls with me, listening to Beatles records in her bedroom. Now the remaining images in my head are the framed prints of Angela hanging on the wall. I considered what Bill said the other day with respect to closure. What can I see that's worse than my imagination?"

The girl's long legs led the way. Stomped by countless feet, the track transformed into muddy slush. Nearing the spot of the buried shoe, my chest constricted. The pathway through the pines to Ceremonies rose to the left. We had arrived.

"Karen!" I hated this place of death.

Taking my arm, she inquired, "Hey, I'm being selfish. Do you want to go home?"

"No, let's do this."

Hand in hand, we approached the open tract. The police had blocked the trail with a sawhorse. Rope coiled around trees cordoning off the plot. Besides some blowflies, we were alone at the crime scene.

Dipping beneath the cord, I towed Karen along. "Come on."

The trench looked wider than on TV and plenty deep. Standing on the edge, gaping into the rent earth, a dank, unpleasant odor turned my stomach. Exposed roots and stones girded the rectangular depressions I assumed were graves. As I mentally counted four, she pointed to a smaller sequestered section.

Recognizing the vicinity where I dug up the shoe, we crawled over an embankment of muck and stood before a vast cavity. The layered soil was richer. In the pit, a pool of murky water reflected the overcast sky. A Styrofoam cup containing coffee dregs bobbed lifelessly. Karen's fingers clenched, eyes brimming with tears. "God, I didn't register I might feel this horrible. Somehow, I thought I could handle seeing this." Studying my profile, she tried to hold in her emotions. "John, I'm happy you're here."

"Me, too," I murmured. "Karen, I'm sorry this happened." Pulling the girl gently into my arms, she sobbed into my shoulder before leaning backwards. As I carefully wiped moisture from her cheeks, Karen guided her lips to mine. Astonished, I returned the kiss.

"Excuse me," an irritable voice interjected. Startled and embarrassed, we separated. "What are you doing? This is a crime scene. Didn't you pay attention to the barriers?" A dark-haired male scowled, black gloves hanging down the seams of a coffee-stained overcoat. For a second, I swore he *was* Columbo.

"Sorry," I stuttered. "We were just—"

"My name is Karen Schmidt. Angela was—"

"I'm quite aware who you are. You're making out with your boyfriend at the grave of your sister? In ten years at the agency, I've seen many heartless things, but this takes the cake."

"It's not like that," I said defiantly, putting a palm out as if to guard Karen. *Boyfriend?* "And it's none of your business. Who are you, anyway?"

The middle-aged man produced a brass badge. "Agent Seth Goldman, Federal Bureau of Investigation. And who may you be, son?"

"John Townsend. Karen needed to see where, you know. . ."

"Morbid curiosity, specifically labeled 'Car Crash Syndrome.' As a special agent, I investigate gruesome murders every day and can't identify why people are so fascinated by death. Twisted. Well, you two run along home. You shouldn't be wandering around on your own."

Karen regained her composure. "I understood the case is closed. What brings you here?"

Goldman's face clouded, and he kicked a rock into the hole with a scuffed wingtip shoe. "Miss, I'm keeping an eye on the site of the felony. It's my job to ascertain who else is interested."

"That murderer is going to be convicted, right? Reynolds will be sent to jail?" I asked.

"Son, you never can predict which way a jury could vote. There are twelve citizens in a room, each looking at the law a different way. That's not my burden. My job is to catch the perp." Goldman gazed sympathetically at Karen. "If it was up to me, I'd love to see that fella fry. Let me escort you out to the pavement."

The FBI agent watched us vacate, his countenance unreadable. Sure we were leaving, he shoved his hands in his pockets and faded into the bushes.

Wheeling alongside, she whirled to ask, "What did that imply?"

"Got me," I replied blushing. "Karen, I was—"

"Not that, silly! Why did he say, 'ascertain who else might be interested'?"

"Oh, I didn't hear that." *I was thinking about kissing you!* Trying to concentrate, I questioned, "You're inferring there's more. Such as?"

Her mood darkened. "When Goldman said he wanted to determine who was attracted to the crime scene, it made me wonder. . . . Conceivably, more than one person is tangled up in this."

At no point considering that angle, my pulse quickened. The ancient vision of the park contained a single individual. *The derby!* "My recollection is of a guy wearing a hat. Reynolds had dozens of them in the closet. You saw them for yourself."

"True," she admitted. Karen looped the Schwinn around me and smiled. "Still hungry for pizza?"

"Hell, yeah!" I grinned, surging ahead.

The Trial

Tuesday Morning—August 8, 1972

I SAT BY KAREN AND HER PARENTS in Room 301 at the Bergen County Court House. Mobbed and tumultuous, the gallery's atmosphere was charged with anticipation at the opening day of the legal proceedings against Martin Reynolds. I was at my inaugural sojourn to a real courtroom, so I was nervous yet excited.

The six months prior to the trial passed swiftly. My grades skyrocketed as I began to appreciate education. I had my study partner to thank for that. Karen and I had officially started dating. For the balance of the high school year, we kept busy hanging out with our friends. During summer recess, my girlfriend and I enjoyed each other's company. Every week, Mom dropped us down at the shore as she visited Grandma in Leisure Village. The lengthy days slipped away, body surfing waves, napping on beach towels, or playing Pong on the Point Pleasant boardwalk. Summertime was nirvana. As we became closer, I prayed seeing my neighbor again wouldn't generate a negative effect.

The tribunal stood in veneration as the bailiff formally introduced Superior Court Judge Charles Wolmar. The tall, grey-haired gentleman entered the chamber wearing a plain black robe. With a flourish of dignity, the somber man settled at the raised bench.

A door swung, and Martin Reynolds came forth, dressed in a navy three-piece suit and dark red tie. Karen grabbed my hand, and I felt her body tense. The portly officer led the suspect shuffling in manacles and leg shackles along the bar to the defense table. The prisoner fixated upon the spectators, exposing the left side of his profile. Appalled gasps of revulsion echoed off the wainscoted walls. Unprepared, I choked back a groan. The right portion of the accused's visage appeared normal; the opposite half was a molten mass of lumpy red flesh. Sunken eye socket, no ear. Shattered teeth hid behind a twitching flap of cheek. The self-administered shotgun blast was sickening. As the man's surviving eyeball scanned for a familiar face, I sunk in my chair.

Forcibly, the bailiff took the defendant's arm, turning him to confront the judge. Wolmar declared, "Martin Reynolds, because of your record of assaultive behavior, you will remain handcuffed for the entire hearing."

The defense lawyer objected, buttoning his jacket while joining the prosecutor at the bench. After the justice added the bailiff to the conference, the officer released the detainee's wrists, leaving the ankle shackles.

Apprehensive, we rose again as Reynolds' destiny filed in, lining seats in the jury box.

Thursday Afternoon—September 28, 1972

The case continued for seven weeks, an emotional rollercoaster. The defense and prosecution attorneys did their utmost to sway the jurists. Seth Goldman was the key witness testifying for the state. Karen's mother and father, as well as other victims' parents, periodically wept in anguish, especially during the horrific autopsy reports and ghastly photos. On separate occasions, a relative belligerently yelled at Reynolds and had to be escorted from the courtroom.

The two of us attended court every weekday. Following the start of school, we eagerly sought the litigation updates disclosed on TV and in the newspapers. The Mad Hatter became a national news item and the foremost topic of conversation in Haworth. The lawyers finished closing statements and the forum remained locked in debate.

As sophomores, our clique confiscated a more prestigious table in the lunchroom. Karen and I carried trays to our classmates.

Ranzetta loudly proclaimed, "The king and queen have arrived!" Outlaw bowed, his hands pressed in feigned reverence.

"Hardy, har, har," I chuckled, sitting. "Where's Melissa?" I asked Bill. The pair spent a lot of time together.

"Melissa's in the girls' room taking care of some business," Karen replied. "If everything goes according to plan, she'll be here shortly."

"Dude, is your lover on the rag?" Vince questioned Bill.

Mortified, he exclaimed, *"Jesus, Ranzetta!"* Comically, I gagged on the stuffed lasagna.

Melissa appeared with her lunch. "What? What are you discussing?" she inquired, smiling.

"Really, you don't want to know," Karen responded, stifling giggles.

"Shit," she glared. "Did you tell these animals that Aunt Flo came to town?"

"No!" Karen blurted. "Vince somehow figured it out, like he always does."

Melissa forked a piece of raw beef off Karen's plate. "Give me that; I need the iron."

As the laughter died, Bill leaned forward. "Any news on the arraignment?"

"Not recently," Karen replied. "The panel has deliberated over four days. Juries can deliver a decision at any moment, but my mom and dad are freaked out since it's unusually long. The prosecutor is nervous about a retrial. When my parents get the word, they'll drive us to the courthouse."

Vince's brow wrinkled. "That's rough. All the waiting."

Outlaw questioned, "What happens when the trial comes to a conclusion? Then what?"

"I'm ready to move on," Karen answered firmly. Head shaking in frustration, she continued waveringly, "At least, that's the idea."

"There's no death penalty in New Jersey, so it's up the judge to ordain the defendant's sentence," I said. "Reynolds will get life imprisonment."

"Better yet, I hope his cellmate slits his fucking throat!" Vince snarled.

"Amen to that, brother," Bill muttered.

Karen and I left the schoolhouse as Mr. Schmidt jerked to a standstill in the loading and unloading zone. Mrs. Schmidt sat rigidly in the passenger seat holding a Bible. "Let's go!" he called urgently. "They're announcing the verdict in an hour."

Inside the hushed car, I considered my part in Reynolds' arrest. Had I done the right thing, ethically? Confident of my neighbor's culpability, I still worried the jurists could find Angela's murderer innocent. What if he got off on a legal technicality? The jurors were sequestered for an extended period, and I imagined burned-out people arguing around a big desk covered with takeout. Antsy to return home, they may agree to any judgment. Pessimistically, I contemplated Henry Fonda's role in *Twelve Angry Men*.

Glancing at Karen facing toward the widow, I hoped she was okay. Although accustomed to the monster's mutilated features during the trial, in nightmares, the grotesque death mask chased me along endless corridors. What might his reaction be, learning the ruling?

Mr. Schmidt's anger intensified as he searched for a parking spot in Hackensack. Checking the clock, he blocked another automobile, telling us to get out. The turn-of-the-century courthouse resembled a miniature version of the state capitol. An unrelenting television crew tried to interview Karen's parents on the way up the steps. Scowling, her father roughly pushed past the press.

Finally indoors, we hurried up the marble stairs to the third floor. A police officer accompanied our group to seats held in the gallery.

We waited anxiously until the jury entered. The female foreman stood, reading the verdict in a shaky voice: "Guilty on six counts of first-degree murder, four counts of sexual assault and one count of resisting arrest."

Courtroom erupting in applause, the prosecutor leapt, pumping hands with the district attorney. As the bailiff shouted for silence, the Schmidts cried and hugged other families. I embraced my girlfriend as the trial adjourned. In a few weeks, Martin Reynolds would be sentenced.

"Thanks for everything, John," Karen whispered in my ear.

"Anything for you," I promised.

Part Three

Bill

Wednesday at Noon—March 19, 1986

FAMISHED, I WAITED IN A CORNER BOOTH at the Blue Jay Diner. "Walk like an Egyptian" played from a tabletop jukebox. Noisy midday crowds filed in, occupying nearby tables. Conspicuously sitting alone, I swiped a crumpled edition of the *Atlanta Journal-Constitution* and scanned the headlines. President Reagan urged Congress to donate $100 million to the Contra rebels in Nicaragua. That was a shitload of cash to fund a dubious war. Irritated, I gave up after a paragraph. Bill slid into the opposite seat as I skimmed an article announcing the recall of 200,000 runaway Audis.

"Christ, this town is hot as hell, and it's not even noon. How can you survive in this furnace?" he chuckled. Two or three years had slipped by since I'd seen my friend. Always stylish, Outlaw wore a dark business suit and eyeglasses.

"Nice goggles, pal!" I replied. Stretching out, he heartily returned the greeting and grabbed a laminated menu.

"My eyesight started to fade, staring at computer monitors," Bill complained. "Whoa, I noticed you grew a beard."

"Too lazy to shave," I smirked. "Are the meetings going smoothly?"

"So boring. What a wasted effort," he groaned. "The banks think debating the fiscal projections for the next quarter is somehow helpful. It's impossible to foretell what's trending on Wall Street. Simply put, the stock market is tanking. At least I get to hang out with you while I'm here."

Bill graduated with a degree at Princeton University and consulted for several major financial institutions in New York City. Fair to say, he prospered.

A waitress appeared and took orders. Surprised that Outlaw requested a Caesar salad, I selected a patty melt.

I asked, "What, are you on a diet?" Obviously the man exercised.

"Yup, gotta be fit for the Missus. With this amount of traveling, it's difficult to eat healthy," he answered, patting his flat stomach.

Laughing, I began to relax. "How's Melissa? What's she up to?"

"Good, fantastic! You know my wife, shaking up things at the advertising agency. I have another announcement. John, you're about to be an uncle."

"What?" I exclaimed, elated. "Melissa's pregnant?"

"Yes, sir. Due date is next month. We're very excited, well, nervous and excited. The kid isn't even born yet, and she's researching private schools midtown."

"Wow, that *is* awesome news, congratulations!" *Bill is soon to be a father!* "Thanks for waiting so long to tell me," I added sarcastically. "The last occasion I saw you guys was at the wedding. Man, how time flies. Anything else happening? Oh, yeah, I wanted to ask if you ran into Vince."

The waitress delivered drinks in red plastic cups. The soda bubbled in my throat.

Bill hesitated a moment, dejected. "This spring, I attempted to call a number of times. The phone is disconnected, and he never replies to any letters. Vince lives in a rundown section of

Newark and looked dreadful this past fall. Strung out. Contrastingly, his brother is out West doing great. Paul created a contracting company in Las Vegas and is raking in the dough from recent casino construction. Ranzetta and Associates specialize in designing and building parking garages."

Grading the high school teenager, I said, "That lad always was a go getter. I'm pleased Paul's staying on the right side of law. That's too bad regarding Vince. Wish there was something I could do." The final encounter with my old chum had been a decade ago and ended in a yelling match.

"Same here. The thing is—" Outlaw exhaled. "Everyone's split up, gone in various directions. So much water under the bridge."

The lunch plates arrived. Fries sparkly with salt, I inquired, "How is Karen? Have you seen or heard from her?"

Glancing up uncomfortably, he pierced a cherry tomato with his fork. "We had dinner with Karen and Eric over the holidays. Your ex-girlfriend appeared happy." Bill continued eating before meeting my glare. "But when we were leaving the restaurant, Karen asked about you."

"What did you say? Who's this Eric?"

"Karen met him on the job in Hackensack. Eric Knapp is an accountant for her law firm. Seems like a nice enough fellow. John, I told her you're cultivating the cure for cancer. She was glad you were doing okay." Bill pushed the dish away in frustration. "That positively sucked, what transpired between you and Karen, but it's time to move on. Apparently, she has." Flustered, he retrieved the salad.

I managed to chew the sandwich, appetite gone. Changing to a related troubling subject, I asked, "Your message stated they're releasing Martin Reynolds in June?"

"Buddy, I admit I'm disturbed. That's one of the reasons I needed to see you now. That prick should serve an entire life sentence, but he was a model inmate working in the Rahway prison library and medical center. Hard to believe that loon aced the psychological exam with flying colors. An associate in the courts says it's rare for a serial killer to be approved by the primary parole board."

"Barely fifteen years. That sociopath ought to be locked up 'til he croaks," I murmured, wondering again why the judge let the murderer off so easy.

"Somebody must have pulled some strings. A dime and a nickel isn't sufficient punishment for that motherfucker!" Outlaw agreed loudly. A few diners stared with concern. "Parolees are not supposed to leave their jurisdiction without court approval, but Mel and I are only living on the other end of the George Washington Bridge."

"We were just kids," I said reassuringly. "No evidence is attached to our names. There's no way Reynolds knows we're accountable for his arrest."

"Sure, I guess," he muttered, dropping the fork into the greens. "I'm still stressed, with a family on the way."

"Are Karen and Vince aware he's getting out?"

"I sent the same letter to Karen, never receiving a reply. As I said, I've no knowledge where Ranzetta is now." Bill reached to his belt, detached a pager, and scowled. "Got to return to this stupid conference. Can we meet later for drinks?"

The address to a local bar noted, he sped off in a sporty BMW rental. Superheated air shimmered, breaching the door to my aging Corolla. The interior was a brick oven. Sweating, I cranked the windows to welcome the moist breeze and sweltered for fifteen minutes reviewing Outlaw's comments. Depressed, I had no desire to start the car, much less drive back to work. The final opportunity Karen and I talked was during the first year of college. Accepted at different schools, we tried to meet each other on the weekends. As the months advanced, we made new friends, and the distance seemed unreasonable. To be completely honest, I became romantically engaged with a female classmate, enjoying the coziness of convenience. Although our relationship fizzled, hardly a day passed when I didn't think of Karen or what could have been.

Swamped with tasks, the afternoon moved swiftly. I toiled for a contract research organization named Quinto Labs. The company supported numerous pharmaceutical companies on research and development projects. I was happy to have a job. My BS in biology hadn't unlocked many doors, and I'd frittered away years doing odd jobs. This position was a hell of a lot better than shaving hair off the asses of pigs.

My boss Katherine was a micromanager, and she stopped by every hour to gauge my progress. The approaching staccato of high heels gave the megalomaniac away.

"John, are you making headway on the latest spreadsheets?" For the last two days, I'd compiled the results of five clinical trials into Lotus 1-2-3.

"Without further interruptions, I should be able to input everything by the close of business. Tomorrow, I'll start cleaning up the data and investigate any anomalies."

Katherine nodded vigorously, thick glasses bouncing on a button nose. "That's terrific. Don't forget; we can't let up for a minute on this one. Countless lives are at stake." Charmed with herself, my boss swiveled and stomped from the office.

Wednesday Evening—March 19, 1986

I met Bill in northeast Atlanta at eight o'clock. Blind Willie's was a newly opened club featuring the best legendary and upcoming blues artists. At a table in the rear, we ordered a pitcher of beer and Buffalo wings. On a narrow stage, musicians set up the sound check for Sunnyland Slim, scheduled to perform later that evening.

Wearing a Hawaiian shirt and shorts, he guzzled the mug of stout and nabbed a deep-fried drumette. "So, how's the job? What exactly are you doing?"

"Jerking off mice," I joked. "Lots of little critters, actually. Just kidding, kind of. . . . El Jefe is a real narcissist, but that's to be expected. On the bright side, I'm learning a few computer skills." I studied the server with mountainous hair and tight vinyl pants.

"Yeah, buddy, that's the future of mankind, computers. I'm already a dinosaur at twenty-nine. I'm enrolled in software classes, trying to keep up with the recent hires." As Outlaw poured the brew, we both saw the aquarium above the bar. "Hey, remember—?"

"That tank at Tiny's with the dead piranha? Woe was the day Tiny realized he became too heavy to stand up and add more water."

"Poor fucking animals, and that Shirley. . ." Bill said, disgusted.

"Paul nearly killed Tiny *and* his wife," I said, reminded of the night that half the drug dealer's apartment complex burned to the ground.

"Oh, my God! I was scared out of my wits for weeks, terrified we might be under suspicion. Paul was totally whacked out of his gourd back then. Luckily, nobody got killed."

I scratched my head, relived the memories, and grinned. "Vince's brother never thought that beached whale could escape that disgusting recliner. Shirley must have rolled that lard ass downstairs." Choking, Outlaw joined my hysterical laughter. In tribute, I raised a glass. "To that fat fuck!"

"Tiny!" he shouted, clinking mugs.

Following the arson, Paul had enlisted with the Marines and spent a few uneventful months in Vietnam. Fortuitous in war, he shipped home once the US troops evacuated.

Bill and I purchased Saint Louis-Style ribs and more brew. Blind Willie's was jam-packed with fans. The band mounted the stage at nine-thirty, riling up the crowd. Sunnyland Slim made a grand entrance, sitting before a well-worn piano. For a gentleman in his seventies, the musician could belt out the blues louder than the PA system. Tonight was truly an awesome performance.

The concert over, we went outdoors to stretch. "John, you should come up," my friend urged. "Melissa wants you to see the baby."

"Sure, Bill." I had mixed feelings about New Jersey. Many memories from my hometown—haunting memories—once, running away to Georgia seemed like a favorable idea. Depressed, I reflected upon Karen and her latest boyfriend. "Okay, I'll find out if I can get the time off. Work's busy, and—"

"Yeah, sure. I'm telling you, buddy, drop in anytime. Stay with us. Maybe we'll take in a Broadway show. Pounding beers will definitely be a required activity." Bill stared soberly. "What about Reynolds?"

The planting of evidence had been my idea, and while my friend went along, I ultimately had to take responsibility. "Don't worry. He doesn't even know who we are," I said, as we parted.

Motoring off in my rickety Corolla, I had plenty to contemplate. My mind spun with what ifs.

New Jersey

Friday Afternoon—June 06, 1986

KATHERINE GOT ON MY NERVES, pushing the right buttons. My boss demonstrated excellence in snatching credit for everything I accomplished. Assessing quite a few practical solutions, I provided suggestions to improve and simplify medical document retention. Katherine offered my concepts as her own to the bigwigs upstairs. As the CEO bestowed my manager with a Horizon award at the May All Hands Meeting, I nearly swallowed my tongue.

I was so engrossed fixing fragmented research data, I hardly registered her entering the room. "Hi, John," she beamed. Katherine cupped the brass trophy, shining the engraving with a tissue. The beast plopped into my visitor's chair. "Whew. What a day! Thought I'd drop by for a status report."

"The results are coming along," I mumbled, rotating back to the monitor. Too much work and in no mood for her bullshit.

"When you're done with whatever you're playing around with, please pop in my office. I'm having an issue with my machine. There's a file I'm trying to copy for Hector. With this updated version of DOS, I'm lost." Eyebrows arched, upturned mouth shaping a sad puppy face, my supervisor resembled a half-idiot.

Sore, I swiveled the seat, deliberately spelling, "DIR."

"Um, what did you just say?"

"Type 'DIR' and the file name. If you don't recall every character, use the star. And be certain you're in the correct directory." A deep gulp of burnt coffee soured my stomach.

"Oh, thanks. At my desk, I'll try that. Please be a dear, and scribble that down for me." Katherine remained settled as I wrote step-by-step instructions. Blood pressure compressed my optic nerves.

Handing over the piece of paper, I said what had been a vague notion during the last few months. "Katherine, I have to use vacation time. Sorry, but I need a couple of weeks to go to New Jersey."

Her hooded eyes widened, unexpectedly conscious. "What? There are mountains of work to do here. The group is very behind in the agenda." The cogs in the magpie's noggin whirled. "New Jersey? What's up there?"

"That's where I grew up, and there's some unfinished business to attend to." My boss knew nothing of my existence, whining only of her own dilemmas.

"John, I'll consider this highly unorthodox request. I'm simply not convinced taking that amount of leave is poss—"

"Katherine," I interrupted, rising. My desk chair pivoted, hit the wall, and knocked a calendar to the floor. "On Monday, I'm heading out and will return when I'm ready." Hooking my Bullwinkle the Moose coffee cup, I marched from the building, leaving the woman openmouthed.

Friday Evening—June 06, 1986

Fleeing Quinto Labs, I hopped on the 285 loop and traveled east. The previous summer, Mom bequeathed the house to Jane and moved south. Mom lived in a comfortable single-level home on the outskirts of Decatur. Adventurously, I suggested eating at an unfamiliar restaurant named Imperial of China.

The hostess sat us in a booth, issuing leather-bound menus.

"How's Jane doing?" I inquired. Exasperatedly, my mother glanced up from the hundreds of numbered choices.

"Jane doesn't call often enough, and when I try to dial, the telephone rings and rings. I worry. That gal has to buy an answering machine."

I ordered General Tso's chicken, and Mom picked the barbecued shrimp.

"As a rookie, we can assume she's particularly busy," I conjectured.

Jane joined the Alpine Police Department last year, a huge shock to everyone. In 1984, my sister graduated college with a degree in economics. After months of not finding employment, she enrolled at the academy. Talking with her, I learned the new occupation was enjoyable. As a recruit, she babysat a multitude of celebrities and "people too stupid to appreciate their money." Despite my concerns, I knew the girl could handle herself.

"Jane told a funny story regarding an Elvis impersonator rolling a Jaguar outside Stevie Wonder's mansion. A neighbor heard the hullabaloo and notified the cops. Your sister arrived as the guy is pounding on Stevie's gate and singing into the intercom, mimicking the king of rock and roll. She had to haul the jamoke off to that puny jail for drunk and disorderly. The numbskull wore the fat Presley rhinestone costume, and the horsehair wig came off when Jane put him in the backseat of the police car. Poor fella was completely bald."

"That's a good one," I laughed. "Shoulda got a photo of that."

"What are you up to, Johnny? Is the new position keeping you out of trouble?" Brow creased, my mother closely examined a shrimp.

"Mom, I've been at Quinto for a year. The job's no longer new." Sometimes, it seemed as if I'd labored there forever.

"What's this, honey?" Exhibiting the shellfish on the prong of a fork, she pointed to something perplexing with an index finger. "What *is* that?"

"No clue. You must realize I never eat anything resembling an insect."

"Yum," my mother murmured, popping the shrimp into her mouth.

Grabbing the rice bowl, I dumped more starch onto the plate. "Just needed to tell you, I'm returning to New Jersey for a bit."

"To find Karen?" she burst out excitedly. I wanted to ferret out Ranzetta, visit the Outlaws and the baby, and. . . . "Johnny, talk to her," Mom implored. Wisely avoiding further inspection, she gobbled the next crustacean.

"Maybe," I sighed. "I'm flying up Monday. That is, if I procure an airline ticket this weekend."

Standing in the driveway, my mother squeezed me tightly. Wistfully, she reminded, "Don't forget to stop by and see your father."

Dad died suddenly in 1973, three months after the Martin Reynolds trial. Complaining of chest pains and refusing to schedule a doctor's appointment, he inescapably went to meet his Maker waiting to pay for antacid at the 7-Eleven—so long ago, resurrecting images of the man was difficult.

"Of course," I vowed. Although the cemetery didn't top my holiday list, how could I deny my own mother?

"Dad's in section 'U' by the Memorial Tower. Go south four trees, and walk toward West Century Road. There is a lovely maple he's resting under. Brush off the grave marker while you're there."

I relived my father chauffeuring the family to Ed's service at George Washington Memorial Park. Now he lay moldering in the same dirt as Bill's brother. Smiling, I pictured my dad yelling at the hippies protesting at the gate. One minute, you're attending a funeral; the next, you *are* the funeral, soon thereafter, forgotten for eternity.

Monday Morning—June 09, 1986

I took an early morning flight and touched down at Newark International Airport at 9:10 a.m. Already hot, sweaty, and cranky, I boosted the AC to MAX and piloted the late-model grey Toyota Cressida up the Turnpike. Exiting in Teaneck, nothing much had changed: the same dated shops and narrow streets. Distracted, I nearly slammed into the tailgate of a delivery truck. *Why exactly did I come back?*

Low on blood sugar and transitive fats, I parked at McDonalds and ordered an Egg McMuffin with hash browns. Savoring a thick cup of Joe, I felt better watching the sun stream through the leaves. At least I wasn't at work. What's my game plan? Impulsively, I hadn't plotted anything out, not even telling Bill of the trip.

Ready to acquire lodging, I checked into a cheap motel in Paramus. After a quick shower, I lay on my back, staring at the popcorn ceiling. *I need to see Jane.* I have to hop into the City to spend time with Bill and Melissa. Vince may be challenging to locate, and what if I couldn't cope with what I found? *Karen!* Did I actually want to barge into her life again? A decade had passed. What was different, and what would I say? Rehearsing inane imaginary conversations, I fell asleep.

Monday Afternoon—June 09, 1986

I awoke in the mid-afternoon with the urge to pee. Annoyed at sleeping the day away, I hunched on the end of the bed, groggy and nauseous. The remnants of a dream pushed me off balance.

Karen and I met in the Woods, floating above fresh mounds of earth. Peering into the pits, I became aware that each rectangular grave held a fully clothed person. The faces watched questioningly, orange owl eyes the size of saucers. I asked her, "Who are they?"

"They're us, silly." Confused, I twisted to see more. On knees squinting into the loam, I recognized Bill in one hole wearing a suit and tie. Flashing a toothy grin, my friend waved. In a deeper hollow, Melissa sat in a nursery rocker, a feline form swaddled in rags cradled to a breast.

Through charred trees, I overheard my name. *"John!"* A body resembling Vince lay head down in the mud. Stringy hair matted pale, speckled cheeks. As I became frantic, the light faded to dark. Where's Karen? I aimed a flashlight into the void. The faltering phosphorescence illuminated two empty graves.

Desperately, I shouted, *"Karen, where are you?"* Distant chanting, a fire burned high upon a hillside. *Ceremonies. She's there!* Stumbling up the path, thrusting aside greedy poisonous vines and branches, I rushed into the defoliated area. Masked and racked across the gigantic sacrificial altar, the lamb's lips pleaded.

A pair of pagan ogres shimmered in the growing flames. "John, we've been waiting. So nice of you to join us."

Monday Evening—June 09, 1986

The shadows spread into the graveyard, sunset sky highlighted with white and pink puffs. The air was muggy, and I studied my father's nameplate. Cast in bold capitals along the top of the coppery brown-colored plaque was "*TOWNSEND*." Fastened to the left side of the marker, a small plate stated: "*Mi-*

chael 1921-1973." On the right, blank metal awaited my mother. Unable to summon Dad's voice or the color of his eyes, I squashed a mosquito buzzing behind an ear.

To ease mowing, the park had installed the nameplates flush to the terrain. On a knee, I tore away the encroaching grass and swept off the humus. The center of the memorial incorporated a recessed bronze vessel that could be reversed for flowers. Curiously, I grabbed the handle and eased the heavy casting from the cylindrical opening. An ivory object gleamed at the bottom.

The bell tower rang the hour. I counted, turning to view the majestic monument bathed in the final golden glow. The sun flared off the glass front doors and the eight windows soaring up the structure. The tail of the rental emerged from a hedge. Fingers shielding my vision, I noticed a figure loitering by the Toyota.

My attention returned to the vase. Fearful of black widows, I cautiously reached into the tube, grasping the smooth sphere. Lurching backwards, I gasped, dropping the cat skull into the grass. *What the fuck?*

I concentrated on the stranger. Before vanishing, the glint of identical tiny circles mirrored the sunlight. Eyeglasses? *No, binoculars!* As I sprung and strode toward the tower, an engine roared to life. Hands clenched, I sprinted after a vehicle leaving in the opposite direction. Against the trunk, I caught my breath, watching an aged sedan exit the gates of the necropolis.

Tuesday Morning—June 10, 1986

Outside Trautwein Farms in Closter, I waited in the Cressida for my sister. The beginning of the day had been spent aimlessly roaming around the locality, killing time.

Jane arrived in a waxed black and white Plymouth Grand Fury, grinning above the "Alpine Police Department" logo. Attaching a mobile radio to her epaulet, she climbed from the cruiser.

"Holy moly!" I exclaimed. My sister wore a blue, short-sleeved uniform. Her blond hair was tied back in a sturdy ponytail; Ray-Bans protected her sight. "Can I hug you?" I requested. "Don't want that thing to go off," I guffawed, pointing at the sidearm.

"The gun's not loaded," Jane joked, patting the holster. Happily, her arms encircled my neck. "What a nice surprise."

Ordering sandwiches and drinks at the farm's deli, I observed two Trautwein sisters gesturing in the storeroom. Beneath the shade of an umbrella, we overlooked the orchard.

"So, what's crackalackin'? What's the real deal? Why are you really up here, big brother?"

"Crackalackin'?" I laughed. "Did you make that up?"

"Nah, that's how I communicate with kids on my beat," my sister replied, removing the glasses. Gazing at me with her penetrating blue-green eyes, she questioned, "Is Mom adapting to the Deep South?"

"Yes, she's doing fine. Always wonders why you don't call."

"Johnny, I chat with her almost every night. Long distance is expensive, and the lady blabs for hours."

I ejected the abundant onions from the sandwich. "This morning, I drove by the house. The old place was never this well maintained."

"Thanks, I had to make it my own. This spring, I painted the exterior and swapped out those overgrown bushes in front. On weekends, I'm working on the inside, scraping off that gross wallpaper. Crates of Mom and Dad's paraphernalia are stored in the basement. Thus far, I haven't determined what to do with it. A pile of that crap is yours. Come by later, and sort through it."

"Rent a dumpster, and throw that rubbish out," I muttered, shaking my head.

"Not as easy as you'd think. You start assigning feelings to the junk and feel awful throwing it away. Sentimentality is the worst emotion. I wind up shoving everything in the box and putting those remembrances back on the shelf."

"No shit," I agreed. "Do you dig being Five-O?"

"So far, so good," Jane answered. "To be candid, the work is usually pretty boring. Occasional B&E cases and DUIs. I applied to the Alpine police force since it's nearby, doubtful I'd be accepted. The salary is first rate, compared to other towns. The chief had to fill the female quota, so here I am. Alpine is a safe town to get my feet wet, but someday, I'll transfer to a different city with more action. How's your job, and what are you planning to achieve while you're up north?"

"That's a swell question. Honestly, there's a possibility I quit—not absolutely clear cut. I kind of left abruptly," I smirked.

"Wow, that's crazy!" she giggled.

Explaining the expedition to the boneyard, I omitted the impression of being under surveillance. The man might be Reynolds; however, I had no indication why he'd follow me. I went over Bill coming to Atlanta and wanting to meet the new family.

"What about Karen?" Jane inquired, biting into a juicy McIntosh.

"Ha! You remind me of Mom. I heard she's with another guy. There's no real point in seeing her."

Skeptically, my sister blinked. "Eric Knapp is a software programmer. For eight months, they've lived together."

"And where did you hear that?"

"Johnny, it's my profession to know the score," she chuckled. "Nowadays, if you have the keys to the kingdom, it's very easy to obtain information."

"Computers?"

"Nope, not this time. Your rich friend told me. I ran into Bill at the post office. The elder Outlaws still reside in Haworth."

"Will you tell me where Karen lives?"

Jane smiled. "Now that's something I *can* look up on the computer."

Karen

Tuesday Evening—June 10, 1986

I LEFT THE MOTOR COURT, stomped on the accelerator, and rocketed up the ramp to Route 17. The Cressida's tires almost rolled off the rims screeching around the cloverleaf onto Route 4. Depeche Mode's *Black Celebration* spun in the CD player, and "World Full of Nothing" matched my dark mood.

Jane provided Karen's current address in Maywood. A fifteen-minute drive didn't leave considerable latitude to contemplate my intentions. On a corner lot, a single-car garage supported the brick-faced structure. Dormers in the roof indicated a second level. An older model white Mercedes sat in the driveway.

Several residences away, I parked and lowered the windows. A few neighbors passed, swiveling to glare. Across the road, a brooding teenager scalped the crabgrass in the cool of the evening. With my supper a bag of chips, I endeavored to nail down why I lost the impetus to keep the relationship with my ex-girlfriend alive. Those college coeds. . . . I imagined Karen seeing me at a distance and running passionately into my arms.

The door of the home opened, killing the fantasy. Sitting up straight, I squinted through the bug-splattered windshield. A blond man plucked a stack of correspondence out of the wall-mounted mailbox and went back inside. *Eric!* In the deepening dusk, a light flickered in the front room window. *The mother-fucker is watching television!* By all accounts, Eric was a decent guy with a good job. *Relax!* Even counting to ten, I yearned to strangle the geeky nerd.

Fuming, I hardly noticed a vehicle slip by and stop. Two young women chatted until the passenger door swung wide and Karen Schmidt exited, holding a briefcase. The driver said a few words and laughed before bidding farewell. As the automobile pulled out, she peered in each direction before crossing the lane. I held my breath and sank into the seat. Flashing a double take, Karen stared in disbelief.

As I fumbled for the handle, she savagely advanced. Cheeks inflamed, her hip blocked my escape.

The love of my life scowled into the Toyota, eyes frigid. "Why the hell are you outside my house? Are you spying on me?"

Fossilized, my mouth froze. Even craving to exterminate me, Karen was the most beautiful creature I had ever seen.

Gazing toward home, she sputtered, "Well? Townsend, you shouldn't be here."

"I was in town, and. . ."

Karen studied me, a sneer softening from blistering hostility to run-of-the-mill loathing. "Jesus, I don't get this. After so many years, you turn up out of nowhere."

This is my chance to talk. Now or never! Kindled, I managed to utter, "Karen, I wanted to see you. I *had* to see you."

Grimacing, she massaged her forehead: in pain, making a decision, or both. "Meet me at noon tomorrow at the Green Olive in Hackensack on Passaic Street. And don't even think of being late," Karen admonished, wagging a blue-tipped finger. Without another glance, she pivoted on stilettos and vanished.

Wednesday at Noon—June 11, 1986

The Green Olive was an Italian restaurant located at the end of a small, rundown strip mall. I waited, wondering what to say. Karen apparently selected this remote neighborhood with a regard for privacy. At the Laundromat, a mother in nurse's scrubs grappled through the entrance with bulky sacks of laundry.

A Mercedes arrived and parked. Waving, I walked forward.

"John, I don't have much time. Yesterday, you caught me at a weak point. This is stupid. Eric and I—"

"Please, let's get lunch. Honestly, I just needed to find out how you're doing."

Entering the chill of the bistro, Karen requested a booth in the rear. Furtively, I examined her over the menu. The woman wore very little makeup and looked absolutely stunning! I couldn't believe she was here.

Eyes downcast, Karen seemed enthralled by the daily specials. "What are you getting?" I asked delicately.

"The calamari's good," she replied, returning my stare. "But you won't try that."

"No, thanks. I'll stick with the ravioli," I smiled, appreciative that Karen recalled my aversion to seafood.

The waitress itemized the orders and delivered garlic bread.

"So, how is Atlanta?" Karen inquired.

"It's okay. Six years, and I'm still not used to living below the Mason-Dixon Line." Passing the basket, I added sarcastically, "They didn't nickname that city Hotlanta for nothing."

"Before Christmas, I dined with the Outlaws. Melissa recently had a baby."

"Yes, I'm excited for them. Tonight, I'll call Bill. They don't realize I'm here."

The conversation died, filled with awkward silence. The table grew terribly long; excessive separation stretched between us.

"Karen," I said softly. "I messed up. Really fucked up big time. Our lives weren't supposed to turn out this way."

"What way, John?" she questioned, biting her lip.

"You know, me in Georgia and you in New Jersey with that—"

"Eric."

"Exactly," I exhaled, clamping the skirt of the tablecloth. "Eric."

Karen glowered with contempt. "John, you're the one that went off to college and decided I wasn't worth the effort. The schools were only two hours apart! And then you took off with that skank!"

Bitter, her volume intensified, pausing as the server distributed our meals. Food never appeared less appetizing. The ravioli resembled bloody hearts, and the calamari looked like . . . like fried squid! *Jesus, it stinks.* Exasperated, she picked up a fork and vigorously stabbed a breaded ring. "You came all the way up here and found me. Now what? What do you want?"

Recognizing what was longed for, yet unable to express my desires, I remembered the cemetery and engraved my own epitaph: *Here lies a pathetic excuse for a man.*

Eager to change the subject, I inquired, "You heard about Martin Reynolds?"

Fear and anxiety flashed across Karen's face. "Damn right, I did. The victim's families had to convene with the parole board." Roll torn asunder, she grabbed a knife. "Those pinheads didn't listen to us. That monster is free to do as he pleases. Your neighbor should've received life imprisonment in the first place, and then those assholes let him loose with ten years left on the sentence. It's not acceptable."

"No, it isn't," I agreed. "Do you have an idea where Reynolds is? Where he's living?"

"Garfield, some shitty halfway house," Karen muttered. "A few legal contacts say his parole officer is keeping a short leash, but I still don't feel safe." Inspecting me intently, she stated, "In fact, Eric and I are thinking of moving."

That took me by surprise. "Where? I assumed you were doing great at your law firm."

"I am, but it's not as if they aim to make me partner any time soon. It sucks that, depending on the state, I may be required to take the bar exam again." Karen's head shook in frustration. "I can't live the rest of my days peering over my shoulder."

This was not the golden opportunity to enlighten her that someone, ostensibly Reynolds, shadowed me at the cemetery. No need putting her even more on edge.

"Aren't you going to finish that?" Eyebrows raised, she pointed to the untouched pasta.

"Maybe later at the motel," I mumbled. After paying the check, I carried the doggie bag from the restaurant.

At the car, Karen asked, "When are you returning to Atlanta?" Attempting to read her temperament, I deduced that it certainly wasn't merry.

"Probably be here for a while. Perhaps we can—"

Karen stuck up a palm, cutting me off. "No, John. Leave! Don't stop by my house. Don't come by my work. Are you listening? Go home to Georgia. That's where you belong."

Moving aside, she swiftly backed out of the parking space.

Thursday Evening—June 12, 1986

I caught the eleven a.m. PATH train from Newark to Penn Station in New York City. Splurging on a corndog and soda, I spent the afternoon wandering around Midtown, absorbing the zesty essence. Mired in a deep funk following the miserable luncheon with Karen, I descended into twilight. The E subway rumbled to Lexington Avenue, where I transferred to the 6 train. At 77th street, the excursion ended with a quick walk five blocks south.

The Outlaws lived in a tall granite building on the Upper East Side. My identity certified, the uniformed guard directed me to a bank of elevators. Bill grinned as the doors parted on the twenty-second floor.

"Brother, I understood you were successful, but this joint is ridiculous!" I exclaimed, clasping his hand.

"Wait until you're inside," my buddy beamed, clapping my shoulder. He led me along a hallway and unlocked the entry. "Mel, look what the cat dragged in!"

Melissa rushed from the kitchen, kissing my cheek and hugging me tight. "John, it's been so long. Did you put on a few pounds?" Appraisingly, she leaned back.

"Those all-you-can-eat southern buffets are killing me," I chuckled, rubbing my gut. "It smells wonderful, whatever you have cooking."

"If you had given us a little more warning. . ." Melissa scolded with a mock frown.

"Sorry. The trip was sort of spur of the moment." I was drawn to the huge picture windows. Before me was a million-dollar view of Manhattan. Breathtaking rows of skyscrapers contrasted against the vivid greenery of Central Park. Bill offered me an ice-cold beer and we clinked bottles. "This is pretty overwhelming. That's the Garden State, right?" I questioned, pointing to the sun setting behind a curtain of pollution.

"The one and only. Glad I can see New Jersey from here, but I sure wouldn't want to live there," he laughed. "Come meet my son."

In a bedroom wallpapered with taxicabs, the infant lay in a crib beneath swaying mobiles. Tenderly, his mother lifted the child, and I clumsily welcomed the small bundle. "Eddie's middle name is Jonathan," she whispered, wiping off his spittle.

"What?" I murmured. The boy gaped inquiringly and gurgled.

Proudly, Bill answered, "In honor of the glorious John Townsend. Ed is obviously for my brother. With Edward Jonathan Outlaw for a name, nobody will dare give him any shit."

"Honey, watch your language around the baby," Melissa reprimanded. "John, we'd like you to be the godfather."

"Thank you, I'm truly honored," I said gratefully. "Eddie is a cute kid, and I'm very happy for you guys."

While Bill put the youngster down for a nap, I followed Melissa to the kitchen.

Opening the oven, she laid a glass pan on a rack. The manicotti steamed and bubbled. "Can I help you with anything?"

Melissa steered to the stove and handed me a bowl. "If you could please set the green beans and these napkins on the table, we'll be ready to eat."

Dinner was excellent. The main course tasted exquisite, and Bill kept pouring fine wine. Nice to loosen up and forget my problems. We cracked up at Melissa's scandalous stories regarding the eccentrics at her Madison Avenue advertising firm. Bill gave valuable pointers on investments. The simple mantra "buy low and sell high" worked for the Outlaws.

The discussion naturally turned to Martin Reynolds, Melissa riled up because of the early release. "That piece of shit shouldn't have gotten loose. Karen's a nervous wreck."

"I saw her yesterday," I grumbled, reaching for more delightful Château Mouton Rothschild.

"Karen phoned this morning, and I heard every gory detail," she groaned. "John, you can be a royal pain in the ass."

"Me?" I simpered, batting my eyelashes.

"Yeah, *you,* fool. She hoped you were about to communicate something real. As usual, you wimped out. The girl still cares for you. God knows why; you're such a putz."

"Melissa, I tried apologizing, but Christ, I'm a jerk." Bill dipped his head perceptively.

"Karen's my best friend, so I don't need you fucking her over again," she warned.

"Sweetie, watch your language around Eddie," my friend reminded his wife.

The Iron Factory

Friday Morning—June 13, 1986

I FROWNED AT THE SMALL TELEVISION SCREEN. The early news rehashed evidence regarding the Chernobyl nuclear disaster, which was immeasurably worse than initially reported. Scientists now projected the human and animal death tolls to be terribly high. The government cover-up of the accident delayed the inevitable exodus of thousands of citizens from Russia, Ukraine, and Belarus. Construction workers slaved on a gargantuan enclosure casing the shunned power plant. In every probability, the radiation would kill the laborers before they completed their job.

Remote tossed on the dresser in disgust, I descended the inn's stairs to the parking lot. Jane relinquished the location of Martin Reynolds' halfway house. She asked why I wanted the address and sounded skeptical of my vague reply. "Johnny, I shouldn't be giving out this information. Don't do anything stupid."

Enduring six miles of Route 17 potholes, I entered Garfield's city limits, driving through a sketchy industrial section of warehouses and used car lots. Colonies of homeless people set up camp below an overpass, roasting a huge animal on a spit. Whatever the beast, the flesh smelled wonderful.

While I paused to read a map, a ring of young boys besieged the Toyota. The children offered to wash the windshield for a quarter. Even after I shook my head, the crew proved persistent. An aggressive kid cavorted on the front, snapping the wiper to and fro. Irked, I yelled, "Get off the hood!" The little bastard jerked the blade until the arm broke in two. The hooligan grinned, sliding onto the asphalt to rejoin the gang. Speeding away, I saw the fresh dent and cursed myself for coming to this hellhole.

The house was on River Drive, abutting the "beautiful" Passaic River. I parked in a deserted dirt lot beside a plumbing and heating supply company. The angle afforded an unobstructed vantage point of the decrepit three-story structure. Narrowing my eyes, I tried to imagine my former neighbor living here. Definitely not the nice home he had in Haworth. Flimsy fire escapes linked the top floors to the ground. Bricks patched missing windows and doorways. In front, a dog rummaged through a row of garbage cans blocking the sidewalk.

The racket of rapping knuckles nearly caused me to hit the roof. A middle-aged woman in a low-cut blouse and hip-hugging silver skirt peered into the glass. "Sugar, come on outta there. How 'bout you and me go to my crib and party?"

Mesmerized by her five o'clock shadow and bobbing Adam's apple, I refused, hastily pushing the locks. A backfire diverted my attention to an ancient sedan merging into traffic from behind the halfway house. It looked like the vehicle at the cemetery. I started the Cressida and gave pursuit, leaving the crack whore in a cloud of dust.

The tan automobile turned onto Outwater Lane and crossed the malodorous Passaic River. I eased off the gas to remain unobserved. Forced to pull close at a stoplight, I stared at the green Carter/Mondale sticker slapped on the Dodge Coronet's fender. The sun's reflection on the rear glass made it impossible to verify the owner. Crushing the steering wheel, I waited for the traffic signal to change. If Reynolds had indeed lurked at George Washington Memorial Park, he probably recognized my rental.

When the light turned green, the car accelerated past the intersection. A sign indicated the town of Clifton. After a few blocks of cheap eats and 99-cent stores, the vehicle passed under the Garden State Parkway, heading down a dead-end street of abandoned factory buildings. Lifting off the pedal, I glided to the curb. A tall male wearing grey-striped coveralls stretched and opened the trunk, removing a duffel bag. The driver must be Reynolds. The side of his face appeared disfigured; yet at fifty yards, the discoloration might be shadow.

Slamming the lid, the man cut over the sidewalk, tugging the chain-link fence wide enough to squeeze into the gap. The figure vanished from sight beyond mounds of rusty scrap metal.

I dawdled, tapping the console. Should I tag along after him on foot or sit tight for his return? Nobody was around. *Fuck it!* Cautiously, I approached the Dodge. In a vacant field, bullet-riddled trucks were submerged in the high grass. The layout of the mill consisted of brick construction connected by overhanging walkways. A humongous water tank on the roof advertised "McKay Iron Works" in flaking white letters.

The inside of the Coronet was empty, save for a blue Virgin Mary statue glued to the dashboard. If this person wasn't Reynolds, what was he doing in this rundown part of town? I pushed apart the barrier and stooped, chafing my skin on a thorny edge. Conceivably walking into an ambush, I crossed grease-soaked earth onto a road sloping between the buildings. The air held the perfume of diesel fuel, and in the mugginess, flies landed on my neck to sip perspiration. Discarded gears and pulleys scattered the fractured cement. At the bottom, the driveway disappeared beneath a slow-moving brook.

Crisp boot prints pressed into the mud, reappearing on the opposite side. A metallic banging echoed faintly in the distance.

To avoid leaving imprints, I hiked upstream, finding an easy section to step across on rocks. The clanging rang from a towering five-level edifice at the far end of the complex. A flock of chattering crows took flight as I crouched behind a rhino-sized oil container. The foundry featured impressive nineteenth-century architecture. Ornate brickwork outlined the rooflines and granite-topped, arched windows. A solitary freight car decayed on the railroad tracks bisecting the property. If I sneaked in the structure to the left, I might gain a viewpoint at the boxcar.

Chained double doors prevented my entry, but an intruder had jimmied a corner window. I eased over the sill, tearing my shirt on the jagged lip. The walls had been stripped naked except for several dated RIDGID tool pinup calendars. A buildup of ash gathering below a smoke smudge retained the odor of a cooking fire. Following a main hallway, I realized this building had once harbored company offices. Outside a filing room, I caught the dull red of the boxcar. The noise increased in cadence and intensity.

Crawling on castoff accounting books, I peeked through filthy glass. With care, I strong-armed the sash and squatted under the railway car. The rhythmic thumping sounded nearby and then stopped.

Ducking lower, I identified Reynolds sprinting on the uneven concrete, ruined face a twisted mask of fury. *That's definitely him. Fuck!* The hammering noise had lured me imprudently close. I slid back into the opening, falling hard on my chest. Winded, I leapt and ran into the hall.

"Johnny, wait up!" he bellowed.

As I sprinted along the passage, the man kept pace outdoors. Swerving toward the rear, I looked for another way out. Reynolds entered the same corner office, screaming. Panting, I stumbled into a chamber covered with dozens of compartment trays. The mailroom's barred jalousies rerouted me to the hallway. A marble staircase led up into light or down into darkness. I chose freedom, three steps at a time, using the banister for balance.

"Come on, I just want to speak with you!" resonated from the stairwell.

The fifth level contained larger suites. Desks for clerical staff furnished a central space. At an exterior window, I glimpsed one of the connecting walkways. Pulling the handgrip, I stepped onto an iron grate. The ramp swung on hanging cables. I walked onto the grid and gawked straight through to the distant pavement. Quickly crossing it, I discovered the facing entryway locked. Frantically, I yanked on the doorknob, using my fading strength.

Reynolds appeared on the bridge, gasping and appreciating my dilemma. "Johnny!"

I used an elbow to shatter a windowpane and reached inside for the lock. *Open!* Barging into the portal, I perched on a catwalk high atop the factory floor. The slender walkway allowed maintenance workers access to the wheels of the rail-mounted gantry cranes.

Door slamming and cranking the lock, Reynolds' blasted mug smushed against the glass, black eye patch sliding to expose a hollow cavity. As he strained into the breach, I sliced the skin of his hand with a window shard. The man hollered in pain, staggering from the fissure. I hefted a casting and snapped off the hasp to the lock. The killer kicked the handle.

Negotiating the footway, I noticed it concluded at a wall. Regrettably choosing the wrong course, I swiveled and rushed past, hoping to pass the maniac before the doorframe ruptured.

Reynolds crashed through the splintered wood, almost cantering over the safety railing. The remaining eye fixed on me. As I retreated, he advanced, clinching the bloody extremity.

"There you are. I finally caught up to you. Let's talk. Gosh, you didn't need to cut me. We're old friends. Were you aware I was acquainted with your father?"

At the edge of my vision, I perceived the yellow of the crane's supporting beam.

"Don't consider going out there. Johnny, you'll kill yourself. That ledge is sixty feet up."

I clambered past the rail and dived on top of an eighteen-inch-wide joist, the surface slippery with gunk. Bending, I utilized an electrical conduit to steady my trembling legs.

Reynolds leaned on the bar. "Kid, that's a fool's errand. Think! I'll meet you on the other side." Crazy or not, my adversary certainly had a point.

A hefty, motor-driven hoist straddled the center of the gantry crane. I questioned if the braided wire might be utilized to lower myself to the bottom. As I arrived at the midpoint, he barreled on the catwalk to the end, footsteps mirroring the musical quality of steel drums. The slick cable was inaccessible and terminated seven yards above an enormous milling machine.

As I reversed direction, so did Reynolds. I sprung, spanning the precarious girder, and climbed to the crossbar. He was at my heels as I touched the door. Shaking off his extended palm, I hotfooted back across the ramp. *If I can just get to the car!* The man's boots pounded on the swaying bridge as I raced into the suites, heading for the exit.

Reynolds grunted and swore as he hounded me. Bounding down the stairwell, I veered toward the office I first entered. While tearing along the hall, I scooped up a metal bar.

I struggled to withdraw, this time catching my blue jeans on the windowsill. *Goddammit!* Reynolds grabbed my shoulders and threw me to the floor. Crab-walking, I scuttled rearwards into the charcoal heap, clutching the shaft.

"Johnny!" Big hands closed in, outspread in a placating gesture. "Hold on. It doesn't have to be this way. I brought you here for a chat."

I swept the two-foot-long piece of rebar below the fanatic's knee and dropped him like a bag of bricks. The man collapsed, wailing and clutching a leg. I leapt through the open window, landing on soft grass and rolling upright. Water splashing, I heard Reynolds bawling my name.

Friday Afternoon—June 13, 1986

"John, you must at least tell Jane," Bill advised.

"I will. Reynolds chased me, but it sounded as if he just wanted to talk." Relocating to a different motor court, I phoned my friend, explaining the incident at the mill and how the parolee followed me to the graveyard.

"Why is he tracking you?"

"God, I wish I knew. Bill, you shoulda seen him. The guy's insane. The face—Reynolds said he met my father."

"That murderer was friends with your dad? What's that supposed to mean?"

"I got no idea. Maybe since we were once neighbors?"

Thoughtfully, he replied, "Or because you were at the trial?"

"Could be. Reynolds sure is in good shape. That fucker really moved."

Outlaw mused, "Prison yards are a great place to exercise. Are you informing Karen?"

"Uh, I don't believe she longs to hear from me," I grumbled.

"John, call Karen ASAP! What if that nutcase comes searching for her? Do you think he figured out what we did? Reynolds knows someone planted that damn shoe in his shed."

"Can you provide Karen's office phone?"

"No, I only have the Maywood number and her business address."

"Bill, I won't telephone her at home. At this hour, she may still be at work. I'll head to the law firm right away."

Most of Hackensack's legal facilities are clustered near the same Bergen County Courthouse that convicted Martin Reynolds. The four-story brick complex stood by an urban park on Main Street. An engraved bronze plaque nailed to the facade read "Block & Ward-Warren, LLC."

Entering the sparse lobby, I requested Karen Schmidt. The sullen young receptionist mumbled that she was at lunch. Annoyed, I asked, "Miss, it's now three-thirty. Does Karen usually eat this late?" The girl shrugged, turning a glossy page in a fashion magazine.

In the waiting area, I mulled over the factory incident. Why did Reynolds desire to see me? If that psycho caught me, what might he do? The man clearly looked angry enough to kill me—*well, yeah, he's a convicted serial murderer!* If I had stayed in Georgia, would that fiend have tried to hurt Karen or Bill? *How did he even find out I was in New Jersey?* Mind swamped with problems and no answers, I stared from the doorway. *Where in the hell was Karen?*

"Sir, we close at five o'clock. Should I leave a message?"

"Yes," I muttered, scribbling the name of the motel. "Please have Ms. Schmidt dial that number as soon as possible. The matter is extremely urgent."

I departed Hackensack, unable to shake a premonition of doom.

In my lodging, I anxiously ate a sandwich, hoping for Karen's call. Restlessly scanning the TV channels, my stomach roiled.

At eight o'clock, the phone rang, and I knocked a can of soda to the floor as I grabbed the receiver.

Bill questioned, "Did you actually speak to her?"

"No, I stuck around the legal firm and left a note. Karen didn't answer my message. I'm thinking of heading to Maywood."

"That's a good idea," he said. "Keep me updated."

Proceeding along Karen's roadway, I saw a black-and-white cruiser stationed at the house. *Crap!* In panic, I shot across the street and up the front steps. At the screen, I viewed two policemen talking to Eric.

"Excuse me!" I said loudly, battering the doorframe. The trio spun my way. "I'm looking for Karen Schmidt. Is she here?"

"And who are you?" the older officer inquired.

"John Townsend," Eric responded bitterly. "That's the ex-boyfriend stalking my fiancé."

Fiancé! "I'm not following her. Where is she?"

Eric spoke tensely through the mesh. "Karen never returned to work and hasn't come home. Do *you* know anything about that?"

The younger officer asked, "This is the same guy you were describing?"

"Yup, that's the one," he replied hotly.

"I was at the law firm all afternoon. You should get ahold of them!" I shouted, losing my mind. *What if Reynolds. . . .*

The patrolmen turned to Eric. "Sir, you'll have to wait twenty-four hours before filing a missing persons report. Ms. Schmidt may be out on the town with a few coworkers, or she has a—"

"This loser has something to do with it. I'm sure of it!" he seethed.

The cops recorded the inn's contact numbers and let me go.

Vincent

Friday Evening—June 13, 1986

I PHONED FROM THE MOTEL. "John, you got to be kidding me," Bill moaned in horror. He muted the receiver and talked hurriedly to his wife. Melissa cursed loudly in the background.

"Bill, I have to find Karen. The cops aren't doing jack."

"Okay, we'll need Vince," he murmured. "We'll get a babysitter to watch Eddie and be right over. At this time of night, the traffic is light. Don't worry, we'll find her," he said encouragingly. Bill furnished Ranzetta's last residence and hung up.

Doors locked, I slowly drove through west Newark peering for Vince's address. Past eleven p.m., most row house numbers were too dark to read or AWOL. I searched for 212 Prince Street, Apartment 405.

A huge, high-rise apartment complex loomed to the sky. *Jesus, I knew it, the projects!* Graffiti tagged signs proclaimed this monstrosity as Stella Wright Homes. Wedged into a parking slot between a pair of dismantled cars, I stood on the verge of scared shitless. The hulking thirteen-story buildings unfolded into the distance. Several thousand people must live on this property. I hopelessly foraged for a map or directory.

Head lowered, I walked toward the treeless courtyards. A cluster of men hung out, smoking on ragged couches. "Hey, friend, can I help you?" one joked. As I continued deeper into the compound, his chums burst into laughter. The raucous sounds of fighting reverberated from the hard walls. The projects were a more fucked up version of Tiny's apartments.

An elderly woman shuffled by, pushing a shopping cart overflowing with trash. Disorientated, I asked for Apartment 405. Squinting, she observed, "Son, Stella isn't a place for a boy such as you. Are you lost, honey?"

"No, ma'am, I'm visiting someone," I replied, extracting a sawbuck.

"Oh, I don't want your money. C is that way." The matron pointed a gnarled forefinger at a rectangular box, an exact architectural duplicate of the rest. "You're lucky it's only four levels up. Damn elevator's busted. As the young folks say, 'Shit happens.'"

Many of the apartments in Building C appeared vacant. Above plywood-sheathed windows on the sixth and seventh stories, the faded trails of soot indicated recent fires.

As I neared the entrance, a rat the size of a cat nonchalantly crossed the sidewalk lugging a half-gnawed bone. As I scampered backwards in fright, a large hand clenched my arm. "That's just a newborn," a deep voice chuckled. "Brother, I can tell you're not from these parts. Is this your initial experience with public housing?"

I had to see Vince and find Karen. Pivoting, I reeled out of the hold. "Listen, pal, I'm meeting somebody. Give me a freakin' break."

A hood shadowed the big man's face. "Who are you looking for? I'm acquainted with everyone in this Shangri-La."

"Vince Ranzetta. As a matter of fact, I'm not convinced he still lives at this location."

"Tall, skinny white dude? Mouthy?"

Excited, I nodded.

"Of course, I know that fella. Follow me through the cabbage patch."

Flyspecked bulbs flickered in the dim lobby as the stranger shepherded me to the stairway. "Elevator screwed the pooch," he complained over a shoulder. In the brightly lit stairwell, I clearly saw my guide slide off the hood. A muscled 300 pounds, the bald man was in his early forties. An undecipherable tattoo encircled his broad neck.

Stepping onto the fourth landing, my new acquaintance extended a hand. "Hey, my name's Sal Harris."

"John," I winced, endeavoring to return the vise grip.

"This is it," he said, standing before a bashed-in metal doorway. "Sorry, I need to ask. Are you here to sell him more dope?"

"No, sir, I'm not."

Sal took a deep breath and hammered on the door with a meaty fist. "Ranzetta!"

Across the hall, a bony gal wearing pink panties and a green halter top appeared to sulk. "There isn't a thing to see, Marjorie," he stated calmly. Vexed, the woman sucked teeth and slammed the door.

With no response, Harris stomped louder. A muffled voice questioned, "Who's there?"

"Vince, it's Sal. You have a fancy uptown visitor. The guy says his name is John."

"Townsend," I added.

"John Townsend!" he shouted.

An eye scrutinized me from the crack in the frame. "Fuck!" a mouth squawked in sudden recognition. Entry swinging wide, Ranzetta rocked on his heels, a burnt-out cigarette held by bearded lips. "John! Man, is that really you?"

Aghast, I responded, "Yes, afraid so." Bill had forewarned me of my former classmate's condition, yet I came unprepared for this emaciated apparition.

Moving aside, a twinkle of embarrassment crossed his face. As Harris entered, I lifted a palm. "Sir, I appreciate that you brought me to the apartment, but I should speak to my friend alone."

The large man nodded, turning to leave. "Stay here!" Vince implored. "Sal's keeping me on the righteous path, getting my soul straight with Jesus."

"Well, he's not doing a very good job. Ranzetta, you resemble shit warm-ups. What the hell are you doing to yourself? Bill has been calling for months, and you never answer." Angry and hurt, I couldn't bear to see my schoolmate degenerated to this mess.

"No telephone," he sneered, scratching inside his elbows. "Disconnected for lack of payment. Those nickel-and-diming prigs!"

Exhausted, I entered the fleapit searching for a spot to unwind. Heaving a hump of blankets, I exposed a futon. Sal leaned against a wall. Ranzetta paced, redistributing garbage to different piles.

"Vincent. Stop it! I'm requesting your assistance."

Ceasing, he stared in wonder. "What happened? What in the world can I possibly do for you, Mr. Big Shot?"

"Martin Reynolds just got released on parole. This afternoon, he attempted to kill me, and now that lunatic has kidnapped Karen Schmidt. We need your support finding her."

Vince slumped, plucking at his facial hair. "What? That can't be—"

"Bill and Melissa are on their way in from the city to lend a hand. We'll return to my place and meet them."

On the matted carpet, he crammed his dirty clothes into a laundry bag. Focused, Ranzetta urged, "Then let's hit the road!"

"Are you up to this? What kind of crap are you on?"

Grinning, he held the sack. "John, I'm into every secret remedy and magical potion known to mankind. Trust me, you don't want to find out; it'll blow your mind. Let's ditch this shithole. Sal's coming along."

"The hell he is!" I exclaimed, rising off the sofa bed. "No offense, buddy, but—"

"None taken," Harris replied, disclosing a snub-nose Beretta and crossing his thick arms. The handgun dangled downwards.

"Whoa," I said, raising both palms. "Man, I'm not looking for trouble—"

"John, he's our enforcer," Vince established. "That's his thing. Sal's a pro, and we'll definitely employ his talents."

I didn't have time to argue. "Fine," I conceded, holding the door wide. Entering the hallway, I muttered, "Come on, Batman and Robin. Let's go save the day."

Karen's rescue team was either rapidly assembling or swiftly falling apart.

Saturday Morning—June 14, 1986

The Outlaws tarried outside the motel. Astounded when Vince exited the passenger side, they were even more bewildered as Sal emerged from the rear.

The ride over was rough. Ranzetta jabbered nonsensically, once pausing to load a glass pipe and ignite the crystals. The cabin filled with the acrid stink of burning plastic. Roaring obscenities, he pitched a fit as Harris stretched forward and threw the narcotics out the window.

Restlessly, I gazed at the stars while Bill and his wife embraced Vince and introduced themselves to our latest member. We needed a strategy. Assorted all-night diners populated the area. Starved and worn out, I suggested getting a bite and discussing our options.

Pressed into a booth at Denny's, I sat across from Sal's intimidating, inked biceps. *Who is this guy?* Dropping the menu, he met my stare. "So what's the score? What are we doing here?"

The others added input as I reviewed Martin Reynolds' homicidal past and convictions. The briefing ended with the factory chase and Karen's disappearance.

Harris remained quiet until the narrative finished. "Thanks for the four-one-one. I can see why this dickhead is bent that you set him up. This woman, is she your girlfriend or something?"

"Or something. . ." Melissa exhaled wearily.

"Karen hates my guts," I concluded.

Antsy, Ranzetta summoned the waitress, ordering a double hamburger and two chocolate milkshakes. "Chief, you're paying?" he asked, and ill-tempered, I acquiesced.

Breakfast on the way, Sal continued, "From what you're telling me, this Reynolds is a real piece of work. The boyfriend should be submitting the missing person's report later today. Then the police will issue a statewide all-points bulletin. What can we do in the meantime?"

Bill leaned on the table. "Let's start searching the haunts Reynolds frequents—that abandoned mill in Clifton and the halfway house in Garfield. The most obvious site is Haworth. That's where your neighbor buried the victims." Crestfallen, he sighed. "What if we're too late?"

Vince snapped to attention. "That fucker's playing head games. There's no denying she's in danger, but from what John said, that screwball wants to talk. Maybe that's the play; he abducts Karen and lies in wait for us to make the next move."

Melissa glared over eggs and sausage. "Ranzetta, to be blunt, you're barfing me out. Christ, you look and smell like my kid's diapers. Sadly, I itch to wrap my fingers around your throat."

Vince's lips curled in amusement. "Ah, Melissa, I always knew you cared." The girl cringed as he spread his arms in a bear hug.

Bill spoke earnestly, "John, you need to engage your sister. Enlisted on the force, she can obtain inside information. Karen may be home at this point."

"Yes, you're right. I'll try giving her a call."

Listening to the pay phone ring, I watched my group in animated conversation.

"Oh, boy," Jane yawned. "Johnny, it's two o'clock in the morning. What's so important?"

Hurriedly, I explained the situation. "It's a lot to request, but time is running out."

"Do you recollect where Reynolds worked or socialized? What was his profession? That could be utilized to determine where he went."

Racking my brain, I tried to remember. "During the trial, I read Reynolds had an affiliation with radios or broadcasting. Before incarceration, he was a member of the Freemasons."

"Great, I'll delve into his records and confirm Karen's status. Buzz me in a few hours at the police station. They'll patch me through. What are you going to do?"

"Not sure, we're working on an approach."

"Don't be a hero, Johnny. This asshole is a certified schizophrenic. Stay out of his way."

After deliberating Jane's warning, I wouldn't put my friends in jeopardy.

Bill questioned, "Did you talk to your sister?"

"Yup. Everybody knows Reynolds is capable of murder. Yesterday, I was stupid enough to walk into a trap. Guys, I can't have you mixed up in anything this dangerous."

Melissa grabbed my elbow, glowering. "We're talking about Karen, correct? Do you honestly believe we're driving home and forgetting her? That won't happen." Dropping my hand, she suggested, "I say we split up and nose around where we can."

The group returned to the inn to retrieve the Outlaws' vehicle. Melissa and Bill were tasked with staking out Reynolds' residence. Vince, Sal, and I would investigate the McKay Iron Works. I decided Jane could meet us later to explore the Woods jointly. There was safety in numbers.

Ranzetta demanded to "beat the piss out of the little guy" before we "blasted off." Taking way too long, Harris glanced at his wristwatch. "We've got to keep a strict eye on that one," he advised, rushing up the stairs.

I banged on the bathroom door. "Wait a sec," Vince mumbled, flushing the toilet. Jiggling the handle, an item clattered to the floor. Locked.

"Move over," Sal grunted, forcing me aside. I thought he might smash the door off its hinges, but the powerful man tricked me by producing a miniature screwdriver set. Dexterously inserting a tool into the knob's minuscule orifice, he swung open the doorway.

Beneath harsh illumination, my friend squatted on the checkered tiles, scurrying to shove fixings into a pocket-sized white case. Standing sheepishly, Vince clutched a Red Cross-emblazoned container to his pale chest.

"What the fuck?" I yelled. Turning, I strained to recall the kid in high school. Vince had wasted away to nothing. An unexpected rage surged as I whirled and kicked a gash in the door. *So much for Sal's finesse!* "Help me," I snarled, tugging the scrawny frame from the commode and onto the bed. "Hold him!" Ranzetta quaked violently as Harris pinned his limbs and sat on his sternum.

Scanning the narrow accommodation, I zeroed in on a line twirling by the curtains. "Use this," Sal offered, passing a well-worn switchblade. The polyester curtain cord worked perfectly, strapping the wrenching hands and feet to the bed frame. For the final touch, I plugged his gob with a sock.

As I regarded my captive, I caught the Outlaws watching from the entryway. Sinking to the desk chair, I cradled my head. "Fuck me," I groaned.

"Wow, Ranzetta, I had no idea you were into S & M," Melissa scorned, shaking her hair in simulated astonishment. Vince looked daggers, twitching for a moment before nodding off into an opioid stupor.

"What now?" Bill exhaled, removing his glasses and rubbing bloodshot eyes.

"Tell me," I lamented. "Is anyone familiar with heroin withdrawal or how long the symptoms last?" Glancing at Sal, I inquired, "Any idea what else Vince is on, besides crack and this poison?" I zipped apart the junkie kit and inventoried the contents.

"Pills, pot, whatever he can get his grubby paws on. Ranzetta maintained until he got a letter concerning some convict released from prison and—" Harris slapped his dome in comprehension. "No doubt that was you guys referring to Reynolds, right? He's been totally fucked up ever since. I try to reason with him, but it's the same as talking to the Berlin Wall." His brow corrugated. "Weaning Vince off scag could take two or three days. In bad cases, drug dependency can continue weeks or even months. Sorry. It's a different story for everyone."

"It's my fault," Bill confessed. "I sent that message. At the time, I didn't—"

"Don't agonize; you're not to blame." Cross at losing members of our search party, I considered Sal. "Do you mind babysitting this idiot for a bit?"

"Okay, if that's what you want. I may be better—"

"John, I'll stay and tend to Vince," Melissa interrupted. "Sal can be more valuable helping you hunt for Karen."

Harris cautioned, "His body needs to mend. An addict starts coming down within six to twelve hours. There probably won't be much to do until the physiological and psychological effects kick in. The dude floats. During this phase, go buy a couple magazines, food, and water. Stage two: predict fever, muscle aches, agitation . . . basically, extreme flu symptoms." He reached into his jeans. "Give him this clonidine for the anxiety. Toward the end, your patient will be puking and shitting himself. While you're shopping, purchase a carton of adult diapers and painkillers. The optimistic news: I think it's a chicken shit habit."

"Chicken shit?" Melissa asked, frowning.

"Vince is a recent friend of Aunt Hazel," he replied. "With a little prayer, maybe he'll bounce back."

Her scowl evolved into a smirk. "Perhaps I shouldn't have volunteered, huh?"

Sal smiled. "Girl, you can handle it. The boy requires soothing dialog and firm handholding. He'll endure a great deal of pain and will be very glad a close friend is nearby." The man turned serious. "When Ranzetta wakes, the inner demon will persuade you to release the bonds. That's the devil himself testing your resolve. Don't do it. Be strong!"

Bill agreed to drive to the halfway house and check for the Dodge Coronet. Sal and I could search the ironworks. Along with monitoring Vince, Melissa would act as our central communications center. Before leaving, I again contacted Jane. She affirmed Karen was still nowhere to be found and an official inquiry had yet to commence. As Bill promised not to approach Reynolds, I wondered why my unusual companion toted a bottle of clonidine.

The Hunt

Saturday Morning—June 14, 1986

WHILE DRIVING THE BACK STREETS TO CLIFTON, I reviewed life in Atlanta: so many wasted years, living in the shadows. A monotonous existence, though compared to searching for a psychopath, boring now seemed very suitable. I realized how much I missed my friends in New Jersey, especially Karen. It was my fault she's in danger. *Please, God, let her be all right!*

"Hey, bro, you okay? For a moment, you looked like you were enjoying a mini-stroke."

"Don't sweat. I'm fine," I replied, glancing at my passenger. "Sal, what do you do in your spare time?"

"A little of this, a bit of that," he answered, flashing teeth. "Currently, I'm taking evening classes at Rutgers to achieve a bachelor's degree. God willing, I'm on target to graduate by the end of this year."

"Oh, yeah?" Intrigued, I inquired, "What's your major?"

"Business Administration. Most critics have concluded that Newark should be put out of her misery. The naysayers may be dead on; not even one cinema remains in that fucking town. In the twenties, Brick City had over forty elegant movie houses. All the theaters and playhouses shut down. On the contrary, I am betting Newark is ripe for a fella knowing his way around a dollar."

"That sounds great. I noticed the tattoos. Were you in the military?"

"A long, long time ago, I did a double tour in Vietnam." Harris frowned at the industrial scenery.

Alone with unpleasant thoughts, we entered Clifton in silence. The iron factory awaited below serene skies. I stopped in the same spot Reynolds had parked his Dodge. "This is the place," I said nervously, frightened of what we might find.

Squeezing past the barrier, we padded downhill to the submerged section of road. In the mud, I indicated the marks made escaping as well as a unique set.

Sal stooped to canvass the footprints. "These lines are created by an individual having difficulty walking," he surmised. "The left heel impression is deeper." Vince's friend peered at my sneaker. "Not yours, so they must be from the person you confronted." Progressing downstream, he urgently beckoned. The husky man knelt again, running a thumb on the edge of a deep boot print. "These are unusual, same sole as the limping imprints." As the Beretta rose, he pulled the slide and chambered a round. "The Mad Hatter may still be here. Show me where you last saw this guy." Harris paused and asked, "Can you give me a description? I don't want to drop the watchman."

"Fair complexion, silvery hair and hopefully limping. Yesterday, he was wearing coveralls. Remarkably good shape for a man in his late sixties."

The two of us followed the rusty train tracks to the structure housing the gantry cranes.

"Stay behind me," he whispered, bending under a partially raised garage door.

We stood on the vast cement floor of the manufacturing plant. High above, sunshine filtered through grimy windows. Just yesterday, I'd fled across one of the massive girders.

The footprints registered Reynolds' recent return. *Why?* "Maybe he's in a different building," I suggested.

"Yeah, could be," Sal replied, guardedly stepping ahead, firearm ready.

Appearing empty, the mill afforded hiding opportunities amongst boxes and machinery. Motes of dust lazily floated in slow-moving air currents, and a lone blackbird fluttered off a rafter. An object glinted in my peripheral vision. A sunbeam illuminated an industrial drill press. A shiny ring swayed at the cylindrical drill chuck. Suspended by a thread, a second elapsed before I recognized the silver tri-pointed star. In disbelief, I became aware how the ornament dangled. I gagged back a shriek.

"Holy crap! What the fuck!" Sal blurted. "Is that what I think it is?"

A human finger was inserted into the triple steel jaws normally used to grip drill bits. *Blue nail polish!* A fishhook pierced the meaty tip of the appendage. The Mercedes hood emblem hovered from a blood-red fishing line. In revulsion, I twisted the chuck key to release the diminutive digit.

"Reynolds, I'll kill you, motherfucker!" My voice boomed, screaming toward the roof. Rage overtook, replaced by numbing defeat. My fists unclenched as I sunk to a packing crate.

"Examine this part of the pinkie. John, I'm no expert, but with the excess amount of blood, the victim may have been conscious during amputation. As Vince deduced, the abductor is playing a perverse game."

Paralyzed, I closed my eyes and leaned against a supporting column. I needed to locate and kill Reynolds, yet was hopelessly outmatched.

"Yo, John," Sal said gently, shaking my knee. Always observant, he pushed aside a box of bolts and eased onto a tipped tool chest. The pistol stayed cocked. "Let me tell you, I witnessed so many ungodly acts of violence in Vietnam. I *never* talk about it, not even with family. But your case is different."

Harris's ardor caught my attention. "In 'Nam, the military employed choppers to ferry troops on missions. Big Hueys. One morning, orders came to pick up a platoon of fellow Marines at an outpost in east bumfuck. The helicopters landed unprotected, no one providing cover. Their comms had just checked in on the radio an hour earlier. The detachment spread out, finding the fortification completely abandoned. Combat equipment littered the place. Creepy as shit—in your soul, you understood something was fucked. I recall the smell of a pot of beans burning on the stove, still can't eat 'em. A soldier starts howling. Rushing into the jungle, everybody locked and loaded. A half a click from the base, we dug up a small-scale National Liberation Front camp. Later, the brass reported the Viet Cong got twenty-eight of our guys. Definitely looked to be a fuckload to me." Falling silent, he gazed at the Beretta.

"What?" I prodded, uncertain how this account related or if I yearned to know the ending.

With haunted eyes, Sal stared. "In the center of that VC camp, we stumbled into a mountain of guts. A huge jumble, a slaughter. Sliced up with machetes. I mean the dead were—a dozen military coroners toiled for weeks figuring out which foot went to which leg. John, the NLF did that to spook us. For a while, the enemy's tactics succeeded. Nobody wanted to go on patrol after that. The corporals, equally scared, made up excuses to keep their squadrons inside the wire. In the end, we had to do our jobs. It's a war. The debilitating fear lessened, overcome by anger."

"The moral of this terrible story is?"

"Retribution. Vengeance. Get up off your ass, Townsend. We're going to rescue your girlfriend and carve up Reynolds like a fucking Thanksgiving turkey."

That, I told myself, I could live with.

Saturday at Noon—June 14, 1986

At a phone booth, I touched base with Melissa, comforted to hear Bill returned safely. There was no sign of Reynolds or his car at the halfway house. A resident leaving the dwelling hadn't seen his housemate since the previous afternoon. She complained that her detainee sweated worse than a pig and begged constantly to be untied. Reassuringly, I swore we'd return soon, bringing lunch.

Missing the pure air of the courtyard, the motel room reeked. Vince tossed and turned on the mattress, wrists raw from straining. "Jesus Christ, open the goddamned window," I beseeched before deflating in a chair. Sal passed around cardboard cartons of Thai food.

The addict's eyes gyrated, pleading for release. "Lay still, shithead!" I commanded. "What are you attempting to do, have us thrown out of this dump?"

Ranzetta ceased thrashing and stared unblinkingly. After I described what we found at the factory, Melissa put a sleeve to her mouth. Bill trotted to the bathroom and vomited noisily.

When my friend returned, I surrendered my seat to him. Inhaling the draft overlooking the pool, I announced, "Jane's coming by at three o'clock. Until then, get a little rest."

Desperate to escape outdoors, Bill offered, "I'll ask if the room next door is available."

"Thanks, I'm tired and can't think straight. When my sister arrives, we'll go to Haworth and search the Woods."

Saturday Afternoon—June 14, 1986

Awaking unsettled, Harris slept on the same bed, eyeballs rolling rapidly under drawn lids. Lips parted by incoherent moans, his nightmares might have been eviler than mine. Shaken awake, my bedmate sprawled over the sheets, grumbling and farting. Bill must have risen to watch Vince, because Melissa replaced the spot on the cot, curled up and snoring.

In the connecting suite, Jane perched on the bed, mopping the "patient's" forehead with a damp cloth. Dressed in civilian clothes, she glanced up, irritated. "Hey, sleepyhead. Tying Ranzetta up, whose smart idea was that?" I raised a palm. "What do you envision the outcome will be, once your friend is released? Vince will run to the nearest street corner and score."

"Yes, I get that I probably acted hastily."

Stiffly, Outlaw pivoted from the window. "I'll get Mel, and we can go."

Jane spoke briskly while driving her Jeep Cherokee, "Johnny, you were on the money. I substantiated that Martin Reynolds worked as a broadcast engineer at different FM radio stations in Bergen County. That was fifteen years back, so I'm not clear if this benefits the investigation, but any information is definitely worth considering." The tires screeched around the exit onto Oradell Avenue. Speeding, we traveled well over the posted limit.

After determining the best area to enter the Woods, my sister stopped on a side road. "Reynolds won't identify my vehicle, but protocol dictates it's always better to take precautions." Jane unlocked the trunk. Hidden beneath a United Airlines blanket, a swollen duffle bag revealed an arsenal of firearms and ammunition. Sternly, she handed me a Winchester 12-gauge. "Pump this, and aim at the bad guy's chest, understand? Prepare for the kick." Presenting Bill an impressive Colt 45 revolver, my sister grabbed a Glock Model 17 for herself. "Mr. Harris, you're good?"

Sal smiled widely and nodded. "Yes, ma'am. Got it covered."

"Folks, I don't know what we'll encounter," Jane said, slamming the hatch. "Johnny is familiar with the trail and can lead the way. These weapons are loaded, so be mindful. Blowing each other's brains out will not help Karen."

Thick with greenery, the Woods were livelier than the frigid day I recovered the shoe. The stagnant air absorbed the musky odor of damp leaves and bark. I cautioned against the skirt of poison ivy edging the path. Even carefully aimed away, the unwieldy shotgun suggested danger. At a fast pace, it didn't take very long to reach the decades-old crime scene.

Even with the remains decades removed, people continued to bestow mementos in remembrance of the victims. A candle flickered within a ring of tacky plastic flowers. Picking up the glass jar, I wondered which family had donated the tribute. The votive possessed an embossed illustration of a guardian angel floating above a mother and infant. The seraph's face had been scratched off.

About to communicate my find, Bill called out, exhibiting a plot of freshly turned soil. Digging rapidly, I excavated a handmade chest a few inches below the clay. The lid's intricate bas-relief depicted a similar winged celestial being, lengthy scroll unrolled by prayerful hands. I unclasped the tiny hook and freed the top. Dozens of engraved metal pet identification tags spilled from the container.

Sal questioned, "What are those things?"

"Guess we forgot to inform you that Reynolds adores dining on neighborhood cats. Karen and I discovered a freezer packed with local meat."

"Back in the '70s, we unearthed animal badges and a cat skull up there," Outlaw added. "It's pretty obvious he was here recently. Perhaps it's time to investigate Ceremonies," my friend proposed, aiming the pistol up the hill.

Heading along the trail, we diverged onto the fork leading up to the place I reviled. Jane took point, weapon ready. The glade appeared less powerful than I remembered. Shrubbery encroached inwards, and the boulder seemed diminished, as if the ground swelled skyward. No one partied here anymore.

Bill and my sister approached the scintillating mica. In a soft voice, he inquired, "What is that?" Tense, my stomach shuddered, picturing what they uncovered.

Piqued, she gestured me close. "What do you make of this?"

Producing a pocketknife, Jane utilized the tip to flip over a miniature article partly concealed by her palm. Moving aside, she exposed a shiny locket lying on the stone. On the rear of the pendant were the engraved words: "*VIRTUS JUNXIT MORS NON SEPARABIT*."

"What's that mean?" Bill asked.

"Resembles Latin," I replied, urging my sister to open the jewelry.

As she used a tissue to pop the case, dripping red liquid traced the quartz veins in the rock's veneer. Jane's fingers slipped, and the disk rolled off the boulder. Sal retrieved the item in the weeds and cleaned the sticky silver with a cloth. "John, you're correct. It's Latin. The text means, '*What virtue has joined together, death shall not separate.*' The motto is Masonic, usually engraved on a member's ring. There's a photo of a woman and child." He held forth the black and white oval.

"Reynolds attended a Freemasons' meeting while we searched his home," I told Sal. "Karen came upon a bedroom decorated for a young girl. Unfortunately, we never authenticated who she was. Is that blood filling the locket?" I didn't know how much more torment my mind could tolerate.

"Possibly," Jane answered deliberately. "The fluid may be animal in origin. The lab would have to run analysis."

"Something else is inside," Harris muttered, reaching for the knife. Using the blade to skin transparent tape underneath the lid, he unfurled a miniscule strip of paper upon the stone's tainted exterior. "THE TOWERS."

"Devil's Tower!" my sister exclaimed excitedly. "That's in Alpine. We need to hurry!" Eyes blazing, she ran from the accursed Gehenna branded Ceremonies. Sun eclipsed by clouds, the afterworld countered with thunder.

Saturday Evening—June 14, 1986

The Cherokee roared up Closter Dock Road toward the Hudson River, a recent downpour wetting the macadam. The sky cleared to steel blue while the sun lowered. Jane asserted over the headrest, overrunning slower traffic, "Devil's Tower is exactly the site this maniac might take Karen. A lot of god-awful folklore surrounds Rio Vista. Allegedly, following World War I, a Cuban sugar baron started erecting a magnificent clock tower for his beloved bride. The newlywed desired an unobstructed panoramic view of the New York skyline. Not positive if this part is true, but legend says the lady rode the elevator to the top to catch a breeze. At that height, she observed her man performing unholy acts with the housekeeper. In shock and dismay, the wife jumped off the edge, plummeting one hundred feet. That put the kibosh on finishing the lookout, so the husband terminated the construction."

"No doubt, the plantation owner felt stupid for building the damned thing in the first place," Sal speculated.

"Ha, you're most likely right." Turning onto 9W, my sister continued, "Honestly, I'm up here at least twice a week, throwing drunken kids off Rio Vista land. The residents are convinced driving an automobile three times in reverse around the tower raises the wife's jealous spirit. A paramedic told me that the ghost commandeered a van head on into a tree, decapitating a female passenger."

"Did you ever test the curse?" I inquired. A daydream induced a manic image of Jane driving rearwards in a squad car.

"No way, Johnny," my sister responded, shaking her head vigorously. "Even if the stories are bullshit, I'm not taking that chance. Once, at high noon, I noticed a column of mist that didn't seem quite kosher. One freaked-out teenager said he circled the tower backwards six times at midnight and met the Prince of Darkness himself—Lucifer. I saw the dread in the young man's eyes and believed him." The Jeep veered onto the Esplanade.

"There she is," Bill breathed.

Devil's Tower rose to Zion, silhouetted by the setting sun. When we proceeded closer, the intricate details of the dramatic gothic architecture became sharply defined.

"The lookout had to be awe-inspiring seventy years ago. Vandals shattered the stained glass and damaged much of the stonework," she grumbled. "On a few occasions, the town tried to tear the structure down, giving up when several workers inexplicably died."

It didn't require considerable imagination to visualize supernatural faces scrutinizing us from the upper windows. Jane stopped the vehicle alongside the bowed opening passing through the tower's base. The day rotated into twilight, and crickets began their chirping chorus. Dispensing the assigned armaments, she reached for a flashlight. The Winchester felt warm and alive in my hands as I contemplated why my sister, the police officer, hadn't phoned in for backup.

"Reynolds left a message, knowing we'd come. Karen has to be at Rio Vista. Be alert. Watch each other's backs," she warned.

A secure gate blocked admittance to the tower. Within the portal, ugly satanic graffiti adorned the walls. Some genius spray-painted "*Salted Babies for Sale*" and a telephone number with a prefix of 666. Sal jogged the gate's ample lock. "There's no entry here. The bottom section is sealed. You'd need an extension ladder to rise any higher."

Jane surveyed the property. "A chapel and mausoleum also reside on the estate. Let's check those out. Supposedly, an underground shaft joins the lookout to the owner's residence, but I assume the entryways are sealed."

In the dying glow, I perceived a pair of rustic buildings across an expanse of lawn. The medium-sized mausoleum was composed of the same granite and design as the tower. Holding the scattergun ready, I hoped to have the courage to react swiftly. As my sister shined the flashlight past the slats in the crusted bars, shadows slid eerily over the surfaces. The tomb was vacant except for ten marble doors stacked on the floor. Although the interiors of the vaults enclosed no bones, a foul odor remained. I warily walked behind the crypt, blocked by huge bushes—nothing besides solid walls. That left the sanctuary plus the tunnel, if we located the openings.

Withstanding the weather, the chapel prevailed as a striking, two-story edifice. With its windows bricked closed and husky bronze doors padlocked, there were no more entrances. "Mr. Harris, do me a favor, and bring the crowbar from the Cherokee," Jane requested. Waiting, I listened to the traffic on 9W.

Out of the murk, Sal reappeared with a substantial wrecking bar. Raising eyebrows to my sister for approval, he hitched up his dungarees and leveraged the claw between the handle and the chain. The muscled man grunted and labored, forearms enlarging. The links held tight, but the brass handgrip popped loudly. Hinges protesting, the heavy doors burst apart. Compared to the burial chamber, the sanctuary smelled abominable.

Jane directed the flashlight into the resonant space, vandalized and in blasphemous disarray. Splintered mahogany pews had been hurled recklessly throughout the house of worship.

Above a modest altar, Jesus hung upside-down, nailed to a wooden cross. The Savior's joyless eyes beseeched salvation.

Climbing the threshold and entering the chapel, I pushed a finger against my nostrils to reduce the stench of corruption. Medieval chandeliers wobbled crookedly from blackened timber. Beer cans and bottles dirtied the planking. The hairs on the base of my neck rose, and my abdomen cramped. The shuddersome sensation was so reminiscent of Ceremonies, I considered fleeing the cell, caterwauling.

"Look at this!" Outlaw hissed, crouched by an eagle-shaped lectern. "Give me the light."

Harris stood watch as we bordered a rectangular crevice. An eddy of cool, dank air flowed out of a stairway sinking into gloom.

"Stay here. I'll go first," Jane ordered. Descending the steps, the crown of her head vanished into the passageway.

"Wait, I'm going too!" Handing Sal the gun, I hurried to stay close. The crawlway was scarcely three feet wide, and I ducked under the rotten framework bolstering the failing roof. Pools of black water flooded the low areas of the earth.

The saucer of brilliance drifted far ahead. Body rigid, my sister halted. The airflow bathing my face intensified. "We're at the tower," Jane said, signifying a dimly lit flight of stairs. *"Come on!"* Ascending, I shortsightedly hankered for my weapon.

Cautiously, we emerged into a high-ceilinged room, previously a library. Sparrows nested on the bare oak shelves lining the walls. A gilded world globe lay bruised in a corner.

An iron spiral staircase stood beside a hollow elevator shaft. The treads attached to a central post, disappearing into the ceiling. Jane aimed the flashlight aloft, emphasizing the blackness of the circular hole. As we clambered up, the steps creaked, yet sustained our weight. The others presumably wondered what transpired.

We advanced onto a narrow landing on the second floor; its curved windows were walled shut.

"Let's keep going!" she urged at the stairway. Rocks and shards of colored glass bejeweled the third level. A slit yielded a peek at the white Jeep parked on the encircling driveway. The outbuildings were visible, but not Sal or Bill.

"Clock room," my sister stated on the next story. The gears of the time mechanism lay scattered in the spacious compartment. An artist had painted an enormous pentagram on the masonry. "Johnny!" she cried, spotting a figure propped against the wall.

"That's a doll," I exhaled, relieved. The blank baby blues of the life-size figurine goggled from a split head contorted the wrong way. A most disturbing visual effect. *Where is Karen?*

In thirty more feet, we'd achieve the lookout's tallest point. "Nothing, nothing at all," I panted, searching the cavernous cubicle. Surpassing the treetops, we watched Manhattan sparkle through the largest arched opening.

"Something has to be here," Jane grumbled wearily. "This is the only tower I know of in Alpine."

"The note said *'THE TOWERS,'* not 'THE TOWER.' What do you think that means?" I pictured the bell tower at the cemetery.

My sister paced the observatory, madly kicking debris. Outlaw's voice echoed below, "John, are you up there?"

"Yeah, buddy, come up. We're at the top."

In the stairwell, red hair appeared, followed by Sal, who silently returned the shotgun. "Find anything? That hole was a deathtrap."

"Not a thing," I growled, turning to stare out a different window.

Bill approached from behind. "Let's go see how Mel is doing. I shouldn't leave her alone for so long. Keeping Vince tied up may not be the most desirable method of treatment."

Utterly spent, I leaned over the flagstone windowsill. What were we doing, squandering valuable minutes? Where was Karen? Reynolds played a demented game that I didn't enjoy or comprehend. I stretched further, glaring downward, and sensed a cold object roll under my forearm. Lifting, I beheld a severed index finger, the marrow plainly discernible. I recoiled—*the same blue nail polish.*

The extremity directed north. *A fresh clue from that sick bastard.* I peered intently outside. *What was out there?* The Hudson extended northward to the horizon. Across the wide river, Yonkers glimmered. On this side, trees and the incandescence of humanity faded into obscurity.

"John," Bill repeated considerately. "We have got to get going. Tomorrow, we might start again to—"

My aching eyes blurred and refocused on three parallel rows of red lights. *What is that?* The pinnacle row of bulbs blinked sequentially. The skeletal structure appeared to be two to three miles distant. I squatted to sight along the length of the digit. Even detached, she pointed the way.

"Another tower," I murmured. "Reynolds has Karen at the Armstrong Tower."

Radio Waves

Saturday Evening—June 14, 1986

"WE'VE GOT TO GET VINCE AND MELISSA!" I shouted, stomping downstairs, ducking into the tunnel.

Jane yelled, "There's a phone booth at the gas station on Closter Dock!"

"Should we notify the police?" Bill asked expectantly.

"I am the police," she snarled. "Let's find that son of a bitch!"

Melissa picked up on the initial ring, unsure of Ranzetta's condition. "Let me talk to him," I snapped. "Can you hear me? Vince?"

"Uh, I'm not deaf. What's up?" My friend practically sounded normal.

"Are you feeling better? Are you—?"

"John, I'm fine. Peaches and cream. How are you folks doing? Having fun yet? Your quivering speech affirms you're ready for my help."

"Yeah, yeah, we'll need everybody. Vince, we've established Reynolds' whereabouts. If Melissa unties you, will . . . are you up to this?"

"Sure, buddy. If you'll kindly instruct Mrs. Outlaw to release these chains, I'll take a quick shit, shower and shave, and be prepared to kick a little psychotic ass."

That was my old classmate!

I requested Melissa to meet us at the State Line Lookout at eleven p.m. Ecstatic to leave the motor court, she agreed to buy supper.

The park deserted at this hour, we sat on the cliffs of the Palisades commanding a vista of the glistening Hudson.

"How far down is that?" Sal questioned nervously. "Jeez, I can't even see the bottom."

"Over five hundred feet," Outlaw answered, flinging a hefty stone into the air. Ear cocked, he leaned precariously on the ledge.

The four of us bent forward, anticipating impact. Silence.

Watching a tugboat languidly pushing a long barge upriver, I wished Karen and I could float away.

"Is our patient improving?" Bill inquired.

"The boy is still a junkie," Jane interjected.

"Ranzetta was quite lucid for someone strapped to a bed," I responded, with no valid interpretation of his present medical or mental state.

"We'll have to mind him closely," Harris cautioned, scooting backwards from the precipice.

"What does Peter think of you being out at all hours of the evening?" Bill asked my sister. I hadn't met her boyfriend in person, secretly glad that he wasn't living in our old home. The idea of an outsider meandering around my former bedroom in underpants was disconcerting.

Jane smiled. "Pete's cool and accepts my schedule is irregular. Once, as a joke, I made up a special word. I explained that, if I mentioned 'Cactus Jack,' it means you're better off not asking any more questions. Tonight is the first time I exercised the code." Hesitant, she petitioned, "Johnny, I considered inviting Pete to move in with me. The house is half yours. Are you okay with that?"

Oh, man. "Of course, Sis. If he's the one for you, go for it." *Karen.* Stretching, I urged, "Let's get this over with!"

In the parking lot, Melissa drove up in a vivid orange Ford Escort. One time, I probed Bill why he didn't own a fancier ride. The Outlaws used public transportation and rarely employed the car to escape the city. Parked on the avenues, the vehicle absorbed a trouncing. No use keeping a nicer automobile.

As Bill's wife dashed to embrace her husband, I apprehensively watched Vince exit the passenger side. Grinning, he wore my travel clothes: black slacks and a decent blue button-down shirt. Clean-shaven and long hair slicked back in a ponytail, the man resembled a yuppie version of a stockbroker.

Ranzetta clenched a hamburger in one fist as I rushed forward. Mouth stuffed, he mumbled into my ear, "Fucking starved for protein. I couldn't wait. Bill, your woman didn't feed me. I hated being an unwilling sex slave."

"In your wet dreams," Melissa rebuked. "Every few hours, I kept giving you food, and you puked up everything! Crackhead, I'm done mopping up your mess." She distributed bags, and we used the Ford's hood as a dinner table. "What's the scoop? On the drive, we passed that giant red-and-white antenna. Do you surmise Karen is held there?"

"For entertainment, Reynolds schlepped us across Bergen County. Today, we learned he worked as an engineer at a number of radio stations before prison. They invented FM technology at the Armstrong Tower, so. . ." Queasily, I contemplated the quarter-pound of beef. "Guys, we need to find Karen soon. I'm not sure what shape she's in or how we might free her. Any ideas?"

Jane mapped a rough diagram on the dirty hood. "The Alpine Tower is an area I patrol. Obviously, surprise can be used to our advantage. There is one driveway in, off of 9W. Reynolds will see us a mile away if we use that. A few trails wind through the adjacent forest, and a fire road ends at the border.

I carry bolt cutters we can use on the security fence. Six or seven structures of different sizes are situated on the complex. The trick is to figure out where Karen's at." Wrapping it up, she pegged a rectangle at the focal point of the sketch. "This is the lab where Edwin Armstrong performed FM research. Any questions?"

"Yeah, I have one," Vince replied, eyes ablaze. "Who gets to take out this motherfucker?"

Emulating the smart kid in school, I was the quickest to raise a palm.

The Escort tailgated us to a new residential development south of the radio aerial. Houses in various stages of completion ringed the cul-de-sac. In the gutter, standing under powerless streetlights, I longed for the moon. Restlessly, I snatched the Winchester, longing to release its wrath.

Metal glinted as my sister dug in the bottomless duffel bag, conveying weapons to Melissa and Vince. Huddled close, she ordered, "Obey my directions. If you get an opportunity to make a shot without harming Karen, don't hesitate. Got it?"

The posse nodded grimly. Single file, we followed her along a firebreak. The colossal tower loomed uphill though gaps in the trees. Noticing the steel lattice creation many times on the highway, I never pondered its purpose or history. Spotlights brightened the three crossbars. The antenna had to be five hundred feet tall.

The compound came into sight. Jane was correct regarding the barrier. Three yards tall and topped with prickly coils of barbed wire, this strong deterrent prevented the adventurous from scaling the aerial. At chain links, I differentiated separate constructions: a couple of Quonset huts to the left and a shed in the foreground. The warehouse blocked our vision of the large two-story brick edifice, which had to be Armstrong's laboratory.

Sal boosted the cutters to the lock of a small gate built into the fence. Touching his arm, I shook my head. "Reynolds might be expecting us to sneak in this way. Let's search for a place less conspicuous."

The group crept to the extreme end of the acreage. The barricade bulged at a jumble of discarded wood and tangled tin. "Here," I suggested.

Snapping though the thick links with the ease of snipping telephone wire, Harris widened the gap as we stepped into the facility. A sizeable water tank was stationed to our left; the Quonset huts were straight ahead. A paved road led to the domed assemblies.

"Scout out that building," I directed to Vince, Bill, and Melissa. Vigilantly, I moved with Sal and my sister along the ridged wall toward the front. I put an ear to the rust. One door open, I peered in the shed. Seeing the tan Coronet, my pulse raced. The hood felt cold under my palm. *Reynolds has been here a while!*

I jumped as Jane grabbed my elbow. "Johnny!" she hissed. "Something's happening in there. The interior went dark."

We rendezvoused with those congregated between the huts. "Reynolds' car is in that garage," I said, forking a thumb past my ear. "My sister saw a lamp go out in the main building. This is probably a trap. If anyone wants out, this is the time." Ranzetta snorted and spat in the dirt. "Check the weapons a final time, we're going in." Chambering a shell, I heard the deadly clicks of bullets loading and hammers cocking. Single-minded expressions waited my command. *Game time!* "One last thing," my voice wavered, "there is no other bunch of people I'd rather be with tonight. Sal, you don't need to be here. I would just like to say—"

"John, everyone knows that we're your best friends, even Sal," Vince sighed, gripping the hulky neck. "Beyond doubt, we're about to die, but what the heck. You sure as shit can't live forever." Laughing, he sprinted toward the largest structure.

"Stop!" I sputtered, chasing the figure running across the vacant parking lot. Sidestepping behind an overflowing dumpster, the team joined us. I cautiously wiggled the knob of the backdoor—locked.

"Bill, bring Melissa and Vince, and investigate the left side. We'll take the right. Try to look inside. Meet at the entrance. Don't go in," Jane instructed.

Sal and I tailed my sister around the corner. Seven sets of windows lined the two levels. "Where did the light turn off?" I questioned.

"Over there, where we were." Jane motioned for a leg up to peek in a windowpane. Lowered to the earth, she whispered, "I recognized Reynolds in the shadows, maybe asleep."

"Did he have a gun? Did you see Karen?" I inquired breathlessly.

"Not that I noticed."

"Are you confident it was him?"

"Johnny, I saw an old guy with half his face missing, wearing a hat. Hmm, does that resemble our neighbor?" My sister sounded irritated at having her word questioned.

"Yes, it does. What do we do next?"

"Move up a few windows, and I'll try again." We inched onward, assured Sal had us covered.

Near the front, I lifted her again, longer before she signaled for me to lower her. "Big room, thirty feet high. He'll hear us entering."

The rest of the gang crouched by a brass globe sculpture. "Anything?" Bill asked.

"Reynolds is situated indoors, no trace of Karen," Jane replied. "What about you?"

Melissa shook her head.

The facade consisted of double doors. The radio station's call sign, W2XMN, was inscribed in the lintel. Ranzetta skulked up the steps and twisted the handle. "Unlocked," he mouthed, easing one squeaky side open.

Heart palpitating, I trailed him into the dim interior, allowing the remainder to enter. Gathered at the midpoint of the expanse, the incessant ticking of a clock amplified the stillness.

The click of a switch flooded the chamber with the blinding glare of fluorescent fixtures. Startled, I squeezed the 12-gauge's trigger. Lead pellets blasted the width, peppering a rack of antique radios and blowing out a window. Bill seized the barrel, aiming the muzzle away.

Martin Reynolds stooped in a hallway at the rear, dressed in the same stained coveralls. A derby topped his grinning visage. Surveying the weapons, he casually stood and raised his empty hands overhead. As Bill freed the shotgun, I pumped once, the spent shell skittering underneath a table. I aimed square at his chest.

Reynolds chuckled. "Whoa, Johnny. No reason to get excited."

Relinquishing his revolver to Jane, Sal darted to frisk the man. "Clear. He's unarmed."

"Sir, it is delightful to make your acquaintance," my former neighbor beamed, extending a palm to Harris. "Hello, my name is Martin Reynolds." Handshake unrequited, he appraised my friends. "Bill, from what I've heard, you are doing strikingly well on Wall Street. Oh, I am very proud of you. And your charming wife has matured nicely!"

"What do you want, Reynolds? Where's Karen?" I exclaimed, ears humming since the bang.

Amused, he turned his full attention to me. "Johnny. Now you hunger to communicate. The other day, you raced off before we got a chance to chat. In case you wanted to know, my leg and hand are killing me."

Springing, I placed the hot shaft of the Winchester firmly beneath the scarred chin. "I don't have time for chitchat, you piece of crap. *Tell me. Where the fuck is Karen?*"

"Go on, shoot. Succeed where I failed." Reynolds enfolded his fingers around my trigger guard. "Kill me, Johnny. Exterminate the vermin!"

Vince slid past the archway to explore the facility. Calling Karen's name, Melissa accompanied him.

"May I rest these weary bones?" Reynolds requested, tugging the barrel from under his jaw.

"Sit over there, chump," Sal directed, leading the man to a chair, handgun to the nape of the neck.

"You doubtlessly want to hear my story. Why I am the way I am. Maybe you youngsters can help get both my oars in the water. Get the bats out of my belfry, so to speak. Become 'cured.' Isn't sanity a miracle taken for granted? In the meantime, we'll bravely wait until your friends return. I won't recite this declaration twice."

Doors slammed, and cries for Karen echoed throughout the building.

"Johnny, she isn't here." Reynolds winked conspiratorially.

I slammed the gunstock into the unblemished side of his mug. Head rocking, a jagged abrasion ripped across a cheek. "Where is she?" I bellowed, retracting an arm to club harder.

The searchers reappeared, bearing scowls of frustration. "Karen isn't here," Melissa grunted, observing the situation. "Honey, let me see that a minute," she demanded, reaching for the Colt. Bill's wife snapped the black patch over Reynolds' missing eye and roughly jammed the barrel into the void. The cannon clacked loudly as she thumbed the hammer. "Talk, fuckface!"

Breathless and in pain, he stammered, "Melissa, Melissa. Johnny already tried to drum some sense into me while you rummaged in the storeroom. Truly, I haven't a thing to lose.

Once I make my confession, I'll disclose exactly where your friend is."

Her face a mask of anger, she withdrew the six-shooter, aiming at Reynolds' nose.

"Grab a chair. Take a load off. Relax. This old man will spin a tale of hardship and heartache." As his audience remained standing, he swung his head in consternation. "You folks presumably think Daddy took me behind the woodshed to sodomize or beat me. Sorry, but my childhood wasn't like that. I had wonderful parents, similar to yours," Reynolds reminisced, glancing my way. "Dad carried out all the normal fatherly pursuits: played catch, brought me fishing, and taught me how to ride a bicycle. Mother helped me with schoolwork. Academically, I earned exemplary grades. The family used to sit and listen to the radio, the *Shadow* our favorite. Those pleasant, intimate moments sparked interest in my professional field of expertise."

His gaze lingered longingly on the enormous antenna outside the window.

"A brother supported everything I did. No, gentle friends, my upbringing had no negative impact on who I grew to be. Following high school, I studied engineering, my supplementary education rudely interrupted when America got suckered into that ludicrous European war. Uncle Sam put a rifle in my right hand, condoms in my left, and sent my ass off to invade France. Shooting Germans was extremely stimulating for a wide-eyed lad, and I quickly became addicted to collecting human lives. As my detachment slept, oftentimes, I made excursions into neighboring villages, seeking the comfort of young ladies." Reynolds leered at Melissa, realigning the cloth pad. "On enchanted evenings, I might happen upon a blossoming *jeune fille* such as your—"

Bill's shoe extended, smashing into Reynolds' sternum. The felt hat flew as the seat toppled rearwards, spilling to the cement. Hunched, my fingers wrapped his trachea. *Choking.* Vince and Sal pulled me aside. Chair upright, they roughly re-seated the captive and crushed the bowler onto his cranium.

"I struck a nerve," Reynolds panted, head sagging and eye-ball mischievously raking upward. "Please excuse me. I must be more respectful telling my biography. Now, where were we?" My friends glowered in reticence as he dramatically watched for a response. "Ah yes, my penchant for the young women. It's fair to say, one date with me, and you won't need another." Hysterical, the man tittered, tears wetting the un-marked cheek.

In a flash, Vince stepped forth, blowing a hole in the murder's knee. Reynolds let out a shrill yowl and tumbled to the floor, keening.

"Jesus, Ranzetta!" Harris blurted, vaulting over the chair. I couldn't believe the size of the crater in the hard surface. Skillfully tearing a rag, he cinched a tourniquet around the bleeding thigh. "Brother, we're trying to find the girl. If this asswipe's pushing up daisies, it's not going to help our mission!"

Shaken, we dragged the shrieking man onto the seat. "Sorry," Vince apologized, yanking Reynolds by the hair. "This stupid fantasy better be winding up pretty damn fast. Chum, I'm strung out and lost my patience when you were rambling about your sick perversities."

Wheezing in anguish, although able to verbalize, he resumed, "Such potential, yet look at what you've become. Mr. Ranzetta is a perfect example of a juvenile growing up in a dysfunctional household who *remained* a failure. People are who we are, and nothing can change that."

Indignantly, my friend began to raise the revolver and then reconsidered.

"Let's skip ahead. The youth of this generation are so impatient, and I'm losing copious amounts of blood." Reynolds managed the pain and haltingly persisted, "The war was won, blah, blah, blah. A veteran, I returned to the United States and moved to Haworth with my new bride." The blanched face glanced at Bill. "Amazingly, I kept it under wraps for a few years. You know, stayed out of trouble. Elizabeth gave birth to sweet Nicole. A damn good daddy, my daughter was my precious jewel. Henceforth, I lived a fairly normal existence until Nicole fell ill with the measles. My princess burned three horrible days with fever. Encephalitis finally reaped my innocent angel."

Reynolds guided his hands to his temples, blood smeared through thinning scalp. "After the funeral, the marriage deteriorated rapidly. One day, my wife came home early and caught me dismembering a stray Siamese in the bathtub. Ironically, that kind of put a fork in it," Reynolds smirked. "Elizabeth packed her belongings and went to live with a spinster sister in Ohio."

"Finished?" I questioned calmly. "You have to tell us where Karen is."

"Johnny, we're nearly done. The house uninhabited, I tried to distract my sinful impulses by joining a men's society."

"The Freemasons," I said, convinced an essential question should be asked.

"Yes, the Masons," Reynolds yelped. "Just a second, please." Eyelids fluttering, he groaned, "The fraternity introduced Brother Christopher. Creatively, my strange mentor illuminated the phenomenal world of pleasure and pain. Ecstasy for me, agony for others . . . before long, I developed profitable side businesses selling finely crafted bondage furniture and accessories to the thriving local S & M community."

"Those torture machines you built in the basement," Vince stated, rapidly pacing.

"And in the garage, I created a haven for those with similar passions."

"Is that when you started killing those women?" Melissa grimaced. "That got you off?"

"By all means, dear one." The man's lips warped in a sneer or smile, horrid to differentiate. "With Elizabeth and Nicole gone, I eventually untethered, a helium balloon floating into outer space. There was no longer any motivation to curb my dark desires. Does that label me a fiend, to give myself a wee bit of enjoyment?" Reynolds' stare met mine. "And Johnny, you will be thrilled to learn your—"

In slow motion, I watched Melissa's slender arm gracefully rise. The woman stood sideways, face in profile toward Reynolds. Hardened green eyes captured the authoritative flash of the Colt's muzzle. *BOOM!* As the gun kicked, a tremendous jet of flame leapt across the divide, tickling the raw side of the man's head. In mid-sentence, the monster of my nightmares evaporated in a vortex of red spray. Jittering, the eyeball curled back as the jaws flopped open in shock. The chair's front legs thumped to the deck, pitching him downwards. The spurting skull bounced against the corner of the steel desk on the journey to oblivion.

"Mel!" Bill wailed in the pandemonium. "Jesus, I thought you only wanted to intimidate him!"

Melissa's arm lowered, focusing wonderingly at the waxing pool of blood and brains. She exhaled and unemotionally turned to Jane. "Trigger's a mite sensitive. May need to have that adjusted." Easing forward the hammer and passing the pistol to her husband, she walked outside. The door slammed.

"Holy mother of God," my sister exclaimed, contemplating the mess.

Ranzetta tucked his handgun in the waist of his trousers. "I counted on putting an end to that cocksucker myself. Old Mr. Reynolds really jangled my nerves." Gazing admiringly at Bill, he complemented, "Your woman sure has some balls. You wouldn't believe the stuff Melissa said at the motel. During our time alone, she provided tons of helpful insights to lead me along the proper road to recovery. Anyone got a cigarette?"

Bill gasped in exasperation and departed to track down his wife.

"Someone should mop this up," I mumbled numbly. With the kidnapper offed, how could we find Karen?

"Got it under control," Harris volunteered. "Luckily, I have experience as a cleaner. There are tools in the carport. Get outdoors, and look for the girl."

"Thanks, Sal. Hopefully, no one heard those gunshots."

Jane mused, "In Alpine, folks keep their yaps shut. We'll have to deal with the Dodge, too."

The Outlaws engaged in a fiery dispute on the patch of grass in front of the lab.

Brandishing her fists, Melissa proclaimed, "Somebody had to do it!" She was pissed.

"Well, why did it have to be you? What if the cops figure it out? Did you forget we recently had a baby?" Bill protested. The 45 and his wife's pistol swayed from his hands.

"Stop it!" Vince appealed. "Later, you kids can debate the thin line between good and evil. Right now, we're going to locate Karen. Fan out, and search the entire property." Agitated, he hastened to reconnoiter the sheds.

The Outlaws argued as I sprinted over the turf, nearing the huge radio tower.

A few locked, shipping containers clustered around the mammoth blocks anchoring the foundation. I craned my neck upwards. The frame of the structure resembled an electrical pylon. A ganglion of conduits packed the interior and dispersed wires to multitudes of aerials and microwave dishes. Circling the bottom, I sighted a staircase zigzagging up the spire. Twenty feet up, a gate prevented further access.

Annoyed, I hustled to the main building to obtain the cutters. Entering the intensely lit room, my stomach reeled. A blue tarp preserved the flooring. Reynolds lay spread-eagled on his posterior, goggling blindly at the ceiling. The corpse jiggled as Sal enthusiastically hacked off a hairy thigh. "What can I do for you, John?" he inquired, pausing to wipe sweat off his brow with a forearm.

"Bolt cropper?" I gestured with fingers, imitating a scissoring motion. The gruesome picture was etched into my memory—more fodder for nightmares.

"Over there," Harris responded, using a bloody digit to point to the bench. "Don't wander too far. I may require that baby again. Small chunks," he murmured. Breathing deeply, he lifted the tree saw and recommenced butchering.

I grabbed the tool and sprinted to the mast. Ascending to the gateway, I snapped the hasp on a brand-new lock. The portal open, I climbed upon the lowest platform. The apex a long way up, I couldn't spot Karen. This effort might be a merry chase. Starting up the first bank of red-painted stairs, each staircase ended at a catwalk crossing to the connecting set of steps. One hundred seventy-five feet above the ground, I began to distinguish the three crossbars jutting from the tower. My knees ached and burned. Through the filigree of angled crossbeam ribs, I identified an object hanging at the tip of a girder. *Karen?*

"John, how are you doing up there?" Vince hollered at the base.

"Get help!" I shouted, continuing up.

As I proceeded, the antenna narrowed, while the red-and-white stairways shortened. Arriving at the buttress of the lowest framework, I observed a ramp heading to a wider platform. The iron grate reminded me of the factory footways. Listening to the metallic ringing of Ranzetta and the crew progressing higher, I advanced one hundred-fifty feet to the terminus. Warning bulbs blinded me as I climbed. A body hung above from the top crossbar. With a surge of adrenalin, I ran up the stairs, moving faster.

I rushed onto the middle trestle, where Karen dangled, strapped into a yellow harness. The girl rotated by a cable attached to the upper scaffolding.

She's four hundred feet in the air!

"Karen!" I screamed hoarsely. "Karen!" The rig spiraled. "Hold on!" Her arms and legs were bound, mouth gagged with silver tape.

"Johnny!" Jane clamored at the aerial's core. "Stay there. We'll determine if she can be pulled up or let down."

Melissa joined me as the others scaled the additional hundred steps to the top. Looking up, she spoke words of encouragement.

Vince and Bill hunched atop the rope suspending Karen, soon united by my sister and Sal. The foursome deliberated various options.

"John, we're in a position to lower her to you!" Bill yelled. "The line should be long enough."

"It better be," Melissa muttered. "Be careful."

Reaching past the lip, Sal released the rope while Bill and Vince braked the descent. Karen jerked downwards, inch by inch. "You're doing great!" I cried, knuckles white. *She's so close!* A robust breeze blew her away from the tower.

The cable suddenly slipped ten feet, jouncing to a standstill twenty feet overhead. "Apologies, Ms. Schmidt!" Ranzetta called. "The view's lovely up in the clouds. What's the weather forecast at fifty thousand feet?" In distress, her eyes rolled.

Karen endured the snaillike trip, now four yards above grasping hands. *So, so near.* "It's all right. You're almost here," I cheered. Level to the catwalk, the hostage sailed out with each gust. I prayed for the wind to subside, *and it did!* As the pendulum veered back, we towed the tackle over the railing and to the grating.

Melissa and I unhooked the rope and waited for Sal to arrive with a switchblade to slice the cable ties restraining Karen's wrists and ankles. As I smoothly peeled off the adhesive, she burst out anxiously, "Where is he?"

"Everything is okay. Melissa handled Mr. Reynolds." A vivid image of exploding grey matter flashed in my mind. "He's gone permanently. Let's bring you home," I said softly, cleaving the bindings.

Karen's appendages were numb from lack of circulation. Carrying her to the center of the tower, I noted spotty bandages wrapping the pinkie and index of her left hand.

As I massaged Karen's calves, she described being accosted at knifepoint in the legal firm's parking garage. "Coming in after lunch, I felt a blade on my throat. He had to be hiding behind a column or vehicle. Reynolds tied my hands, took my keys and forced me into the trunk of his automobile. I heard my Mercedes' engine start and he left. Ten minutes later, he returned and drove us onto the street. As I attempted to kick out a taillight, the motor stopped. The lid opened, and that asshole gave me a choice: fingers or my head." Karen winced. "I assumed he'd fillet me right then. When I didn't give an answer, the prick slashed my fingers, saying I got off easy. The creep said I was lucky to still be alive." Puzzled, she examined my face. "Reynolds couldn't kill me because 'John wouldn't appreciate that.' What did he mean?"

"I'm honestly not certain. That crackpot left enough clues for us to ultimately locate him holed up in Armstrong's laboratory. Seemingly eager to confess, Reynolds told his life story and the reasons for his terrible crimes. In fact, I suspect he was confiding something specific when Ms. Trigger-happy ended the conversation." I glanced disapprovingly at the executioner.

Melissa shrugged and wrapped an arm around Bill. "Even that turd understood you two ought to be together."

"We have to get down and finish cleaning up," Jane urged. "Can you walk?"

Karen smiled in gratitude and rose shakily. "Ah, I can feel my legs. Get me off this birdcage."

Helping her descend the tower's stairs, we crossed the green to the lab. "Wow," she breathed, seeing Reynolds carved into a baker's dozen.

"Who wants to wrap up this garbage?" Sal asked. Vince, Bill, and I kneeled and rolled chunks of meat into strips of plastic. Duct-taping the packages, my sister threw the pieces into trash bags.

Melissa found Karen a bottle of water and mopped the gore off the floor, walls, and furniture. Without the resources or time to replace the damaged sash or fill in buckshot and bullet holes, there was a boatload of evidence left to be discovered by the morning shift. It was time to go; we'd have to take our chances.

The Gates of Hell

Sunday Morning—June 15, 1986

OUTSIDE ARMSTRONG'S LAB, the morning sky brightened. Hurriedly, we rammed the garbage sacks, saw, and blood-stained chair into the Coronet's trunk and exited via the front gate. At the cars, Jane suggested meeting at the river to "Give that turd the sendoff."

As I steered the Dodge along the sloping Henry Hudson Drive to the base of the Palisades cliffs, the Outlaws followed in the Jeep. Karen looked pale and withdrawn. "How are you?" I inquired, reaching for her hand.

Motionlessly, she stared ahead. "I should call Eric to inform him I'm safe. He must be flipping out."

"Your fiancé?"

"Eric told you that?" Karen responded, turning away.

Feeling rejected, I fixated on the raw pain. "That makes sense. As soon as this piece of business is settled, we can find a phone."

Dense fog seeped over the banks of the Hudson. The Alpine Boat Basin was empty, apart from a handful of coffee-drinking anglers sitting in lawn chairs by the seawall.

In the rear seat, Jane instructed, "Park at the north part of the marina." Harris and Ranzetta dozed around her. "There," she added, guiding us onto a narrow path leading to the end of a stone wharf.

Exhausted, we assembled around the Coronet. Screeching seagulls circled skyward as Sal and Bill began hauling out the trash.

"Hold on a sec," I requested. "Put the bags back in. I thought of a better idea." Slamming the lid, I opened the driver's side doors and cranked down the glass. "Lower the windows, please."

Before shifting into neutral, I yanked the Blessed Virgin Mary off the dashboard. *My souvenir!* After a quick glance, we pushed the automobile to the jetty's edge, and it splashed hood-first into the river. Murky water gushed past the windowsills as the Dodge floated through the grey mist. A few seconds later, the tip of the radio antenna sunk below the ripples.

"Does anyone want to say a few last words?" Vince asked, smirking. "Ashes to ashes, dust to dust. . ."

"Fare thee well, douche bag," I muttered.

"Ditto," Bill concurred. "Rot in hell."

Sal's closing benediction was "Fuck him—and the horse he rode in on."

"That was very moving," Jane said sarcastically, retreating to the Cherokee. "Let's blow this pop stand."

Karen lingered on the shore, focusing downstream at the few oily bubbles marking the spot. Nudging her arm, I coaxed, "We really need to go."

En route to the Escort, we discussed alibis. "Stick to the same story," Bill advised, yawning.

"Yeah, I spent the night dancing in a punk club downtown," Melissa rehearsed. "That's all I remember."

"Karen's version is the most important," I emphasized. "The particulars have to be plausible."

"Okay, I'll keep the facts vague and won't even mention Reynolds. An unknown person grabbed me at work and held me captive. Something interrupted his course of action, and I escaped."

Jane pondered a moment, slapping the steering wheel. "That's perfect. Tell the detectives you were blindfolded and didn't see anything. Where did they hold you prisoner? I mean, before you got loose and called for help?"

"The police will connect her to the mess in Armstrong's laboratory," Bill murmured.

"Not necessarily," Ranzetta mused. "Not if she turns up far from here. Any of you heard of the 'Gates of Hell'?"

"Those foul sewers in Clifton?" Jane replied skeptically.

"The one and only. A natural hiding place for a freak like Reynolds."

Wearily, Bill questioned, "What are you talking about?"

"Over the years, I've slogged those storm drains and never explored the entire layout. The underground channels unwind everywhere beneath the Black Prince Distillery. There were multiple times when I've run outta there screaming."

Bill started laughing, "You're joking, right?"

"I'm serious. The Gates of Hell have worse juju than Ceremonies."

Displeased, Melissa inquired, "And why should you bring Karen there?"

Vince snapped the sweaty shirt off his neck. "Honestly, I'm not sure. The notion just popped into my mind."

"Cops are always reporting stories regarding the Gates, so I know they're located by the Pathmark. Access is illegal, but juveniles enjoy venturing down there for kicks." Jane ruminated, "Ranzetta could be correct. They may be an excellent venue to stage a hostage scenario."

"Tell us, Vince, what makes that sewage system unusually scary?" Bill asked.

"First off, nobody has determined how old they are or who built them. The walls and roof are ancient. The earlier sections are stone blocks, and the newer parts are brick. It's all completely covered with demonic graffiti and upside-down crosses. A lot of it's pretty offensive. Urban legend states that the Gates of Hell are comprised of seven levels. The further you descend, the closer you get to meeting Satan."

Grimacing, I said, "I thought he dwelled at Devil's Tower. I'm not taking Karen anywhere dangerous. Don't you think she's been through enough?"

"John, evil is omnipresent," Melissa said.

I questioned, "Karen, will escaping from the storm drains work?"

"If Vince and Jane consider the tunnels safe, I'm fine with their opinions." She breathed heavily. "At this point, I want the whole ordeal done with. For evidence, I'd leave rope or tape. What if the authorities don't accept my account?"

"You're lacking two fingers. What's not to believe? Such a shame the cops will waste time searching and never find your kidnapper," Melissa answered, scrubbing blood spots out of her palms.

The Ford's bumper sticker depicted a woman swinging below a multicolored hang glider advertising Cypress Gardens. Amazingly, the car made a round trip to Florida.

"What a day. Now we must tend to our son," Bill groaned, pushing himself out the door. "Good luck, Karen."

"Hey, thanks, buddy," I said, reaching to grip my friend's shoulder. "We'll drop off these fellas and drive her to Clifton."

As the Outlaws headed to the George Washington Bridge, I wondered to what degree our future relationship might be affected by today's horrors.

On the quiet ride to the Newark projects, I strained to stay awake. Harris slept, lolling against the passenger window. Squashed between Vince and Jane, Karen nodded to herself, deep in reflection.

Peering in the rearview mirror, I inquired, "Are your fingers hurting? We should stop at a drug store and buy a bottle of pain medication."

Karen's eyes met mine. "The stumps ache like hell, and that's the way I want them when the police arrive. If I'm lucky, they'll allow me to go to my house."

"I truly regret what happened. This isn't exactly how I envisioned my visit to New Jersey. For a while, I hoped—"

"John, I'm mixed up right now. When I originally saw you, I was so angry. Still am, I suppose. The thing is, I'm also happy to see you." She certainly did look confused.

"Karen, I didn't come here to screw up your life. I don't intend to interfere. Back in college, I abandoned you. I was a jackass," I mumbled.

"Agreed, but you saved me, risking everything to come to the rescue. Not everyone would do that." Scowling, she studied the red welts encircling her wrists.

"Yes, and I wasn't the only one. The whole team had a key role in finding you." The Stella Wright Homes complex came into view, appearance unimproved by daylight. A pair of demolished pickups elevated on cinderblocks marked the last parking spot.

Karen sighed, "It took Reynolds to bring us together. Twice."

We woke Sal, and his eyelids popped open. "Home sweet home," he grumbled, exiting the automobile.

"Thanks," I said, hugging the powerful man. "Sal, you're an awesome dude, and we wouldn't have freed Karen without your support. I'll always be grateful and in your debt."

"Glad to assist. John, in the near future, I may request that you make a small financial investment." Harris grinned. "Trust me, you won't be sorry." Waving a hand, he shooed away a gaggle of kids vying to sell meth.

The sun soared in the azure sky, and heat was already radiating from the gummy sidewalk. I asked Ranzetta how he was feeling.

Pensively, my friend gazed at the brick buildings. "Maybe it's time to move the hell out of this rathole and start again someplace nicer. I appreciate what you folks did." He advised Karen, "Give this blockhead a break. Life's too short to spend pissed off."

Nodding into his shoulder, she wiped away a teardrop. "Take care of yourself, Vince. Sal, if you ever require any legal advice, please contact me."

"Ma'am, it's been a pleasure," Harris stated, bowing deeply.

Vince frowned. "Watch yourself in the sewers. The main entryway is a big concrete outlet in the side of the hill. A mile inside, there are a few enormous square chambers. Your tootsies will get soaked, but as long as it doesn't rain, those rooms feature elevated ledges that are dry. Tell the cops that's where Reynolds kept you hostage. This is important. Once you enter, go straight, and don't turn onto any secondary passageways. Seriously, you'd be lost forever. Oh yeah, here's one final detail." Frazzled, he rubbed his knuckles on the back of his skull. "A spirit guards the Gates of Hell. There are railroad ties above the mouth. Knock three times. Don't disrespect Red-Eyed Mike."

The two men disappeared within the bleakness of the projects.

Route 21 followed the Passaic River toward Clifton. "Sal and I can help Vince. I'll enroll him in a drug rehabilitation program," Jane pledged. "The guy is no dummy. We simply have to keep him on the right track."

My sister told Karen of my clumsy attempt at drug rehabilitation. Melissa's nursing skills had really improved Ranzetta's rapid recuperation.

"After school, we left him behind. I didn't stay in touch," Karen said regretfully. "But, as you're well aware, life goes on."

"What's the strategy? We bring Karen to the Gates of Hell. Then what?"

Jane's brows knit in concentration. "Assuming law enforcement commenced the search," she beamed widely, "a concerned citizen might tip off the police, reporting a suspicious man dragging a young woman into a storm drain."

"Tie me up," Karen said. "When the cops show up, I'll say the kidnapper left me alone for some reason."

"Sounds like a done deal," Jane concluded with satisfaction. "There's a coil of rope in my gear. When we near the Pathmark, watch for a pay phone."

"There's one!" Karen exclaimed, pointing at a glass booth.

"Have the authorities transport you to an emergency room," my sister requested. "Those fingers demand medical attention. What did that crazy fuck use?"

"Pruning shears, the kind at the hardware store. So, I presume this ends my piano-playing career," Karen responded ruefully. "Words can't express my gratitude, Jane." Over the front seat, she clung to my sister. "Don't worry; I'll leave your names out of my statement."

I parked at the supermarket. Leaving Jane in the vehicle, we scrambled up the gravel ballast onto the railway. Aimed south, I led the way to a railcar stationed a mile along the track. The midday sun scorched.

"John, are you okay?" Karen asked, tugging my sleeve.

Looking up from the endless creosote-soaked ties, I noted the sheen of sweat shimmering on her colorless face. "Yup, just famished, I guess. Sure is hot. What about you?"

She replied, smiling wanly, "Hanging in there. I must rest soon."

At the switch, we trailed the siding to a black tank railroad car.

"There!" Karen indicated a manmade structure shaded by twisted elms. On the border of the park, Weasel Creek trickled between moss-covered rocks.

Negotiating the steep, rugged slope, we stood on a bulkhead overlooking a broad drainage ditch. One-handed, she swung past the lip, grasping the descending iron rungs. To the left, a huge oval culvert spewed filthy soup. Directly ahead, the rectangular entrance to the sewer had been clearly marked. In crude block letters, an intellectual had spray-painted the warning: "THOSE THAT ENTER THESE GATES OF HELL ARE DOOMED! YES THAT MEANS YOU TOO STUPID!" During many decades, generations had contributed layers of exceedingly sordid proclamations.

Flashlight and backpack of supplies checked, I took Karen's arm and entered. A ripening wind blew back our hair as the boxlike threshold tapered into a smaller tunnel. The floor was horizontal and bare, but flowing liquid gurgled somewhere distant.

"We forgot to tap on the railroad ties!" she exclaimed, turning to peer at the waning oblong of daylight.

"We ticked off Red-Eyed Mike," I answered uneasily. Disgusted, I aimed the beam downward, hoping she hadn't noticed the monstrous albino spiders plastering the ceiling. "Let's continue moving."

The disturbing graffiti coating the reinforced arched ceiling became increasing graphic. A horn blared far inside the shaft. The deep chord reverberated throughout the hub of tunnels.

"What in the hell was that?" Karen cried, clutching my elbow.

"That's a New Jersey Transit train passing overhead," I responded with false confidence.

A black pool mirrored a crosspiece proclaiming: "NINE DEAD CHILREN BURRIED ON LEVEL THREE."

Initially, we were able to progress moisture-free, sliding to the edges of the tube. Now, groundwater splashed out of various corrugated and precast plumbing fixtures jutting at different heights from the walls.

"Keep your fingers dry," I cautioned, escorting her into the ankle-deep effluent.

Debris cluttered the crawlways, forcing us to maneuver around logjams of garbage, snarls of wire, and what resembled an old-fashioned mining cart filled with broken moonshine bottles. A grated hole illuminated a long tree limb propped against the cement. I glimpsed a patch of smudged sky.

"Wait!" Karen hollered to be heard, arms girdling my waist. The swill roared past, chunks of offal smashing our knees. A bloated raccoon raced by, glazed eyes watching us huddle in the tunnel's intersection. "Give me a second to catch my breath." Pulse slowing, she asked, "Which way?"

"Straight. Vince said to avoid any offshoots," I replied, ignoring the steadily intensifying growls.

"John, what's that howling?" Trembling, her temple pressed against my chest.

"It's water. There's something up ahead!" We entered a cavernous space. Assorted pipes surged dreck, but I no longer had to shout. "This must be the room Ranzetta described. There's the ledge." Eight feet off the floor, a wide concrete shelf spanned joined walls. "Can you remain here until I carry back that branch? We can use it to get up there."

"Are you kidding? If you take that flashlight, it'll be pitch dark!"

"I'll scarcely be gone a minute. I promise."

Karen crouched on a mound of sludge. "Be quick," she pleaded.

Ducking into the passage, I toppled the timber to the ground. I pinned the wood under an armpit and lugged it upstream. Frantic shrieks echoed from the underworld. "Karen!" I yelled, dashing to the chamber. The tiny bulb spotlighted the girl cowering in a niche, palms raised in defense. "What is it?"

"A man ran by. I felt—"

Hastily, I swept the beacon around the desolate compartment. "Nothing here. These drains are too tight to crawl through, and they would've had to pass me." Stressed, I retrieved the limb and braced the makeshift ladder in the corner. "Let me help you climb up."

The grimy mantle proved spacious enough to spread Jane's blanket. Securing the rope, I trussed Karen's wrists and ankles. "Do you want to lie flat or sit?" I questioned, judging my handiwork.

"There's no way I'm laying down. A rat will run across my face!" she stammered.

"What else can I do?" I inquired.

"Don't forget, I couldn't see the abductor."

Utilizing the adhesive, I fashioned a blindfold and slid the mask on her forehead.

"Will you be all right?" In the ray of the flashlight, Karen appeared so frightened. Dazed, I realized I was about to abandon her again. Alone in this hellhole, I'd go mad. *What had Vince been thinking?*

"John, hurry and phone the police. Then return to Georgia until this blows over." Bravely, she held her chin high. "Tape me up, and make it look credible."

Carefully, I sealed Karen's lips and clumsily squeezed her shoulder, a shitty way to say goodbye. Finally, I hurled away the branch and rushed toward the light.

The Visit

Saturday Morning—November 22, 1986

"VINCE, I'M GLAD YOU'RE DOING OKAY." The inexpensive cordless handset picked up the signals of another exchange. To improve my reception, I shifted to a different location on the tiny patio. The combination of weekend, temperature in the mid-sixties and upcoming holiday put me in an unusually good state of mind.

"I resemble the Incredible Hulk, except for the green part," he joked. "Paul is working my butt off, but I'm fine. Eating healthy and staying off the dope. 'Just say no,' that's what Nancy Reagan preaches. I quit smoking cancer sticks. Can you believe that? Once I learn the ropes, he'll promote me to foreman."

"Wow, that's fantastic news. Hot as hell there?"

"This desert is so parched, I caught two trees fighting over a dog," Ranzetta guffawed. "Seriously, the weather's perfect this fall in Las Vegas. You should jet out to Sin City. Sal stopped by a few weeks ago, and Bill and Melissa are bringing their kid here in the spring. Brother, we'll paint the town! I'll drink ginger ale, of course. Meet my sponsor—what a babe! You should accompany Amber and me to an AA meeting."

Really happy, I laughed. "Karen's coming to visit on Monday for Thanksgiving. She's—"

"Bullshit!" my friend interjected in mock astonishment. "Mon Dieu! The sky is falling; dogs and cats are cohabiting as one—"

"Don't get starry-eyed. This is kind of a test run, you know, to see if I fuck up. We've talked on the phone for months, every night for hours. In the wake of the 'incident,' she stayed with her parents in Haworth to convalesce. No one is saying anything out loud; nevertheless, I'm hoping Karen decides to move down here."

"What about the nerd fiancé?"

"Well, you see, Eric didn't save her," I replied.

"Ha, ha! John, you cad!" Vince ribbed. "I hope it works out for you both. Gotta go. Paul even has me busting my hump on the weekends. The big cheese is trying to keep me on the straight and narrow, but I'm too damn freakin' beat to find any mischief."

"Later, buddy." Hanging up, I went indoors.

I spent the remainder of the afternoon cleaning the apartment. Smokey's green eyes tracked me warily as I vacuumed near his couch. "Someone has to brush you," I complained, dusting clumps of cat hair off the kitchen table.

Taking in the queen-sized bed filling the single bedroom, I prayed that the awaited evenings wouldn't be spent sleeping on the sofa with Smokey.

As I popped a rental into the VCR, the telephone rang. "Hello?"

"John, what are you doing?" Karen asked.

"Relaxing after a busy day preparing the palace for your visitation. Actually, I started *Back to the Future.* Have you seen it?"

"Last year, I saw it in the theater. Michael J. Fox almost gets frisky with his own mother."

"Please tell me you're pulling my leg. Thanks for spoiling the film," I chuckled. "Anyway, I'd prefer to watch the movie with you."

"The studio made a heap of money. Perhaps they'll make a sequel. Hopefully, we can check that out together."

"A man may simply dream," I sighed. "What's going on? You sound tense." My stomach clenched in concern, I fretted that the trip was canceled. "Karen, you're still—?"

"Don't worry; I'm coming down. Just warning you ahead of time, I'm bringing a small surprise."

"What type of present?" I questioned, relieved. "Is it bigger than a breadbasket?"

"Yes, your gift is slightly larger. You'll find out Monday afternoon at Atlanta Airport. Remember, US Airways, 2:27 p.m., Gate D21."

"Karen, I'm excited to see you and the surprise!" Fantasizing all sorts of scenarios, I hung up.

Monday Morning—November 24, 1986

Standing before a wide plate-glass window, I watched the airplane taxiing to the gate. Bedtime had been spent tossing and turning in hope and anxiety. I'd love to report the nightmares stopped since Reynolds' death, but that was wishful thinking. The dreams altered in nature, yet stayed malevolent.

As the jetway extended to the plane's portal, I envisioned Karen in the cabin unbuckling the seatbelt and pulling carry-on luggage from overhead bins. Fidgeting with the roses, I speculated what her revelation could be.

An airline attendant released the door, and a flood of travelers dispersed into the airport. Remaining calm, I scanned each passenger. *There she is!* Waving wildly, I advanced, ready to scoop the woman into my arms. *Somebody is with her, someone rather short!* Smiling, she bent and whispered in the boy's ear while pointing in my direction. *Maybe that's her cousin's son.* Despair fell as I selfishly comprehended my precious moments with Karen might be shared with another person, specifically a kid. This epiphany was quite a jolt.

The pair split from the line, and we met by the arrival and departure monitors. The youth had blondish hair and was nine or ten years old. Gently, she said, "Johnny, this is Mr. Townsend, the man I told you about. This week, he's showing us around Atlanta."

Oh, my God. "Correctamundo, my young lad," I babbled, leaning forward to shake the child's hand. "Johnny, we'll have a splendid time. Be assured, I've arraigned gobs of thrilling activities." Panicked, my brain whirled. *Like what?* "Tomorrow, we're taking a trip to the zoo. Six Flags over Georgia is out of this world, and the Jimmy Carter Library and Museum is a few miles away." Resting a palm on his shoulder, I appeased, "Only kidding regarding the Carter thing. Stone Mountain is oodles more fun. Naturally, on Thanksgiving, turkey is—"

"It certainly appears Mr. Townsend has everything well organized," Karen murmured, a pleased expression pursed on her lips.

"Mom, he's not as tall as you described," Johnny noted.

What the...? Mom? Mom! What's that mean?

"Don't be rude," she reprimanded, studying my reaction.

"Your son is one hundred percent right. Joints compress as humans age and the spine shrinks. I used to be seven feet high and had difficulty passing through doors," I said, hunching to enhance the effect. "Life has immeasurably improved at this elevation." The boy hardly smirked.

Bestowing the flowers and giving Karen an awkward hug, I had a million questions, but this wasn't the occasion for them. On the ride home, we talked of our families and jobs. Johnny sat in the back, listening intently. Mr. Schmidt had been elected as the new mayor of Haworth. Karen had experienced discrimination as the lone female lawyer at the firm, gradually earning admiration by her peers. I chronicled an animated account of Katherine screwing up a major research project. Upper management had decided I might do a better job than she. The humorous tale ended with the punch line: "My boss now works for me!"

Waking to guests, Smokey leapt from the couch in greeting. Johnny gathered up the elongated grey rag doll and paraded around the living room.

Embarrassed, I gave the fifty-cent tour: the kitchen, bathroom and bedroom. "Too bad this place isn't any bigger. Towels are in that closet; you guys use the bed. Smokey and I will camp out here." A huge phony grin stretched my mug.

"Thanks, John. We are most grateful for your hospitality," Karen said, smiling. "This is a nice apartment, and I adore what you've done with the decorating." Its walls bare, the cubbyhole was ultra-depressing.

We went to dinner at Chin Chin Chinese restaurant. "It seems you're doing better?" I inquired, examining her healed nubs.

"Lying quietly, I sometimes feel phantom pain," she mused, touching her thumb between the surviving digits. "Slowly, I'm becoming adept at hiding the disability. Most people do not even notice the fingers are missing."

"Mom slammed her hand in a car door," Johnny muttered skeptically. Chopsticks snapped at a chunk of Mongolian beef. "That's what happened, right?"

"Sure. Your mother's been through a lot, but she's strong. Nothing will hold her back. You're very lucky to have her for a mom."

The tone of the conversation changed instantly when he asked, "So, are you my father? Is that why we're here in Atlanta?"

A spoonful of sweet-and-sour soup went down the wrong pipe, triggering a coughing fit.

"Drink more water, Mr. Townsend!" the boy urged, sliding over the cup.

At this stage, I shouldn't be flabbergasted at his question; nonetheless, the answer remained unclear.

"Johnny, your mom and I need a quick chat," I stammered, glaring at Karen. "Sit tight; we'll be right outside," I promised, pushing away my seat.

Hurrying past the hostess stand, I went outdoors to pace tempestuously beneath an awning. Traffic streamed by as the late sun glittered off storefronts. Karen approached me, her countenance unreadable.

"Is that true?" I questioned, sitting on a low rock ledge.

"Do you want it to be?"

"I don't know, Karen. You just sprung this 'small surprise.' Christ Almighty, I wasn't expecting—"

"That's a good choice of words! I did not *expect* to get knocked up in my freshman year of college. I hardly anticipated my boyfriend, my best friend to dump me. And I definitely wasn't equipped to look after a child, go to school and earn a paycheck at the same time!"

"Why didn't you say something? Didn't you realize, I would—?"

"I had no idea what the great John Townsend might do. I trusted that I could rely on you, but obviously, I was mistaken. Many days, my parents helped babysit my son."

A lively party of customers entered the restaurant.

"What can I do?"

"Come inside, and finish supper. I imagine this news is a shock, but consider how Johnny feels. Your son figured out for himself that you were his father. The boy is no idiot."

Despite the frown, Karen looked gorgeous. Extending a palm, I implored, "Pull me up, buttercup!" The mood suddenly brightened. Reborn, I lost myself in her embrace. "Sorry, baby, I love you so much," I whispered.

"That's grody," Johnny groaned from the doorway. "I'm too grownup to care for a little sister."

Reluctantly, we broke apart, trailing the youngster indoors. Karen and I held hands under the table, unable to bottle up our exhilaration.

"Well?" my son inquired, assessing each of us in turn. "What's the verdict?"

Karen glanced questioningly at me before I responded. "The original plan was to spend this holiday together sightseeing the amazing local attractions. We can still do that. The rides are cool, and it will be fun. On Thursday, we'll feast on turkey and mashed potatoes, topped by a nap. The question is: What happens on Saturday? Do I drop you both off at the airport and we figure out our relationship sometime later? Or do we avoid all that stress and wasted time by solving this problem immediately? Like, right now over fortune cookies. Don't get me wrong; this pledge is a big decision, not to be taken lightly. There is no turning back."

Pausing, I pondered what they contemplated. "Do you understand what I am requesting?" Both nodded solemnly, Johnny peeking at his mom.

"Okay, then, on the count of three, put your hand forward if we're to become a family. If you don't, there are no hard feelings. Agreed?" Eyelids closed, I inhaled deeply. "One . . . two. . ."

Part Four

Road Trip

Tuesday Morning—June 24, 2014

AMERICA LOOKED TOWARD THE PACIFIC SKIES the afternoon the Democratic People's Republic of Korea detonated two suitcase nukes in New York City—one in Times Square and the other in New York Harbor. Our generation's Pearl Harbor, 4/24/2012, took the nation by complete surprise.

"When are we leaving?" my son asked, raptly watching Al Jazeera news.

"This Friday," I replied. "The New Jersey Exclusion Zone opens on June thirtieth. That gives us three days to make Parsippany and get in line."

Unloading the dishwasher, my wife questioned, "Is that enough time?"

"Who knows?" I answered. "Hope so. Did your parents provide the final list? I'm presuming that—"

"Check this out, Dad," John Jr. interrupted impatiently.

The television beamed images of burly troopers netting squatters on the lower east side of Manhattan. Yellow hazmat suits advertised the National Guard. An iPhone must have been used to capture the jerky clips.

"That one's running!" my son exclaimed, rising on the couch. He resembled a younger version of me, but was taller and topped with the thick, dark hair of his mother. "Go, buddy, go!" he cheered at the pixels.

"Calm down, John!" Karen called at the doorway. "That's a female, and she won't get very far."

As usual, my wife was accurate. Air-charged net-guns launched into the sky simultaneously. Large webs trapped the fleeing woman. Tumbling to the trash-covered sidewalk, she bucked like a wild animal. A soldier came into the frame and briskly sprayed a soapy substance on her.

"Gotcha!" John Jr. whooped, falling into the cushions. "That's the nitty-gritty they don't want the public to see."

"As I was saying, I'm worried your parents' salvage list is too long for this trip."

"Honey, Mom and Dad respect the limit is one vehicle. With the three of us going, plus necessities, that leaves room in the trunk and on top. Most of the requests will be for sentimental items such as photos and important papers."

"You're probably right," I conceded, passing through the kitchen and into the garage. Reading the checklist, I surveyed the camping gear massed against the green Honda CRV. The weather forecaster had predicted mild temperatures, so keeping warm shouldn't be a problem. Shrewdly, I monitored the door before reaching onto a shelf and plucking a Glock 19 with boxes of ammo from below a drop cloth. Raising the SUV's rear seat, I hid the firearm and two knives. Weapons were not permitted in the exclusion zones.

Ready for lunch, I re-entered the house. "What's cookin', good lookin'?" I inquired softly, grabbing Karen's backside as she slid pizzas out of the oven.

"Jesus, John!" my wife hissed, twisting away. "What are you trying to do, get me burned?"

"Undoubtedly," I chortled, moving in again.

Grinning, she wielded a serrated pizza wheel from a drawer and held me at bay. "Here, make yourself useful."

Beside the TV, we ate cheese pizza and drank filtrated water.

"Yummy," John Jr. uttered, between mouthfuls. "Where did you manage to find these?"

"Craigslist," his mother replied. "A lady named Mary bakes pizzas from scratch in her basement. Quite an efficient setup. By the way, I traded your stamp collection."

"These are well worth it. Mom, you can't eat stamps."

"Or mail letters," I added. The bombings had been the final straw for the failing US Post Office.

"At least the Internet is still working," Karen sighed, powering up the iPad.

Al Jazeera looped the same old footage of nuclear mushroom clouds towering over New York and telescopic helicopter shots of the aftermath.

"John, turn the channel," I requested in disgust. Viewing those dreadful scenes a thousand times, I never wanted to see the destruction again.

"Dad, there's nothing on except reruns," my son grumbled. Surfing through the limited stations, he settled on a replay of the *Walking Dead*. The half-crazed sheriff drew a 45 and blew the lids off two lurching zombies.

"Just received an email from your sister," Karen announced. "Although Jane's currently committed to law-enforcement work at the Zone, she can meet us in Parsippany."

I questioned hesitantly, "Did she mention how they're feeling?"

"No, your sister hopes we're doing okay. Pete is responding to the treatments. That's all she wrote."

"Oh," I said. "Reply that I can't wait to see her."

The television went dark and silent.

"Christ," John Jr. complained. "That's the second blackout today. The utilities claim they're fixing the issues, but I'm not noticing any improvement."

"Things will get worse before they get better," Karen declared, laying aside the tablet. "You watch too much TV anyway."

"Maybe you're right," he smirked. "I suppose I'll go take a nice extended nap."

"John, on the way to your siesta, please start the generator!" I yelled down the hallway.

A few months after the attack, my son had moved back into the house. Ann, his longtime girlfriend, had left for Los Angeles to be with her parents. John Jr. held onto his job as a copy editor at the *Atlanta Journal-Constitution* until the newspaper ultimately rolled belly up. Now, at age thirty-seven, he was trying to reinvent himself as a blogger. With the national unemployment rate zooming past twenty-two percent, I hoped my son found a more stable livelihood.

"Are you nervous?" Karen asked, needing to talk.

"Nervous of what?" I replied, having a hint of what she referred to.

"This trip to New Jersey. Witnessing the real devastation, not purely what's on television? Radiation, hurtful memories, the journey won't be easy."

The video flickered as voltage returned. "Don't bother!" I shouted. Grabbing the remote, I ended the escalating zombie carnage. "Experts state if the twelve allowable hours in the NJ Zone are not exceeded, the risks are low. The Authority loans radiation detectors and dosimeters to monitor the levels. Radioactivity troubles me, yet it's the people I'm most concerned with. Karen, you read the bulletins."

"If it's so dangerous, why are we going? Mom and Dad aren't hurting for that stuff."

"This is a perfect time to get away," I chuckled. "This year's Townsend family vacation is to Hell!"

"Definitely not Hawaii," my wife exhaled, kicking off her shoes and reclining on the sofa.

Ready for a nap, I tossed extra pillows on the floor and joined her on the cushions. Wrapping my arms around Karen's waist, I murmured into her fragrant hair, "Not this holiday, baby."

Friday Morning—June 27, 2014

Karen jarred me awake. "John, get up," she whispered.

"Didn't hear the alarm," I croaked. "Oh, man." Beat and bleary, I glared at the clock: 3:30 a.m.

In the dream, Martin Reynolds spoke in unknown tongues, shoveling clay on my open casket. The nightmare premiered a disturbing segment exhibiting our cat lying in the bottom of a litter box. Spooky wasn't moving. Frantically, I prodded the limp body with the scoop.

"The boy is busy packing up the car with the ice chest and auxiliary gas cans."

"Oh, swell," I exhaled, tugging on my jeans. "Got the papers?"

"In the bag," she answered, drawing the sheets to make the bed. To enter the Zone, an online appeal was submitted six months ahead of the actual admittance date. One hundred thousand valid lottery applications were tendered, and the Authority drew five thousand. More than four million people in New Jersey had been displaced by tidal wave flooding and radioactive fallout. We were very lucky to be awarded the two-day pass.

In the brightness of the garage, I found my son ratcheting the cargo container straps to the top of the CRV. For the increased capacity, I traded one of the neighbors a surplus rake and packets of tomato seeds.

"Nice job, kid. Are we bringing the whole kit and caboodle?"

"I'm thinking of taking this axe for self-defense. Out on the road, it's better to be prepared."

"That's for sure. Superb idea. Might as well tote this." I handed John Jr. a spade and continued in a lower voice, "A gun and machetes are cached beneath the seat. Don't tell Mom."

Elaborately zippering two fingers across his lips, he threw away the key. "The secret is in the vault. Why, do you reckon we'll need to defend ourselves?"

"Hopefully not, but as you said, can't be too careful."

Karen entered, bearing a tray of coffee and a bag bursting with food. "Ready?"

"Get while the gettin' is good," I responded, setting the cup in the center console.

My wife occupied the passenger seat, and our son curled up on the bench. "Notify me when it's my turn to drive," he requested, fluffing a jacket under his head.

Backing out the automobile, I proceeded north from our sleeping development. The goal was to reach Charlotte, North Carolina, by nightfall. I merged into the influx stalling I-85. Ninety minutes crawled reaching the initial National Guard checkpoint.

The sky started to glow as John Jr. appeared between the front seats. "Are we there yet?" he whined groggily. "I got to drain my dragon."

"Yeah, me too," I agreed, searching for a space to take a break. The rest areas were closed due to lack of state funds. Signaling to cross two lanes, I pulled over a quarter of a mile down a maintenance tract.

In unison, we flooded the depths of a gully. "Ah. . ." my son exhaled. "Where in tarnation are we?"

"Recently passed the marvelous city of Braselton. Long way to go."

"John!" Karen waved. A raised pickup truck came to a standstill behind the Honda. A pair of unkempt males in their twenties lowered themselves to the pavement.

"Howdy, folks!" the tall driver hollered in a southern drawl. He wore camouflage overalls, a black T-shirt, and a Bass Pro Shops cap. "Everything okeydokey here?"

"Yes," I replied, zipping my fly and approaching the men. "We stopped to stretch our legs. The traffic's a bitch."

The passenger resembled a youthful version of the driver. "You can say that again," he admitted, hooking thumbs into his belt. "Do you happen to have any food or gasoline to share with a couple of fellow travelers? We're getting low on rations, and we're a mite hungry."

"Sorry, but we didn't bring anything to spare," John Jr. said in a deep voice. "Excuse me; we'll be on our way."

"Hold up, hold up, my friend," the man pleaded. "My brother and I just need food or, as I stated before, a can of unleaded. Then we can get home."

We shortened the distance to the car, blocked by the driver.

"Take your mitts off of me," I bluffed. "Didn't you hear we didn't pack any extra rations? Get the fuck out of the way. We're leaving." The highway sounded far away.

"That's no way to speak to a—"

Karen brought the heel of the axe onto the driver's skull with a sickening snap. The cap sailed through the air as the broad-shouldered bandit thudded to the earth, felled like a great sequoia.

"Shit!" the younger brother screeched, falling to his knees. "Dale!" he cried, cradling his sibling's bleeding scalp. "Lady, why did you go and do that? We simply wanted food."

John Jr. reached around the blubbering man, locking the stubby neck in a chokehold. Clamping tight, the man's legs kicked dirt before he slumped unconscious.

Dumbfounded, I questioned, "Where did you learn to do that?"

"MMA, Dad," he answered. "Controlled restraint is critical with a sleeper hold. Normally, it's advisable to relax the clench once your opponent passes out."

I glanced at my wife. Judiciously, she toweled the axe clean and stowed the tool between the seats. At the wheel, my son joined the vehicles on the roadway. Karen furnished us with breakfast bars.

"Mom, you almost cracked Dale's coconut," John Jr. said with wonder. "Do you think that guy will live?"

"Hard to say. I choked up on the handle and chose not to use the sharp side. Those morons will rise and shine with headaches, whatever." His mother shrugged. "Parting with our supplies wasn't an option, and those two smelled of danger."

"In the future, we'll be more cautious," I muttered in the rear seat. "Time for a bit of shuteye. Wake me up in an hour."

"Roger, Captain!" my son saluted.

The Honda wallowed and rattled. Sitting up, I became attentive, noticing we were no longer on the interstate. "What's happening up there?" I inquired, squinting at the plume of black smoke.

"Several miles ago, the police made us detour onto this frontage lane," John Jr. responded. The car shuddered over a series of potholes. "A cop said a fire caused the delay."

Above a berm of highway, flames belched from a huge vehicle surrounded by smaller automobiles.

"That's a fuel tanker truck," Karen observed, craning for a clearer perspective. Heads bobbed as an explosion vibrated the chassis, scorching our skin.

A surly policeman directed traffic up an entrance ramp returning to the freeway. Peering backwards, I saw a squad of armored SWAT officers standing by numerous carcasses sprawled across the concrete.

"Possibly a shootout," I hypothesized, turning forward.

"Hijacking gone wrong," my son reasoned. "In the current market, gas is more valuable than gold. What a waste of ten thousand gallons."

Now brooding about the next fill-up, I asked, "What's the gauge indicating?"

"Still got half a tank. Tomorrow, we'll have to get juice."

"No coverage here," my wife groaned, shoving the iPhone in her purse.

"Why, who were you attempting to call?" Keeping the AC shut off to improve mileage, I opened the rear window to suck in air.

"Your mom and my parents, just to let them believe everything is hunky-dory."

"No news is good news," I concluded. Drowsy again, a dull headache pushed behind my eyes. This undertaking had started off badly.

Friday Evening—June 27, 2014

John Jr. and I swapped seats in the humidity of mid-afternoon. Fourteen miles from Charlotte, I exited in Belmont.

"Thanks," I said, accepting the bottle of insect repellant. "Lovely, reeks of pure DEET." Thirsty mosquitoes attacked as we set up the tent in a woodland by the CRV. "This is the life," I joked, scratching the itchy welts rising around my ankles. Propped on a log, we ate sandwiches. Although the hour neared twilight, the riverbank presented an unimpeded view of the big homes and boathouses lining the opposite side of the Catawba.

Half-seriously, my son questioned, "Dad, will we ever be able to stay in a hotel again?" Along with thousands of trailers, FEMA used any available lodging to harbor the millions of people uprooted by the evacuations. Analysts criticized that, without jobs, the motels and hotels could never be emptied of government-sponsored guests. Landlords savored the fat checks.

"Perhaps, John, but not in our lifetimes," I smiled, tossing the water jug. "Remember the time we went to Disney World? The motor court lost the reservation, so we had to sleep in the rental the first night. That goddamn alligator biting the fender at two a.m.?"

Able to obtain reception, Karen quietly updated her parents, wisely omitting our troublesome rest stop. She hung up and passed the phone. "Your mother."

"Hey, Mom," I articulated loudly into the mouthpiece. Simple communication with my eighty-four-year-old mother was onerous. "Wanted to inform you, we're still alive and should be in New Jersey on Sunday."

"Don't forget to visit your father," she urged. "Do you recall where the grave is?"

"Of course I do," I answered. "Dad's by the bell tower. Section U." I didn't clarify my apprehension of dropping by the cemetery. For a few more minutes, she described Scruffy, the neighbor's unruly dog.

"How is your mother doing?" my wife inquired, casting a handful of pebbles into the swift current.

"Mom's doing well, considering. I'm glad she already lived in Atlanta when all this crap happened." Coincidentally, the lights on the distant shore winked out.

Saturday Morning—June 28, 2014

"Let's try to find gasoline," I suggested, decamping. In the early morning fog, I followed the waterway upstream to Belmont's tiny Main Street.

Two open filling stations sold fuel at the same outrageous price of $14.75 per gallon. Pulling up to the single pump at Tony's Emporium, I jammed in the nozzle.

"May I check your oil, sir?" John Jr. laughed, popping the hood. "Can't have a breakdown now, can we?"

With Japanese parts in high demand, I nodded. "While you're at it, see if you can scrape those June bugs off the windshield." My son assigned to the disgusting task, I entered the convenience store to make payment and peruse the available provisions.

The dim establishment boasted a meager selection of groceries and snacks. Once an Exxon station, the Emporium still advertised the defunct Food Mart logo on the working freezers. The bored clerk rubbernecked as I strolled to the rear. From sparsely stocked shelves, I grabbed two containers of purified water and a trio of wrapped bran muffins. Smiling, I laid the purchases on the counter before a mulleted fella labeled "Anthony."

I produced a credit card as the cashier used a calculator to tally the total. "$162.50," Tony said unenthusiastically, shaking a forefinger at the plastic. "Sir, I require cash. The sign outside says so."

After I shelled out the money in my wallet, half the bills would be gone with this one acquisition. "Come on man, can't—?"

"The credit card's server is offline, has been for five days. Sir, you must pay with currency."

"That leaves me short," I disclosed.

"Pal, you should have thought of that before filling up that fucking mini-SUV with my gas."

"What if I remove the muffins?"

"$152.50," Tony growled, feeling under the bench.

"Fine," I capitulated, holding up my left wrist. "This chronometer is worth over four hundred bucks."

"Give me the watch, plus $100, and we'll call it even. Keep the muffins; they're stale."

I forked over the greenbacks and unfastened the band. Long ago, I acquired the Wenger at Costco for $49. "Here," I said desolately, slapping the timepiece into Tony's outstretched palm. "My dad died wearing this wristwatch. Enjoy it in good health."

John Jr. glanced up as the door slammed. "Dad, you okay?" he asked, seeing my expression.

"Yeah, let's get out of this cesspool." Scowling, I handed Karen the pastries and motored along Main Street.

"Would you like to stop and get breakfast?" she questioned, reading the poster in front of Jolene's Cafe. Everything in this podunk town had a first name.

Learning from previous experiences, if my wife asked if *I* wanted to do something, the proper reply was always affirmative. "Please," I answered, parking before the large, decorated windows.

The cafe stood empty, except for a pudgy woman washing tables. I was not shocked when she rose, revealing a "Jolene"-embroidered nametag. "Sit anywhere," she directed.

By the window, we maintained an eye on our luggage. Two geezers unhurriedly crossed through the misty sunshine and entered the restaurant. The gents looked us over before seizing a table in the corner.

"Here you go, folks," Jolene said, offering menus. "So you know, I got the eggs, but no bacon. Johnnycakes are on special. Eight dollars, includes coffee. What can I get for you?"

"We'll take the pancakes," I responded. "Do you have any orange juice?"

"Sorry, I had OJ last week. It went fast, even though the cartons were past the recommended dates. There is a pitcher of fresh wolfberry extract. Pastor Don made it himself from shrubs in the yard."

"Just water, please, filtered." The owner noted the elderly men's orders and withdrew to the kitchen.

"What was that about?" Karen inquired. "The poached eggs sounded delectable."

I explained our monetary status. "With lots of asphalt ahead, I don't wish to get stuck, that's all."

Jolene eventually reappeared, balancing three plates of stacked flapjacks. No syrup, although she served pads of butter and a jar of "Don's Heavenly Homemade Berry Jelly." The jam turned out to be very tasty, indeed.

The geezer's voices had risen exponentially. Cramming pancake mix into my piehole, I eavesdropped on the conversation.

Geezer Number One bellowed, "You don't comprehend what the hell you're sayin', Ernie. The Koreans bought the farm. There ain't nobody left."

"Some is still breathing. Our guys didn't get all-a-them. That fuckin' UN didn't let us. It's our duty to find the stragglers, the ones hiding in caves," reasoned Geezer Number Two. "Finish 'em off, this time, permanently."

"What should the government do, Ernie, drop another hundred mega-whatever bomb on them? China's completely pissed off, and what of them dying youngsters in South Korea? Those kiddies hadn't a thing to do with politics. That poison ruins the whole enchilada. New York, does that ring a bell?"

Ernest glanced irritably at us before replying, "Go to hell, Ralph. You know damn well I was at Inchon in fifty-two. Deep in the action, the hot shit. Why we couldn't vaporize them then, I'll never understand. Fucking gooks."

Intrigued, we watched Jolene's efforts to pacify the diners.

Standing, Ernest pushed aside the untouched omelet. "Lost my appetite. Gotta go." The man flung a few bucks on the tablecloth and stormed out.

"Wow!" John Jr. exclaimed. "The one duffer seemed ready to throttle the grumpy old coot. Small-town gossip is particularly exciting."

"Forewarn me to skip Belmont on the return trip," I grumbled, counting cash for the bill.

For the remaining daylight, we drove in shifts. Keeping between the lines, I reviewed the aging men's heated bickering, reminded of when I discovered the United States of America retaliated against the DPRK. Branded in the homeland's psyche, it was impossible to forget where and what you were doing on May 7, 2012. Analogous to the most vivid memory, 4/24—the day New York City disintegrated, 5/7 became an overwhelming lifetime experience, similar to the Kennedy assassination, the Challenger and Columbia explosions, and 9/11.

On that horrible day, I kneeled, weeding the vegetable garden as Karen descended the rear steps, shouting, "John, they did it. Our government bombed North Korea! The story is all over the press."

"What's that?" I stuttered, dropping the hoe. Although I clearly caught the words, their weight didn't register.

"Come indoors," she coaxed, nervously scanning the cloudless sky. Pulling me toward the house, my wife's face lost color. "Oh, we need to phone John. Get inside!" Karen spun and ran into the kitchen.

Opening the screen, she conversed with our son. "I can't say. Yes, I heard a few minutes ago on the radio." My wife listened intently and solicited, "Bring Ann. In uncertain times, family should be together."

"The kids should be here in a while," Karen spoke anxiously into my shoulder. "John, what will happen?"

"Baby, I have no clue," I replied, turning on the TV. Every cable channel recounted the breaking announcement.

John Jr. and Ann arrived shortly thereafter, spending a tense afternoon watching various news broadcasts. The spotty facts were jumbled and vague. A stoic Pentagon spokeswoman verified multiple military strikes were executed against North

Korea in response to the unwarranted attack against the United States. An NBC reporter blatantly questioned if nuclear weapons had been utilized. The government had no comment.

The news stations used social media as credible sources for information. Dozens of major Korean cities and military sites were leveled, including the capital city of Pyongyang. Personal video and live webcams transmitted graphic pictures of expanding radioactive clouds spewing dust high into the stratosphere.

Slack jawed, Ann sobbed, "Oh, my God. . ." Transfixed, we stared at a repeating clip of a congested Wonsan intersection. Beginning as a normal workday, Koreans pushed baby carriages or escorted youngsters to school. Pedestrians, automobiles, and bicycles overflowed the sidewalks and streets. A blinding flash froze men, women, and children in their tracks. An instant later, everyone and everything swept horizontally off the road and out of view, as if by a giant whisking a monstrous broom. Incredibly, the webcam streamed content another quarter hour, unemotionally recording the wounded staggering amid the rubble.

The same medical and climatology experts who charted radiation fallout during the New York City detonations gave opinions on how civilization could be affected. "We are talking about ten of the Democratic People's Republic of Korea's major cities," a professor from MIT intoned gravely into the camera. "No entity has ever run simulations for that degree of damage. The populated areas are gone, uninhabitable for the ensuing millennium. Remote villages may continue as they did for the last thousand years. So far off the grid, those agrarian cultures might not have any notion what occurred until the natives start feeling ill."

Republican and Democrat representatives lambasted our leader for not using diplomacy to promote a peaceful solution or lauded the courage to stand up to a despicable antagonist. The debates were exhausting and depressing to behold.

Cross-legged on the carpet, John Jr. swallowed. "The president had to adopt extreme measures." Unconvinced, he glanced at us. "True?"

"History will tell," I answered uneasily. "We'll see if North Korea is a cooked goose or if they have any more tricks up their sleeves."

Days and weeks passed as we anticipated our enemy's next move. On multiple occasions, the Emergency Alert System interrupted television programming with DEFCON 2 warnings or triggered hair-raising sirens during bedtime. People were on edge. Throughout the world, protesting countries characterized our actions as criminal, and the surviving members of the United Nations threatened sanctions.

Like anything else, subsequently, the predominant menace appeared to be past, and we forgot the enemy, or at best, shoved the fear to the backs of our minds. Evening satellite images illustrated before and after lighting comparisons. A communist regime with hardly enough energy for a single nightlight was now completely dark. Nothing, nada. Resolutely, we set about our hectic lives, worrying and working around America's prevailing internal matters.

Saturday Evening—June 28, 2014

Despite gridlock, we reached Richmond, Virginia, before four-thirty p.m., earlier than predicted.

"What should we get for supper?" I inquired, filling the fuel tank and gas cans. After two hours sweating in the smoggy queue of a military checkpoint, I was starving and annoyed. "I'm so hungry, I'm angry!"

"Can we afford it?" Karen responded dryly. "You know, did the Townsends bring enough wampum?"

"Baby, we may have to trade your services for steaks," I winked. Brow furrowed in thought, she considered my proposal.

"Dad, you are so crude," my son scolded. "How 'bout we trade that old shiny gold crown in your mouth instead? The toolbox has a set of pliers."

"Do I select the clients?" my wife retorted with conviction. "I'm game, if I get to pick. Hmm, some nice big—"

"Aww, no. . ." he moaned, clapping palms over reddening cheeks.

"Jeez, I wasn't serious. Merely trying to lighten the mood after a hard day on the dusty trail." Even at this age, viewing John Jr. cover his ears, I still envisioned the skinny ten-year-old I first met.

"Yes, we have the funds for dinner. Let's splurge tonight. Keep your eyes peeled for a Sizzler or Black Angus. Maybe those restaurants continue to exist." Karen and I luckily managed to hold onto our jobs, while millions of others were out of work. Furthermore, we'd accrued sizeable financial returns investing in Sal Harris's lucrative projects. Being very frugal to conserve our savings, I kept a substantial portion of currency and gold concealed in a plastic drum buried in the garden, hoarding for the inevitable rainy day.

With proximity to Washington, DC, Richmond remained in decent shape. No chain chophouses, but we did find a busy barbecue shack aptly named Awesome Bob's. Waiting in line, I noticed the amazing numbers of customers displaying side arms. Following 4/24, the National Rifle Association shoved through state bills permitting openly bearing firearms in public places. One dude topped with a worn cowboy hat sported two vintage six-shooters strapped to a fancy leather cartridge belt. No person with half a brain was idiotic enough to rob Bob.

We carried trays outside to sit below twinkling Christmas lights strung between sweet-gum trees. "Must make the Exclusion Zone gate tomorrow," I mumbled, using my teeth to shred a pork rib. "Wonder if the line is super long."

"Did you see all those guns?" Karen asked. "They made me uncomfortable." Wistfully, she tossed a drumstick upon the flourishing boneyard centerpiece.

"Mom, should we have brought protection?" John Jr. probed, sending me an amused glance.

"Who said we didn't?" his mother replied, methodically stripping a golden corncob. Ladylike, she brushed off a kernel on her upper lip. "I know your father well enough to realize he took his Glock, and I got a little sumpin'-sumpin' stashed in this purse. Let's just say it was a recent birthday gift from your Aunt Jane."

"Shit," he grinned. "You guys are too much. Looks like I'm saddled with a rusty machete." Our son had no inkling what Karen went through at the hands of Martin Reynolds. John Jr. still thought his mother had lost two fingers in an automobile's door, and no one in the family was about to inform otherwise.

Afterwards, we searched the outskirts of Richmond for an adequate locality to shelter the dark hours. Many open regions had evolved into long-term refugee tent cities for the homeless, including recreation areas and parks. As the sun dipped beyond the horizon, we decided on a playground in a residential neighborhood. Slapdash lean-tos and shanties haphazardly covered the trampled grass. Despondent men and women sat on crates or lawn chairs illuminated by smoky bonfires. Fidgety children and dogs scampered noisily around the habitats. The woeful scene reminded me of John Steinbeck's *Grapes of Wrath*. While Karen reorganized the contents inside the car, my son and I erected the tepee.

"Dad, you missed out on my formative tot lot years," he grumbled, assembling the aluminum support poles.

Confident John Jr. was clowning, I tried to remain sensitive. "Sorry, kiddo, can I push you on the swing?" This father-and-son bonding activity might be difficult to achieve. The campers used the colorful equipment as a jumbo clothes drying rack.

"Don't you want to play with me, Daddy?" he moped, forcing stakes into the solid ground. Face hidden, I couldn't determine his disposition.

"Are you kidding?" I answered, arranging the cooler and a bucket for seating. "You turned out fine without me there to wipe your nose and change your diaper."

Karen perched on the icebox, reeling out dental floss. "What are you boys chattering about?"

"Nothing, Mom. Just giving Dad a hard time regarding his early absenteeism." Tearing off a length of waxed line, John Jr. fished for leftovers amongst his wisdom teeth.

"Your father wasn't aware you existed. Honey, you were my little secret. It worked out, right?"

"Guess so," he responded indecisively. "Come on, don't you think I'm pretty fucked up?"

"No, not at all. You're no worse than the rest of us. Dad and I also had rough times. Now, you're mature enough to hear the truth."

A soccer ball rolled into the campsite, closely chased by a string of giggling kids.

"Always had a curious feeling you were hiding something important. Is it that serious? I was always afraid to ask."

"What transpired was unpleasant. There are specific aspects involving your parents that you shouldn't be aware of," I replied gently. "To sleep peacefully, naiveté is generally preferred."

Our son rocked back and gazed into the great unknown, as if seeking divine guidance.

"Some other time," John Jr. chuckled weakly. "Is it related to Aunt Angela?"

Wondering if he had seen an article posted on the Web, I answered, "Correct."

"It's late, and I'm bushed. I'll turn in—long day."

"John, we'll sit outside and discuss you for a spell, if you don't mind," his mother said, smiling.

"No worries. This thin ripstop nylon ensures your complete privacy. And Dad, I was busting your balls about you being a deadbeat. Once you put in an appearance—to be honest, we dropped anchor on your doorstep—you were always there for me."

"Best day of my life, Johnny. Get a good night's sleep."

Karen and I sat closely, tuned into the sounds of the camp. At the curb, drunken men argued in a recreational vehicle, while in a nearby minivan, an amorous couple bumped uglies.

"That won't be happening for us," my wife breathed, nodding over her shoulder.

"Mom, I hear that. You're only sitting two—"

Without preamble, a resonant voice emerged from the murk, announcing a visitor, "How y'all doing this evening?" A heavyset man in his sixties stood cross-armed, etched features plainly visible in the moonlight.

"We're fine," I responded, glancing at the sidearm.

"As superintendent of this campground, I guarantee everyone under my care feels safe and secure. Getting straight to the point, I demand a modest upfront fee for these services."

"And that is?" Karen asked sarcastically.

"Seventy-five dollars a night. It's a bargain. You'd spend more than that to stay at a regular camp."

Angrily, I said, "Pal, this park is public domain. Unless you provide official identification, I think we'll pass." *Why does everybody have to be such a prick?*

"All joshing aside, if you don't pay, I'll help you pack up. Obviously, you folks will reimburse me for the time you spent here," the peppery-haired man asserted. Intimidatingly placing a palm on the pistol, he peered around the campsite searching for objects of worth.

The door unzipped. John Jr. grazed my back, standing to full height. "Mister, I am going to close my eyes and count to three. When I open these peepers, you ought to be long gone," he rumbled, clutching the same plastic mallet used to wallop stakes.

Eager to defuse the situation, I drove a mitt into the intruder's crotch. The brute gasped and grabbed for the handgun as the business end of the hammer flashed swiftly overhead. Karen darted sideways as he fell, crushing the tent.

Applause erupted in the encampment. A circle of refugees approached out of the shadows, patting our shoulders and shaking fists. "That cheat has milked us dry since we arrived. Every time we start preparing to leave, he threatens us," a gaunt camper protested, ringed by wide-eyed offspring.

Karen bent to rifle the immobilized crook's pockets. Holding up a thick wad to the mob, she shaved off banknotes to unfolded hands. "Robin Hood takes from the rich and gives to the poor!" a child hysterically hooted.

A fair-haired teenage boy flipped the inert man, liberating the holster. Booting the racketeer vigorously in the kidney, the juvenile disappeared into the gloom, cherishing the prize. The adolescent's actions ignited a frenzy. Furiously, the growing legion kicked and clubbed the prone figure, swinging anything handy.

The riotous scene induced a flashback to a time in college when I hitchhiked with a few friends to Watkins Glen, New York, for a Grand Prix race. It was autumn, and the sky poured buckets the entire weekend. The weather was miserable. Wandering drunkenly throughout the racetrack, we happened upon the "Bog." Mired recreational vehicles and automobiles burned in the bottomless pit. Hundreds of spectators caged the mud hole chanting, "The Bog wants a car!" Under a hail of stones, a motorcycle gang poked roadside flares into gasoline tanks. An enormous Winnebago smoldered while the bikers worked on a red Corvette. I never forgot the tableau of a throng acting insanely.

The rawboned father advised, "Mister, your family should scram." He held a red can of Coleman fuel. "We'll handle Mr. Keppler."

Hurriedly throwing the tent and ice chests into the Honda, we wheeled by the screaming horde, past the jungle gym and over the edge. The side mirror reflected oily flames billowing into the sky.

Hushed, we bolted into the blackness, inserting mile markers between us and Richmond.

The Zone

Sunday Morning—June 29, 2014

THE DIGITAL CLOCK DISPLAYED 4:05 A.M., exiting to an all-night travel center outside Baltimore, Maryland. Even at this hour, the traffic remained heavy, especially on the Beltway bypassing Washington, DC. Amped with adrenalin, I stayed alert; however, for the previous twenty minutes, sleep had beckoned me.

I rolled to the gas pumps, wife and son still asleep. Watching hookers hawk their wares amongst the eighteen-wheelers, dollars poured into the tank. In light of what transpired at the campground, we were fortunate to slip away untouched. *I think they roasted that asshole alive!* Mind spinning with troubling thoughts, I wondered when my family became so adept at laying transgressors out cold. *Two in two days!* Is this crippled world all we had to look forward to?

"Time to go, John," Karen urged, shaking me.

"Where are we?" I yawned, the sun hot on my stubble. My eyes were crusty. I vaguely recalled backing into a parking spot.

"Some skeezy truck stop. I woke up here at the Neverland Ranch to the musical harmonies of two transvestites fighting. The GPS says our position is south of Baltimore."

"I filled up. What's the time?" Everything felt dreamlike.

"Late. Let's pick up takeout and hit the road. The traffic's already horrible." Observing the highway, she grouched, "We'll eat while I drive."

Sunday Afternoon—June 29, 2014

Thirty miles from New York City, the Authority had set up access to the New Jersey Exclusion Zone in Parsippany, New Jersey. Picturing a tall fence or wall raised around the perimeter of the contaminated cities, I had been astonished to merely see warning signs posted at major intersections.

"The Zone is enormous!" John Jr. exclaimed, sailing by nearly two miles of cars waiting for passage. At three-thirty in the afternoon, my son U-turned and shut off the engine behind a Chevy Suburban. I stared at the chrome Jesus Fish swimming on the rear door. Back of the line. The gate opened tomorrow morning.

"This is so lame," I bellyached, lowering a window. The sticky air smelled tainted. Outside the Exclusion Zone and considered harmless, most Parsippany residents refused to recover their assets. The public didn't stock any faith in the Government's radiation data.

"We get a break from driving," Karen responded optimistically, tilting the headrest. "Tomorrow, we go in, get what's needed, and clear out. With luck, we won't have to make a second trip on Tuesday."

John Jr. noted, "Grandma and Grandpa's home is in the farthest area of the NJ Zone. And as a result of Haworth being so close to the City, it's on top of the nuclear fallout list. Six hours doesn't leave any leeway."

"No, that sure doesn't," I acknowledged. "And I want to visit my old house. Oh man, check this out," I chuckled. A converted school bus leisurely passed the lengthy chain of parked automobiles. Covering the side, a handmade banner proclaimed: "Since there is NO GOD—DON'T Blame Him for this Mess, BLAME YOURSELF!" Drunken men and women leaned out windows or capered to booming disco music on the attached party deck. The revelers reminded me of the bacchanalian floats at New Orleans' Mardi Gras.

My grin paled as the doors of the Suburban swung wide, and a rock-throwing tribe of four bird-dogged the lemon-tinted coach. As the atheist's vehicle accelerated to dodge the bombardment, a good-sized missile pegged an adolescent merrymaker in the eye. The girl's fingers flew to her shrieking face as the bus cut the corner. In disbelief, we watched as the parents fervently high-fived the son and daughter, returning to the Chevy.

"Wow, everyone is so unglued," Karen said sadly, setting the lock. "This was my dumb idea. We should never have come north. Don't you think we ought to get the hell out of New Jersey and go home?"

In the fall, my wife had suggested this excursion, wishing to help her parents, who'd shed everything in the mad rush to vacate. I needed to stop by the house on Franklin to repossess valuable items. Back then, I thought this trip might be an adventure bonding the family closer together.

"Let's stick around," I replied halfheartedly. Clinching Karen's hand, I stared into her brown eyes. "We drove all this way." I nodded wearily. "Jesus, maybe you're right. We became embroiled in two violent confrontations on the way here. Getting hurt or losing our lives isn't worth a few material possessions."

"Come on, don't give up," John Jr. implored. "This vacation isn't a complete fiasco, and we're not even certain what befell those hoodlums. Those losers are probably up and about causing new funny business. There were many gratifying times too." My son smirked. "Like when Mom cracked that hillbilly's melon with the axe or how Dad punched the tot lot bully in the balls. Remember the crowd roaring 'Robin Hood' as she gave those poor people their cash? Another day or two, and we'll be driving to Atlanta, bearing the memories of a lifetime!"

Karen's phone rang. "Jane's almost here, fifteen minutes out." Resting on the sidewalk, we flagged down the police cruiser. My sister parked in a driveway, trotting across the street wearing grey NJ Zone fatigues and toting an assault rifle.

"What a sight for sore eyes!" Jane exclaimed, happily embracing us. "Gosh, it's been way too long."

"Can't agree more, Aunt Jane," my son concurred exuberantly. "When are you moving to Georgia? The northeast is ridiculous."

"Not for a while, Johnny," my sister answered. "Securing the border of the Zone pays well, and since losing the house and car, I'm broke. The banks demand mortgage payments, even though the structures are condemned. The insurance companies aren't giving up a cent either, utilizing the 'Act of War' clause hidden in the tiny print."

"Didn't the Supreme Court rule in favor of canceling debt for those formally living in the affected regions?" I inquired. Reparation had become a regular topic on the nightly news.

"That's true, big brother, but the financial institutions took huge losses and are litigating to overturn the decision. Furthermore, Peter is an issue. For now, we can't wander too far from the treatment facilities. He's hanging in there, but it's just a waiting game at this point," she responded dejectedly.

Succeeding the attack, the military set up provisional field hospitals to oversee and minister to the civilian victims of radiation poisoning. Jane was successful in evading the direct path of the black rain. Her husband hadn't been as blessed.

"Jane, I'm sorry to hear the status of Pete's well-being," Karen said sympathetically. "How have you been? Aren't you being exposed to radiation at work?"

"Thanks for asking. I'm fine. After the bombs hit, I was nauseous and drained for days. For a couple of weeks, I popped potassium iodide tablets like M&Ms. Every vehicle patrolling the Zone is outfitted with full-time radiation detectors, and we wear dosimeters," she specified, patting the round gadget underneath the badge. "The same as civilians, law enforcement isn't allowed into harmful areas without special permits. Guarding the boundary, the goal is to keep people away. As you see, there are no physical barriers; nevertheless, the Authority spent a fortune on electronic surveillance. The department's task is maintaining an official police presence to prevent illegal entry and curtail looting. Trust me, Karen, while caring for Pete, I learned to be very cautious regarding my health."

"We worry about you up here," I said. "Atlanta isn't the city it used to be, yet it's far nicer than this insane asylum. Coming north, we ran into a few problems." Keyed up, we gave a summary of the trip.

Jane shrugged in amazement. "The Townsends seem to attract chaos." Turning to her nephew, she asked, "So, Johnny, you knocked out that scam artist with a plastic hammer? That's a sight I would've loved witnessing for myself."

"Yeah, I hit him right here," he indicated, pointing at the ridge of his brow. "That jerk went down like a sack of potatoes."

"There are various vendors setting up near the Zone entryway. Tonight, I'll treat you to delicious rat shish kabobs," my sister wisecracked.

"Go ahead, I'll stay with the car," my son volunteered. "Get me something filling; I'm starving for sweet rodent."

Following the string of automobiles toward the colorful tents, the atmosphere grew festive. A young man with a red Mohawk had opened a tattoo parlor under a tarp. The artist inked a black-and-yellow radiation symbol on the lower back of a bikini-clad woman. A gallery of shirtless men admired the trefoil tramp stamp.

On a milk crate, a silver-faced humanoid was wrapped in foil, miming for an apathetic audience. At his feet, a placard advertised: "Get your photo with Dorothy's Tin Man. Donations Accepted." The statue's bloodshot eyes tracked our every movement.

Two pimply teenagers leaning on tipped-up skateboards dickered with a boy for a bag of multicolored pills. Eying our uniformed escort warily, the adolescents completed the transaction. "Kids know the cops won't make an arrest," Jane confided, adjusting the strap of the MP5. "The Authority has bigger fish to fry."

Closer, the smoky essence of roasting poultry and pork drifted with the breeze. Randomly positioned food service trucks sold everything from Greek food to kettle corn. The territory adjacent to the Zone gateway even hosted a giant Oktoberfest beer pavilion, replete with rowdy patrons. A hardworking band rendered Led Zeppelin cover songs for the gyrating crowd. Prices were astronomical, but unless you brought your own vittles to gobble, this was dinner.

A sunburned gentleman approached Karen. "Linda, do you like it?" he wheezed into her face, baring blackened gums. "Oh, Linda, do you want it? Do you love it like that?"

Disgusted at the ripe odor and erupting facial sores, my wife backpedaled.

Fishing a fin out of my wallet, I pleaded, "Buddy, maybe you should—"

Jane stood between us and the deranged man. "Have you illegally entered the New Jersey Exclusion Zone? Seriously, stay out. It's toxic. Those lesions are radiation sickness. Sir, it will not cost you a dime to check into a medical center."

The wizened man's lungs hitched, laboring to stifle a spasm. Agonizingly, he forcibly coughed up a bloody mass onto his sleeve. Jaundiced eyes homed in on my sister. The bum muttered, "Gail, do you want it? Don't you love it like that?"

"Not so hungry anymore," I moaned, rubbing my tummy. "Do you run into a lot of that?"

"Every day," Jane replied, thoroughly examining her shiny boots for gore. "Pete's in pretty much the same shape as this guy, but at least he's being prescribed medication. The specialists give Pete a fifty-fifty chance. Without any treatment, this dude's a goner."

Contemplating that sobering announcement, I waited as my sister procured jerk chicken at Stone's. A mass of boisterous youngsters materialized as we unhurriedly carried the Styrofoam boxes to the car. "Watch your pocketbooks," Jane cautioned, as the squealing group encircled us.

Resembling a jockey, a skin-and-bones girl mounted my shoulders, using my hair for reins. "Sir, can I get some money for Mommy? Mama needs to buy medicine for my little brother. Mickey's got the clap! Please, Mister, please," she breathed hotly into an ear. Embarrassed, I struggled to shake the tenacious child loose.

"Scat!" Karen growled, swatting a diminutive paw straining for her purse. Twisting a set of tentacles resulted in a high-pitched screech of pain. "You made me do that, you—"

"Run!" I barked, waving the billfold aloft. *There must be twenty munchkins!* What could I do, hit one of the tykes in the snout?

The ragamuffins pursued a short range before dispersing and searching for fresh prey.

"That tiny street urchin latched onto me like a suckerfish," my wife panted, slowing to walk.

Jane doubled over, spluttering, "That was priceless. Karen, did you spot Johnny running from those kids? He looked terrified."

"Ha, I don't deny being scared. That's the same as being attacked by a swarm of bees. And you shouldn't be talking. For God's sake, you're a cop!" I retorted, snorting with laughter. "Too old for this crap. Who are they?"

"No idea," my sister answered soberly. "Usually, the juveniles are runaway or abandoned tweens controlled by a degenerate adult providing food and shelter in exchange for a daily quota of stolen valuables. These thieves were quite immature."

We returned to the car by dusk. John Jr. awoke, thankful for nourishment.

Supper finished, Jane shut the takeout box. "See you for breakfast."

"You're going into the Zone with us?" I inquired, thrilled, yet surprised. Back in Atlanta, we discussed this topic, but my sister was unusually noncommittal.

"Wouldn't miss this reunion for the world," she promised. "But I ought to mention it's the wild, wild, west inside the Zone, and I will not be permitted to lug this," Jane said fondly, caressing the machine gun. "Tomorrow, I'll be off duty."

Monday Morning—June 30, 2014

The portal opened at sunup. The line moved slowly as Jane dropped into the Honda's rear seat. "Morning, everybody!" she brightly exclaimed, allocating coffee and pastries. "Did you guys sleep well?"

Beholden for hot caffeine and not intending to damper my sister's mood, I responded with equal zeal, "Fantastic, Jane. Everything's delightful. Nothing compares to sitting wide-awake all night in a stuffy car, afraid to leave the windows cracked!"

"Yeah, and Mr. Farty Pants up here didn't help," my son complained, tugging a shirt to cover his nose.

Karen, mid-bite into a jelly-filled doughnut, choked on her giggles.

The National Guard unit assigned to the Zone had erected a dozen booths at the fence to validate paperwork and inspect vehicles. Approaching the checkpoint, my wife located the necessary documentation and presented forms and IDs to the official.

"There are passes for three people." The sentry peered inside. "Ma'am, I require one for you."

Jane held out her badge to the woman. "Sergeant, I'm here unofficially accompanying my family to salvage personal property. As authorized when off duty, I'm bringing a sidearm."

The officer uploaded four permits into a tablet, affixing the sticker to the interior of the windshield. A dome-shaped object stuck magnetically to the CRV's roof.

"Folks, I'm glad the gas tank is full. Pull up to the next station to be outfitted with mandatory apparel. Keep in mind, as you depart below the flag, make note of the time. In six hours, you must be back here to egress. If the National Guard initiates a rescue mission, you will incur a hefty five thousand-dollar penalty. The Authority tracks all activity with GPS, so stay within the residences or businesses approved for admittance."

At the safety booth, we donned white hazmat suits, blue booties, dust masks, and goggles. Dosimeters swayed from our necks as a pleasant civilian gave the group a succinct course on using the radiation detectors.

The Honda slid under the huge Stars and Stripes hanging above the New Jersey Exclusion Zone archway. "We have to return by one-thirty," John Jr. established. As instructed in the training, he affixed duct tape on the air-conditioning vents. With windows sealed, the temperature in the cabin exceeded ninety degrees.

"Wonder why the cops didn't search us," I mused.

"Maybe because I'm Zone Police and openly carrying," my sister conjectured.

Thirty miles to Haworth, the lack of traffic on Route 80 was unnatural. After the van we followed exited to Fairfield, the roads remained unoccupied. Taking it slow, I periodically swerved around sidelined automobiles or debris.

"This is surreal," Karen said, lowering the visor to shield the glare. "That eerie landscape makes me edgy."

I had to agree. Twenty-six months since the expulsion, Nature had made significant progress redeeming what had been hers. Cracks in the pavement widened, encouraging weeds and even trees to spring up everywhere. Vast flocks of geese wheeled higher. Once, I stomped the pedal as coyotes leapt the guard rail, blending into the dense median. Glumly, I prophesied what the Zone might resemble in one hundred years, a thousand. . . .

"Look at that!" Jane exclaimed, gesturing out the window. A formation of Apache helicopters swooped low over a shopping mall, landing in the huge parking lot. Miniature commandos ran in the direction of Sears.

"Illegals?" I assumed, steering by a charred Greyhound bus blocking two lanes.

"You've seen the roundup clips on TV?" my sister asked. "The rumor is that tens of thousands are living here and in New York, scrounging off the remaining food supplies. The military is apprehending squatters one by one. Plenty are armed and resist relocation. Many are certifiably mad or hopped up on pharmaceuticals raided from drug stores or hospitals. In reality, the Zone can furnish a luxurious lifestyle, if you're willing to withstand a daily dose of gamma rays."

"All clowning aside, I'd hole up in a dope crib with a harem of glowin' honeys, cruisin' the godforsaken streets with the top lowered," John Jr. chuckled, glancing up from the radiation meter. "Same as that Heston character in that movie—"

"Omega Man!" I finished, laughing. "I mean, how dangerous can the environment still be?"

Karen peered through safety glasses. "See me, John? Inside this body bag, I'm sweating like a pig, but I'm definitely not taking it off, even for an instant." Her voice sounded muffled in the mask.

"Excellent point," I admitted. "Let's make a quick stopover at the cemetery. George Washington is off the next exit."

My eyes burned, yet received no relief from the tears. Some things really have to be seen to be believed. Overwhelmed, I squeezed my wife's hand, hoping to not lose it. A quartet of aliens on a bizarre mission to a corrupted planet circled the graves.

The family name spelled: "*OUTLAW*." On the left part of the bronze marker, a rectangular plaque stated: "*William 5/27/1957-4/24/2012*." The plate on the right read: "*Melissa 11/2/1957-4/24/2012*."

Below, my friend's son, my godson: "*Edward 4/13/1986-4/24/2012*."

A likeness of Bill and Melissa holding a smiling Eddie flashed for a millisecond, replaced with nothing. Too fucking final. Hyperventilating, I tore off the elastic filter.

Karen laid a palm lightly on my shoulder. "Come on, honey. Put the mask back on."

As Jane traversed the highway overpass, I fumed, furious at the arrogance of the Koreans. In the distance, objects glimmered.

"Motorcycles!" John Jr. bellowed, startling me from the funk.

On Route 17, bikes approached swiftly, mechanical thunder echoing off stark buildings. "Did they see us?" I questioned, suspecting the worst.

On the gas, my sister made a hard turn onto Spring Valley Road. Tires screeching, the Honda skidded into the entrance of the Van Saun Park Zoo and braked alongside a dilapidated maintenance shed. The cages were unlocked. I theorized the zookeepers set the animals loose before fleeing.

Outside, we caught the raw revving of engines.

The SUV's bench angled forward, I extracted the Glock, poking the piece in my waist and pocketing the ammo. Handing my son a machete, he dubiously assayed the corroded blade.

"Nephew, here's something more useful," Jane said grimly, withdrawing a long shiny weapon from under the front seat.

"How did that get there?" I stuttered. "I thought, I thought you had—"

"Naturally, I planned to dispose of the gun. Still, a girl can always change her mind," she said, giving the Colt 45 revolver to John Jr. "I don't know who those punks are, but I definitely have no desire to meet them. Head for high ground; we're extremely visible in these damned white suits."

Through the thicket, we followed my sister beside a row of fenced pens. Several held the skeletal remains of large mammals. The motorcycles close, we hid in a stand of maples behind a children's carousel. The low knoll afforded an unhindered view of three Harleys swooping into the zoo's parking lot. It became obvious as the leather-jacketed riders dismounted that sawed-off shotguns were the only protective gear they wore.

"Who are those people, and how did they even find out we are here?" I whispered.

"Satan's Chosen MC from Jersey City. This gang is snooping around, robbing residents trying to reclaim their belongings. Normally, they solely harass squatters. The rest of the mob could be searching elsewhere," Jane answered.

Lighting cigarettes, the bearded men split up. Two hurried toward the menagerie as the tallest male slung the scattergun across a shoulder and ambled to the merry-go-round. Karen withdrew a small Ruger revolver. Calmly checking the cylinder, she pulled the hammer and released the safety. "On Thursdays, I went to the shooting range while you were bowling," my wife confessed softly, sighting on the approaching individual.

"Hold on, we can't risk the sound of a gunshot," John Jr. declared, hefting the machete. Swiftly, he stripped off the hazmat suit.

"What are you doing?" I rasped, as he grabbed a branch and began climbing.

Passing up the cleaver, my son requested, "Just get him over here."

"Well, then, I guess I'm having a heart attack," I responded. Clutching my chest and grimacing, I dropped against the roots.

"Help us!" my sister blubbered to the oncoming man. "Please, my brother is not breathing. Roger was fine a minute ago. He said his arm hurt and collapsed. Oh, God, I have no idea what's wrong!"

Pumping the shotgun, the long-haired biker crept warily into the brush. "Who's in those trees? Come out now!"

Karen knelt, administering CPR. "Please sir," she wailed, "my husband's unwell."

Thrusting Jane roughly aside, the scruffy man stood above me. From slit eyes, I watched her reach for the weapon.

"The old guy looks baked to me," he pronounced.

John Jr. plunged, blade scything through the air and landing solidly in the broad man's clavicle. Although he missed the muscular neck by inches, a vital connection severed. As my son fought to his feet, the goon took aim. The sawed-off slid to the earth as the bicep relaxed and flapped limply. In shock, he tottered and turned to run, grasping hand seeking to stem the gushing wound.

"John, we've got to finish him off before he calls the others!" I shouted, leaping unsteadily. Tackling the weaving man, we wrested in the dirt. Even with one working wing, the biker proved scads stronger. Straddling my ribs, he mashed my windpipe with a tattooed forearm.

With a warrior's cry, my son yanked the man's pigtail, sawing into the gristle of the thick throat. Warm blood drenched my mask and goggles as he convulsed, sputtering a final gasp.

"Get off me!" I groaned, pulling away the clogged filter and wiggling under the beefy corpse.

Irritated barks of "Filthy Phil, where the hell are you?" brought us back to reality. Removing the smeared lenses, I observed the two outstanding men yelling as they charged into the meadow.

"Spread out in the grass," my sister directed. "Someone at the Battle of Bunker Hill once ordered, 'Don't fire until you see the whites of their motherfucking eyes!'" She slithered from sight between flowering weeds.

Lying in the hot sun, I fixated on the converging men. The blood-filled paper hood stuck to my skin. *I can't see anything!* Head rising, a dumbfounded unshaven face locked eyes with mine. Quickly, I elevated the Glock and blasted the man twice in the stomach. Pirouetting, he staggered out of view.

In a volley, I ducked, witnessing the final gunman attempt escape to the motorcycles. In the grassy field, Jane and Karen equidistantly kneeled on both sides of the fleeing man. The gang member fell flat on his mug when the women mowed him down in a hail of crossfire.

Overwrought, I hollered, spotting my wife and sister, "Is everyone okay?" *Where's my son!* "John!"

"This, way Dad!" I spun to see John Jr. standing above a prone body. Sprinting, I heard the gut-shot man beg for his life. Or that's the way it sounded; I couldn't discern the inarticulate whimpering. The leather-clad figure lay on his backside, flannel shirt soaked in blood, dark puddle inflicting the evacuation of an anthill.

Joined by Jane and Karen, we held vigil by the dying man. "What should we do?" my wife asked, mesmerized. Tears streaked the biker's chin, while bloody claws roamed in pitiful cramped movements around the heaving abdomen. The spectacle bore the resemblance of a surgeon performing his own operation.

John Jr. glanced at his watch. "Three hours remaining. We've blown too much time here."

I jumped as the Colt barked very loudly.

Deliberately lowered the hammer, he clasped the big 45. "May be time to get out the carving knife," my son suggested to his aunt, stroking a thumb across the three notches chiseled in the checkered grip.

After dragging the men through the meadow, we disposed of the bodies in the monkey pit. John Jr. dumped the motorcycles behind bushes and hid the machines with straw. As we prepared to leave, a thin donkey wearing a bridle arrived from nowhere hoping for a free meal. With nothing to offer, Jane detached the harness.

In silence, we preceded east on Oradell Avenue toward Haworth and the in-laws' house. I stopped the Honda by the large green Victorian, the wraparound porch steeped in shadow.

Karen didn't move. The concerns that bothered me likewise weighed heavily on her mind. "Go on," I prodded. Currently, no one wore a hazmat suit.

"Something's not right. I'm a lawyer; your sister is police. A half-hour ago, we shot three people, plus beat those two men on the trip up. John, I'm having difficulty relating picking up a shoebox of old family pictures and tax papers to killing. It's not logical, is it? What if one of us had been hurt, or worse? What if we run into more grief driving home?"

Numbly, I searched for a plausible reply and found no words to fix the situation or even give comfort. "Karen, I don't have a worthy answer. Straightaway, we must gather the things your parents wanted and return to the gate as soon as possible. That gang will look for their buddies. Out of danger and with added time, we can consider the implications of what occurred. This trip will be a complete loss if we come back empty-handed. Baby, I'm sorry, that justification totally sucked."

"Your response is better than I expected," my wife smiled, herself again. "Sister-in-law, when you're finished with your pistol grip, let me borrow that knife," she grinned. Opening the car door, Karen approached the house, Ruger ready.

The lock on the front entry was pried apart, the interior hastily ransacked. The living room's TV entertainment center lay face down, and hollow jewelry boxes strewed the floor of the master bedroom. Otherwise, the dwelling endured as a spooky time capsule.

It didn't take long for my wife to cover the residence's two stories and finalize her parents' request list. She retrieved a bundle of important documents from the closet safe along with a chest filled with portraits. I found Karen in the dining room, gazing at a discolored picture of her sister. The girl posed beside two plaid-skirted friends, beneath the Statue of Liberty. "So many years past. . ." she murmured, smudging a knuckle along the glass. "The sole remnant that outlasts Angela is this photograph."

Recognizing how Martin Reynolds cut her sister's life short, I tenderly put an arm around my wife. "Angela never had a chance to grow up. I wonder what she would say about all this," I said, looking into the overrun backyard. "Without people, the houses are so vacant, barren." I questioned if the Zone might ever become inhabitable or if this structure would eventually deteriorate into dust over the eons. An uncontrollable wildfire wiping the slate clean was a credible possibility.

On the sundeck, my sister and son rocked in chairs, drinking water. Exhausted, we set the cartons on the stoop and sat on the steps.

John Jr. dispensed refreshment. "Salute!" he exclaimed, raising the bottle high.

"A mob of dogs crossed the golf course hunting an animal. Mixed breeds, Dobermans, poodles and even a teeny Chihuahua," Jane reported, pointing beyond the vegetation. "There were over thirty."

"The pack didn't notice you?" Karen inquired in disbelief. "I've heard feral dogs attack."

"Hopefully the muties won't chase the car," I added, half-jokingly.

"Oh, shit," my son cursed. "In the excitement, I haven't monitored the radiation detector. Check your dosimeters!" he shouted, dashing to the CRV.

Astounded the instrument stayed looped to my neck, I squinted into the tube at the graduated scale. The needle pushed the 15 mark. "What are fifteen milliroentgens?" I asked curiously. The gauge peaked at 200.

"Apparently, not good," John Jr. replied, fingering a chart received during orientation. "There's a reading of three milliroentgens an hour on the radiation meter. When we passed the gateway, the device recorded point-five milliroentgens. This table says an adult should not absorb greater than two in any one hour or one hundred millirems of artificial irradiation for the entire year."

"Marvelous, one must tolerate the dosage of a thousand x-rays," I said, standing. "Let's get going. There's one more stop."

The boxes stowed in the trunk, I requested for Jane and Karen to wear their hazmat suits. My son and I left our ruined shields at the zoo.

The house where my sister and I lived was on the other side of town. Sentimentally, I yearned to see our homestead one last time. Honestly, I didn't reckon we would ever return to New Jersey.

Gliding through deserted downtown Haworth, I imagined movement in the darkened storefront windows, mirages from the past. Memories of the fun times Vince, Bill, and I enjoyed as youths: attending school, purchasing sweets at Jim's Market, and riding, happy-go-lucky, on our bicycles. In the mirror, I focused on the lines creasing my eyes. *Where had the time gone?*

I talk to Vince every few months on the telephone, and we journey to Las Vegas whenever convenient. My friend is now married to Amber and has twins. Financially and emotionally, he's doing fine. As a partner, he helps Paul run the construction business. Ranzetta never got used to the heat.

Bill and Melissa! I can't even think about them without getting choked up, so I don't. Just two days before the attack, I emailed Bill an amusing picture. The non-delivery notification abides in the inbox for me to hit the deletion key.

The only humans that mattered were right here in this car, soaking up radioactivity.

"There's the Woods," Karen said uneasily, eying the abyss where numerous hideous things happened. "Hmm, it appears considerably smaller than I remembered." Sponging her forehead, she coiled away.

I envisioned the Shack, Ceremonies, the graves, all those murdered girls. I recalled teenage Karen clicking a snapshot of me with her dead sister's shoe. Today, the Woods seemed bigger, *expanded*. The menacing trees and sickly-sweet overgrowth crawled over the sidewalk and devoured the pavement. In the future, the township will evolve into one giant nature preserve. No matter what, Ceremonies will always be an evil longitude and latitude of terrible hoodoo. Funny, how our perceptions differed.

"Yes, it is smaller," I lied, a chill descending my spine.

Cresting Tank Hill, I navigated around a skewed tower of baby carriages. A crumpled cardboard sign at the top advertised: "SWEET AND SOUR BABIES FOR SALE TAKE A LEFT." The disturbing verbiage looked oddly familiar.

Coasting down the slope brought to mind chasing Karen to Closter and dropping off the film containing the images of Reynolds' home. That day was fun. In retrospect, we were so carefree and naive.

We approached the turn onto my road. Franklin Street triggered a slew of good and bad memories and I was nervous to revisit the place where I had been raised. Mouth dry, I scanned for 268, not wanting to glimpse where he lived, but fighting the same urge people get passing a horrendous accident.

Karen's fists tightened in her lap. "Where is it?" she questioned, anxiously pressing on the dashboard.

"Right there," Jane answered, designating a bare lot. "Don't you remember? Nobody would buy the building. The city council ultimately razed the eyesore, preventing the creep's house from becoming the final destination on the 'Where Do the Psychos Live' tour map. No one even bid on the land, unsellable."

I switched off the ignition and leaned on the hood, listening to the engine tick. Inhaling deeply, I walked to the epicenter of the lot, bounded by weeds and stunted saplings. I discovered conjuring up a replica of the split-level laborious. We were indoors, practically caught when Reynolds returned early from the meeting at the Masons. Regretfully, I bent toward the overcast sky, reaping the fallout.

"This is the site?" John Jr. inquired. "Martin Reynolds lived here? A few years back, I found old photos in news articles on the Internet. A juror also wrote a book describing the trial."

"Yeah, he did. We were just kids—me, Vince, Bill, Melissa, your mom." I pivoted to study my son. Where might I be if I hadn't met him? Lost. After a slight hesitation, I continued,

"Aunt Melissa took care of Mr. Reynolds with that pistol you're holding. A close friend named Sal sliced and diced, and we all fed the son of a bitch to the eels in the Hudson River. That monster murdered your Aunt Angela and nearly killed your mother. By the way, John, Mom didn't lose those fingers in the car door."

"Oh that's. . ." my son mumbled, digesting the words. Frowning, he scratched a nail into the deep grooves in the 45's rosewood handle.

"Do you feel better knowing?" I asked, coercing the transmission into drive. Karen waited for a reaction.

"Aunt Jane, what about these other two notches on the gun's grip?" John Jr. questioned thoughtfully. "Or is that a subject I—?"

"The Colt had those marks when I got it," my sister answered, staring into space. "How are those radiation levels?"

Grateful for the change in topic, we rolled into the driveway.

Back Home

Monday Afternoon—June 30, 2014

THE RESIDENCE WHERE I LIVED most of my formative years had changed. Jane had altered the exterior paint scheme from yellow with white trim to a pleasing combination of tan siding and green shutters. The original forsythia hiding the facade had been chopped down and replanted with younger shrubs. The yard might be restored to its former splendor following an extended visit by an energetic landscaping crew. Abruptly, I realized that would never happen.

"Looks different, doesn't it?" John Jr. commented, surveying the property. My initial impression of the building's condition was wrong. Up close, it became easy to discern the effects weather had on a structure left vacant. The black driveway sealer crumbled, and weeds sprouted in deep cracks. Paint flaked from the garage, and woodpeckers drilled cavities in dozens of shingles.

"Let's walk around the outside," I suggested, treading on the molehills pockmarking the side yard.

Sixty-year-old trees still existed, while others were felled. In the backyard, a recent-model air conditioner squatted on the same concrete pad. My earlier recollections conflicted with these raw images.

"This place is a wreck," Jane muttered dejectedly. "I expended tons of money renovating, and now, feast your eyes on this shithole. What a disaster." As she hauled a fallen branch across the yard, I didn't have the heart to restrain her.

Circling the dwelling, we stood on the flagstone stoop. From her jeans, my sister removed a tarnished key and silently enclosed it in my hand.

I weighed the familiar brass token before unlocking the front door. The interior was warm and smelled musty. A plumbing leak caused much of the living room ceiling to cave in. Couches and chairs corralled the heap of moldy sheetrock and insulation.

Normally the most active space, the kitchen appeared dull and lifeless. Today, the modern appliances were as functional as props on a movie set.

"How can we help? Jane, do you want any of these?" Karen asked quietly, indicating a police academy graduation picture and a wedding book of our parents. Nobody lived within miles, yet I understood her compulsion to speak softly. A shrine for human memories, this dying house lingered, eternally haunted.

Unhooking the photo from the wall, my sister laid the frame with the album on the dining room tablecloth. "Thanks for reminding me of these. I'll check for more mementos." Drained, she climbed the staircase to the bedrooms.

Karen and John Jr. stood uneasily by the sink. "Stay here," I said. "After a quick peek downstairs, we'll leave."

I descended the steps into the russet-tiled laundry room. Except for the new washer and dryer, the pinewood paneling and cabinets were original. An open doorway revealed Jane's automobile. A thick layer of soot coated the hood as rubber flattened to the cement. Reminiscing about the thousands of days coming through this garage, delighted to be home, I also reflected upon the shoe once hidden in the tires.

Depressed, I shut the door, taking the wooden stairs to the basement. Comfortable below ground, the air remained cool and damp. The narrow casement windows failed to fight the gloom. Clinging to the washing machine, I found my mother's age-old magnetic red and silver Eveready. Although dented, the flashlight's powerful glare endured.

A Ping-Pong table dominated the center of the cellar, a paddle reclining atop an orange ball. I speculated who won the last tournament. Stacks of cardboard containers filled a metal shelf on the far wall. Five cartons had been marked "Mom and Dad," and two additional were labeled "John's Junk."

I moved my boxes by the net. One consisted of a complete set of Lionel toy trains wrapped in 1964 newspapers. Tears stung my cheeks as I recalled the moments Dad and I assembled the train tracks beneath the Christmas tree. At year's end, he reveled in running the miniature steam locomotive on the oval railway more than I did. Sniffling, I wiped my nose on a sleeve. It was odd how particular sentimental flashbacks can suddenly blind.

The other crate encompassed the items a teenager collected: baseballs, mix cassette tapes, playing cards, and old magazines. Amongst the rubbish, I saved a faded snapshot of my sister and myself standing beside a beaming stranger in a cowboy outfit.

Dad's workshop appeared the same as the day he had died in 1973. Screwdrivers and files precisely lined the racks spanning the workbench. Packed underneath were scrap iron and storage bins for nails and fasteners. To the side, the flashlight illuminated a partially disassembled General Electric toaster from the '50s or '60s. A note taped to the chrome defined the part needing replacement. Analyzing my father's unique handwriting, I slid the paper into a pocket alongside the photo. A newish weed-whacker, engine in pieces, took a break on the opposite end of the bench. Apparently, Jane and Pete worked on their own projects.

The drafting table waited, wedged in an alcove behind the furnace. Exhausted pulling out the high chair, I sat, resting forearms on the slanted oak. I pondered why Dad spent so many nights in the basement while his wife and children watched television. Gazing up at the heating conduit, I wondered if hearing us laugh made him lonely.

As I slowly sweep the light, the shadow of a ledger became visible above a galvanized steel duct. Intrigued, I impulsively reached upwards.

Startling me, my sister questioned, "What you got there?" Immersed, I hadn't heard her come near.

"Not sure. This was up in the rafters, and I just happened to notice it."

I brushed caked dust off the burgundy leather cover. Stamped in gold script along the lower corner were the words: "*The Family Album*." An elastic band was threaded between two eyelets in the spine.

"Holy cow!" she exclaimed. "That looks archaic. Let's take a gander."

With trepidation, I exhaled and opened the book. The first page held a black-and-white portrait of a serious man in uniform.

"So young then," Jane mused, fondly touching the face. "Johnny, you should cart this home for Mom."

Peeling away the clear film, I unstuck the photograph and flipped it over—nothing.

I paged to a bleached *New York Times* story describing the US invasion of the French Republic. Below the text was a grainy depiction of the same somber man leaning against a shuttered window. He cradled a worn rifle, the strap looping toward the rubble. At the bottom, the jagged white border cut off the uncurled fingers of a fist emerging from a darkly stained sleeve. Scrawled on the posterior: "Grenoble - August 22, 1944." Not my father's methodical longhand.

"Doesn't seem too happy, does he?" my sister brooded, turning the sheet. "World War II must have been terrible. Dad never really mentioned it."

Occasionally, my mother discussed my father serving in Korea; however, I wasn't aware he had served in both wars.

On the next page was a crinkled, handwritten letter pressed taut by plastic.

> Mikey,
>
> Hope this message finds you, Mom, and Dad in good health and spirits. I don't want you to worry about me. Trust me, the fighting is no walk in the park, but I am still alive so that is saying something right? The army is doing important work over here throwing the fascists out of France. In a few weeks I may be standing on the Eiffel Tower! Who knows! HA!
>
> The French women are beautiful, Mikey. When this war is finished, I'll fly you to Europe. The local people drink wine all day long. Even the kiddies. HA! We'll enjoy a swell time. Can't wait to show you the sights. Everything!
>
> The men in my unit are great guys. You would like them a lot.
>
> Do you remember when we went to the county fair and saw that girl in the glass fish tank? The barker said she was a real live mermaid. That night we learned that she wasn't. Just a big fake! [scratched out sentence] HA! HA! Lately I think of that carnival for some reason.

> Well gotta go. Chowtime. Then tomorrow I'll kill more Nazis. I'll bring home a helmet with a bullet hole or German Lugar for you little brother.
>
> Take care and write soon. Tell the folks I am fine.
>
> Martin

Annoyed, Jane inquired, "What is this, Johnny? Who is Martin, and why is he corresponding with Dad? Why does a stranger act like a relative?" She rapidly flipped through the remaining leafs.

One sheet preserved a nuptial invitation for Martin Reynolds and Elizabeth Albrecht, accompanied by a brief newspaper blurb. Another displayed a color reproduction of the blissful couple cuddling a baby.

A heartbreaking obituary announcement for six-year-old Nicole Reynolds.

Disturbing articles and posters for missing women.

Umpteen news stories recounting the trial.

The scrapbook only included pictures and clippings concerning Martin Reynolds.

Violently flinging the album, my sister marched side to side muttering obscenities. Grabbing her firmly by the shoulders, I strove to make eye contact. "Jane, you can't argue this. Karen and John will never find out!" I hissed. "This is just between you and me. Do you understand?"

"You knew that Martin Reynolds was Dad's brother, our uncle?"

"No, I couldn't be certain until I saw this," I replied, picking up the book and shoving the damned relic up in the beams. "Something always felt funny. Before Melissa blew his brains out, Reynolds attempted to talk to me. After examining these photographs, the resemblance to our father is obvious."

"Why the dissimilar last names? Why did Dad keep his brother a secret? How come that psychopath approached you and not me? Reynolds lived up our street, for God's sake. What about Mom?"

"Jane, I can't answer those questions, and I doubt you'll ask our mother. Even if she knows, why stir up nasty memories at this stage of life?" I held my sister tight, until her heartbeat gradually slowed to normal. "Please, we need to go upstairs and hurry to the gate. Are you able to do that?"

Barely composed, we returned to the daylight.

"Ready?" I called. Not prepared to meet my family's scrutiny, I quickly scooped up the small pile of framed photos on the table. Relaxing outdoors, John Jr. raised the rear hatch.

Retracing the drive to the New Jersey Exclusion Zone exit was quick and uneventful. No breakdowns, no bikers, no reason to kill anyone. This afternoon may be a pleasant jaunt in the country, if we weren't driving past miles and miles of uninhabitable wasteland.

"Very close to natural radiation levels," my son reported. "If we wear lead underwear for the next few years, we'll survive."

"Ha, I'll fashion a tinfoil helmet," I chuckled, peering at Jane in the mirror. Eyes red, she remained expressionless.

"I'm contemplating trekking to LA to see if Ann misses me," John Jr. said. "Possibly move west. What are your thoughts?"

"Go for it," I answered, glancing at Karen. "If she's the right one, don't squander another minute." *As I did!*

"What if it's too late? I mean, what if she's with another dude? Plus, what will you do without me to defend you?" my son smirked.

"John, we'll be fine," his mother responded. "Of course, we'll visit. You never can tell. Your father and I might relocate to California someday. They say San Diego has wonderful weather. Ann's a nice girl. What if she's been expecting *you* to ride to the rescue?"

"There's always a chance. How about you, Aunt Jane? Ever consider migrating to the West Coast?"

"Now, my primary priority is getting Pete back on his feet. I'm trying to stay positive and hope for the best. Once he finishes therapy, well, that's a different story. Perhaps California requires a sheriff to round up all those dangerous outlaws? Definitely would be a sensible change from this," she replied, facing the window.

Nearing the gateway, I envisioned my father sitting alone in the cellar, listening to his family through the heating ducts while updating the scrapbook. What if Karen and John Jr. heard us discussing Reynolds? *Sound travels both ways!*

Nervously, I gazed at my wife, who was staring fixedly at the highway. "Karen, I believe you should—"

She turned to study me. Imperceptibly, the woman I married shook her head and smiled. "Oh, I know exactly what you're going tell me. We're your best friends, and you love us very much. That's old news."

"Yes, that is precisely what I was about to say. Baby, you read my mind."

The car bounced on a pothole as I careened around an abandoned catering truck.

Karen clung to the strap and grinned. "John, this trip's not over yet!"

www.ingramcontent.com/pod-product-compliance
Lightning Source LLC
Chambersburg PA
CBHW020554310726
48979CB00008B/1214/J

* 9 7 8 0 9 9 1 4 2 4 8 1 8 *